ON WAVES OF GLORY

The Quest of Captain Guy de Kersaint

On Waves of Glory: Tween Sea and Shore, Book 3 by D. E. Stockman

Copyright © 2024 D. E. Stockman

All rights reserved. No part of this book may be used or reproduced by any means without the written permission of the publisher except in the case of brief quotation embodied in critical articles and reviews.

This is a work of historical fiction. While based upon actual events, any similarity to any person, circumstance or event is purely coincidental and related to the efforts of the author to portray the characters in historically accurate representations.

Cover design by D. E. Stockman and Jacqueline Cook

Interior design by Jacqueline Cook

ISBN: 978-1-61179-428-1 (Paperback)

ISBN: 978-1-61179-429-8 (e-book)

BISAC Subject Headings:
FIC002000 FICTION / Action & Adventure
FIC014000 FICTION / Historical / General
FIC047000 FICTION / Sea Stories

Address all correspondence to:
Fireship Press, LLC
P.O. Box 68412
Tucson, AZ 85737

Visit our website at:
www.fireshippress.com

Visit the author's website at:
www.stockmanbooks.com

This book is dedicated with much appreciation and thanks to those whose help brought this book to publication.

Nothing is easier than self-deceit. For what each man wishes that he also believes to be true. —Demosthenes

A Note to the Reader

This novel is based upon the life of Captain Guy de Coëtnempren, Count de Kersaint. The narrative fills with speculation what the limited historical documents tell us about this great French ship commander. It aims to entertain and enlighten, and the reader should not consider it a factual biography. Although much is fictional license, it rests upon the recorded foundation of his remarkable career. Archives inform us of his adventures in life, and the basics of when and where he played his role in the mid-1700s French wars. To those points, this accounting attempts to remain true.

This is the third book of the *Tween Sea & Shore Series*. Many of the characters mentioned in this book can also be found in the previous two books: *The Ship's Carpenter* and *Captains of the Renown*.

A helpful *Addendum* to the series, containing ship terms definitions, foreign word pronunciations, maps, and much more, is available at the author's website and may be downloaded for free in PDF format at: https://stockmanbooks.com/downloads It is an excellent aid in reading the series' books.

ON WAVES OF GLORY

The Quest of Captain Guy de Kersaint

D. E. STOCKMAN

FIRESHIP
PRESS

THE CARIBBEAN SEA AND MARIE
1710-1727

Sunlight poured through tall windows and crept over the limestone mantle in the salon. The brilliance bathed the old mantel clock, reflecting off its fittings and cut-glass panes to dapple the room's walls with rainbows.

The harpsichord pinged as someone offered to play in the nearby library while guests gathered. They had come to celebrate Guy's seventh birthday, the firstborn son of Count de Kersaint. The previous day, the boy's favorite friend, Marie, had also arrived at the manor and they played together without let-up.

Guy, shorter than Marie, scurried past the paintings hanging in the hallway, and he peeked back around the corner. "Hurry Marie, we'll miss it!" He halted, staring at the timepiece that sat on the mantel, a tribute to de Kersaint's glory.

Mesmerized by the bright ivory dial, he focused on the hour hand. "See, it's going to strike," he said as his playmate stopped by his side. Marie and her little sister visited often, but he had never shared this secret ritual with anyone.

Marie's blond hair glowed in the sunbeams and distracted him as he pointed to the clock. Guy's attention swept between his companion and the family relic above the fireplace.

When the delicate brass pointer ticked onto the twelve, mechanical clicks and whirs sounded. Clear and high, a silver bell proclaimed the hour with chimes. Guy smiled, satisfied, and turned to her.

Marie returned a momentary blank glance with a quick shrug, and then went to the straight-back chair near the wall and dragged it before the hearth.

Guy's eyes widened. "What are you doing?"

"I want to see it better." Marie hopped up onto the upholstered seat on tiptoes.

"No, Papa forbids it!" said Guy and stepped forward, but too late to stop her. Her arm reached for the base.

Guy's voice grew stern. "The king gave it to grandfather. Don't, we aren't allowed!"

Marie ignored him as her small fingers glided over the smooth tortoiseshell case and tapped the gold acanthus leaf garland along its edges. "Who's the lady on the front?" Two of her fingertips stroked the bas-relief figure of a tunic-draped woman clutching a trumpet with one hand and an upraised laurel wreath with the other.

"That's the Goddess of Fame; she's beautiful," he said in veneration, barely audible. Someday, he thought, he'd get one from the king, too. "Papa says it's for grandfather's bravery in a sea battle." Guy glowered as she explored the family's hallowed object.

Marie climbed down just before Guy's father walked into the room.

The count's brows furrowed as he fixed on the out-of-place chair and then on his young son. "Why is this here?" He glanced again at the seat.

"I watched it strike, Father." Guy wrinkled his forehead and bit his lower lip. "But I didn't touch it."

Marie's head cocked. "That's so, Count de Kersaint, he didn't." The half-truth eased the count's suspicions as her blue eyes twinkled in innocence.

"Put it back where it belongs, Guy-François." The count pointed to the empty place for it.

After pulling the chair to the side, Guy snatched Marie's wrist, and they ran out together.

As the two raced up the stone stairway toward his bedroom, she slowed. "Why did you tell the count you moved it?"

"I didn't want Father to yell at you." Guy paused to answer.

Marie scoffed, "But I wouldn't care if he had," and darted ahead.

By the age of nineteen, Guy had learned how to read his father's eyes in an instant. They always showed the count's temperament, and that morning, tight slits glared at his year-younger brother Joseph as they sat at breakfast.

"So, Joseph, your brother Guy leaves on an active posting aboard ship soon." The count's eyes stared hard at Joseph. "But your performance at the academy is dismal, I've been told." A scowling face made both sons sit straighter. "Our family has captained for generations. Just what do you intend to do?"

Joseph dipped his head low. "Papa, I want to become a priest." He put his fork on the plate without a clatter.

Guy sat motionless at the table, barely breathing.

The count's glare softened a bit. "A priest, huh? You realize that your grandfather and I wanted the two of you to follow our careers. As a de Kersaint, you're expected to go to sea, not a pulpit. I spent a great deal of money for the *Garde de la Marine* to prepare you."

"Yes, sir." Joseph, eyes down, avoided him. "For me to continue in that direction serves neither you, me, nor the navy any benefit. I'd make a poor ship commander."

Guy spoke up, "Papa, he's doing terribly. Once in navigation class, Brother Lefon scolded Joseph as only good for ditch-digging."

"Lefon said that?" The count focused on Guy. "Does he know what stock Joseph comes from? Outrageous! Lefons are commoners." Their father stirred and hunched forward, his hands curled. "Whatever a de Kersaint puts his mind to is successful. If Joseph becomes a cleric, he'll be a great one, perhaps a bishop."

Joseph sneaked a glance at Guy and mouthed the word *thanks*.

Again, turning to Joseph, he continued, "Yesterday, when I arrived in Brest, the academy director informed me you lacked a certain, hmm, stature for becoming a military officer."

"Better words would be *arrogance of command*. It's not in me." Joseph's face reddened as he squirmed. The sons strove to please him and anything less ended in harsh lectures or even punishment.

That morning, though, the count remained silent for nearly a minute. "Perhaps you're right." He nodded as his finger traced his jaw. "If your heart has guided you to the church, start at the seminary at once. Given time, you may be Brother Lefon's rector." He gave a snort, reached for a dessert, and set his gaze on Guy.

"Marie and her father are in Brest this week and I asked them to our dinner tonight. She gives him such headaches. He wants her to learn the violin, but she only wants to study art. At the Chateau de Bézal, he told her to dress for supper with the marquise and viscount, and she wore her day clothes. When he says one thing, she does another. His daughter is so unlike both of you or any young woman I've known."

"Oh, it's her obstinacy." Guy stared upward.

"Obstinacy is also disrespect," his father said and took a bite of the apple compote-filled crepe. The count waved a syrupy fork in the air. "She'd not get away with that under this roof."

"Sir, I find her behavior curious, almost a mystery, and don't think she is doing it to be rebellious or hurtful, but independent." Guy reached for the dessert plate.

Count de Kersaint, chewing, pointed his fork at Guy. "Uh-huh, you've always fancied that girl, but I have yet to see why. At least you're consistent in your actions, although one never knows about hers." He wagged his head.

Guy put two crepes on his plate. "Marie thrives on pluckiness, and I've thought it refreshing compared to others I meet."

Joseph glanced sideways at Guy and grinned. "Marie is blossoming into a fine-looking mademoiselle, too, and popular among navy officers, Father."

"At least I have my eye on someone." Guy's foot kicked Joseph's shin under the table. "Maybe someday, she'll grow fonder of me."

Hours later, Guy and a classmate leaned against a low stone wall on Rue de Mer alongside Brest's docks, their flashy cadet uniforms standing out among the townspeople. Nearby, vendors hawked their various goods as buyers drifted from one handcart to another to bicker over prices. Guy's fingers brushed back and forth over the rough stones behind him as he brooded over his soon-to-come nautical career and the dinner celebrating his graduation that evening. He ignored his friend's chatter and the crowd noises.

The other cadet whistled, drawing his attention. "Who's that pretty woman with the officer?" he said, pivoting the tip of his scabbard toward her.

Marie and a navy ensign walked together fifty feet off, accompanied by a chaperone. When the man spoke, she put a fingertip on her cheek and replied, her teeth glistening.

"Marie de Bruc." Guy winced at seeing her with him. "She's a family friend who lives in the Chateau de Brézal most of the time. The viscount and marquise are godparents to us both. When in town, she and her father live in their house across the river."

He never considered she might develop feelings for anyone other than himself. "Let's go. This is so boring." Guy's mind filled with speculation as he led his friend in the opposite direction along the stone pier. The upcoming graduation and Marie's ignorance of his affection for her compounded the stressful uncertainties of his future.

To honor Guy's commission as a cadet aboard a warship, the de Kersaints invited kin and guests to their house in Brest, rather than to the mansion in Cléder. When Guy returned home, his brother devilishly teased him. "So, Marie is coming tonight," Joseph said. "Since you'll not see her again for some time after going to sea, be sure to tell her about your lust."

"You dolt! Lust has nothing to do with it." Guy gave him a soft punch in the shoulder and then looked down and sighed. "She may find others more suitable, anyway. I saw her on Rue de Mer with someone. Maybe I waited too long to tell her my feelings." He turned away from his brother, visualizing the ensign with her.

"Wouldn't it be ironic if she found you as appealing but never mentioned it?" Joseph laughed. "Two blind mules pulling the same wagon, each oblivious to the other."

"*Mules*, huh?" Guy reached over and grabbed him, his brawny frame enveloping his brother's slim body, and swung him around in a playful tussle.

By evening, the guests arrived, filling the smaller house. Guy had asked his stepmother to seat Marie next to him for dinner. Fine china and silver-plated candelabras punctuated the length of the table. The burning candles' warm glow made Marie appear even more radiant and captivating as he turned to her. "The navy has assigned me to a two-decker, *le Griffon*." He swallowed hard. "I'll be leaving soon." Guy shifted in his chair, as he reconstructed phrases to express his love to her.

"So I was told. Couldn't you ask for an assignment ashore? Aren't you worried about battles and storms, Guy?" Her face scrunched. "I want you forever to be my favorite friend, not a martyr or name on a lost-at-sea list."

"Since we're not at war, I'm not afraid of that, and all de Kersaints take positions at sea, not ashore. Besides, *le Griffon* will just escort a convoy to the West Indies, and before the hurricane season begins."

Marie poured wine into the water in the crystal before her to purify it. "Will you be attending the holiday ball in two weeks, or already be aboard ship?" Her eyes stared at the glass, her finger rubbing the stem.

"I should still be here, but it depends on nature when we'll depart. We can sail only when the wind is out of the northeast, and that's unusual in December." A pensive look preceded his next words. "Is anyone accompanying you?" Guy's jaw clamped tight, waiting.

"Several of our friends are going. François de Saint-Alouarn will be there. His shyness amuses me. Every time I talk to him, he blushes. He's so awkward with women." She giggled while shaking her head. "He's mature in his conversations, though, almost as much as you." Her gaze drifted again to him.

"I believe you're more polished than either François or I." His brow creased. "We're still hesitant in divulging our thoughts, but you express yourself with confidence and without hesitation. Perhaps someday we'll achieve that boldness in revealing our true selves."

Marie sat back in her chair, her necklace glittering from the candlelight as she breathed. "Hah, you are both far bolder. You've chosen a profession that takes bravery, risk and resolve. I shudder, thinking of the dangers to come in your futures."

The joy left her lips, and she closed her eyes for a moment. "My outspokenness is my burden, not my boon. I've long realized my tendency to act rashly and speak my mind. Often I pay in regret twice as much as any contentment I might get from it." She halted again. "You follow a steadfast path of wise choices, tempered words, and reason. How I wish my seedling had grown in the same manner, but it's life's little joke that each of us must pocket the talents given, not those preferred." Marie looked downward, unfocused.

"Marie, of those I know, you have risen so far above inhibitions. It's an uncommon thing to be so free from the foolish constraints of propriety and still remain loved." He hesitated, fighting what cried out from his heart to say. But she needed encouragement, not his forlorn amorous confessions, he decided.

"Loved by whom? Those who call upon me?" She sighed and wagged her finger. "No, to me they're mere distractions and don't love me as much as want me." Marie's fingernail tapped the water goblet before her, frowning. "It's strange that we think love and ardor mix like water and wine when they are more like water and oil, ever separate. One may love and desire, love and not desire, or desire and not love, but they are always apart and seldom in equal proportions."

As Guy opened his mouth to respond, his father rose at the head of the table. All present turned to their host.

"My friends, I must give notice to my son's academy graduation. Guy has begun his seafaring in the tradition of other distinguished sailors from Brittany. At nineteen, he is now a cadet officer upon a vessel of our great royal navy to serve the king. Had not my wound curtailed my service aboard ships, I'd have added to that glory. Yet, I'm sure Guy, as part of our maritime heritage, will surpass his ancestors' achievements. Please raise a glass to his new station." With that, he held his drink high, and everyone stood and faced Guy.

After the toast, they sat and Guy got to his feet and coughed lightly. "Dear all, thank you for the gesture of support and honor. I hope my duty on board shall fulfill not only the king's expectations, but yours and, I trust, my own. Pray that my voyage returns me safely to Brest from Saint-Domingue's fevers and hazards ... and their women."

The crowd roared and applauded as Guy returned to his seat. Marie put her hand over her mouth in jest and glimpsed up at him.

"Should I regard you as lascivious as those wishing to court me?" She crinkled her eyes and mocked at clutching her heart while laughing. "I never imagined you harbored such notions toward the fairer gender."

He chuckled. "Like you, I'm old enough where your peculiar breed is no longer viewed as pests but embraced as intimates. You mentioned François earlier. Is he a pest or a beau?" A lump swelled in his throat.

"François? No. He's just a friend," she answered quickly.

Guy's face melted as her's turned crimson and she looked away. An aunt to his left asked for the saltshaker, and he conversed with her for most of the dinner.

⚘

At the end of December, the yearly academy dance gathered navy officials, wives and older daughters, local nobility, and junior officers and cadets who strove to impress them.

François, taller than Guy and less muscular, had a lanky stride. Guy saw him coming from a distance and waited for him to catch up outside Brest's naval hall. Despite his jealousy over Marie, he liked the younger cadet who always wore a greeting on his face.

"It must be exciting for you," François said as he came closer, his charming beam rewarding Guy's wait. "You're done with schooling. I wish it were me." His uniform, too short for his gangly arms, already needed lengthening to adjust to his teen-years' growth.

"Now the hard part has begun onboard," Guy moaned. "Until we leave, they have us climbing to the tops, memorizing spar dimensions, and learning sea charts and flags."

François rose a finger. "Still, it's better than sitting at attention and listening to the Jesuits all day at the academy. Did they say where you're bound?"

"To Saint-Domingue and other Caribbean islands, of course." Guy glanced past him into the distance, and for a second, his spirits stirred. "Oh, Marie just arrived." He pointed as she and her father strode up the stairs from the sidewalk. "She mentioned you. I suspect she favors you." Guy encouraged his mouth into a bow.

"Yes, we've become close companions." François peered in her direction. "When she visits Brest, we stroll and talk. She's delightful." He beamed when spying Marie.

Guy's voice tightened. "She is that. Has she expressed any deeper feelings for you?" The tactless question made him blink hard.

"For me?!" François's eyes enlarged. "No, we're just friends. She has many officers lining up for her. What chance do I have?" He stood watching her ascend the stairs to the entrance.

"I suppose you're right. No sense hoisting a jib at anchor." Then he turned away and went off to mingle with others.

Not fifteen minutes later, he noticed François and Marie talking and cheerful in a group of friends. Guy sulked and left the dance. Within a week, *le Griffon* set out to sea.

⁂

Lieutenant de Santec, their mentor aboard ship and a dozen years older than most of the cadets, gestured with his hand to pale dots of land still leagues afar. "There they are, gentlemen, the Canaries. Remember them. They're nature's signal to bear for the West Indies." His suntanned complexion stood out in contrast to the pale flesh of his charges, as much as his taller, well-muscled body did.

"Are we far from Morocco, sir?" asked one.

De Santec then pointed east toward the portside. "The African coast is a few days that way."

Guy and two others put spyglasses to their eyes to try to remember the shapes, colors, and alignment of the closest islands.

Sailors above and on deck shifted the huge sails as the creaking rudder swung to catch the wind to proceed southwest.

"Sir, how many times have you made the trip from France to the West Indies?"

"More than I can recall," De Santec said to Guy and turned to the others. "Each of you won't be able to count the number of crossings, either, when you're lieutenants. Our colonies need our constant protection and service."

Then de Santec's deep-brown eyes grew serious. "Our squadron's mission is important. The rebellion that sprang up last year in Saint-Domingue wasn't caused by slaves or runaway Maroons but by free inhabitants. Our navy must put an end to it before it becomes a bigger concern or spreads to other colonies." The seriousness of the voyage forced the cadets out of their childish fantasies.

After two more weeks on the Atlantic, they approached the Windward Islands, with Martinique resting on the horizon. Guy tingled at the thought of exotic foreign lands. Then six hours passed, and their squadron of warships glided toward its main harbor, Fort Royal.

Later, Guy turned to de Santec as the warship tacked windward for anchorage. "Sir, I can smell it." His nose lifted up and outward.

"What do you smell?" asked the officer, chuckling.

Guy appeared in a trance. "It's so sweet." He continued sniffing the air. "Is it the sugar makers?"

The lieutenant nodded toward the rising steam coming from the various vats outside the shoreline factories. "Slaves are boiling the juices they squeezed from the cane. Most they dry and press into sugarloaf, and what's left over they distill into rum. This island's commerce, though, is nothing compared to what flows from Saint-Domingue. From there, we get not only sugar products, but tobacco, cocoa, indigo, and coconuts. It's Saint-Domingue that is France's treasure chest."

Guy looked puzzled. "I've never drunk rum, sir."

De Santec scrunched his mouth to one side. "We'll only be in Fort Royal for two days to transfer sick ashore and take on water, so you'll not get the opportunity. But after we berth at Petit-Goâve in Saint-Domingue, the captain will let you disembark and you can try it."

They sailed northwest and stopped at low-lying islands en route until *le Griffon* dropped anchor in Petit-Goâve's Bay. The principal town rested inland from the harbor a quarter mile with a collection of shops, taverns, and factories along the road to it. A small mountain sprung up in the distance behind all.

Guy and a fellow cadet, Emeric, sat beside each other as a longboat took them to a pier where they clambered out and set off to explore. The dockside street held many little buildings with plastered walls and bright-colored doors. The port bustled with people as slaves and free folk busied themselves with tasks. Wealthy French gentlemen and White or mixed-blood ladies with parasols strolled arm-in-arm along the quay. Everywhere, sweetness permeated the tropical air. Guy's eyes sped from one new curiosity to another.

More men landed from other ships, and soon the streets filled with uniformed officers and raggedy sailors. The island's citizens retreated from the day's heat to their homes and shops, giving way to the boisterous invading crewmen who only craved alcohol and sex. Guy and his friend meandered along a dusty street and watched the seamen cram the drinking establishments.

"Too crowded here for a drink." Guy sighed and motioned. "Let's search further to avoid this mob."

They turned up an unpaved road leading away from the waterfront. The sun, straight above, covered everything in a brilliant, hot blanket of white rays. Guy's dark uniform soon soaked him and the two young men sought relief. Cooler shadows under the thatched palm fronds of an open-sided tavern beckoned. Flanked by wood benches, a well-stained plank table occupied the entire center of the small hut. The Black owner stood with crossed arms next to a short counter holding a keg of rum, one of ale, and wooden tankards.

"Good day, Admirals!" The barkeeper flashed a grin as they approached. "Please, shelter from the forge and rest your burning bones under my cool sunshade."

"It's sweltering, we shall," answered Emeric. "Give us two rums."

The man poured the drinks into the vessels as he eyed them. "You are brave sailors."

"Pardon, sir, why do you say that?" Guy said as he wiped sweat from his forehead and they set their hats on the table.

"Young seamen never venture this far from the docks. Most are afraid of Maroons. But the escaped slaves live in the distant hills and mountains, and only raid at night to slit French throats." His eyes bulged, and he drew his thumb across his throat.

"Ha, Maroons wouldn't attack with a fleet in port." Guy chuckled and shook his head. "This is our first visit. I didn't expect such heat." He lifted the tankard and stared at the clear liquor inside, hesitating to take a drink. Emeric grabbed his, took a too-large gulp, and coughed as the rum seared its way down. Tears formed in his eyes and he grimaced.

"Petit-Goâve is not always this warm. Usually, it is much hotter." The tavern keeper winked and picked up the Spanish pistareen Guy had placed on the table and gave him back a few copper coins.

Emeric pulled his wig off and plopped it into his hat, running a palm over his wet, short hair. Such a faux pas seemed tempting to Guy, too, but he kept his wig on and suffered. The pair sipped their rum as it burned to their stomachs. Then, after twenty minutes, they bought another they swallowed with more ease.

The owner brought a small wooden plate with two whitish lumps on it sprinkled with powdered sugar. "Celebrate your first visit with these, the pride of Petit-Goâve, our candy. It's a gift." He tapped his finger next to them.

"Mmm, they look good," said Emeric, who snatched up the tiny mound and popped it whole into his mouth. His eyes enlarged, and he smacked his lips crudely.

Guy bit into the other and understood his friend's reaction. "My God, this is incredible. I've never eaten a sweet as delicious."

The owner's chest swelled as his eyelids closed. "It's worth the extra climb from the dock's taverns, no?"

"Where can we get more of these?" asked Emeric. "I want more."

"You'll find them anywhere in town, although people buy the best on this road." He motioned up the wide, sloping dirt path. "The place with a green door. She makes coconut bonbons better than anyone else on the island."

The cadets finished their beverages and bade goodbye, leaving to search for the shop. Not a mile along the way, they came upon a small shack, painted pink with a green entrance. A stone chimney pushed up from one end and a gentle swirl of gray smoke lifted from it, lacing the air with a syrupy scent.

Guy knocked on the faded boards, and a voice from inside called, "Come in, come in! Shut the door after." Her accent, like the tavern owner's, took a second to comprehend.

The two entered, and divine vapors overcame them. "Oh, God," Emeric gasped. The hot room had large pots and vats on short ovens, boiling and bubbling off more of the delectable fragrance. An attractive, dark-skinned woman, bent over one cauldron, looked up and scanned them.

"Good afternoon, madam." Guy greeted, beaming at the smells. "A man down the street said you sell sweets."

"At the tavern." It was not a question. She wiped her hand on a color-smeared cloth and straightened, arms akimbo. Sweat glistened on her flesh, and her blouse, open low, showed much cleavage. "Ah, you want my goodies, then." The woman wore a friendly face and waved them over toward a shelf hanging on the wall. It supported tin trays of smooth treats like those they ate but coated red and yellow. "Those taste lemony and these of hot spices. Choose which you desire."

With fingers at their mouths, they inspected her offerings and pointed to those they fancied. She picked them up and laid them on a green banana tree leaf cut into a square.

"Are you enjoying your stay in Petit-Goâve?"

"Yes," both said eagerly.

"Then entertain yourselves." Her eyes sparkled. "Opportunities for fun are rare in the navy."

"We intend to," Emeric replied, still looking over the selections.

"You're in luck." She pointed outside. "This very day, my neighbor is having a party. You must come to see how we enjoy our afternoons."

"That's a cordial offer, madam." After searching for another pistareen in his pocket, Guy pulled one out to pay.

The candy maker snatched up the money and dropped it into a purse at her side but offered no copper in change. Then she grabbed a forearm of each and led them across the street toward a small, whitewashed house. After she ushered them before the threshold, she rapped.

An older fellow's upper body popped out of the doorway and looked at the Frenchmen. His dark muscular arm reached out and pulled each by a shoulder into the building. He patted them on the back when they stood inside as the vendor waved and left.

"Sit down, my lords. Sit." The enormous man swept his hand dramatically toward stools against the wall. A small, amateurish painting of the Virgin Mary hung opposite between two doors.

Their heads still swimming from the rum, they gawked at each other, bewildered. As Emeric opened his mouth to ask a question, a young lady exited the left room, wearing the flimsiest of nightshirts. It flowed to her knees and showed her features beneath. The female sashayed up to Guy and rubbed his neck.

"Please tell me about your adventures. I love navy officers. Call me Marie." She pulled him from the seat into her chamber.

Guy followed her without protest as he glanced back at his mate, eager. Then another young beauty emerged, and Emeric bolted from his stool for the other bedroom.

Once inside, the lovely woman assisted Guy in undressing, and he settled onto a small bed. She helped him into arousal and into the mysteries of lovemaking. When they finished, she showed him outside and he sat again.

"Five pistareens, good sir." The big man loomed in front of him with his huge hand open before Guy's face. Guy shot his fingers into his waistcoat pocket in a quick search to comply. He pulled a handful of French and Spanish coins from it and held them to find the right ones. In a flash, the flesh-peddler plucked five from Guy's palm.

"Thank you, and please return on your next trip. I hope you enjoy the dainties." He motioned to the small, leaf-wrapped package Guy carried.

"Y-yes, we will," he stammered and waited for Emeric to finish. A few loud groans came from the second boudoir, and as Guy expected, Emeric emerged from his frolic to join him, grinning like a fool.

After his shipmate paid the brothel keeper, they strutted along the road to the docks in silence as they reflected on their emergence into full adulthood.

Aboard their ship, they bragged to the other cadets about their experience without a hint of shame. It had no bearing on Guy's love for Marie, although the seducer having the same name as his beloved in France seemed to defile it somehow.

◦∞◦

The stormy season had started on the southern coast of the island, with frequent squalls passing with dark gray swaths of sky. The rain came heavy with strong winds that whistled in the rigging and rocked the ships. Still in Petit-Goâve, de Santec and Guy spoke of the uprising on another steamy, wet afternoon below decks.

"Once our infantry debarks in all the ports, sir, they'll round up the rebels," Guy said, frowning.

"Some of them, yes." The lieutenant went on. "There are too many to imprison, although most colonials oppose the rebellion. How would troops sort them out?"

Guy squinted and cocked his head. *"Sort them out,* sir?"

"Some of the Small Whites, the White commoners, shopkeepers, tradesmen, and farmers rebelled. But fewer of the untitled Frenchmen, who come to the islands to marry wealthy Black and mixed-blood women. Probably even a Big White or two, those officeholders, nobles, and large business and plantation owners may support the insurrection. They have more to gain by freeing up the controls than anyone else. They give the king his greatest worry. In attacking the trading center house in Le Cap, though, they crossed the king's line of tolerance."

Guy put on a stern face. "But they're French, sir, even if they live in the West Indies. They should follow the decrees passed down to them and be thankful we protect them."

De Santec's features darkened. "Patriotism is the color of gold. The decrees forbid dealing with any other country except France and control prices for almost everything. The colonists claim the regulations stifle freedoms and handicap their economy." He frowned. "The French East

India Company has exclusive rights to buy and sell slaves, sugar and rum, and food exports. It buys low from the plantations and factories and resells for much higher profits elsewhere. Distilleries get less for their product unless they smuggle it to the English colonies. Rum-running is a lucrative business here."

"At least, sir, we won't be in danger cleaning up this mess other than getting the troops ashore," Guy said with certainty.

"True, we'll be at sea, but there are other ways to take down one's adversary. You may discover, Guy, in revolts, as in naval battles, any method to defeat an enemy overshadows moral codes we claim to embrace but few practice. Watch your tankard; poisoning is common," he warned with a wag of his finger.

The next month dragged by for Guy in the stifling tropical heat. As the weather cooled, the ships embarked for Le Cap, about 30 leagues north. After making port, infantry went ashore to prevent another revolt.
Leaning on a thick stay line, Guy surveyed the capital as it sprawled beside the ocean. The city appeared much larger than Petit-Goâve. Someone approached behind him and he turned.

"Brush off your uniform, Guy. All officers must attend a welcoming reception at the governor's mansion, except those on duty." De Santec picked lint off his tricorn hat. "I'll show you the way this evening."

After the early December sunset, he and others trailed Lieutenant de Santec to the house. It sat a mile inland on an overlooking hill. Every French fleet that arrived received the customary soiree.

Upon entering, Guy stood to the side watching the island's wealthy, port administrators, and most of the fleet's officers within the room. Everyone exchanged the news from France and the colonies with the revolt dominating the conversations. The French East India Company magistrate discussed issues with the governor of the isle. Other dignitaries spoke in hushed, fearful tones about the attacks and upheaval. Their wives also huddled in groups, whispering descriptions of atrocities they feared might happen.

Guy stood with the other cadets and sidled over to the table holding the rum punch bowl. A house slave served him a ladleful in a goblet. He eyed the contents for a second, sipped the drink, and then took a deeper gulp before returning to his spot along the wall.

"Welcome to Le Cap, young man," said an older aristocrat standing three feet away. "I take it this is your first trip to the island." Aged near fifty, he had a rotund physique and fleshy jowls.

Guy made a half-bow to the gentleman. "Sir, yes. It's my first to your port."

"Ah-ha, then you've never tasted our rum, no doubt. France forbids its import as a threat to the brandy trade. How do you like it?" The heavy man beamed at him.

"I had some earlier, that, well, left a lifetime impression." Guy's face lit up. "To be honest, the fruit juices dilute this one. But the beverage is good."

"My name is Baron de Courseuil. My distillery produces the finest on the island." His eyes gleamed with pride. "What you hold is a poor imitation. You should have mine before you depart for France." He paused and added, "But wait, I have a bottle in my coach if you care to test my boast. Come, it's there with the other carriages. You're in for a treat, my friend." He beckoned with a curled finger and Guy followed him.

"I'm Guy de Kersaint off of *le Griffon*. Everything is a fresh experience for me in the West Indies. I'd love to try yours." He trailed in the baron's footsteps. Before the entrance stretched a long row of two-wheeled curricles, simple carts, and fine coaches in a slight sea breeze cooling the evening.

"Over here." The baron pointed and strutted toward the sixth in a line of dozens parked in the fading light. Atop each sat a Black coachman awaiting his master or mistress. The rum-maker ignored his driver, opened its door, and fetched a leather-covered decanter with a large stopper from a pocket beside the seat. "Now toss that swill in your cup away and sample this. You mustn't leave the island without partaking of the best." He poured Guy's goblet full and put the bottle back. "Guy, who is your father? Perhaps I've met him."

"My father is Jacques de Coëtnempren, Count de Kersaint, and Régisseur de Brézal." Guy swallowed and it stung downward. "My, what a wonderful flavor," he said, not really tasting anything but liquor.

"Oh, *de Coëtnemprens*, I know of them. That's an old family we've heard of, even in Paris." The baron's eyes widened. "What do navy officers make of the trouble here in Saint-Domingue? What did you hear on the ship coming over?"

"The revolt, I've been told, is a top priority for the king. He's aware of the complaints against the East India Company and their strict monopoly but believes those here must take into consideration his perspective. If he gives in to the demands, it'll force him to do likewise in all French colonies."

"Did your officers tell you exactly whom the king is blaming for this uprising?" he asked, studying his face.

Guy answered, sampling more of the liquid, "No, they said some in the upper class may have instigated the actions."

"How's the governor planning on resolving the issue?" The baron motioned for them to return to the hall and began walking. "Did they mention arrests?"

Guy attempted to consume the rum as fast as the baron but settled for sips. "Infantrymen will guard the docks and quell any rioting or sabotage. Yes, they mentioned even arresting nobles." He touched his numbing nose.

"Ah, I see," the baron said but stopped short as his gaze fell upon movement near the entrance. A squad of colonial soldiers entered the building, led by a tall Black infantry captain. With each word crashing into the next, he spurted, "Well, Guy, I'm afraid this night has worn on me and I'll depart. Good luck on your return voyage, my boy."

"Yes, sir. Have a pleasant evening. Your product is exquisite." Guy spoke to the gentleman's back as the baron rushed to his coach, departing under whip with the horses clopping and speeding to a gallop.

When Guy returned to the hall, he found his shipmates befuddled. "What's happened?" Guy asked a fellow cadet.

"The governor tried to capture someone here tonight, but the nobleman suddenly vanished!" the cadet replied.

Guy scanned the crowd as he saw the soldiers searching the rooms. "Who did they want to arrest?"

"A baron whom they'd invited here as a trap," he said.

Guy's jaw dropped. *"Baron?"*

He hurried to de Santec. "Sir, is the name of the person they're seeking *Baron de Courseuil?*"

"Yes. Have you seen him?" The lieutenant's attention fixed on Guy.

"The baron saw the troops arrive and raced away in his carriage, sir."

Without commenting, the lieutenant sped to the colonial in charge and told him the fugitive's whereabouts. A second later he shouted, "Guy, come here! Tell this officer what you saw."

He stood before them and related the conversation with the baron and the fast departure on the road toward the harbor. In seconds, the captain and infantrymen ran from the hall. Everyone's eyes watched them leave and then settled on Guy. The lieutenant patted him on the back and returned to his group.

"Good thinking, sir. We'll catch him at the docks before he can flee on a boat or into the hills." Guy turned to see the governor addressing him, looking pleased. "I'll commend your quick action to your captain. Enjoy the rest of the evening."

Guy swaggered back to his friends, his chin up and chesty, and answered their questions about the baron. Until he left, he strutted around as the little drama's hero.

Later that night, the colonial lieutenant nabbed Baron Courseuil at the docks and brought him before the governor, who informed the defiant rascal of the king's great displeasure.

Over the ensuing months, troops seized others with most feeling the whip on their backs or awaiting trials. The slave masters and rum and sugar makers still demanded regulation reforms, but the French East India Company kept control of its monopoly and gave them few concessions.

On his third day at sea after leaving Santo-Domingue, Guy stood watch one evening. Light winds near the Windward Passage eased the fleet westward on their circular route back to France. Crewmen blew handmade wood, bone, or metal flutes to an old shanty in the midships, and others smoked pipes or talked in small groups. Civilians who worked for the government strolled the deck in the cool twilight.

Guy noticed one twice the size of most, approaching. It was the baron.

"Good evening, sir. I see you're returning with us." He tipped his hat. "I'm Guy de Kersaint. We met at the naval social at the governor's mansion."

"Why I do recall." Baron de Courseuil bowed slightly and beamed. "So, tell me my rum isn't the best you've had. Am I correct, my friend?" His jocularity seemed infectious.

"Yes, sir, it was. Are you headed home for a visit?" Guy guessed the nobleman was far too powerful to be confined in chains.

"One might say that, but my visit will be permanent, I fear. As you probably learned, the king and I disagree on the commercial parameters of the East India Company. He's forcing me back and banished me from Saint-Domingue." The baron shrugged.

Guy's lips pulled to the side. "It is unfortunate you won't be there to oversee your distillery."

"It's fine. I'll run my business from Nantes." The gentleman waved his hand before him, dismissing the concerns. "My son-in-law will take care of the details on the island."

"Nantes is close to Brest, sir. I thought you mentioned you lived in Paris?" he asked.

The nobleman flinched and squinted one eye. "Yes, but he also barred me from Paris and royal residences. For the titled, it is the worst a king might do other than putting a sword across one's neck or inviting him to Rue Saint Antoine."

"Sir, *Rue Saint Antoine?*" Guy wrinkled his forehead.

"The Bastille's street, my boy. Still, it came from my own doing. My actions upset the king over one of his key investments. You see, he owns most of the French East India Company."

Guy clucked and said, "Sir, had you known that beforehand, surely you wouldn't have caused him such concern."

"Oh, my dear young man, but I did know." The baron's lips curled. "Yet, with rights and property, a person must choose either to obey unjust laws or do what one may to amend them. We brought the issue to Versailles with our little upheaval. It had lean prospects of success, but perhaps it will spread and change the king's unfair perspective on trade someday," he said, still smiling.

"But now they've punished you for standing up to a greater authority, sir. A lone rook should never check a king or queen without the protection of other chess pieces." He rethought his presumptuous reply. "Oh, I'm sorry."

"Ha, ha! It's true, Guy," the baron boomed. "Knights and bishops, though, can still be played. The game continues, and even pawns topple kings with the right moves. A ruler's power exists as long as people support and have confidence in his decisions." With that, he waved his hand, turned, and walked sternward, leaving Guy to ponder his words.

In the chilled air of a pearl-gray dawn weeks later, in the higher latitudes, *le Griffon* crept toward France. Before the sun in its rise broke free of the blue expanse, a topman glimpsed a shadowy violet smudge along the sweep, and shouted out, "Land afore!"

Guy, like every crewman on the ship, rushed to the bulwarks to catch a look at their distant homeland. The moment he spotted it, a tingle ran up his back and he noticeably quivered. He spun around when de Santec, behind, spoke. "So, what thoughts now that you're ending your first mission?"

Guy grabbed a nearby line and paused. "Sir, I loved it." A smile spread. "To serve aboard an actual warship, not one of the academy's small training vessels has changed me. Before, I viewed myself as a landsman pretending to be a seaman. Now I'm a real one with important tasks. Although I have so much to learn, I share in my family's tradition."

"You're justified in those ideas, Guy," said de Santec. "A man can embrace sea lore and the maritime arts with his mind or his heart. In the mind, it's only a momentary amusement, but in the heart, it takes hold and never let's go. How you imagine yourself is the difference.

"We'll be anchoring in less than a week. The captain allows cadets to take leave after their first trip. I'm sure your father, or anyone else, will be delighted to hear of your accomplishments." The lieutenant raised an eyebrow. "Perhaps any young lady that has been waiting for your return as well."

Guy glanced aside before answering, his face warming. "Yes, sir. There is someone, Marie, to whom I've yet to confess my feelings. But I'm resolved to clear up that upon landing."

Le Griffon moved at a frustrating horse-walk through the currents for days, and Guy centered on Marie every free moment. The wintry night they moored in Brest's Bay, he lay awake on his cot with eyes open, trying to sleep. He chided himself for voyaging aboard a warship and prepared to meet any enemy, yet, fearing to utter that one intimate sentence to the woman he loved.

Soon after making berth, the captain permitted him to cross the bay to Brest. A boat rowed the cadets past the large citadel that dominated the landscape at the port's gateway and guarded the Penfeld River's outlet.

Ashore, he trotted up the sloping street with a vanishing haze following every breath to their family's smaller port house. For over a hundred years, it sheltered de Kersaint sailors while in Brest.

He opened the door with the single iron key he carried, and it squeaked a welcome before he called, "Is anyone here?" No one replied until a distant sound came from the garden courtyard. Their houseman, Pascal, had answered.

The familiar voice comforted his ear. "It's Guy, I'm home!" He hurried to the kitchen where the servant had laid out food for a breakfast.

The shuffling, aged fellow, thin and frail, entered through the rear exit. "Welcome, Master Guy. I was feeding the cat outside. How was your cruise?" He smelled of garlic and wine.

Guy enjoyed Pascal, who had a whimsical nature. "The voyage was of little consequence. Is my father in Brest?"

The old servant brushed a lock of white hair from his balding forehead and patted Guy's arm. "Afraid not, sir. The count's at the manor in Cléder." Then he toddled to the hallway and touched a cloak hanging on a peg. "It'd have bitten you if you had passed it closer. Joseph is back from the seminary."

"Is he here now?"

"Since Tuesday." The elderly man splayed his lips wide and pointed upward with his wrinkled finger. "In the bedroom, still asleep, I suspect."

Guy scrambled up the stairs. Joseph lay on his stomach, hidden under the covers. "Hey, get up, lazy dog!" Guy playfully let out as he tugged on the blanket.

His brother stirred and propped himself up on an arm. "Oh, it's you." He yawned and dropped back down, moaning as he stretched his legs.

Guy put a fist on his hip. "I traveled thousands of miles and that's the way you greet me?" He slapped at his brother's rear with his hat.

"When I am half-asleep, yes. After I eat, I'll give you all the attention you need." Joseph rubbed his eyes with the heels of his palms and crawled from under the bedcovers, setting his feet on a small wolf-skin rug.

Guy raised his brows. "How is everyone? How's Father?"

"Fine. Father is healthy, and everyone has been eager to see you." Joseph yawned once more, walked to an armoire, and pulled out a pale green chamber robe. It was their father's, and the sleeves hung to his thumb tips. "Did everything go well at sea?" He stretched again and tied the silk sash around his waist.

"Yes, and I have lots to tell you. I helped capture a rebel in Saint-Domingue!" The boast over the minor triumph sprang from Guy's mouth. He hesitated and wondered why it popped into his mind, recognizing it as the only thing he might claim sole credit for on the trip.

"Did you fight him?" Joseph's head leaned sideways.

Guy looked downward. "No. We had a drink together. I'll explain later." His face lit. "Has Marie been at the manor?"

Joseph placed a finger on his chin and paused. "Hmm, *Marie? Marie?* I'm not sure of whom …."

"You damn chimney sweep!" Guy joked with a threatening fist. "Tell me!"

"Ha-ha," Joseph pushed him away as he made for the door. "She visited there a month or two ago. Father said she inquired when you'd return." He headed for the stairs, with Guy trailing. "Anyway, she's here in Brest. I saw her by the vendors on Rue de Mer on Tuesday."

By the time the brothers reached the main floor, Guy's heart pounded faster. "Oh, perhaps I'll take a walk to visit her."

"*Perhaps?*" Joseph snorted and strode to the kitchen, where Pascal was preparing another plate for Guy.

That morning, after filling in Pascal and Joseph on the voyage, Guy cleaned himself up and left. He followed the route leading downward toward the docks, stopping after two blocks to scan the huddled buildings on the other side of the Penfeld. The de Bruc house lay halfway up the hill in Recouvrance, the worker section of Brest straight over the river, and he could see it from where he stood.

A small ferry boat took him across, and he ascended toward Marie's home, his confidence swinging like a pendulum from swollen to deflated. The confession he prepared to make had lain rooted deep in his heart and mind since childhood. Regardless of the outcome, Guy concluded his revelation of love finally should free him from a decade of fearful procrastination.

When he reached the door, he knocked, and the sound of the brass latch clicking made his eyes pierce into the darkness within the opening.

"Why Guy, so good of you to pay a call." Marie's father stood in the doorway. "Please, come in. Give me your cloak and hat." The same height as Guy, he wore no wig and his temples showed white streaks. His waistcoat flapped unbuttoned.

Guy entered and followed him to the only salon the small house contained. "Sir, I pray you are well. I'm hoping Marie is here." He kept his hat and didn't take off the cloak.

Marie's father bore a friendly expression. "I'll fetch her. She's here in the kitchen with Charlotte." He faced down the hallway. "Marie, come greet Guy."

The dish clattering stopped and Marie emerged through the doorway, wiping her hands on her apron. "Guy, you're home safe, thank God!" She beamed and ran on tiptoe.

Guy hurried forward, grabbed her outstretched arms, and bussed her cheek. "I arrived three days ago and came ashore today. There's so much to tell. Might we stroll?" If not for her father nearby, he'd have opened his heart on the spot.

"Let me get a wrap and bonnet." Marie moved to the clothing hanging on pegs in the salon. "Father, we'll be home before long." Moments later, they stepped onto the cobblestone street southward toward the bay.

"Marie, before I describe the West Indies trip, I have things that have weighed upon me for a long, long time." Guy's left eyelid twitched every few seconds, and he hoped she didn't notice.

She kept her head tilted upward as they went. The late morning sun, full on her face, made her appear more angelic than ever. Humbled by the plainness of his own looks, Guy stopped once again to speak. Then a flurry of words rushed out.

"Marie, I've held deep feelings for you for ages and wonder if I'm worthy to court you. I realize my present position in the navy complicates matters. Still, a strong relationship can overcome many obstacles. I always hoped our bond might build into something more permanent."

Guy had a wave of relief wash over him after spilling his long-hidden passions and felt an actual physical lightness. His eyelid stopped quivering.

"Guy, those are the fastest and most endearing sentences I've ever heard." Spoken softly, her caring demeanor implied to him no ridicule of his confession. "I have known for years you liked me. Although, I assumed you knew my feelings. Of those men I've met, you remain the most appealing." Marie had turned to him and put her arm under his. "The truth is, I'm not interested in commencing a courtship with anyone yet. I can say in honesty, however, you stand out among those I've ever met." Her sparkling eyes and quick banter stole back his wandering gaze.

Guy realized his errors: first, she had been aware of his pining; second, she was not refusing his advances; but third, he must wait longer. The unresolved nature of it overwhelmed him and he said nothing for a full half minute.

Guy swallowed and exposed the last concern. "I feared you favored François over me."

They continued along arm in arm, toward a small cannon battery wall that faced the great chateau across the river. Marie stopped and gazed up into his face and pulled him down, kissing his cheek.

"I'm just twenty years of age, a year younger than you. With a lifetime ahead, we shouldn't rush into a commitment so early. I enjoy François's company almost as much as I do yours, Guy. My heart will tell my head when it's ready to accept a genuine relationship and marriage. One thing I am convinced of is when I do decide whom I shall spend my days with, it'll be a partnership for life. I cannot ask that you wait for me to declare. We both must go on. If fate brings us together, then that is what should be." Her eyes squinted.

"Then I'll hold off on my expectations. When you choose, if in my favor, my total being is yours. I have stood by this long. What do weeks or decades mean, if it bears the fruit of our hearts?" Guy felt an ache in the pit of his gut but stroked her face with his fingertips.

"I'm happy you agree." Marie placed hers on his neck. "So, now that we've exchanged our heartfelt thoughts, tell me of the voyage to the Americas."

By the time he finished, they had returned to the house. After bidding a sincere *adieu* with a long hug, he departed for home.

Joseph called to him moments after getting back. "Guy, come to the salon!" Holding a book on theology, Joseph had spread on the divan arranged parallel to the fireplace. When Guy stood near, he sat upright and patted the cushion beside him. "Sit. How was your visit with Marie?"

"A mix of emotions." Guy sighed and plopped next to him. "I proposed my affection, but she doesn't want to consider serious courting yet." He wondered if Marie had told him that to lessen a rejection's blow. "She gave me reasons to expect her attention when the time comes."

"Marie would treat you like a mule driver leads his beast." Joseph quipped, merriment on his face. "She's a demanding and spirited young woman. Are you certain you'd want to pursue her?"

"At the moment, yes. Still, as she mentioned, we both must temper our desires until we mature more." He pulled off his wig and scratched his shorter brown hair.

Joseph placed the text on the table nearby. He spent much time reading Latin and Greek assignments while attending Brest's Jesuit seminary, only blocks away, sneaking home when he could. "When do you think she'd be ready?"

"Not for a while. Which is fine, I suppose. My career is just beginning, and naval officers need permission from the navy to marry."

"Well, you'll be at sea soon, going back to Saint-Domingue. Who knows what her thoughts will be when you see her next?"

"That bothers me. It's difficult to maintain a calm resolve when not here to check what is happening. Someone may interfere. I'd appreciate any news from you." Guy scowled and put the wig on his crossed knee, gently thumping the top of it repeatedly with his fist. "I'll be leaving in two weeks after we take on supplies, and have no idea when we'll return."

―――

For the next three years aboard *le Griffon*, Guy studied the seaman's lore as they traveled to the West Indies, Spain, and South America in convoys, infrequently returning to Brest. Once more, in the summer of 1727, they were heading home.

"Half a decade as a cadet and you still get that knot wrong." De Santec wagged his finger at Guy and grabbed the rope Guy played with, and slid the first pass over the loop, not under it.

"Yes, sorry, sir. When will we be making port in Brest?"

"With these winds holding, perhaps a week." De Santec pursed his lips. "I guess we're all eager to see our families. Or is it that woman you spoke of, ah, *Marie*, correct?" He glanced sideways at Guy, hiding his amusement over young love.

"I do long for both. My brother wrote a few months ago that she's seeing other men." Guy frowned. "These lengthy trips wear on her feelings for me, I'm sure, sir."

"That is the curse of all sea-bound. We either lose them while away, or keep them, but never know who's the father of our children." De Santec smacked Guy on the shoulder and laughed.

A few days after the ship harbored in Brest's Bay, Guy walked up from the quays to a livery and rented a horse to visit his family in Cléder. The ride began just after dawn as he rode out through the gate of the high port walls.

When he arrived, he answered questions and learned all the recent news. Then he and Joseph wandered outside to the garden.

"Has Marie visited?" Guy stood beside Joseph, facing a square reflection pool, where short yews traced the perimeter.

"Here? About a month ago. She spends most of her time now in Brest, not at the viscount's chateau. Ask father to invite them to dinner and she'll come." He nodded knowingly.

Guy hoped his brother was right. "I liked it better when you were at the seminary before becoming a priest. You could report on her for me in Brest. Now you're in that small village far away, leaving me with no way of knowing what's happening."

"True, but I've heard nothing to imply she's fallen for anyone. You'll find out for yourself shortly."

Two days later, Marie's family, the de Brucs, arrived. When describing his voyages during their meal, her every response still titillated him. After dinner, Guy took Marie aside. "Shall we take in the orchard?"

"Of course," she replied. "Now tell me about that officer who instructs you. De Santec, you told us."

As they left the house and walked along the short dirt road to the apple trees, Guy hesitated in asking once more about wooing her. "The lieutenant treats all the junior officers with respect, which few superiors do. He takes an interest in cadets' private lives rather than treating us as an added burden to his regular tasks. I like him." Guy put his hand in hers and held it. Marie squeezed it.

"I don't know the family name." Her eyebrows arched.

"De Santecs are lesser nobles and have little wealth or lands. The lieutenant has been patient and should receive a promotion soon." Guy had always sympathized with the lieutenant's long wait. "From what he admits, they live frugally and his wife and two children do without common luxuries. Father said he recalls a rumor the family lost their remaining worth when the East India Company share prices collapsed and paper money devalued."

"How tragic." Marie's face sagged. "I hope to never endure that. We've both had enough funds to support our status since birth. Surely it devastates one to enjoy a lifestyle and then be torn from it."

"Yes, but de Santec's adapted well." As they walked, spring breezes covered the path with the soft white and pink petals of the orchard's apple trees.

After three years of absence, Guy's patience in waiting for a word of approval to court her had dwindled into a dark foreboding. He wondered why she seemed not to regard their future as paramount as he, but did not wish to pressure her. She might rebuff him altogether.

"Another thing I admire about de Santec is having a family, whom he talks about often. It must comfort him to know there's someone waiting." Guy glanced down at her, hoping to catch a reaction.

Without looking up, she said, "Yes."

The path ended under an old oak tree where the previous year's acorns crunched and flattened as they trod across them. The closer they got to the trunk, the louder the noise the bursting nuts made. Guy walked a few more paces and then slowed and stopped in the darkness under its massive limbs.

"Marie," he paused, "are you open to the prospect of an affair of the heart, yet?" His free hand's thumb rubbed the inside of his waistcoat pocket. "I don't wish to force you to decide about our relationship, but just wondered."

Faced downward still, her words drifted to him.

"Certainly I have, Guy, a great deal." Her face crept upward with her voice sincere. "I recall I was about twelve, hmm, or thirteen when I first felt love for you. Of course, I didn't know how you regarded me, yet meeting you at mass or at your manor was the highlight of the week. You haunted my thoughts. I envisioned how we'd marry and live here with a family. It was a child's fantasy." She stared directly into his eyes without blinking. "But then we became adults and realized how complicated things are."

"That didn't answer my question," Guy mumbled, more to himself than to her. His face lost all expression as she gulped before speaking.

Marie glanced aside. "No, it didn't. This is the reason we came to dinner today, Guy," saying nothing for a while, tears formed. "Both my father and François's believe we would make a fine match. Papa has offered the de Saint-Alouarns a dowry."

Like lightning, the words blazed, burning to ash his expectations. Silence followed as his mind refused to accept it. A few moments passed before he spit out, "Is this what you want?" A caustic ember grew in his chest.

Turned away, Marie went on, "I told Father that François and I had formed a deep friendship. It's true I am quite fond of him. Still, I've never indicated to anyone I viewed François as a lover or prospective husband." She stopped speaking and faced Guy. "This is nothing I expected or desired. I'm sure he'd make a wonderful spouse, although I do not want to wed yet. Father's insistence over the matter has thrust me into a dreadful position." Marie placed her palms on his chest. "This must hurt you so."

Guy, his face flushing, took a step back. Marie's hands fell, and she looked away again.

"I realize that neither you nor François hold any blame for this distressing event. Not even your fathers. I'll turn the rage upon myself for harboring these dreams for so long. I'm a fool." His head dropped.

A sound of gasping came from Marie's throat. She turned back toward him with wet stains streaking her gown. "Oh, Guy. You mustn't put this on yourself. For most of my life, I held the same dream." She sniffed. "How it's wounded you. I am so, so sorry."

Tears blurred his vision. "At sea, I feared this might happen. Where is François now?"

"He's awaiting assignment to another ship in Brest."

"This grieves me more than any words that have passed into my ears." Guy placed his hand over his eyes. "There's no hope for me, is there?"

Without hesitating, she spoke. "Unless something were to happen or my father and François's father change their minds—no." She dabbed her nose with her handkerchief.

Guy assumed her answer. "Damn it!" Fists tightening, he summoned up the strength to overcome his anger. "Marie, I shall forever remember this day as my undoing. Fate has dealt me a foul hand."

She touched his arm. "I have cried every night since my father told me of their plan, for you and for myself. Believe me, I had no desire to wed yet. This is as much a disruption to my dreams as it is yours, Guy." She swung her head back and forth. "We both suffer this terrible misfortune. François accepted our parents' decision without regret, it shocked even him. Please hold no ill feelings toward him."

"No, I can't. Had I been him, I would have been ecstatic hearing of it. You are a treasure everyone seeks, Marie. Had I known before what was to transpire, I'd have not made the decisions I did earlier, even if my father would disapprove. You are more important than any of that." Guy shuffled his feet toward the house. "Let's return."

They shambled along the path in silence.

Guy's brother, that night, approached their father in the salon. "Marie and François de Saint-Alouarn may marry soon, Father. Guy told me after she left and then he went straight to bed. He's heartbroken over it and said that Marie doesn't love François." Joseph's forehead wrinkled. "I have no idea how to help other than prayer."

"*Help?* This is out of our hands, and I doubt God would interfere. I'm aware of his feelings toward Marie, but there is nothing to do. Besides, it's between families." The count clamped shut his mouth while weighing it all. "Officers need consent, so there's a chance the navy will refuse. The port intendant and I are friends, and a word from me …." He rejected the idea with a quick shake of the head. "That seems ungentlemanly and devious, though."

Over the next few days, Guy's depression shrouded the family with concern, and his glum disposition wore on his father.

When Guy returned to *le Griffon* for duty, the cool, sunny, spring air had turned wet with days of rainy weather. As the ship took on provisions, every glance to shore carried the reminder he was still in Brittany, where the core of his problems lay. Brest's citadel, standing dominant, conjured up his strolls with Marie. The tall church spires pointed upward to salvation brought back only memories of masses and festivals they'd enjoyed together. Nothing could be better than if they hauled anchor and left, he deduced. That week, the warship set out again for Saint-Domingue.

The Barbary Coast and Émile
1728–1737

The great peak of Gibraltar jutted above the sea like Triton rising from the depths as *le Griffon* entered the Mediterranean. For Guy, the shape registered as another navigation landmark he needed to remember. He watched it disappear as they continued eastward on sparkling, sunlit waves. The humid scorching of the West Indies lay months in the past.

Other warships stood off to the starboard, their timbers creaking with each passing gust. Whatever campaign the navy planned thrilled him. Like his superior, de Santec, he wanted to show his martial skills, but not solely for advancement. Often he imagined François still ashore, while he, cutlass in hand, fought against the nation's foes. The fantasies ended, always, with him saving Marie as she swooned in his arms, her blond hair dazzling against a background of blue sky and sea. He longed to prove his valor in battle to all, but especially to her and himself.

Soon they put in along France's Mediterranean coast at Toulon. Its thick fortifications ascended from the shoreline that encircled the walled harbor.

A week passed and de Santec finished a meeting on the admiral's flagship. He grinned. "Where we're going should delight you."

"Sir?" Guy's face lifted with the hope of action.

"The Barbary Coast to quell pirating." De Santec rubbed his hands together. "Although sultans rule the Barbary countries, the pashas and beys in control of the local regions govern as they feel fit, often at odds with the sultans. To make things more complicated, renegade corsairs ignore their pashas' and beys' commands. The lack of structure and discipline has been a problem for European shipping for hundreds of years.

"Last year, we sent an emissary to Bey Hussein of Tunis, and he promised to stop the pirates from attacking our ships. Barbary corsairs from there had anchored near an island off our coast and raided villages and looted vessels all along the shoreline. Two months ago, they seized three French merchantmen, sailed them to Tripoli, sold off the cargos, took their crews prisoners, and now demand ransoms. The assaults were a horrific breach of our treaty. The king wants to force the Pasha of Tripoli to return the ships and prisoners, and bring all the beys like Hussein back into line."

"So, we're bound for the Barbary Coast." The thought of battle made Guy's pulse quicken.

A month slipped by, and in June, the small fleet departed, heading south-by-southeast. After three days passed, they caught sight of Africa off their bow.

The port of Tunis drew close as the French warships ran parallel along the coast. A large Tunisian naval fleet of warships lay before the town. Low, sleek xebecs, a few with their sails unfurled, outnumbered the other ships in the harbor. The xebecs' shallow draft, small crews, and light construction presented no challenge to a sturdy European warship in a one-on-one clash on fair seas. Although a xebec could outmaneuver a European vessel in rough waves. They were a serious threat in a fight.

Guy's sighting of his first one under sail brought to mind the tales and stories of the horrors inflicted by the Barbary pirates. Hair rose on his neck as the distant, trim craft flew across the water, its flowing, smooth lines so unlike French ships. Triangular canvas hung on three masts, and a yellow, green, and red striped pennant raised high flapped in the wind.

Guy said, "Never had I thought of seeing Tunis, the ancient city of Carthage."

"And conquered many times. But we aren't to strike unless they challenge us." De Santec lifted and dropped his sword in its scabbard every few seconds, the hilt guard clinking as he watched for movement with a spyglass in his other hand.

When the squadron came to rest before the harbor, twenty minutes passed before a launch lowered and left the commander's man-of-war to head shoreward. Sailors pulled at the oars, and a young lieutenant mounted the bow with fists on his hips. Another sat at the stern by the tiller. When the boat reached the distant dock, Guy saw through his spyglass a throng of men accompanying the two Frenchmen toward the bey's palace. The Moorish-styled fortification stood higher and a quarter of a mile inland from the shore.

"If they meant to start a war, they'd have taken the crew prisoners." De Santec mentioned out loud. "See, our oarsmen are still sitting in the launch." He pointed as he peered shoreward.

"Yes, sir," Guy agreed. "That's a good sign. Perhaps they fear us."

"And they should. The bey would be wise to grant our mandates."

Before long, the two French officers came back to the squadron commander, de Grandpré. The bey had pledged to abide by their demands and release any captives.

In a second, Guy's hopes of proving himself in combat vanished.

By evening, turbaned sailors delivered the prisoners. Once the freed crewmen climbed aboard, the French set sails and departed.

Tripoli, the pasha's capital and dwelling, lay less than a hundred and fifty miles to the southeast of Tunis. Early the next morning, the hills, ramparts, and grand buildings of the city stood before them. The climbing sun's rays pierced through the sea's blue-gray mists and made gold the far eastern walls and sides of the structures upon the ivory-tan desert sands. It was a glorious phantasmal sight. Glowing tall minarets, towers, the castle, and domed mansions sprinkled throughout the port, contrasted with the deep azures of those in shadow. It reminded Guy of the stories of Arabian adventures his father had read to him as a child.

As in Tunis, Guy saw the same routine repeat. First, a boat rowed to the harbor with two officers on board. Then a crowd met them at the dock and escorted them elsewhere.

Besides Barbary craft, three merchantmen of European design sat in the port, the French ships the pirates had seized months before, lying tethered against a wharf.

None of the xebecs undertook to flee. A signal cannon sounded somewhere in the city and heightened the crew's alertness, but nothing more showed a need to prepare for a fight.

After hours of waiting, Guy sought de Santec. "Sir, what's happening and why is it taking so long?" He leaned on his musket, rubbing his chin on its barrel.

"We could be here for days while they debate the release of the French merchantmen, passengers, crews, and cargo. What happened in Tunis with Bey Hussein is unlikely to happen here. Pasha Husayn ibn Ali is far more powerful and a prime ruler." His head wagged as he explained. "His sons and nephews are the beys all up and down the Barbary Coast and he might call upon their aid. At this very minute, their fleets may be on the way to attack us. We must stay watchful both toward shore and seaward."

Guy's eyes narrowed as he surveyed the distant sea in search of the fore-and-aft sails of xebecs.

By midday, a crowd gathered on the dock and the two emissaries embarked back to de Grandpré's warship to inform the captains of the pasha's decision.

Crewmen stood around in silence as they awaited what the Barbary leader had decided. The returning officers' grim faces showed them the answer.

The pasha had refused.

Drums rolled, and every man sped to his assigned battle post. Guy kept watch in the bow on the forecastle with his musket, checking and rechecking if he'd loaded the gun's powder pan. His lips pressed hard, and he imagined swarms of turbaned fiends crawling over the ship's sides. It was one thing to daydream a part in a furious clash, but another to face others who sought to kill you.

De Santec shouted from the quarterdeck to the gun captains. "Target the xebecs, the fortress, and dock areas, men. Our bomb galiots will aim for the farther positions." He scanned the crews. Every soul anticipated the next command. "Fire until a cease order."

At once, a rolling broadside exploded across the waves as thirty cannons belched flashes, shot, and smoke at the city. Then, as each gunner adjusted the aim, the firing became an uncoordinated staccato. The repeating blasts pounded Guy's body. Other warships opened up as well, the cacophony of thundering weapons consuming his senses. He remembered the cotton he had shoved in his pocket for the occasion, spit on it, and pushed a thick wad into both his ears to dampen the roar.

While Guy watched the destruction unfolding in front of him, Tripoli's defensive shore batteries began hitting them. As enemy cannoneers improved the elevation and range, balls hit *le Griffon's* hull.

"Cadets, if gun captains fall, replace them! There'll be no need for musketry!" De Santec shouted to them above the racket from the main deck.

Hour after hour, the heavy balls pummeled down and Tripoli's damages grew as the assault lasted into the night. "Almost half the xebecs have sunk or are damaged, sir." Guy turned his attention to the harbor's direction. "They must surrender shortly."

De Santec stared landward, his voice burdened. "The pasha's pride is at stake here. Regardless if his navy and people suffer, he will resist as long as possible. What you've seen so far is nothing compared to a day or two more," De Santec scowled.

The battering proceeded into the next day, and the next, without a sign of surrender. For five full days, the capitol bore the onslaught of iron falling from heaven, dawn through night. On the sixth morning, a xebec, emblazoned with colorful flags, left the harbor for the French fleet. De Grandpré's ship raised a signal to cease the ruinous cascade until after meeting with the delegation.

Guy, accustomed to the unending roars from the guns, peered shoreward in the stillness. Acrid cannon smoke filled the air near the ships, but as the gray haze lifted, he beheld jagged walls, burned-out storehouses, blackened windows, and smashed abodes covering the hillside. Even the pasha's own residence, far beyond normal gun range, showed gaping holes in its domed towers from the pounding by the mortars on the galiots. It seemed few of the thousands of buildings had avoided their barrage. Glorious Tripoli sat in ruins.

Not twenty minutes later, a squad of marines departed for shore in a launch with three lieutenants. By day's end, over a hundred men reached the quay in a continuous stream of launches and climbed aboard the captive French ships.

After dinner that night, the officers stood talking about the details of the surrender. The pasha had consented to a 100,000 livres reparation and promised to send an ambassador to apologize to the *Most Very-Christian King Louis*. Between decks, once the word spread, relieved crewmen joined priests in prayer, giving thanks they had not faced the fierce Barbary marauders in a naval battle.

Guy thought about the entire mission before sleeping. The ominous feelings during the bombardment had lifted. He reflected how before, he had welcomed the chance to fight. Now, he realized the consequences of those actions, the waste of effort, lives, and money. Still, the pasha had caused the situation, and King Louis responded the only way he could.

He also wondered what Marie and François's thoughts on it might have been. François held the same duty-bound beliefs as he, yet Marie was more likely to have pitied the people and cursed the pasha and her king, he mused. As man and wife, he reminded himself as his spirit crashed, both now placed importance more on married life than foreign countries or rulers' stupidity.

The next day, Pasha Husayn released all the captives to their ships, and boats ferried ill ones to the fleet. The warships continued to blockade the port as more quarrelsome negotiations dragged on for weeks. By mid-August, he'd agreed to a new treaty, like the earlier one, and the French fleet shoved off for Toulon.

Six months had elapsed since Marie had spoken to François. His last words resounded in her mind; *"Perhaps not now, yet it may be."* The navy had rejected his request to marry.

"Marie, why didn't you and François try again to get permission to wed?" asked her sister Charlotte.

Often Marie imagined what being a wife to François might be like with the financial stability and his appealing personality. Still, when the port intendant denied him an exception to the age limit for marriage, she considered it a blessing. "It wasn't as if I loved him. Besides, most women don't take a husband until their mid-twenties or even thirties!" Marie knitted her brows. "I hold him dear, but I had no powerful urge to accept him as my spouse."

"But Papa …" her sister said.

Marie's snicker interrupted her. "Father tried to cajole me into the plan, telling me how lucky a marriage I'd have with a pleasant and wealthy de Saint-Alouarn." She rolled her eyes. "François is a close, close friend to me, nothing more and less than another."

"Oh, I can guess," Charlotte replied, smiling. "Guy's always been your darling."

The pace of Marie's words slowed. "Yes, but we'll never wed either. As much as I prefer him, he's like most of the suitors in Brittany, a sailor. Since a child, I've watched naval wives waiting for husbands to return from the sea, until one day, the men don't." Charlotte nodded. Marie added, "Then, the rest of their lives are spent alone. That's not for me."

Charlotte sighed and went about her chores. The sisters hadn't the luxury of servants like the de Kersaints or de Saint-Alouarns.

Yet, the mystery of the navy's refusal continued to bother Marie. Other officers received the intendant's blessings, regardless of being too young, and the de Saint-Alouarns were prominent nobles. Did her family, the de Brucs, cause the rejection of such a minor petition? Their lower status and declining income might have influenced the decision. She mulled it over while washing the kitchen table.

That evening, as her father read in the salon, she asked, "Papa, when the intendant refused my betrothal, did the navy give a reason?"

He squirmed in the chair and set his broadsheet aside. "Well, I hesitated to tell you. Someone mentioned to me a letter opposing it." He sulked as he spoke the words. "I presumed whoever interfered desired you for his own. What's curious is nothing came of it later. No one offered his hand."

Marie's head jerked back. She recounted those who courted her during that time, but none were privy to her and François's plans to wed. The only person she had revealed it to was Guy.

"No," she whispered to herself. Such an underhanded act lay beneath his standards. Moreover, he had left just days after she told him, weeks before François sent the application. After all, what influence does a cadet have with the Port Intendant of Brest? Then Marie recalled Guy's father's close connection to the navy. Often she saw the intendant conversing with him at length at formal functions.

"How well does Count de Kersaint know the intendant, Papa?" Was Guy aware of what his father could have done, she wondered, or did he pressure him into it?

"Oh," he said and looked away. "Yes, they're friends." His eyes closed. "I long suspected the count had intervened and hoped it might lead to, well, an arrangement for you and Guy, but he never approached me."

"I see." Marie put her hands on her hips, thinking. Guy's father, she knew, never liked her much. Regardless, someone had meddled. Although upsetting, it worked out well for her, and she had avoided an arranged marriage to a mariner. Still, Marie felt as if she had been haggled over like a peck of vegetables. She believed such demeaned the concept of love and freedom.

As Marie prepared to go out the next morning, she grabbed her cloak, flung it around her shoulders, and stepped to the door. Unseen, the bottom hem snagged on a hook near the fireplace, and as she moved forward, it pulled. "Oh, dear!" she cried, as it ripped.

"What happened?" her father asked, lifting his eyes from paperwork.

She bit her lip, groaning. "I've torn my cloak. Now I'll need to buy some matching yarn."

She left for Rue de Mer and crossed over the river, searching the small carts for an identical strand. When she found none, Marie climbed the road to the shops. A colder wind than normal for spring showed each breath she took along the way as she hurried to the tailor's shop a few blocks up the hill.

"Good morning," Marie greeted the elderly tailor. As she pointed out the rip, another person entered behind her. The handsome man, dressed in fashionable attire, had broad shoulders and strong-looking calves, and she had never seen him earlier in town.

Marie faced the owner again. "I'll darn it myself, though I've no wool to match it and can't find any at the carts by the river."

"That shouldn't be a problem, mademoiselle." The tailor picked up the garment, placing it on top of the workbench as he examined the thread.

"That's worsted wool, and looks like an English twill," said the customer as he stepped forward, pulled a folding magnifying glass from a pocket, and spied through it. "Hmm. It'll take darning well, especially English worsted. The fibers are longer, compacted, and twisted. Just use a running stitch and it should be fine." He spoke with a Parisian accent and turned to the tailor. "Do you agree?"

The craftsman inspected the fabric on both sides while humming to himself. "Yes, that's correct. I have yarn to blend with this," he said with twinkling eyes and walked to a case of pigeon-holes filled with skeins.

"Oh, thank you." Marie wondered how the newcomer knew woolen fabrics.

The shopkeeper, old but spritely, returned with a small ball of thread in his hand. "That is one denier, mademoiselle."

Marie paid him and stood back from the table to put on the cloak.

Next, the tailor faced the male patron. "What may I do for you, sir?"

"Umm," said the customer. "My breeches need mending right away."

The shop owner noticed the man's empty hands. "Ah-ha. A predicament then, I presume?"

The gentleman peeped, "Yes, very much so."

"There's a dressing closet behind the curtains where you can take them off." The tailor pointed to it, a smile on his face.

Marie giggled and covered her mouth as the man trotted over to the little changing room, holding his frock coattails to hide the embarrassing accident.

"Split backsides happen more often than people might guess." The owner winked at Marie and continued in a whisper. "During the spring, the cold draft brings in more of them than during the summer." He laughed and placed his bony fingers over his mouth.

Marie chuckled as she buttoned her wrap.

"For my billing record, what is your name, sir?" asked the tailor.

"Émile Gardinier."

"You have in-depth knowledge of textiles, Monsieur Gardinier. Do you work in the trade?" asked Marie, adjusting the cloak's front. He seemed about five or six years older than she.

Émile answered through the screen, "Yes, I'm a fabric merchant and sail canvas chandler. I hope to sell to the navy here."

"The senior naval stores supervisor, Monsieur Pierre Chatroen, is a family acquaintance," she said. "Do you have dealings with Monsieur Chatroen?"

"No, I don't. But I'd like to meet him." The pace of Émile's speech quickened. "Is there a chance I can talk to you about him? I'm here on business and would appreciate your help. We could chat later, after the tailor finishes, and I feel more presentable."

At first, Marie wavered whether to consent to the stranger's request, then replied, "Um, we can meet at the café which is four streets west on the corner. Say, in an hour?"

"That's superb." His face lit. "I'd love to buy you coffee for your kindness."

Marie wrinkled her nose. "They make a better cocoa. Until then, I'll be at the market. Oh, I'm Mademoiselle Marie de Bruc, by the way. See you shortly." She left again for the Rue de Mer stalls.

After browsing for a while, she entered the café and noticed Émile sitting near the door, sipping his drink. He got up from his seat when he saw her. "Ah, Mademoiselle de Bruc, I'm so thankful you've come and didn't forget." Émile bowed and gestured to a place for her.

"Of course, it wouldn't slip my mind. By introducing you to Monsieur Chatroen, I may be of service to him as well as to you." She joined him at the table.

They conversed over their drinks about the season's ever-wet weather in Brittany. Émile relaxed in the chair. "Do you live in Brest?"

"Most of the time," Marie replied. "We have a small home on the other side of the river in Recouvrance and also stay sometimes in the Chateau de Brézal. We're related to the marquise. She and the viscount are my godparents."

Émile grinned. "Oh, you're nobility?"

"Not very, or at least in name only," Marie chirped timidly. "And you? I assume your office is in Paris, and you've been to Brest before."

Émile pursed his lips. "No. This is my first visit, and yes, the business is in Paris. Although Father and I own a small warehouse in Rennes. I'm here to inquire if the navy could use more hemp or canvas. Unfortunately, getting to talk to someone of importance is almost impossible without connections or a vendor's license."

"Monsieur Chatroen could help with that. Allow me to contact him." Marie's gaze wandered to his ring finger. The newcomer wore none, and she glanced up at his soft brown eyes.

He leaned forward and pushed his cup and saucer closer to hers. "How can I refuse the offer? Please, call me *Émile*. Even though this day started out by splitting my breeches, meeting you restarted it fresh. You're my second dawn and as beautiful, giving me hope after a week of disappointments."

Marie blushed. "No one has ever compared me to the sun before, Émile. To rush to compliments might discredit your sincerity."

"In business, it *is* poor form to flatter a client too soon." Perfect teeth showed between smiling lips. "In the presence of lovely women, on the contrary, it is *never* too soon to offer accolades to their beauty."

Marie roared, hands clapping and shaking her head at his fawning puffery. "You must leave every woman you meet breathless!"

Émile joined her laughter and reddened at his own brash attempt. "You never know who will yield to flirtatious patter. The timing is all." An eyebrow rose. "Once one learns how to pace and stress the comments, success is inevitable. Proper oration assures credibility, whether in selling a bolt of fabric or buying another's trust."

"Ah, so you've learned this skill in your business, huh?" Marie laughed aloud. "Should I infer I'm of no more value than a roll of cloth, sold and bought with timed intonations?"

Émile sat back again, placing a hand on his heart. "I'm wounded you'd think me insincere, my dear." He guffawed and then grew still, staring into her blue eyes. "The moment I saw you at the shop, I had to engage with you somehow." He spoke in a serious, earnest tone. "When you suggested coming here, my emotions soared."

Marie swallowed, her pulse throbbing. "Émile, I have to be honest, too. For years now, I've resisted intimacy from admirers and for myself. Today at the tailor's, I sensed a change in the wind." Her gaze stayed steady on Émile's.

∽

Weeks later, Marie and her father spoke after dinner. "Marie, Count de Kersaint said you introduced Émile to Monsieur Chatroen. Your antics embarrass me. Is it wise to involve yourself in business matters?" He leaned his jaw on his fist. The vendor had called on Marie practically every night since the first meeting.

With a blank face, she replied, "Émile had difficulty in seeing Monsieur Chatroen, and I helped. At the end of an hour, he'd gotten a vendor's license and an order for hemp."

"Over the past month, you've been spending much time with him." His brows hung low and concerned. "How unlike you to act as a trade liaison for strangers."

The moment had arrived, and she locked her fingers together before her on the tabletop. Marie stared at him, joy radiating from her face. "Papa, Émile and I are forming a special bond, and I believe I'm falling in love."

Without speaking, he frowned and thrummed the table with his fingertips, glaring. "I feared so. You've had countless men of respectable character and nobility try to court you, and refused them!" His voice grew to a thunder as he turned scarlet. "Now you're in love with a shopkeeper?" He rubbed his forehead.

The attack forced Marie back in her seat. "A merchant he may be, Father. At least Émile isn't a conceited, overbearing officer like those the academy churns out!" she barked with eyes narrowed. "I almost married François. He's on a ship somewhere and won't come home for weeks, maybe years. Should I have spent my days praying for his return while raising children in loneliness as the other wives in Brittany?" Her woven fingers turned into fists.

Smacking the surface hard and making her jerk, he shouted, "Don't you understand that marriage is more than a personal choice?! It's also a family decision. Marrying well should benefit all, not just oneself. The same applied to Mama and me. If she were alive, she'd say the same." He paused and became still, speaking more softly. "The de Brucs walk the edge between poverty and prosperity. By wedding a noble rather than a commoner, you could help." Then he rose and clomped from the room.

Marie sat in silence. No friend or suitor had touched her heart like Émile. He came from a world of commerce and the glamor of Paris, not from her unrefined province of fishing nets and warships. Gentle and caring, Émile's honesty toward her, she weighed, was lacking in others. Her destiny lay either with him, or living for the financial stability of the de Bruc household. Marie decided she had to choose which and make a stand.

The next day, she stood before her father in the salon. "Papa, Émile may be the only chance for a satisfied future." Marie held her head high. "This will upset you, but my relatives' welfare mustn't be the single motive for deciding the directions I must take. If he asks you for my hand, I pray you give your blessing. Can you accept my resolve?"

He looked down, placing the quill on the escritoire's top. "Before bed, I debated the situation a great deal. I understand you believe our lives in this world seem too short to dedicate to anything other than what is in our hearts. Later, we learn the importance of one's kin and unemotional objectivity." Seldom did her defiant nature allow options for him. Focused on her, he said, "Be aware we have but limited funds. I shall give my consent, but not a dowry, not to a commoner."

Delighted, she said, "Yes, I thought not. Émile's family may not demand one. Save it for Charlotte. Perhaps she'll find a nobleman who can help us."

"That's what we'll do, then. Nevertheless, I am happy you've found someone who suits you." He stared skyward. "God knows Émile needs divine guidance to put up with you." He took her hands, holding them. "But I've learned and he will, too."

"Oh, I'm not that headstrong. After I move, without me around, Brest will bore you," Marie giggled.

After a slight titter, he sighed. "Dear, I suppose I miss you already. Paris is so far from here."

⁜

The port in Toulon hosted the typical entertainment venues of most naval stations: taverns, brothels, and gambling houses. Once the ships returned from Tripoli, the crews made use of the establishments while waiting for new assignments. Guy joined de Santec in a tavern to exchange thoughts on their next mission. They had just sat with their mugs of ale when the lieutenant, bemused and saying nothing, pulled out a folded paper from his pocket, its seal unbroken. Slowly, he held it up.

Guy caught his name on the front.

"When the packet boat landed, you were ashore, and I knew you'd want it right away." The letter dropped next to Guy.

"Yes, sir. That's my brother's writing. Thank you." Guy read it as they sipped their drinks.

> *My Most Honorable and Dearest Brother Guy-François,*
>
> *I hope these tidings arrive to you swiftly, for they bear good news. As I suspect you have not yet learned, this information will shock you. The marriage between Mademoiselle Marie de Bruc and Monsieur François de Saint-Alouarn did not take place, as the intendant denied the request because of his age. Authorities usually overlook the requirement and it begs why the navy rejected his application. I hastened to inform you of this because her situation in this area no doubt affects your marital ambitions.*

The letter then mentioned items not half as interesting as the first paragraph. Guy reread it twice to make sure of what it said. The nagging and depressing brooding over her marriage to François lifted in seconds as hope rekindled.

Guy's expression lit and he looked up at de Santec. "Sir, Marie didn't wed."

"Well, that'll delight everyone you know on board. We hated your gloominess," he laughed.

Guy gulped his drink, head high. "Sir, this changes everything for me. Marie had said she didn't love him and preferred me. After we make port in Brest, I'll press again for her hand. This must have devastated François!"

De Santec raised a brow. "When did this occur? The navy may have reversed the decision. It's happened before."

"Joseph wrote the letter three months ago. I doubt Marie encouraged François to appeal since she didn't want to marry." Guy's cheerfulness hadn't lessened one bit after de Santec's warning.

For days, his mind created increasingly complex steps to win her. As the daydreaming grew, so did his expectations and humor, confident that Marie's next betrothal would fulfill both their desires.

⁓

As Marie foretold, Émile asked her father for permission to wed. Using his persuasive talents, his affable character awed and won over the elder's assent.

A month later, Émile and the de Brucs rode together in a coach as it approached Paris for the ceremony. The carriage rocked and swayed on the rutted road, just miles from the capital's western gate. Émile turned to her father and sister. "Edouard, my older brother, is opening his house for you to stay there. He's a lawyer, new in his practice, but has a promising career, and attended the University of Paris." The de Brucs returned impressed glances.

"Had you hoped to go to the university, also?" Charlotte asked with a peaked brow.

"Charlotte!" Marie snapped. "One doesn't ask such intimate questions. As his fiancée, I can, but you shouldn't."

Charlotte lowered her head. "I just wondered if …."

Émile's gaze wandered onto the passing landscape, unable to face her with the lie as he finished her sentence. "If I had higher aspirations? Oh, no. I never intended to become anything other than a merchant like my father. 'Trade is in my blood,' as Father would say." He turned back to Marie. "Anyway, he couldn't have afforded two sons at the Sorbonne. He taught me everything I'd need to take over his establishment or open my own. Then I struck out and opened my fabric and fiber store, five years ago."

Four days later, the families gathered for the small wedding at Saint-Sulpice. Before they took their vows, hammering from workers echoed through the nave of the yet unfinished church. Except for Marie's sister and father, the front pews were filled with the Gardiniers' friends, relatives, and acquaintances.

Marie stood in a side chapel as the organ shook the air with processional music. She trembled and her father placed his arms around her. "Calm, my dear. We're here for you," he whispered and kissed her cheek. As a child, in an imaginary wedlock, it was Guy, not Émile. When she recalled the memory, a slight shock ran through her. Had she made the right choice?

The deep bass of the organ's pipes grew and her father held her elbow, leading her toward the altar, where the priest waited to invoke the sacrament.

Incessantly throughout the rite, Edouard's children made noises, and he argued over a legal point with an invited fellow lawyer. When it ended, the attendees poured outside to wish the newlyweds a blessed union.

Charlotte ran to Marie in the square before the enormous church. "Masons banging, kids shouting, and people bickering the whole while, no ceremony in Brest could equal it." She laughed and threw a flower at her sister.

Marie, smiling, answered, "Ha! It might be an omen of things to come, and far from what a simple life in Brittany offers. I'll take it!"

The first week after the service, she forced herself to write Guy. The letter was brief.

> *My Dearest & Beloved Guy,*
> *This missive brings a joyous announcement of transformation. On the 18th of this month, I became the wife of Émile Gardinier, a shop owner in Paris, whom I met*

in Brest. We took our vows at Saint-Sulpice. As mentioned long ago, my heart would tell me when to marry and it has. But I remember the fondness you carried for me earlier and pray you consider my extreme happiness before harboring regrets over my actions. Life with Émile has soothed that part of my spirit needing the comforts I could never find with any other. If these words evoke sadness on your part or anger, I am truly sorry. My greatest hope is the day will come when you also discover your heart's love as I have.

Wishing you fair seas and the opportunity to see you soon, Your Most Loving, Obedient, and Respectful Friend, Marie de Bruc Gardinier, the 22nd of May 1729, Paris.

With every stroke of the pen, she wondered how it would affect him. This forced her again to question if Guy might have been a better husband, someone to temper her wild impulses, rather than match them as Émile did. Despite that, it remained her mate must live within reach and without danger.

⁂

The months drifted by as Guy patrolled the southern coast of France on *le Griffon*. One day, de Santec informed him they would not be returning to Brest.

"It seems once again, the Barbary corsairs are causing trouble. We'll patrol for some time here in the Mediterranean." His mouth drooped. "I've written to my wife about this sad circumstance. It may be a while before we head homeward."

Guy lifted his shoulders. The navy controlled his life. "Yes, sir. I'll write my father and brother of the delay, too."

"And Marie?" de Santec posed.

"No, sir. I won't send her any letters. My arrival remains unpredictable anyway, and if I surprise her, that may excite her enough to accept my proposal. Alerting her beforehand might cool her emotions." Guy held up his index finger. "I've been giving it all a great deal of consideration. I shall win her over."

De Santec leaned against a nearby staircase. "Ah, I see." Over the years, he'd gotten to sympathize with Guy's relentless yearnings for Marie. "What makes you so enamored of her?"

Guy plunked down on the end of a cannon and put a foot on each of the back carriage wheels. His brow furrowed when he recounted his reasons. "First, I understand her better than a sister, sir. We grew up together either at the manor in Cléder or when we stayed at our godparents' chateau in Brézal. She's beautiful and so different with an independent nature. I don't consider myself a fearful man except in dire circumstances, but she's never shown an instant of dread or panic. If she wants to do something, nothing stops her. I admire her for always speaking her mind, though not cruelly. Marie takes care of her word choices, but cares not what others may think of them once spoken." Guy's face lit. "When we played as children and in our teen years, every moment with her somehow opened my eyes to a new perspective. As if she dragged me along on untried adventures, things I'd never attempted or even thought of. The two of us seem fitted—she, the hand, and I, the glove. Marie directed, and I protected."

"My, Guy," replied de Santec, "you've described her well. Marie must be quite a woman. My wife has few of those qualities but possesses others I find remarkable. To miss far away lovers gives us purpose for the day when we can go home to them. Otherwise, our lives might end up meaningless or selfish."

"Sir, I'll stop at nothing to marry her."

Two months later, they returned to Toulon where letters had arrived for each of the mariners.

Guy recognized Marie's handwriting and yanked at the flap to open it. As the words of her wedding stabbed his mind, each sentence tore away a scene from his imagined life with her. His romanticized world collapsed, and its bright hopes vanished into blackness. He stood in the midships and re-read it one last time before throwing her penned catastrophe overboard into the wind.

The abominable sheet of paper ended his pursuit for Marie's affections, and before him lay a void.

Only four months had passed since their wedding, but the opposing personalities between Émile's father and Marie grated on one another more each day. She was a constant reminder to the old man he didn't get the dowry he wanted, which to him was as defeating as a lost business opportunity. To Marie, her father-in-law's never-ending snips and curt replies became insufferable, and she responded in kind. The two's steady bickering trapped Émile between paternal and spousal loyalty.

Émile's forehead wrinkled as he suggested an idea to Marie. "If possible, we should move to our own home, somewhere nearer to where I work. First renting and then we'll save until we buy a place."

Marie grinned. "Yes, of course, it's time we planned for our future and even for children."

"Another sale with the navy would ensure it if I go to Brest and talk to Chatroen. The purchase may not be much since he only purchases enough to cover a lack from regular contracted suppliers." Honed by his father's crafty acumen, his mind churned ways to increase earnings. "Why don't we leave soon? When I'm with Chatroen, you can visit your family and friends."

Within the month, the couple departed for Brest, and Chatroen welcomed Émile with smiles.

"So, I learned you married Marie de Bruc. Congratulations and you look fed and happy." His grin widened. "Now, what have you got for the navy?"

"Sail duck I imported from Holland through Scotland at a good price. And I'll have it shipped here immediately if you're in the need." Émile winked. "Made from the finest hemp available."

"Hmm, that sounds fetching. Though the naval warehouse is almost full. There's no incentive to buy more at present." Chatroen glanced at Émile and raised an eyebrow.

The word *incentive* cued Émile, and he came prepared. He reached into his satchel and pulled out a small leather bag holding two gold coins, sliding them across the desktop.

The naval procurer lifted and peeked inside the pouch. The metal glimmered at the bottom. "Shortages can come fast. Hmm, best if we prepare. So, we need more after all. Perhaps double what we ordered last time." Chatroen chortled, "Monsieur Gardinier, I believe you and I shall be dealing a lot with one another."

When Émile returned to the de Bruc's home, he omitted to mention the bribe. Worth months of his salary, it wiped out half of the profit from the transaction. But he needed to lure the buyer to rely on him.

Émile left for Rennes to arrange the shipments of the canvas to Brest, leaving Marie behind to enjoy time with her father, Charlotte, and visit old acquaintances.

One day, as Marie climbed the road to a friend's house atop the hill above the slips, she stopped. In an instant, she recognized the shape and motions of the person approaching. Backlit by the bright blue sky came Guy.

When he saw her, he sped. "Marie! No, I mean *Madame Gardinier*." He bowed low with his hat in hand, exaggerating the movements with a flourish.

Marie giggled and then made a deep curtsy to him. "Come, give me a hug and kiss, you idiot," she said, eyes smiling.

He grabbed her waist, and they kissed one another's cheeks.

Marie spied his eyelids tearing as he turned aside. "You got my letter?" she asked.

"Phew! When you decide to make a change, you don't waste your time. But that's nothing new, is it?" He kept his mouth fixed, and added, "You seemed so set on remaining unmarried. He must be quite an impressive man. Will you be in Brest for much longer? We just anchored yesterday after leaving Toulon, but I'll be here for less than a week."

She heard his voice tighten, on the verge of cracking. He coughed with deep breaths.

Marie took his hand, and they began a walk along the street above the river. "I'm only staying until Émile returns and then we're off to Paris again."

As they went, she told him about the wedding, how her father-in-law behaved like a curmudgeon, and the plans for a home.

Marie put the other hand on top of his. "My marriage upset you. Surely, it must have. I've been worried since I wrote. You didn't write back or wish us well."

Guy paused, blushing. "Yes, of course."

She heard him breathing hard before continuing.

"I imagined a different life than the one awaiting me now," he said. "Over the last few months, I've reflected on my irrational obsession with unfounded beliefs. To assume too much only brings pain." Guy's head hung. "Or perhaps my aspirations are too far beyond my talents. In either case, those are problems I must solve myself."

"I'm sorry I contributed to these things that bedevil you," said Marie, tightening her handhold. "When we spoke last, I didn't mean to encourage your feelings toward me. I said you stood above the others. It wasn't just because of my fondness for you. Everyone thinks you are an exceptional person. You'll find a more suitable companion without trouble if you let it happen."

"Oh, I'm certain I shall. Still, I wish you and Émile all the best in your lives together." A forced smile followed.

The words sounded flat to her when he spoke. Marie looked off, unfocused. "Guy, I know this has all been very hard on you. I love Émile very much, but shall never try to forget or diminish the feelings I've had for you. Nothing will ever undo the golden link between us. Still, we go on and must both abandon unfulfilled dreams."

"Perhaps. Regardless, you'll always be the closest to my heart," he said.

Guy's solemn face reflected her words hadn't soothed him. "What warship are you on?"

"*Le Lys*. Over there in the bay." He thumbed in the direction of the vessel's anchorage. "She's a fine, big ship of seventy-two guns. If the wind holds, we'll be leaving again for the Barbary Coast." Then, turning to the northeast breeze, he inhaled deeply.

"Oh, it must be wonderful to experience all the foreign sights and faraway lands that you have." She kept the topic going on seafaring. "The strange foods, alone, I'd find a thrill."

The inflection of his speaking came out with less strain, and he rambled on, describing missions and the African cities until they reached the citadel. They stopped and gazed past it at the crystal cyan sky over deeper blue water. Hundreds of ships lay at anchor and smaller fishing boats coasted with white sails. Gulls cried and somewhere a ship fired its signal cannon.

"There's *le Lys*, the third more distant of those larger warships." Guy pointed to the vessel, and she noted a calmness in his voice. Marie hoped she had quieted his clashing emotions after seeing her. But she didn't find out. Guy left in two days without talking to her again.

———

Marie and Émile returned to Paris with his success delighting his father, who for at least a few hours refrained from quarreling with her.

The next day, she sneaked up on Émile from behind, putting her arms around him. "Where shall we find a house to rent?"

He faced her. "Somewhere in the Cordeliers area close to the shop. Although not a fashionable part of town, it's a start. Your relationship with my father should improve once we live apart." He placed his lips on her forehead.

In little time, they began the search for a house which they found and moved into. The number of rooms included one for children, making the cost higher than they intended. Somehow, Émile always came up with the money for rent each month.

A devastating letter arrived from her sister not long after, telling how their father had passed away while climbing the hill to their home in Recouvrance. She and Émile sat in their salon as she fidgeted with the folded news.

"Take heart, your father left the world with both of his closest in loving hands. Your sister is courting a fine nobleman now, and you are married to a poor commoner who loves you more than life. He's pleased." Émile hugged her as she curled up in his arms on the divan.

"Nevertheless, I miss him. Not saying *goodbye* will haunt me forever." Marie said, sniffing and dabbing her lashes with a handkerchief. "It's tragic he didn't get the chance to see my sister marry, nor hold grandchildren. Papa died too soon." She pulled another handkerchief from the stack on the nearby table and wiped her eyes and nose.

Émile took her hand. "Your poor sister isn't going through this alone. Charlotte has her fiancé to comfort her."

"They'd just settled the dowry and gotten engaged when Papa died. She'll be fine after they marry since he comes from a wealthy, titled family."

"Then she will be moving out of the Recouvrance house?" he asked.

Marie wagged her head. "Oh, no. She wants to live in that tiny place. Charlotte's so sentimental."

"Well," Émile looked downward, "at least she has a home without paying rent. We'll have to wait."

"Not for long, dear," she whispered. "My inheritance, with a bit more, should allow us to get a house. Papa would have liked that." Marie sniffed again and tried to smile. "Will the navy be placing any new orders?"

Émile pursed his lips and slumped. "Not likely. They've purchased from me, well, more cloth than what they need. Chatroen can justify only so much."

He knew from other vendors that Chatroen's superiors were growing upset about the amount of fraud and bribery at the port.

"Give me some time and I may gather what's needed," he added.

∽

As *le Lys* departed Brest, Guy tagged along with de Santec, the new first lieutenant, as he called commands while they passed through Brest's narrows to open water. Although Guy now acted as a senior training cadet, he still had much to learn even after seven years at sea. The voyage's purpose sent them back to Tunis, once again to confront the bey over breaking treaties.

Guy asked, "Sir, shall I check the cribs below?"

"No, another cadet will do it. Accompany me until the pilot clears the Goulet and we've passed into the outer bays," de Santec replied. The narrows between the harbor and sea included many hazards. Both de Santec and Guy watched the passing shoreline for landmarks to remember the pilot's meanderings around treacherous unseen pinnacles.

Guy held the envied post of a cadet assisting the first lieutenant, but it was not without good reason. He had performed his duties well and his reputation already earned the respect of even *le Lys's* senior officers.

"Sir, will we be seeing a bombardment like two years ago at Tripoli?"

De Santec stood near the mainmast. "You're aware how rascally the bey is. Corsairs attacked Genoese transports last November. They kidnapped the noblemen, asking for ransom. In addition, corsairs pillaged a few small villages on our coast again. The bey must hold the brigands to the agreements, as his own navy does." His fist thumped the railing. "Commander de Gencien must use tact to free the Genoese, not force. In the end, war costs outweigh those of simple diplomacy."

Le Lys arrived at Toulon for supplies. When the squadron embarked, eight more ships accompanied them.

Spring winds hurried their passage across the Mediterranean Sea, and they floated off Tunisia in days. As before, the warships anchored outside Tunis's xebec-filled harbor.

Guy waited on the forecastle with other cadets and masters for officers to debark for shore. But after two hours, nobody had lowered a launch.

"Look, the bey has sent a boat," the sail master said to Guy, standing beside him and pointing as a flag-festooned xebec left the dock for the French ships.

As it drew nearer, emissaries stood at the prow wearing long silk robes and colored turbans. They oared straight to Commander de Gencien's ship.

"Hmm, he's forced them to come to him. That's a clever trick to begin a negotiation," said Guy.

The sail master lifted his brows. "Right. He'll teach the bey who's in proper control of the situation."

Within an hour, the xebec withdrew back toward the port. Onboard sat Commander de Gencien, surrounded by four other naval officers. When reaching the quay, the entire delegation disembarked and set off to the palace, guarded by the bey's tallest soldiers, carrying long-barreled muskets of Arabic make. That evening the xebec returned to the fleet bearing a single French lieutenant, who brought the message de Gencien would spend a few days conferring with the bey.

Much like the earlier confrontation, Bey Hussein released the Genoese noblemen and concurred with the demands at once. De Gencien, staying in Tunis, assisted the French consular to make sure the corsairs would uphold the bey's treaty through added negotiations and agreements.

A week after arriving, de Santec located Guy below deck. "Clean up your uniform and wear your good shoes, Guy. We're going into Tunis to carry a message to Commander de Gencien. Be quick."

Guy hurried and also slipped on a powdered wig, and proceeded to the boat.

"Sir, are you aware of what the communiqué concerns?"

"It's about Genoese sailors still in captivity. They released the nobles but not the crewmen whom they had no right to enslave." De Santec smirked at the treachery. "Just follow my lead. If I bow, you bow. If I'm silent, you remain silent. Better still, be quiet the whole time." He didn't smile.

When the launch bumped up against a pier, Guy expected the same mob of guards to surround them. To his surprise, no soldiers met them, and even the fishermen and commoners ignored them as they climbed up to the dock.

"Which way the palace is, I can only guess." De Santec lifted his head and looked around for it. "Let's take this widest road upward from the waterfront and find out where it leads."

In a short time, they strode to the palace's front where four sentries stood before an enormous, dark wooden entrance covered in brass design work. The guards stared at them.

"Monsieur de Gencien, please." De Santec pronounced the words slowly so they might understand. When none of them responded, he repeated, "De Gencien."

A soldier moved to the portal, cracked it open a bit, and spoke to someone. Within a minute, a young monk standing inside addressed them after the sentries pulled the immense doors apart.

"Welcome to the palace." The friar waved them forward, and the two entered the marble-floored vestibule.

"Oh, you're French. Thank God, I didn't know how they'd figure out we had to see Commander de Gencien." With a grateful face, De Santec tipped his hat.

No emotion showed, and he eyed them with care. "I speak several languages, although I come from Florence, not France."

Guy noticed three knots in the cord girdle around his robe. "You're a Franciscan. I wasn't aware they were in Tunis."

"I'm the only Franciscan, sent to service Christians as a translator and Latin scribe for the bey. There are other orders here, but like Saint Anthony, I travel alone." He led them up a staircase to a set of smaller doors. "Commander de Gencien and the bey confer at the moment. Is your information critical?" he asked, stone-faced.

The lieutenant answered with palms raised. "The acting commander told me to deliver a document at once to de Gencien. I have no idea of its contents."

"That suffices to make it important enough." The Franciscan curled his finger to follow him into another closed space. The narrow hall was even darker, with dim light filtering in from two small windows high on opposite walls. After their eyes adjusted, a guard blocked the entrance before them, a massive man with a scimitar in his belt and a long, thin musket in his hands.

The monk turned to them. "When we enter, we must pay tribute to Bey Hussein by kneeling and touching our foreheads to the floor." He tapped his forehead twice. "He will then motion for us to rise. Once I translate what your visit is for, he may or may not allow you to approach. Come." He spoke to the giant sentinel, who opened the entryway and stepped in first.

The three followed the guard into an octagonal chamber. Rays streamed through broad windows, so bright they squinted to see. Guy caught sight of ornaments on the walls and tall brass lantern holders ten feet high standing around the immense reception room. Surfaces covered in mosaic tiles of geometric design glistened and reflected the brilliant sunlight throughout. Across the space, the bey rested in a large chair before a small table where de Gencien sat opposite him. A scribe, positioned between the two, finished translating what the commander had just said.

The Franciscan fell to his knees and bent down low, placing his brow on the marble. Guy and de Santec imitated his movement without a pause.

The bey pronounced what seemed one very long word, then the scribe translated the bey's comment. "Rise and explain."

After they stood, de Santec said, "May Your Highness allow us to deliver an important message to your honored guest, Commander de Gencien?"

Bey Hussein raised his finger, and the assistant again interpreted. "Yes, approach."

The monk and doorkeeper left as de Santec and Guy stepped forward.

They made a small courtesy bow to the bey and then to their commander. "Sir, this document is to be delivered to you immediately." The lieutenant held it out. The fleet commander took it and broke the seal.

He scanned the paper with a deep grunt. "My, my." Then he looked up at the messengers. "You may return to the ships, gentlemen. It needs no response."

"Yes, sir." De Santec touched Guy's arm to follow.

Mumbled to him, the scribe translated for the bey. "His Highness asks if the visiting officers would like to partake of a meal before leaving. It is time for refreshments."

They stopped and turned to answer. "Sir, if you permit," said de Santec to de Gencien. Guy stood at his side with a grin.

"Oh, by all means, men. You'll have two treats. One will be the food and the other telling those aboard what they missed." He smirked and looked at the bey, who listened to the scribe restate. Then the commander glanced at the lieutenant and winked.

Bey Hussein let out a loud, "Hah!"

"Stand here by the pillar and wait until I conclude my business and we shall dine soon after." De Gencien turned back to the bey.

"As our king has informed me," the commander spoke in the scribe's direction, "our government will not compensate the surgeon from Marseille for his services in Tunis. One hundred and fifty piasters is extreme and others have made residence here without subsidy from our monarch. Surely the bey agrees you'll profit from the tax when foreign visitors and inhabitants need his skills."

The bey listened and answered through the scribe. "True, Jews and English who come to Tunis and do not trust our doctors will reward him for his work. But we tax more for practitioners of European medicine. And the little we ask of the Great King Louis should cover the extra fee."

"The French government cannot ...." The commander paused when the bey held up his hand and imparted something to the translator.

"Our Highness has decided it is time to eat. He said he needs strength to fight off the demands of the French." The scribe spoke with no intonation, although the bey had laughed saying it.

De Gencien chuckled and nodded his approval, too, for a break.

They rose and walked through the larger opening leading from the hall. Guy and the lieutenant followed, making their way through many rooms to a dining area. Large red tasseled cushions surrounded a low oblong table of inlaid mother-of-pearl and silver wire patterns in wood.

The men settled on the cushions while a servant in aqua pantaloons carried a steaming coffee urn, filling etched glass cups in gold cradles before each person.

Guy, not fond of coffee's bitter taste, pretended to, licking his lips as he sipped. No one spoke, waiting for the bey to begin.

The scribe listened and repeated in French his master's words. "Our Highness asks if you gentlemen have been in Tunis before?"

The lieutenant answered, "No."

Guy realized de Santec did not want to remind the bey of Tripoli's bombardment two years earlier and also lied, shaking his head. "Nor I, Your Highness."

"Then you must enjoy our dancers," the translator relayed. The bey ordered a servant to get them and thrust out his chin.

As they sat drinking their coffee, a group of three young women, veiled, came into the room. They wore pastel-colored skirts that ended mid-calf and sheer puffy blouses. Two carried cymbals, a stringed instrument, a small drum, and tambourines as the third stepped into an open space.

Most striking for Guy was a European woman, obviously not from Tunis. Her blond hair peeked out from under her headscarf and her white skin contrasted with the others' olive tones. They played, and the dancer moved in swaying and suggestive motions to the music, keeping her eyes on the bey. Her bare arms waved like slender reeds in a breeze, almost hypnotic, with a graceful rising and falling to the beat. As she did, servants brought food to the table. Strong spicy and meaty aromas filled the room, and Guy's nose coaxed his attention away from the entertainment.

Guy tried the first served, a delicious lamb glazed with mint and other spices. A second mutton dish came with much more vigor and zest of cinnamon and ginger flavors with prune and almond garnishes. After months of naval food, he put more on his plate.

Attendants then placed nearby rice blended with okra in a creamy sauce. Fresh quartered tomatoes, flavorful beans, and slim wedges of sweet peppers sprinkled with oil and goat's milk dressing sat on a tray before each. *Drah* bread, corn-based, lay in the center for dipping into couscous, spiced olive oils, or *marga*, a reddish tomato stew. With every dish unique, scrumptious, and new, Guy had difficulty deciding which to retry.

While he ate, he turned once again to watch the performer as she began another dance. Her body, now glimmering in perspiration after half an hour, titillated his thoughts. The woman kept her focus on the bey. The musicians also stared at their master, but often peeked at their instruments. Guy thought the rhythm sounded strange but enticing when coupled with the female spinning with seductive motions before him.

For a bit, Guy envied the bey's lifestyle in his luxurious palace. His gaze drifted to the European woman making music, and she, for an instant, glanced at him and raised an eyebrow. She appeared no older than his twenty-seven years and had appealing features that the loose silk clothing didn't hide. He wondered how she came to be in Tunis.

Once the bey completed his main course, two new servants emerged and hurried to clear the table. Another brought in the dessert, baklava puffed pastry swimming in honey and nuts on an ornate brass serving platter. After everyone finished the sweets, slaves placed a cotton towel and a Chinese porcelain bowl filled with lemony water beside each person.

As they wiped their mouths and cleaned their hands, the music and dancing ended. The old bey waved the dancer over and clapped in appreciation. She stood next to him and bowed. When she did, the bey put fingertips on her calf and rubbed it up and down. The woman ignored it until he stopped and then departed with the musicians.

Bey Hussein burst to the scribe, who said, "You see, gentlemen, this is how we celebrate our lives, with good food and beautiful dancers!" The ruler's smug face and eyes drifted from one guest to the next.

The three Frenchmen, ignoring the slight, over-spoke each other with praises for the cooking and performance. After rising, the commander faced them.

"You can return to the ship. The bey and I have much to discuss before I leave," De Gencien pointed to a doorway and walked away.

"I suppose that's the way to the exit," said de Santec, trying to retrace their steps. He headed down a hall toward what he believed to be the front of the palace, passing through a smaller room. In it, the performers were packing up their instruments in a box.

Guy complimented them, not knowing if they spoke French. "Nicely done, ladies." Again, his gaze settled on the European.

"To make music for you is our joy." The blond stepped forward, speaking a poor *lingua franca*, a mixed language of mostly Spanish and French used on the Barbary Coast to speak to foreigners. "I am Sofia, a Saxon."

Her accent sounded Germanic, but Guy understood. "Oh, from where?"

"Transylvania." Sofia looked back, but the other women had turned away. She lowered the veil covering her face and spoke in hushed tones. "For many years, I am a slave. Help me."

Guy stood staring, unable to talk.

With an appalled look, de Santec rushed to ask, "How may we assist you?"

Her deep blue eyes pleaded for help. "Give my name to my momma,

Sofia Schumaker, from Hermannstadt. Tell Momma, *ja?*" She reached out, glancing around in fear, and grabbed a hand of each and squeezed them hard. "*Bitte.*" Then she turned, replacing the veil.

The Frenchmen gaped at her, unsure how to respond. When she returned to the others, the dancer pointed at the men, accusing Sofia of misconduct, and gave her a gentle head slap. As the three walked away, Sofia looked at the Frenchmen, raising her brows piteously as if to say, *will you?*

They nodded and waved as the women left. Guy spoke first. "How the devil did she get herself into this plight, sir? What can we do to free her?"

De Santec lifted a shoulder and sighed. "We'll try to pass the information on to her mother. Other than that, there is nothing we can, or should, do."

"Nothing, sir?" Guy frowned.

"Slaves cost a lot and abetting an escape might create a political situation. Just the paltry allowance for a physician's tax upset the bey. Imagine if a musician escaped!" He quickened his steps for the way out of the palace.

Guy slammed his hat on as they reached the big wooden exit doors and spat, "What a terrible ending to a glorious day, sir."

"Glorious or glorifying? Surely you realize that everything we saw, ate, or heard, the bey contrived for two results."

"Sir, I don't understand what you mean."

De Santec slowed his steps and explained. "From the moment we arrived, all of it either belittled France or glorified the bey. Even going from the darkened anteroom into the radiant stateroom, they designed to awe a visitor. He asked us to dine, so we'd describe his luxurious life to the crew. Nothing demoralizes men faster than riches, good food, and lovely women they can't have. He's a cunning old bastard."

"It hadn't occurred to me." Guy's eyes widened in surprise and then glared.

"Scheming and creating disruptions are the tools and strategies of politicians. It's all they know. So, you must remember to suspect everything they do." De Santec stopped in his steps. "Guy, you can't tell anyone on board what happened today at the palace. Make up a story if you wish, but say nothing to crush morale."

He replied with a resolute, "I won't, sir."

Halfway to the harbor, the men entered a market filled with the exotic goods of the Barbary Coast and Ottoman Empire. Their pace slowed as they perused the various textiles and trinkets sold. One old woman, whose ancient, wrinkled face spoke of surviving many beys, wars, and rebellions, addressed them in French. "Come, gentle sirs, see the finest of shawls for your wives."

Startled by her perfect speech, they entered her open-air shop under a large green-and-yellow striped awning. Her long silk scarves and woolen garments hung in rainbows on racks throughout, fluttering in the dry afternoon breeze.

"For you fine captains, I'll give you a special price of only five piasters for these, the best of my wares." She grinned, showing many missing teeth.

De Santec paused and fingered a yellow-and-red wool scarf. "How much is this?"

"Ah, that good sir, we make of the finest yarn from Tunis sheep." She pulled others off the rack and laid them across her arms to view.

"*Tunis sheep*, huh?" he replied.

She pointed to four of the creatures across the courtyard being led toward the butcher shops. The fat tails and copper-colored faces and legs looked unlike the sheep in France. "Only two piasters for such fine Christian men."

Guy thought for a moment and considered a wedding gift for Marie. "Where did you learn French so well, may I ask?"

"I was born in Marseilles and landed in Tunis with my parents long ago."

"They were merchants?" Guy eyed her tanned skin, wondering if she came from Moorish or Southern French descent.

"My father was a French ironmonger. The commodity, rare here, is imported for blacksmiths." She paused and looked around suspiciously. "Later, the bey imprisoned my father and made me a slave for years until the bey's brother killed him to become the new bey. Then a Turk bought and married me, but died after opening this bazaar."

Still upset over the musicians' incident, Guy mentioned it. "We chanced upon another enslaved woman at the palace today, a musician. So many seem destined for that fate here." His face darkened.

The old vendor whispered, drawing closer. "Did you meet one named *Sofia?*" She looked up in sadness.

"Why yes, that is whom we saw!" de Santec replied with a surprised look. "She asked we send her name to her mother in Transylvania."

"I've known Sofia for years." The woman then related the tragic story of her capture at sea by Barbary pirates with her sister and brother when children. The devils had slaughtered all adults on board, including her father, right before their eyes. By the end of the tale, the brutalities dumbfounded the two Frenchmen.

"By God, there must be something we can do, sir," Guy said.

"We don't understand the circumstances, Guy. Perhaps she prefers to live here at the palace now and just wants her mother to know her whereabouts. To interfere in other's lives, especially when dealing with state matters, is unwise."

The merchant stared at both. "Sofia wishes to leave and return to her country. As I did. Often I wonder how my life would have been in France. If you're able, help her. Place your mind in hers and open your heart to her grief."

De Santec sighed. "Yes, madame, I'd assist if I could." He paused. "But I don't know if I will be back in the city. This may be our only visit."

The woman placed a finger against her temple. "Perhaps if you might wait a few hours before returning to your ship, we can manage this. I'll send a message to the palace and inform her of this chance."

Guy's heart pounded faster. "We are obligated through our faith to aid another, sir. To hell with politics, this is a Catholic life at stake."

"Conspiring to free a slave is punishable by court-martial and maybe by death here. Also, she's probably a Protestant." De Santec frowned. "Although every Christian deserves freedom from these mosque-goers. If we smuggle her aboard with no one knowing, we might do it."

"Sofia's not permitted to visit the market when foreign ships are in the harbor," the vendor told them. "Perhaps she can sneak out."

"And then?" asked de Santec. "How do we conceal a woman on our ship? We'll have to hide her in case the bey sends people to search." His eyes held a thoughtful look. "First, she has to escape the palace. Afterward, we must come up with a plan to slip her onboard."

The old shopkeeper spoke, her finger raised. "I'll hire a messenger boy to deliver a note to Sofia. If any read it, it'll mention the special goods ready to go that she asked to send on the French fleet. She'll get the idea."

De Santec looked skyward, a hand on his brow. "This all seems so ill-prepared. If they trace it back to you, it will cost your life."

She cackled, "Ha! The bey can chop off this old head if he wants. It'll plop into the basket, mocking him after getting Sofia free."

"Nothing prevents us from trying, save horrible punishments if caught." Guy winced. "Write your message, madam."

A boy arrived minutes later and scampered off with the note to the palace, and told to tell no one. The three waited for a reply. It came within half an hour when the lad returned to say he gave Sofia the paper.

Then half an hour passed and two more dirty young boys wandered into the shop. The hand of the tallest slipped up and pulled at his head wrap. Blond hair tumbled down. It was Sofia. Beside her stood her younger sister, also dressed as a male. They rubbed off the wax and tallow onto their sleeves that had made their skin appear darker.

"Oh, God," Guy stammered. "You've escaped!"

The bazaar owner showed her wide-gapped teeth and clapped her hands, speaking in Arabic to the girls and then in French to de Santec. "They fooled everyone. I'm so happy they're trying to run away."

De Santec laughed at their disguises but then knitted his brows. "Those *kaftans* were good enough to sneak from the palace, but now we have to hide you on one of our warships."

"Hmm, that complicates things." Guy put his hands on his waist. "They don't look like sailors."

"Oh please, we must board a ship today. They will search the city for us when we are missing tonight. The bey is so horrible." Sofia's eyes teared up as she searched their faces.

"Leave this to me. I have an idea!" cried the old lady. She rushed from the shop and up the stairs, returning with pairs of her husband's old

Turkish pantaloons. Her hands snatched a measuring tape and scissors. When she finished sewing, Sofia and her sister, Anna, took the altered garments upstairs. They hurried back, looking every bit like French crewmen in short trousers, their blond hair tucked neatly up under quickly sewn wool caps.

Embracing packaged scarves to hide their bosoms and blouses hanging to cover their hips, the two new sailors followed the Frenchmen to the dock.

In minutes, they climbed into the waiting boat. Without explaining where the new seamen came from, de Santec ordered the oarsmen to row to the fleet. Everyone stared at her when Sofia spoke in *lingua franca*. "Thank you so much. You shall forever be in our prayers."

The lieutenant steered the launch, not to *le Lys*, but toward a galiot. Once alongside, he climbed aboard and whispered to the captain, who leaned over the side and peered down at the two boyish crewmen at the boat's bow.

"Well, can you help them get away?" De Santec said.

Captain Daniel smirked. "This could put us in prison, de Santec."

"Then I'm calling in the debt for helping you pass the exams." He playfully poked Daniel in the chest.

"Ha, you're using that to save two women you don't even know? You could use it for a much better deal." Daniel returned the smile. "I owe my commission to your tutoring. Fine, let them come aboard. But if I'm caught, I can't promise not to tell them who asked for the favor."

De Santec waved the two to climb on board. Then he escorted them to the captain's cabin to introduce them.

Daniel eyed the Saxons as they sat across from him.

"Ladies, welcome to my galiot." Daniel's stare stayed on Sofia. "I'm agreeing to help you at my friend Lieutenant de Santec's request. He said you require passage to France. So, you are my guests until we arrive in Toulon."

Sofia and Anna didn't understand a word he spoke, and de Santec translated it into *lingua franca*.

"*Danke*," Sofia said in German with her hand on her heart. "You're saving our lives."

"Oh, you speak German?" Daniel said in her language. "I know German."

A conversation sprang up about the sisters' upbringing in Transylvania. Then Sofia and Anna told how the corsairs had captured them and their brother and sold them as slaves to the bey.

After fifteen minutes of talk, de Santec excused himself to return to his boat. Both Sofia and Anna jumped up and rushed to him, hugging and kissing his face. As he left the cabin, Daniel eyed him, spread his lips broadly, and shook his head.

On *le Lys's* deck, Guy asked de Santec, "Why did you take them aboard Captain Daniel's bomb galiot, sir? Wouldn't they have been safer here?"

"Ours might be the first searched when they discover the escape. No one from the galiots has gone into the city, and I know Captain Daniel better than any other captain. He and I attended Garde de la Marine together, so I can trust him." His head nodded. "He'll shepherd them to France, where they should make their way back to Transylvania."

"Sir, I hope they pray for you for everything you've done." Guy exhaled loudly.

De Santec guffawed and said, "We'll only need the prayers if we get caught!"

A few days passed, and as de Santec predicted, the bey asked Commander de Gencien to search the ships for the runaway women. The bey's slave master, escorted by British officers, went deck by deck through the squadron. Yet they didn't notice two youthful sailors high in the shrouds, clinging to ropes as fearful of the height as of the beatings if recaptured.

When the galiots departed for Toulon, Guy clucked his tongue. "Imagine, sir, how they feel at this very moment going home after years of slavery under a Barbary bey."

"Not as cheerful as one might expect." De Santec looked away. "They left behind their brother."

"*Brother?*" Guy let out a slight gasp. "Did they mention him?"

"When we were on the galiot, I mentioned the vendor related they had one. Sofia said the bey's army took him to train and told her they'd lash him near to death if she or Anna ever escaped." De Santec then grinned. "But her brother had replied he'd happily take the whipping if either got the opportunity for freedom."

The first cool September wind portended the coming fall seas. Rains soon accompanied the breezes, and the fleet journeyed back to Toulon.

The navy had promoted both when they returned from Tunis. Guy became an *enseigne de vaisseau* to be transferred, when returning to Brest, onto *la Venus*, a 26-gun frigate, and de Santec would leave to captain a ship.

"I meant to tell you what I heard," said de Santec a month later. He seemed bothered. "The Bey of Tunis somehow uncovered his slaves had fled on the galiot, and wrote a letter to King Louis, asking that they severely discipline Captain Daniel. How the old bastard discovered the Saxons were on board, I'll never figure out. But I'm not worried; it's unlikely the king will do anything to a French officer for rescuing two Christian women from a barbaric tyrant. Though I'm surprised my name wasn't dragged into it."

Guy stirred on his barrel header seat. "I'd like to have thanked Captain Daniel myself for his help. Perhaps he'll return to Toulon before I leave on *la Venus*."

"If he comes, it may be as a galley slave." De Santec laughed. "Still, I hope the affair doesn't harm Daniel or affect his rank."

De Santec left for his new ship soon after, and Guy departed within days on *la Venus*, arriving in Brest in time for the year-end holidays. While they resupplied the frigate, he visited Charlotte in Recouvrance. She told him that during his three-year absence, Marie hadn't yet returned to Brest. The few letters he'd received spoke of a quiet, married life. Guy found it hard to believe she happily accepted a settled, domestic routine.

Mid-spring rains came and *la Venus* left Brest to escort a fleet of merchant ships to Québec. His first cruise as an ensign allowed him to ease into the tasks without stress or putting his new authority to the test.

While there, he spoke to a cadet friend from the academy. In trading experiences, he related the escape of the two women from the bey, still thrilled by their daring feat.

"My God, that involved you?!" The other paused with a look of concern. "Then you did not hear. The navy punished Captain Daniel in La Rochelle for his actions. They've relieved him of his command and put him on shore duties as an officer-of-the-pen, never to sail the blue again."

"No! Oh, such a horrible reward for our pure intents." Guilt flooded Guy's face. Had their gallantry, he asked himself, been worth the penalty to the captain who only helped?

Dreary weather continued with a constant rain as his frigate with a few merchantmen set out for Louisbourg on Cape Breton, two days south of Québec.

The Louisbourg fortress was situated beside a bay along the southeastern coast of the island. Surrounded by marshes, it was home to warships guarding the entrance into the Gulf of Saint Lawrence and the river to Québec. Considered the Gibraltar of New France, it appeared invincible, with armed land-side walls rising thirty feet high and forty feet thick at the base. More gun batteries dominated the harbor on islets and facing shores to deter enemy vessels. Over 250 cannons, mortars, and swivel guns defended the port.

While ambling along its waterfront, the two months of dull sea and landscape hues, and glum clouds obscuring the sun, drained Guy's cheerfulness. Sounds of masons' chisels and carpenters' hammers of the ongoing building in Louisbourg disrupted the babel of fishermen, natives, merchants, and soldiers who filled the roadways. As he walked toward the main street, Guy's morale improved with each step of another's approach. It was de Santec.

"We landed yesterday after a trip to Saint-Domingue. How fare you?" De Santec threw up his hands.

"I'm well! *La Venus* came from Québec a week ago." Guy's hand pounded his friend's shoulder. "If you have time, we can eat at the Royal Sword."

Across the table from one another, they talked over plates of *tourtiere* and stewed cabbage. The men enjoyed the well-seasoned, steaming pork meat pies and drank wine between mouthfuls. Crowded with midday customers, the café hummed with jabbering patrons, punctuated by outbursts of laughter.

After catching up on the news, de Santec went silent and squinted at Guy. "What's wrong? You seem unhappy."

"There's something you must know, regrettably I learned Captain Daniel lost his ship posting as an officer-of-the-sword. The court put him ashore in La Rochelle because of the Saxon women's escape. Now he's an officer-of-the-pen, scribbling in books and records."

De Santec said nothing and sat staring at his drink with a noticeably deeper breath. "This devastates me," de Santec whispered. His eyes lowered and his hands went limp on the table. "I owe him a greater debt than what I can repay. I forced him through an abuse of friendship." He slowly shook his head. "He was not as willing and did it only to please me."

"The guilt is mine, too, sir. I pressed you into the act. Life is disappointing," Guy said, frowning.

They spent the rest of the night at the tavern playing dice with little enthusiasm.

‧｡‧

By fall, a letter came to Guy while in Brest. It arrived three weeks after he left Louisbourg. His father had come from Cléder to see him at the house after coming ashore.

"Sir," Pascal said, "a message has come for you."

Guy opened the folded paper.

> *Dearest Beloved Friend Guy,*
> *Six months have passed since my last posting to you and I have been negligent for too long.*
> *Émile, whose business is flourishing beyond our expectations, is often in Brest attending to the navy's needs. A recent plan is to expand sales into other naval shortages, besides his fiber-based merchandise. This, unfortunately, requires more trips away from our home. Perhaps one day you will catch Émile in the port for more explicit details. He*

is well acquainted with our friendship and wishes to meet you.

Life in Paris is not without the gaiety of theaters, grand parks, and, the most magical of all, the operas. Émile and I visit them when possible. The gossip from Versailles accompanying these entertainments is as amusing as the performances.

I must admit to fancying the political intrigues abounding in this great city. Seldom the sun sets that prattle does not circulate, although a long time may pass before hearing your exciting sea stories.

A note of interest, our dear friend François de Saint Alouarn is to be married next January to Marie-Josephe Pélagie. I am joyous about the news. Perhaps he will find happiness in his union as I have in mine. For years, I assumed the refusal of the navy to grant François to wed me resulted from your father's doing. If true, he crafted a blessed intervention. The consequences ended fortuitous to all.

Until you come or I return to Brest, I pray the seas carry you gently and the winds blow your ship home safely.

Your Most Loving and Respectful Confidant, Marie de Bruc Gardinier, the 14th of November, 1733, Paris.

Guy's face brightened, and he paced the salon, tapping the letter upon his fingertips as he digested her words. Émile's business success eased his worries over her welfare. Her suspicions, though, that his father interfered in their engagement wrinkled his brow.

That night at dinner, looking serious, he opened the issue. "Papa, several years ago, when François and Marie de Bruc planned to wed, the navy disapproved, and it ended. Did you, by chance, play a part in the intendant's decision?"

The count swallowed hard. "Guy, I had hoped the two of you might marry in time. Although the marriage would not benefit you financially or socially, you had given your heart to Marie since childhood. To see it breaking saddened me and forced me into a lapse of ethics."

"That, dear Father, is in one act the most despicable and the nicest thing you've ever done for me." Guy's lips turned upward. "To relieve you of any guilt you carry, Marie is happily married and François weds next month." Everyone's dreams were achieved, except for Guy's.

―――

Six months after admitting to intruding in their futures, his father caught a cold with deep coughing spasms. Guy returned to Brest one evening from a voyage to discover him in bed, asleep, with Joseph kneeling by his side.

Joseph glanced up and tiptoed out of the bedroom. "It's good you're home. Father's been quite ill for days and Stepmother is coming from Cléder. The physician said it is pneumonia." He stood in front of Guy, face downcast.

"Is he in danger?" asked Guy, as he placed his hand on his brother's shoulder.

Joseph looked away. "Many whom I've prayed with recovered, but they were younger. In case he worsens, I performed the *Viaticum*. All we can do is wait." A tear formed in his eye as he spoke.

Guy's slumped shoulders matched Joseph's. "When I last saw him, he seemed healthy. It changes so fast when one gets old."

"Yes, God prepares the way. In my parish, the elderly come to pay respects for a departed friend or spouse, and soon they are passing." Joseph's voice cracked, and he turned away.

Guy gently grabbed his brother's neck. "If it must be, he'll be with Mother, Joseph."

"You know, Guy, we've no idea what she looked like other than what Papa has told us. I almost look forward to seeing her. She died giving me birth. All I can repay her with is my love," Joseph confided.

"No, you gave her much more." From behind, Guy squeezed his brother's shoulders. "I've always wondered if you chose ministry as repayment to her. You've given hope and solace to hundreds. Papa will be far prouder of your work when telling Mother than of my feeble accomplishments."

The harsh noise of coughing came from the bedroom and they

both reentered. Their father's eyes opened with barely the whites visible as sweat poured off his bluish-pale face. "Come, my boys," he said breathlessly.

The two knelt beside him, waiting for him to speak again.

"Where's Yvonne?" the count, hallucinating and confused, asked.

"Mama's in heaven, Papa," answered Joseph, tears streaking his cheeks.

"Oh ... yes." He coughed and gasped for air.

As he did, the door creaked open and Pascal's head slid through the crack. "Your stepmother's carriage has arrived, sirs."

Guy stood and left the bedchamber to meet her in the foyer, and filled her in on his father's illness. She rushed upstairs to the bedside with Joseph.

Staying in the salon, he hesitated to rejoin the family, not wanting to witness the end, and paced the room. Then, in seconds, Guy raced above to be with them.

That night, his father died in his sleep. Guy wandered around the house, speechless and solemn. As the elder of the siblings, he mourned more deeply. He had let his father down, he reflected, by not having achieved the fame they both expected.

"Joseph, I never became what father desired of me. I failed him and shall forever feel guilty," Guy told his brother in the garden one morning, his hands locked behind him and shaking his head.

"What? You did nothing of the kind," Joseph replied. "Guy, you did exactly what he wanted. It was I who rejected his plans. Nevertheless, I place no blame on myself. What paths we follow with our lives is determined by a far greater power than even our beloved father."

Guy's dour expression did not change. "We have a duty to our parents while on this earth. If I had tried harder, I may have achieved more before he died. Certainly producing a son was within my grasp if I had respected his wishes."

Joseph, adept at philosophical debate, countered, "You think you didn't please him. We'll never know. To fail in your own goals might dissatisfy you, but wouldn't necessarily have bothered him. In either case, flagellating yourself with guilt does nothing. It's meaningless."

True, Guy accepted he had gained no relief by reproaching himself and had always done his best. Fate had kept him from those things he believed his father expected of him.

He spent the week helping his stepmother mourn the loss, preparing for the funeral in Cléder, and handling the legalities. Naturally, Guy inherited the estate and titles, Count of Kersaint, Count of Coëtnempen, and Lord de Crec'h-Morvan. With it came the extra responsibility of overseeing the finances besides frequent voyages aboard *la Venus* to the colonies.

In the early summer of 1736, Marie walked to the table where Émile sat waiting for breakfast. The kitchen window was open and birds twittered outside as she wore a devilish expression and settled in across from him. She picked up a fresh brioche, poked a hole in it, and forced jam inside until it bulged. Émile stared curiously as she continued stuffing in more. Then she held it up before her and chimed, "What do I have in common with this?" Marie glanced from it to him and back. When no answer came from his bewildered look, she shook her head.

Émile watched, unspeaking.

"Sweetness in a roll." A smile stretched across her face. "I'm with child. I think by three months."

"Oh God! This is the greatest news. I'll be a father!" He clapped his hands, got up, and rushed behind her, kissing her forehead. "We must travel to Brest to let your sister know. You'll be able to, won't you?"

"Of course, if we go soon before I get larger." Marie beamed at the idea.

A half-month later, the couple climbed into a coach-and-six for Brest, arriving in mid-July after a warm and bouncy journey. The house in Recouvrance filled with glee after the announcement.

Charlotte, learning it, said, "Marie, I never thought my willful sister would ever wed, let alone take to married life so well and become a mother!"

As Marie visited friends to show off her enlarged middle, she stopped by the de Kersaint house, rapping at the entrance. Pascal answered and led her to the salon where she sat upon the divan next to the fireplace. Moments later, Guy walked in, putting on his frock coat and beaming.

"No notice about your trip here? You're lucky to have caught me. Only yesterday, my ship arrived." Guy clasped her hands as she rose from the seat to peck his cheeks. Then he stared at Marie with a side glance, noticing her belly. "Oh, mercy, you're going to give birth."

She tossed her head and scoffed. "Yes, but not for another four or five months."

The child in her womb manifested her commitment to Émile, not a mental or social one, but a physical, tangible, biological sign. Did it affect him, she mulled.

Marie paid attention to every nuance in his voice and gesture as they talked, trying to find if he hid disappointment or anger in her condition. Although Guy's face expressed happiness for her, she wondered if he wished it had been his child.

"If there's anything you need for the baby, please tell me, Marie," Guy gushed. "A crib from Spain, perhaps? Let me help you."

She detected no emotions other than joy for her. "If you agree," Marie looked into his eyes, "I would love you to be the child's godfather." The consolation could ease any negative feelings he might hold, she hoped. "I can think of no other I'd prefer. My sister will be her godmother."

"I'm not a relative, though," answered Guy, squinting.

Her look begged consent. "No, but you're like a brother to me, at least! Please?"

"Yes," he said. "It's an honor."

"Fine, we'll have the christening here in Brest when you know your voyage departures."

When she left his house, she reviewed the visit. Nothing showed any regret or displeasure in his behavior. Marie crossed back to Recouvrance, confident he was truly pleased for her.

Near mid-winter, Marie gave birth to their first child, and as the midwife foretold, a daughter. In January, they traveled again to Brest and had the baptism at her old church with her sister, but Guy, called away to sea, missed the ceremony.

∞

The year began with *la Venus* setting out to a new destination for an old cause. The Pasha of Salé in Morocco brutally tortured and imprisoned hundreds of Europeans under horrendous conditions to sell as slaves. Six warships, including *la Venus*, made up the squadron that sped southward. The pasha relented and soon after *la Venus* returned to France.

"I learned Versailles plans to unburden that ongoing problem in Louisiana," Guy said to his brother, now the rector of his parish, at the house in Brest.

"The Chickasaw of South Carolina and Georgia, under British support, have attacked French interests along the Mississippi again," Guy explained, lowering his brows. "River shipping, trade routes, and settlements suffer from their raids."

Joseph kept up with national events and shook his head. "This has been going on for decades, though."

Guy continued. "Two years ago, we assaulted Chickasaw villages, and the natives rebuffed our infantry. That embarrassed King Louis. Now he hopes to remedy it." Guy relaxed his face. "For me to achieve any recognition, I have to go where the possibilities exist. I plan to volunteer my services there."

"What? Louisiana?" Joseph, eyes tired after a full day's ride to be with his brother, pulled his mouth to one side. "Why in heaven's name would you venture into that mess? You know nothing of land tactics."

Guy wagged his finger. "Hah, when did hard study ever stop me? I have books on war strategies to read. Then I'll pay for an infantry company in Louisiana and find an experienced sergeant to handle them."

"Do you have permission?" Joseph asked, frowning.

"First, I have to go to Paris for the approval where I'll recruit a veteran who fought in those terrible places."

"It seems ill-advised if you ask me." Joseph grimaced.

∞

The week-long rainy spring trip to Paris teased Guy's patience at seeing Marie again. Her infrequent letter, albeit informative, did not replace her presence, and he had written about visiting her and Émile. They planned to get together at the public garden, Jardin des Tuileries.

Crossing the Seine, the garden entrance came into view. In its center, a tall, flamboyant statue of La Renommée, the Goddess of Fame, upon Pegasus glorified the greatness of the Sun King.

Shadowed by the monument stood Marie, equally beautiful. When their eyes met, she strode in Guy's direction as the carriage stopped.

"Oh, dear!" She said as they met. "You look more handsome in bright sunshine and amid flowers, a rarity in Brest."

They hugged, and he kissed her cheeks and put her arm in his to begin their stroll. "How I've missed you since we last talked, and you seem fit, as always. I have so much to tell." Guy's face lit. "Where's your child and Émile? I looked forward to meeting them, too."

"Émile is traveling and won't return for another week, first to Brest and then Le Havre." She rolled her eyes.

Guy took her arm in his. "When can I see my godchild?"

"Camille, our servant, tends to her when I leave for errands or visits, and she takes care of me, too, on my bad days," she joked.

"So, a servant? Émile is providing for you in luxury. Good." Guy held his gaze on her for a few moments. "For years, I've worried about your well-being, Marie. I still do, I suppose."

Marie looked downward, smiling. "Often, no, I always worry about your daring life."

"Then my next voyage will truly unsettle you." He closed one eye and put a finger on his chin. "I'm going to raise a troop of infantry to fight the Chickasaw in Louisiana."

Her mouth dropped open. "Guy, are you out of your senses? Those are warriors you'll be battling, not gentlemen with court swords dangling from their sides!"

He let out a soft, "True," then added, "but the king needs to settle the conflict. Besides, in order to gain recognition and promotions, I have to go where we're fighting. So, I'm here to enlist an experienced sergeant."

"Please be careful. It's one thing to be ordered into harm, another to seek it out." Marie patted his arm. "At least Émile will suffer no dangers in his profession. So far, his competitors don't carry weapons." She laughed.

"What is he doing in Brest, still selling canvas?"

Marie's brows rose. "Both sail cloth and to see if they need other goods, as I mentioned to you in my last letter. There are shortages in some areas."

"Yes, there are. If he can find sources, he'll make a fortune. The Polish War disrupts the supplies routes, especially timber. I so wanted to meet him." Guy pouted.

When their tour of the garden ended, they separated, promising one another more letters.

That week, Guy introduced himself to officials at the Admiralty and promised to fund a company of infantrymen. In a records department, he came upon an officer filling in paperwork. The clerk was Captain Daniel.

Guy at once moved to turn away and leave, but he gripped his portfolio tighter and walked forward. Heat sprang to his forehead as he stopped to reconcile with the person he had wronged.

Before the desk, he wobbled with downcast eyes. "Excuse me, sir. You're Captain Daniel, are you not?"

The officer looked up and scanned Guy. "Yes. And who are you, sir?"

Guy shifted his feet and wiped his brow with a kerchief before admitting the crime. He took a deep breath. "My name is Ensign Guy de Coëtnempen de Kersaint, and I owe you a great apology, sir. I'm afraid it was I who pushed Lieutenant de Santec to rescue the two Saxon women from the bey. Had we known of the grave consequences you'd face, we surely would not have attempted such a desperate act. For this, I beg forgiveness."

The admission out, Guy's saddened eyes crawled up to meet Daniel's.

Daniel's mouth stretched open. Then, without warning, he jumped forward and grabbed both of Guy's shoulders. "So, it was you who upended my life?" With his lips pulled wide, he roared, "Thank you, my new friend! Thank you!"

Guy leaned back, head pitched back. "Sir?"

The man said with a grin, "You two changed me for the better. I've gained much more in Paris, both personally and career-wise." He spread his arms out. "Because of you and de Santec, I enjoyed the pleasures of Paris, an improved life, and relief from the tedium of watching over sailors like a hen tending chicks. I miss not a bit of gales and foam."

Guy relaxed his body. "That is incredible news and relieves me so much, sir. Did the two Saxons leave for Transylvania? It has long bothered my mind."

"Anna, the younger woman, lives once more in Hermannstadt with her mother. Sofia, the older one, did not." Captain Daniel paused, his lips held tight.

Guy's eyes narrowed. "Did they send her back? Is she a slave again, sir?"

"No, though she now lives with a new nobleman … me." Joy spread across his face. "I married Sofia when we returned to La Rochelle! We live in Paris and are expecting a baby in two months."

"Sir, congratulations." Guy lit up hearing the words. "This takes a burden off my mind, and I'm sure Captain de Santec will be equally pleased."

"I haven't seen him since Tunis." Daniel sat and motioned for Guy to do the same. "If you run into him before I do, please tell him to forget his worries."

Then Guy told him of his intentions. Captain Daniel praised him for his courage and suggested an ex-soldier to consider as sergeant. He advised Guy to hire an equal number of native Choctaws, just as other French captains had done.

Guy signed up the seasoned man-at-arms, Ernest Dupré, who soon created a supply list and pay book for thirty men.

By summer, Guy and Dupré set out from Brest for Louisiana. The sergeant had fought the Chickasaw years earlier, knew the territory, the native tribes, some of their languages, and importantly, many of the officials, infantrymen, and Choctaw there.

Halfway across the Atlantic, he became more familiar with Dupré. The veteran looked muscular and healthy at forty-five and carried a long scar running from his graying hairline down the left side of his face to his neck. He had a habit of tracing the cleft with his little finger when he contemplated but never mentioned its cause. Dupré expressed an additional problem one day while Guy discussed hiring native Choctaws to accompany them.

"There's plenty of ex-infantrymen in New Orleans. And it'll be easy to get Choctaw warriors to fight for us, sir. The worry is, who the hell will go with them?" Dupré's mouth turned downward.

"What do you mean?" Guy stared at the rough soldier. "Do we require a chief?"

"We need someone to keep the young bucks in line. There's one if he's still alive, but he may not wish to join us. Damn, it's been ten years since I last saw him." Dupré shrugged. "He's clever as they come, though. The warriors will listen to him, by God!"

"Then I'll leave that up to you," Guy resolved. "Are any payments needed besides the blankets, bullets, and gunpowder we've brought?"

"That's plenty. Hell, they'll want nothing more. It's what we can offer old Hashi Humma to agree." The sergeant's eyes squinted in thought.

Guy rubbed his lips with his finger. "If an elder when you last saw him a decade ago, will he keep up with us on a march?"

"Oh, horse's ass, he's able to out-pace us both, Captain," Dupré claimed with a confident smile at Guy. "Hashi Humma has a lot of experience fighting the damn Chickasaw. He's maybe ten or fifteen years older than me. But shit, Hashi Humma will die of a musket ball or pox before dying of old age."

"I suppose you met him on your campaign. If he's alive, then do whatever you must to hire him to guide us and handle the Choctaw."

"Actually, Captain, he saved me from damn near bleeding to death." His hand went to his scar again. "It happened when I picked up this." Dupré stroked it.

He continued, his eyes focused on the distant memory. "I married a Choctaw woman, Fala. And we were happy until an enemy warrior raped and killed her. Then I tracked the bastard, found him, and we fought." He tapped the marred flesh. "He bellied away, wounded, nearly dead. I crawled, too, blood half gone, and Hashi Humma nursed me back to strength."

"Did the killer ever come to justice?"

Dupré shook his head. "He belonged to the damn Nachez or Yazoo, I think. I don't know what tribe the son-of-a-bitch came from." He snorted. "We didn't talk, only fought like hell. But I remember his goddamned face and if I find him ...."

The incident recalled the brutish lives people lived in the wilds of America. Guy wouldn't ask Dupré to expose more of his pain and led the conversation away.

Weeks later, they anchored in New Orleans and stored the supplies near the dock. Dupré left to inquire where a particular Choctaw trapper hunted and set out to find him. Guy enlisted his infantry company from the many unemployed and enjoyed in the town what he assumed were the last comforts of frontier civilization.

When Dupré returned, he introduced Guy to Hashi Humma, the Choctaw he wanted to guide them.

Guy bowed and extended his hand to shake with the tall, slender elder. The native had long graying hair that hung loosely over his shoulders, and the arm he put out carried no fat, only sinewy muscle. For a moment, their eyes met with a penetrating scan. In an instant, the stranger had stripped the wall of pretenses every man builds to guard his deficiencies. Guy realized the Choctaw experienced far, far more in life than he, yielding wisdom and perception beyond that of an entitled Frenchman.

Guy said in Common French, "I am Guy de Coëtnempren de Kersaint, the company commander. I'm happy you've chosen to lead us. Sergeant Dupré assured me you are the finest guide among the Choctaw."

The old man again stared at him, expressionless for a moment. "*Ah,*" he responded in his language, "yes." Then he added in French, "I will go with you to save Choctaw from dying. Perhaps it will keep your men from dying, too."

"Do you know the route well?"

Hashi Humma lifted up his palms. "Paths change with great river. If Mississippi favors us, I will follow way."

The simplicity of his speech and tenor made Guy glad Dupré had coaxed him into going, even if for the substantial cost of a horse. The amount was far more than what he offered the other warriors, but then, they were not leaders, Guy reminded himself.

The Mississippi River and Red Moon
1738-1740

The British and French disputes over colonial trade and land along the Mississippi River rekindled every few years, pulling many regional tribes into the fray. The Nachez, Quapaw, Osage, Caddos, Missouri, and Yazoo came to fight, and even the Illinois, Miami, Kickapoo, and Michigamies from the far northern woodlands and prairies. Allied with either France and the Choctaw, or with Great Britain and the Chickasaw, warriors battled for riches, glory, or revenge.

A month after setting foot in Louisiana in 1738, Guy's squad began a trek along the Mississippi's eastern shoreline, four hundred miles north to the half-built Fort Assumption. Army commanders in New Orleans ordered Guy to find a way to the stockade that could accommodate field pieces drawn by oxen or slaves. Twelve Choctaw warriors accompanied them deep into the forests on hidden trails no European ever saw or could have seen. Hashi Humma, who knew the route well, led on the winding path.

Moon rays split the fog and filtered between branches as Guy and his Choctaw guide crouched low in the underbrush. Near the stream they had crossed earlier, the frogs again stopped croaking, and Hashi Humma's long, slender hand touched Guy's wrist as he pointed into the darkness.

"Kersaint, Chickasaw come." Hashi Humma's voice sounded no louder than a tumbling leaf and he signaled others, pointing toward the creek. "*Ushta*," he whispered to the other Choctaw and held up four fingers.

Silence followed, although Guy saw nothing but gray, trusting in the old Choctaw's instincts. Hashi Humma had not been wrong before, not once in six weeks of trudging through the thick of the Mississippi Valley woodlands. Guy turned and motioned to the nearest French infantryman near him. All down the line, men kneeled along the trail and clicked musket hammers into position.

The musty, damp smell of the earth drifted up to Guy's nostrils and his knee felt the cool wetness of the ground. Moments later, four silhouettes slid through the heavy shroud of late evening mist fifty feet away. In the beat of a heart, the sergeant signaled and explosive flashes highlighted the figures as the sound of many muskets firing in unison cracked. Just as fast, dense, surrounding trees swallowed up the roars. Each ghostly stalker had dropped in place, and Dupré hopped up to confirm the kills.

As he did, two Choctaw came to Hashi Humma and spoke in their language. He rose and said in a louder voice. "No more Chickasaw are coming, Kersaint."

The rest then stood, confident in Hashi Humma's announcement. They gathered around the fallen Chickasaw, just boys of sixteen or seventeen, each pierced by more than a single ball. One still breathed in uneven gasps until a Choctaw tomahawk to the skull stilled him. Tasked to follow the Frenchmen and Choctaw, the young braves would never report back to their tribe. Hashi Humma knelt beside the dead and mumbled words Guy couldn't hear.

Guy placed a fist on his waist and turned to Dupré. "I think it'll be safe now to make camp and set pickets." His trousers, wet from crossing the muddy water, stank, and he wanted nothing more than to dry them by a fire. "Have the Choctaws close by."

"Yes, sir." The sergeant strode away.

In half an hour, campfires burned within circles, one of natives and another of Frenchmen. Carlos, the Black servant whom Guy had hired in New Orleans, hung Guy's clothing near their blaze and pitched the tent so radiating heat entered the opening. All others lay on the open ground.

Later that night, as they prepared to sleep, Guy found Hashi Humma a hundred feet from the camp, gazing at stars.

"Well, Hashi Humma, we made excellent progress today. Almost twenty-five miles, I calculate." Guy smiled as he approached. "Fort Assumption can't be more than a couple of months away."

"Two full moons more and we'll come to fort. No Chickasaw are near here now." The Choctaw's reply eased any fear of attack. "In north, there will be many more."

Guy paused beside the native leader, and his brows rose. "When those Chickasaw warriors died, you gave them a last rite or prayer."

"No, Kersaint. I told their spirits to forgive us and cause no harm." He showed no expression.

Turned away, Guy nearly laughed aloud. "I thought Jesuits raised you as a Catholic? Didn't they force you to abandon those old beliefs?"

"Monks and priests taught French tongue and your gods, Jesus and Marie. But we have our gods, too." Hashi Humma looked again at the dark sky. "Those dead warriors do not sleep in bone houses and will not go to *Aba pilla*, our heaven, home of Aba. They died in violence and bloodshed and must wander trails at night as *shilups*, ghosts."

Guy smirked over their pagan practice of removing flesh from the dead and putting bones in little huts to be cared for and given offerings. "Shilups, huh? There's a purgatory for everyone, I imagine. A hell, too, no doubt."

The native grunted. "Choctaw have no fire hell. That is somewhere Christians go," he teased, side-glancing at Guy. "There is only one heaven,

Kersaint, far beyond mountains with Aba, where it is springtime forever and always shining."

Guy ignored the sarcasm. "Aba is like our God, then?"

Hashi Humma pursed his lips. "No, Aba is our sun god. Above live many gods and our greatest is Nanishta, who created Choctaw and Chickasaw people."

The two leaders returned to sit fireside and succumbed to the hypnotic power of glowing embers and dancing flames.

A loud popping cinder yanked Guy to awareness, and he stared down before speaking. "I suppose many of your men have died since the war started again."

"*Ah*, many have become shilups. More will be before war ends. But warriors are not mine. Warriors belong to chief." The aged leader shook his head.

"Oh, aren't you a chief? The warriors always obey you and call you *humma*."

"Choctaw obey wise men, Kersaint. I do not need to be chief. I need to be wise." Hashi Humma told him and continued. "*Humma* means red in your tongue, not chief. It is high honor. I have no power, only words. You are chief with power."

"Yes, I am a chief of my troops. Although, I'm not the king. The king wants the Chickasaw off of our land. I do what our king tells me." He pulled his shoulders back.

"French leader must be wise if so many soldiers listen."

Guy paused. "Mmm, people don't think that often."

"Why do soldiers follow king if he is not wise, Kersaint?" he asked, his brows lowered.

"In Europe, we obey or we're punished, exiled, or even killed. Also, the king gives one more power and wealth if you do as he says." A moment later, Guy also frowned.

"Hashi Humma, you didn't shoot your musket today at the trackers." Guy wondered if the native had lost his knack for battle and if they could count on him in a future fight.

"Chickasaw did not attack me. I use weapons only if I am in danger." His face, most often serious, hid a grin. "You decided to kill them. Their shilups will haunt you if they wish, not me."

"I don't believe in ghosts, my friend, since I've never seen one and never will," Guy huffed. "I do not fear what I cannot see."

"There are many kinds of shilups." Hashi Humma put two fingers on his head. "Some walk on trails, others walk in the mind."

Guy snapped back, "War forces us to take others' lives. There can be no regrets over necessary actions. We had no choice but to keep the trackers from reporting our position to the English."

Hashi Humma snorted. "Words hide paths for doing what is right. War is little sound but covers many trails. It's difficult to find straight track when hidden by big war idea." The old man waved his hand before his eyes. "Each of us must decide what to hold or cast aside to follow best path." He then lay down on his leather ground cover and pulled a wool cape up to his shoulders.

Guy stood and went to his cot in the tent, passing Carlos, who was already asleep on a mound of leaves, curled up in a blanket reaching his ears. Just his gray hair showed. What the Choctaw said about war stayed with Guy as he tried to sleep. But he had decided years ago to become a naval commander, as his father wanted. Vested in his career, he couldn't change it now. The navy counted on him, and he on it.

◦○◦

Dupré saw it first, a faint blur of movement across the pond. The soggy ground, mixed with rotted vegetation, had hampered their progress for miles and offered no signs of enemy tracks. The sergeant's still-keen eyesight had picked out the person sixty yards away. His arm rose and everyone in the company froze in place, even the Choctaw. Slowly, he lowered it, pointing toward the spot of his intense stare. Someone, far ahead, had spied them and ran.

Without a word, Hashi Humma lifted his hand and held up a pair of fingers. He pointed and waved them from side to side, then curved his arm above his head. Four Choctaw warriors silently sprinted off, two to the left and two to the right.

Only trills of redwing blackbirds reached their ears as the company spread out in a long defensive line without a sound. Guy crouched down, and the rest did likewise. Kneeling in the mud and on the puddled, swampy path, he expected whoever had seen them to be far already.

They waited for ten minutes before the scouts returned from both sides, appearing out of the giant reed wall before them, not making a rustle. The oldest of them spoke to Hashi Humma, who turned to Guy and Dupré. "Woman getting cattail stems saw us and ran. We must go now. Many Chickasaw will come fast."

Guy stared at Dupré, both grasping their dangerous predicament with no real cover on the boggy ground. A fight amongst six-foot reeds and standing in mud offered little chance of either a secure defense or effective offense.

"Follow," the wise man said as he dashed forward into the dense green and brown growth. The narrow leaves swallowed him. Everyone joined in a line, one behind the other, running as fast as they could in the ankle-deep muck.

Onward they pushed, water up to their knees or mud sucking at their boots. Although in late November, the day had been warm. With the extra effort of fighting the soft earth, the crowded quarters amid the stalks felt like a sweat lodge. The stench of decaying plants filled their noses as they slogged for half an hour, grunting and panting with each step.

At last, solid ground supported their feet, and the wetland gave way to a dry, raised strand next to a narrow river. There they rested, tired from their flight. Dupré sent Frenchmen out as guards in both directions from the river's edge. Three Choctaw warriors stood on the perimeter of their group with their ears turned toward the fen.

"We must get across. Here it is too deep. Ahead is portage." Hashi Humma told them, looking around, alert for the slightest noise. "Chickasaw know we are here and come."

"Fine," Guy said between gasps. "Lead the way to a good defensive location."

"*Ah*," confirmed Hashi Humma. "Crossing place is not far, Kersaint. Come, we must go now."

Guy had always considered himself healthy and strong, but he understood his limits. His legs weakened and lungs burned. He couldn't see how the ancient Choctaw sped mile after mile without rest, never tiring. They jumped up and trailed behind him again in a string, glancing rearward every few moments.

When Hashi Humma stopped ten minutes later, the river showed a sandbar from one bank to the other, with deep channels on either side near the shores. He bound across the waterway to the sandy stretch in a long leap. Without pausing, he ran the bar's width and sprang over the water to the far side.

Others did the same until the entire company crossed. Still, Hashi Humma led them on for a quarter-hour more. When the men couldn't take another step, he stopped along the riverbank, his eyes searching the opposite shoreline.

"We must be safe now," Guy panted to Dupré, who stood behind him.

Sweat dribbled from Dupré's brow. "I'm not too sure, Captain," he said between breaths, attention riveted on their native leader.

The warriors knelt on one knee, silent, and eyed the other side, listening for pursuing footfalls. The Frenchmen, on their rears, gasped air into their burning lungs.

Floods had washed away enough growth from the bank to make for a firm footpath, but no side trails existed through the thick, short shrubs beside it.

"Hashi Humma, are there woods nearby we can reach?" Guy asked as he stared at the waterway ahead, searching for a safer location.

"*Ah*," the Choctaw replied. "Chickasaw will go there as well. They know, too."

At that moment, a warrior clapped his hands and pointed across the river. He had heard something.

On the other side, a crow's cawing downstream caught their attention, and another answered upstream.

"Shit!" said Dupré, frowning. "They've found us. We'll have to make a goddamned stand here."

Guy looked around him at their hopeless position with thick, close-growing, low shrubs on one side, and water on the other. They stood on the only tenable spot between both and out in the open.

"Men, create a half-circle facing downstream," Guy ordered. His eyes darted from cattails to bushes on the distant bank, waiting for the onslaught. "We'll retreat no more and deal with them." He glanced at Hashi Humma and waved him inside the arc. "You must join me here to command."

"I stay with my warriors, Kersaint. We will fight those coming from ahead." He pointed up the channel, not a concern showed, as he turned and spoke to his Choctaw brothers.

The two groups, divided by a dozen yards, waited for any signs of the enemy. It came from the sound and smoke of a musket hidden by bulrushes and a puff of dirt kicked up by the ball ten feet from them.

"Steady, men. Fire by command when they appear!" Guy shouted with a sure voice. "Sergeant Dupré, if they cross, fix bayonets."

"Yes, Captain." Dupré made a quick salute while staring downstream.

Along the distant bank, a line of Chickasaw crossed a closer sandbar and approached at a run. Guy tried to count them, but there were too many, perhaps twenty or thirty.

"Bayonets!" Dupré shouted, and the troops pulled them from their belts and fixed them to the tops of their guns in unison.

Upstream appeared three canoes, drifting with the flow to arrive at the same time as the attack from the other direction.

When Hashi Humma spied them, he led his fighters at a run toward them, whooping and screaming war cries. A minute passed before they were within a hundred feet and stopped as if by command. The Choctaw knelt and let loose their muskets. Those in the canoes returned it, and men fell on both sides.

The boats carried twenty-two, with three of them now wounded or dead. One of the Choctaw suffered a musket ball in his thigh, and another tried to stop the bleeding.

With a raised arm, Hashi Humma directed their focus on the last canoe, the larger of them. Nine foes crouched in it, six of them firing their weapons.

The Choctaw spaced themselves apart, and on solid ground, their shots landed far more accurately than those in the swaying enemy's boats.

Gunfire from the two leading canoes took down another Choctaw, hit in his throat, and gone straightaway.

At the onset of the skirmish, Guy kept his attention upstream, but hearing piercing cries closer, swung around his head. The Chickasaw sprinted at full speed toward them, their eyes threatening over gritted teeth. Most had muskets, the rest carried war clubs and tomahawks.

"Form lines facing the bastards, front kneeling!" Dupré called out, and the arc became two rows. "Prepare. Aim. Fire!" he shouted in sequence. The guns roared and four onrushing warriors at the fore of the enemy column collapsed.

Only a few hundred feet separated them as the French infantry reloaded their weapons. They could volley just once more before the Chickasaw would be upon them.

Guy drew his pistol from his belt with his right hand and his left held a saber. Hammer cocked, he waited until they came closer, aiming at the warrior with the largest frame. His eyes shifted from one enemy to another and although his own grimaced face expressed determination and ferocity, fearful thoughts flooded his mind. Aim well. Wait. Pull the trigger.

When he did, the biggest of the foes dropped only twenty feet away. This was followed by the second volley from their line, and five more enemies fell.

The infantrymen stood in a practiced European defensive formation, with weapons at the ready. The Chickasaw wave crashed upon them, swinging their war clubs. Two Frenchmen tumbled from blows as bayonets and musket butts sent warriors sprawling onto the bank. The melee that ensued broke into individual engagements with two enemies for each infantryman. Then Dupré, a veteran of frontier tactics, formed them into a tight circle for a unified defense.

Guy, trying to get to the group, took on a foe wielding a long mace with antler tips jutting from its top. The opponent's hands gripped the handle and swung it high to come down on him. Guy sidestepped and drew his sword across the man's abdomen, slicing through skin and muscle, almost eviscerating him. The club, continuing on a downward angle, glanced off the hilt, and struck Guy's forearm with a crack. Guy dropped his arm, thinking it broke. In a second, he raised it, throbbing, but not fractured.

Upstream, the Choctaw had killed all the Chickasaw on the larger canoe and a few were swimming out to it while the others aimed at the remaining two craft. Another of their tribe had fallen, but only injured.

When the swimmers reached the canoe, they threw the enemy warriors into the water and paddled to shore as the smaller Chickasaw canoes flowed downstream toward the French.

Hashi Humma and his men hopped into the big one and set off at a fast pace. Three worked paddles while the rest targeted the other canoes.

Further away at the sandbar, more foes crossed to join the fight.

Screaming warriors surrounded Guy's close-grouped troop on the bank, who used their bayonets to keep the attackers' tomahawks and clubs from reaching them. Guy lunged and slashed with his blade from the center of the small group.

As the attacking enemy boats reached the hand-to-hand clash, for fear of hitting their comrades, they jumped ashore, using guns as clubs. When they did, Hashi Humma arrived at their backs. Firing into the Chickasaw crowd, every ball hit home and half a dozen fell.

Aware of Hashi Humma's success, Guy shouted above the tumult, "Move to the river!"

His men inched their way as a group downward to the water's edge. Hashi Humma headed his canoe to the abandoned boats, now pulled up on land. Four of his warriors leaped out and dragged them back into the water, paddling toward the Frenchmen.

A deadly volley from the Choctaw guns cleared the Chickasaw, and the infantrymen waded to the canoes. As Guy's men crawled into the boats, the Choctaws on them sent many of the enemy, chasing chest-deep in water, to their gods.

With shots flying by them, the Choctaw and French paddled in a frenzy upstream along the opposite side until its bend shielded them from the attackers. The Chickasaw continued the pursuit, trailing them on the far bank and firing when in view.

For twenty more minutes, their paddles drew quick, deep strokes to leave their stalkers downstream.

Guy counted heads to discover they lost eight men, five of his infantrymen and three Choctaw. The enemy had given others serious wounds, and many had cuts, punctures, and bruising injuries. Even Carlos suffered a missing finger and a slashed wrist in the fight. Thirty left New Orleans, with twenty-two remaining, and more might pass from infections, Guy feared.

Still, considering the circumstances of the clash, the losses seemed bearable, he calculated. The Chickasaw outnumbered them by almost three to one. If not for Hashi Humma, the enemy would have slaughtered them. Dupré's tactics, Guy reflected, also deserved praise. He regretted the fallen, of whom he knew little, except for the last names of the French dead, and nothing of the Choctaw but their faces.

The party moved faster in the boats, and by the end of the next week, they had gone a hundred miles north. Guy considered his mission to scout out a path for cannons completed. From the start, he had found the woods, marshes, and terrain far too difficult for transporting fieldpieces on his assigned route. If the governor wanted big guns there, he'd have to transport them by boat or find another way. Guy's goal now was to deliver his men to Fort Assumption, fit enough to fight.

By the end of the next month, the party had traveled through dense forest, on the river, and along open native trails. Hashi Humma had led them hundreds of miles.

"How many more days to the fort? We've gone a very long distance already," Guy asked.

After spreading out his hide to sleep, Hashi Humma stood and faced Guy. "Tomorrow we will be in Chisa Foka, halfway from New Orleans. Village is one day east of great river." Then he wandered away.

Guy hurried to catch up to Hashi Humma when he saw the campfires being lit. "Why are we building a fire for every man?"

"We are near Choctaw village but also closer to enemy's land, and in more danger. Tonight we must create much flame and smoke. Chickasaw watching will think warriors from Chisa Foka joined us." He let out a grunt, once more showing little emotion, something that puzzled Guy.

Hashi Humma stopped and stared skyward as Guy walked up next to him.

"I suppose everyone everywhere finds beauty in those." He pointed with smiling eyes. "Look at the bright one there. Mars, I believe."

The old man looked at the shining orb. "Ah, that is *fichik homma*. In my tongue, *fichik* is star and *homma* is …"

Guy finished his sentence. "Is red, like your name. Of course, the red star. For us, it is the planet of war."

The native lowered his chin. "*Fichik homma* is powerful and cursed. I quit following warpath long ago."

"But you are on our expedition, one of war. How can you say you don't go on it when you're leading us?"

In the dark, his eyes appeared black as he stared back. "No, Kersaint, I am showing you trail you asked me to show you. I do not intend to kill Chickasaw or others. Only if they attack me, will I fight. My path is straight like tree trunk, not tree root. War only makes more shilups. I need horse you promised to me."

Guy grimaced. "So, you're saying I'm cursed because I am on that crooked path?"

The Choctaw elder paused. "Each chooses how to go through life. Then he forgets he chose. All pathways are equal and different, not bad, not good. Everything is in balance." He hesitated again, then added. "You decided to protect others. I want to help people. Both are needed and must be. Your choice is not cursed. But you travel cursed trail."

"Huh," Guy said, "True. Mine is a rough and treacherous career. Joseph, my brother, is a cleric and lives on that peaceful, helpful road. I suppose had he been born before me, he'd be the fighter." Then he asked, "Do you have a brother, Hashi Humma?"

"*Ah*," he affirmed. "Brothers live in Bishassa village east of Chisa Foka one day's ride. Sisters died and are in Aba pilla now."

"I never asked before. Are you a father?"

Hashi Humma burst into a rare grin. "Yes, two boys and three girls. All live in Bishassa village. Wife, too." He added, "Children have children, and soon, they will have children. Why are you not married, Kersaint?

You do not wear ring." He pointed to Guy's hand.

In the darkness, nobody saw him flush. "I haven't found the right woman. There was one I loved, but she wed a merchant many years ago." His thoughts drifted to Marie's face, doubting she'd find the deep wilderness to her liking.

The elder native tilted his head. "Do not wait too long. Get woman to grow old with. They give you what you need and do not have." He turned and headed to their camp, and Guy followed.

"Dupré mentioned you had another wife earlier," Guy said.

Hashi Humma mumbled to himself and answered, "Everyone makes mistakes, Kersaint."

"Oh? You're fallible then?"

"Pretty hair and faces make us fools. She left me for brave warrior. Like your woman who married trader." He stopped talking and remained that way until they got back.

In the morning, three Choctaws walked into the campsite, slipping past the French sentries. A few warriors greeted them.

Dupré came to Guy as Carlos packed their supplies into backpacks to prepare for the day's march. "They're from Chisha Foka. One is the brother of a Choctaw in our party. He claimed they heard about our coming days ago."

Guy closed his eyes, wagging his head. "Days ago, you say?" he scoffed. "I'm glad we weren't trying to sneak up on Chickasaw."

"We're easy to sniff out, sir. Twice earlier over the last week, I saw Choctaw hunters watch us pass." Dupré's nose and chin lifted. "But hell, if they're not enemies, I don't mention things like that, and neither does Hashi Humma. He spied them, too."

"So, many stalkers roam these woods. I'll try to detect them from now on." Guy felt a slight tingling as he cringed over his ignorance of the backwoods.

"Fewer than if we were passing damn Chickasaw camps." The sergeant's eyes glowered. "They're skilled hunters and Choctaw are great farmers. You'll notice that when we come to Chisha Foka, Captain."

In the late afternoon, they drew closer to the village and passed planted fields, most empty after harvesting earlier in the fall. A few still had squash on the ground and beans on vines hanging from dried-up corn plants, already stripped of their ears. Curling, blue-gray smoke rose over the distant trees from assorted spots.

Fifteen minutes later, villagers, all Choctaw except for a few French trappers, gathered along the road to watch the troop enter the settlement. They found a sizable establishment of many hundreds or even a few thousand, with scattered round shelters of sticks covered with hides, or long, dried reed leaves. A few log cabins stood amid the dwellings, their presence clashing with building skills. No wide streets existed, just horse-width and narrow walking paths from one group of lodges to another. Hashi Humma led them toward the center of the village and stopped when they came upon an open area, the closest they had to a town square. Huts flanked each side, and a crowd of natives encircled them.

As Hashi Humma stood in front, he raised his hand and spoke in Choctaw a long, loud pronouncement, facing the largest hut.

"What did he say, Dupré?" Guy asked, eyebrows lifted.

Dupré shifted slightly to hear, and he summarized it. "He's telling the people to welcome us as friends and protectors while we stay. Hashi Humma asked the healers to care for our wounded and women to tend to the men." He snickered and then added, "I'm sure he meant for them just to cook food for us." While he translated, a Choctaw elder with three feathers hanging in his long hair left the bigger hut and walked toward Hashi Humma.

"Come, Kersaint. Meet chief of village," said Hashi Humma, beckoning him with a wave.

Guy and Dupré stepped forward as the leader drew nearer. Without a word, the tribal head grabbed his friend, and they hugged.

Hashi Humma then went into a lengthy description of something that ended by pointing toward Guy. The chief turned and put his hand on Guy's shoulder, squeezing it. "Welcome, Frenchman Kersaint," he spoke in French.

Dupré whispered, "Place both of yours on his shoulders, sir."

Guy did as told and the village leader let out a loud, "*Ah.*" Then he walked back into his hut.

"We're not in Paris, sir," joked Dupré, "but hell, at least it isn't another soggy overnight in the woods. Someone here may have some damn brandy or liquor."

Much to Guy's and Dupré's joy, that night one of the French trappers joined them in their camp and shared a jug of rum. Earlier, Choctaw women had made them a delicious stew of root vegetables and venison, unlike anything the Frenchmen had ever tasted. Hashi Humma brought a female healer who inspected the wounds of the men and applied poultices of herbs and honey spread on weed leaves and bound by red mud.

As they sat around the campfire, an infantryman sang an old song about returning home after a war. Those who knew the refrain joined in singing. Most of the Choctaw warriors listened and the melody even moved them.

For the first time since leaving New Orleans, Guy felt secure and safe. They were among allies, fed, and resting without the worry of a nighttime attack. He sat away from the other French soldiers with Carlos. The stump of the man's small finger had become infected during the journey. Choctaw and Hashi Humma effectively applied grasses, greases, and bandages that soon healed it. Now, he'd have a souvenir of his adventure.

"Pull your boots?" he asked.

"No, I may go for a walk, yet." Guy pointed toward him. "I noticed lash scars on your back a few weeks ago. I'm guessing you served aboard a warship or were a slave?"

In his strong, mixed Spanish-French-African accent, Carlos explained. "I was Spanish slave in Cuba. Try to escape and they flog me. When master die, his mistress, mixed-blood, she free me." His eyes stared at Guy without any hint of regret. "When they bring us from Africa and chain us slaves, my boy too young to work fields. They sell him to be mansion servant here. Afterward, I make to go New Orleans to find my son."

Guy imagined the pain of loss Carlos felt. "Did you find him?"

"No. Master change his name. After fifteen years I pass him in street and not know him. He be twenty-three now if he live." He looked away from his captain.

"Perhaps someday." Guy put his hand on the older man's knee and patted it. Whether sailor, slave, servant, or tradesman, the incessant flow of travelers through the great ports of the world passed like air in lungs, forever in and out. So many people came and left, it seemed impossible Carlos could find his son, he concluded.

"I wonder where Hashi Humma is?" Guy looked around and pointed at the Choctaw group. "I haven't seen him with the others."

"He by chief hut when I get water." Carlos tilted his head toward the center of town. "It dark, maybe come back now."

Guy stood and strolled among the homes and night fires fringing the paths in every direction. For the first time, he heard women speaking their strange language. Dogs barked, and the occasional snort or neigh of a horse reached him. A cool evening breeze had begun late and carried wood smoke, sometimes food odors, but often fouler smells from the latrines.

When he got to the gathering place, he saw a group of Choctaw elders sitting on logs around glowing embers in the middle pit. Hashi Humma sat two men away from the chief as others passed a pipe to one another.

When their eyes met, the Choctaw's bore delight in seeing him. "Come join us, Kersaint. Here." He placed his hand on the log space next to him.

"Will I offend the chief if I take a seat without permission?" Guy asked. In France, it would be an insult.

"No. You are with me and I am welcome here." Hashi Humma had a strange expression on his face. "Sit."

As Guy did, he recognized the acrid smell coming from the pipe and chuckled to himself. He had become familiar with it in the camps on the trail. The Choctaw used the hemp plant as medicine and often to relax with, much like tobacco. In New Orleans, people with syphilis chewed it and swallowed the juices for a cure.

They heard a distant hooting and the group's talk died for a moment. No one spoke.

Guy looked around, and every elder sat still as if thinking. "My presence must have offended them," he whispered to Hashi Humma.

"It is owl, Kersaint." His eyes glanced in the sound's direction. "They bring omen. Someone will go to Aba pilla soon."

Many of the group tried to hide their peeks at Guy and Hashi Humma. Both men caught them.

Guy leaned close to his friend's ear. "They think one of us will die next."

"*Ah*. It may be." Hashi Humma's face turned blissful. "That is way. If it must be, it is what we chose before we came."

Guy frowned. "I didn't choose to end my life in Louisiana. Besides, it's just a bird, not a prophet or Sybil." He rolled his eyes.

His friend sat and echoed, "*Ah*, it is only bird. Or maybe owl is telling us. Either way, it is truth; we come and die. It can be tonight or another day, but it is truth." Then he spoke to the others, and they laughed.

He faced Guy again with a serious expression. "Kersaint, we must finish what we began in mother's womb before birth. When it is done, we go see Aba. There is no more for us to do. It is perfect."

Guy, tired, yawned. "Whatever reason I have for living, no one told me about it. At least I don't remember. I have enough unfinished goals and unsettling memories, anyway."

The Choctaw seemed to read his mind and grunted. "Hmm. Me, too. Memories circle around like stallions in corral. If you mount wild memory, get off before it hurts you. Ride only tame, pleasant ones."

When the pipe passed to Guy, he handed it off to Hashi Humma and yawned again. "It's late. We have a long day's travel tomorrow, so I'll return to our camp. Do you want to come with me?" Guy stood.

"*Ah*, I follow you. My head is strange." The elderly Choctaw got up and waved his hand toward his brethren, and wished them well in their language.

More than once, Guy had to pull Hashi Humma back onto the path. As they walked, neither spoke. The tribal beliefs had upset Guy, although his companion seemed unbothered by the hoots. He realized he'd never understand how the Choctaw thought, even one whom Catholic monks raised.

When he crept under his blanket, he relegated the portent of death and predestination to the rubbish heap in his mind and fell asleep in minutes, as usual.

※

Three weeks had passed, and the troop of French and Choctaw men drew closer to their destination. The fort lay still eighty miles north. As they made their way on the trails, many times, Chickasaw appeared in the distance and, in a flash, withdrew into the thick forest. Every night they posted twice as many pickets and native sentries in fear of a raid.

The third full moon of their journey broke through the clouds, low and venous red, above the trees when darkness came. Dupré and Hashi Humma decided on a camp beneath pines. The dense boughs dispersed campfire smoke and the needle-covered ground muffled footsteps and dampened noises. They kept the fires small and everyone talked in quiet tones. Out beyond, the enemy searched for them in the nocturnal gloom in numbers they could not match.

Guy had lost his tent during the earlier run-in with the Chickasaw. He spread out his blanket near the others with his pistol and sword by his side. The infantrymen slept with their loaded muskets cradled in their arms, each prepared to fight in the instant of waking.

Hashi Humma did without bedding. He crouched, his back leaning against a large pine, saying nothing, peering into the soot-black darkness for any lunar reflection glinting off a tomahawk or gun barrel.

Tired but unable to sleep, Guy's nerves forced his eyes open, looking under tree limbs to the distant field where insects buzzed in flight. The night was humid, warm, and still.

Finally, Guy's lids slowly closed. He began to dream when an unusual sound woke him. Someone had gasped deeply, loudly, and far away.

In seconds, the men jumped to their feet or kneeled, spaced apart, encircling the dull glow of their campfire.

Hashi Humma motioned and three warriors headed for the noise.

Guy counted his troops as Dupré came and whispered. "One of our sentries, Henri, I think. The bastards got him by surprise." He needed to say no more. Henri, they knew, lay scalped and lifeless. Everyone wondered if the Chickasaw dared a nighttime assault or wanted to pick them off along the trail in the morning. Each hoped for the latter rather than a moonlit fight.

Moments later, the scouts returned and spoke in hushed voices to Hashi Humma, who crouched by Guy and Dupré. "Frenchman is dead. Chickasaw will strike tonight. Do we battle here or go?"

It was up to Guy. Both Dupré and Hashi Humma, searching the blackness, waited for the answer.

"Do you know the way in the dark?" Guy asked.

The elder dipped his head twice. "Ah." Then he added, "They will come from everywhere on trail. We must get to base of rock cliff ahead to keep attack on one side."

"Good plan, my friend," Guy said low, his brow glistening with droplets, like the others.

Guy wiped the sweat from his upper lip. "Dupré, tell the men and warriors we'll follow Hashi Humma for the bluff to make our stand. Leave the packs behind and just run fast as hell on my order."

The sergeant knelt by every person and repeated the instructions. When he finished, he returned to Guy and the Choctaw. "We're ready, sir."

Guy scanned deep into the shadows, wishing the morning sun could rise ten hours early. As he did, something hooted. It could have been a Chickasaw or a real owl, but the effect was the same. The warriors' eyes widened, gawking at one another, and then straight at Hashi Humma.

Hashi Humma leaned toward Guy. "Men are afraid. Time to go, Kersaint."

Hesitating, as he opened his mouth to speak, an arrow found its mark in an infantryman's chest, dropping him in an instant. Then dark moving shadows in the surrounding black reflected the filtered, dim moonlight off the arms and bare legs of many figures coming at them.

"Now! Run!" Guy heard himself yell. In unison, the company turned toward Hashi Humma, who sprang like a deer, twenty feet ahead on the path before anyone left the campsite.

War cries filled their ears from behind as they crowded down the trail in a mass of bumping and shoving men fleeing for their lives. The

Chickasaw converged on them, and the escaping defenders slashed and stabbed those attacking from the trail's sides.

The retreating juggernaut forced itself in a beeline toward the rock face, with the trailing enemy forty feet behind the last man. Tomahawks and spears flew past and over their heads; shots drowned out the yelling and screaming of the vicious pursuers. Two men fell, one Frenchman and one Choctaw. Still, on they ran, fear driving them faster than their foe's deadly thirst.

After a quarter mile, they gained distance from the Chickasaw, and the trail-side onslaughts ceased. As they sped, Dupré and Guy exchanged ideas on how to defend themselves once they reached the cliff wall. Every man's legs and lungs ached. Each recognized the uphill climb yet ahead to reach the face of the bluff. Even if making it, they might be too exhausted for an effective resistance.

"Hashi Humma, you're pushing the men too hard!" shouted Guy at the native ahead of everyone.

Hashi Humma turned his head to the followers. "I run to save my life. Go faster to save yours, too!"

The frequent glances back at their adversaries' contorted faces in the moonshine showed the enemy's determination to destroy them. To Guy, the jagged and dreadful streaks painted across their foreheads and cheeks represented marks of a grisly commitment to kill or be killed. He'd never met such fierce, determined fighters in his travels, who looked far more threatening than any Barbary pirate.

At last, the goal appeared a hundred yards ahead as they slowed while crossing the stoney hill that lay before it. After they stumbled over unseen rocks and boulders, they emerged near the ridge. Guy and Dupré formed a line of men, and Hashi Humma positioned his warriors to the left. With their rear protected by the cliff face, they might stand a chance with just one front to defend against the horde.

The rushing Chickasaw felt the first bite when three enemies tumbled from hits by the French infantry. Part of the onrushing pack split to the right as eleven others veered left. Around fifty in the main body advanced slowly upward, allowing the flanks to get in position.

This slight delay gave Guy's infantrymen a chance for another musket volley, and for a fast reload. Dupré looked at Hashi Humma and at the warriors converging on his flank as if exchanging unspoken thoughts.

Dupré ordered, "Target the left. Make every ball count, by God!"

The Frenchmen and Choctaw turned, facing those scrambling up the incline, and fired. Of the eleven enemies, only two remained when the night air cleared the gun smoke.

Hashi Humma shouted and his warriors raced downward for the last standing. This drew the majority leftward instead of up the hill. Guy, grasping the tactic, pointed his sword to the right and ordered, "Bayonet attack!" The Frenchmen hurled themselves at the fewer advancing on the other flank. Both attacks had blunted the enemy's unified forward offense.

The Choctaws dispatched the last and reversed, running full speed back as the main Chickasaw group swung to chase them. Dupré's infantrymen then fell upon about ten on the right with a bayonet charge that sent the enemy falling under the blades or racing away. Guy and Dupré's troops, too, climbed hurriedly again toward the summit. In all, they had lost only one man during the cliff skirmish, a Choctaw.

At the top of the hill, both the French and their allied natives formed a semicircle to await the climbing Chickasaw. The men tried to reload, with more than fifty enemies spreading outward and pushing uphill.

Suddenly, Dupré stepped out before the line and pointed, glaring at one of the foremost native foes in the moon's rays. He slowly placed his finger on his facial scar, tracing it downward, and released his musket to fall on the ground. His eyes held an insane ferocity never seen. He stood there, straight and stiff, pointing. Every infantryman stared at him, jaw dropped.

The oncoming Chickasaw also questioned the mad Frenchman, who defied sense and exposed himself without his weapon. A loud cry came from a leader wearing many feathers in his hair at the front of the Chickasaw line. The entire advancing mass stopped when he spread out his arms and streaked forward, focused on Dupré.

Dupré stepped downward toward the chief and then sprinted in a full dash. Halfway between, the two adversaries met, knives in hands, spilling onto the ground in a dusty brawl, grasping and slashing until both withdrew with gashes. Guy and Hashi Humma stood in wonder at the scene, as did all others.

They lifted themselves up, holding their wounds, and stared at one another again, both only yards away from Guy. Then Dupré ran and dove into the enemy's midsection with enough force to topple a horse. Both fell, and the Frenchman landed on top with his left hand grasping the other's left hand and lying across his chest, pinning the Chickasaw's right beneath. As the chief kicked his legs, Dupré caught sight of a knife tucked in the foe's buckskin boot. He dropped his own and snatched it out with his right hand.

Dupré held the blade for a second before him. Reforged from a bayonet, it was long and slender. Not made for skinning or scalping, an English blacksmith had crafted it for one purpose—to kill, like the weapon that took his wife. He brought it slowly down between the native's legs, saying, "For Fala." Then he thrust the dagger upward and sideways into the Chickasaw's groin and twisted it. Blood spurted out in a rhythmic flow, covering Dupré's hand. He had sliced an artery. The chief cried out in pain and jerked free his right arm, swinging his knife high and then down into the sergeant's back. The Frenchman arched and grimaced, but spoke not a word.

Only two understood why the duel happened. Guy looked at Hashi Humma. "Let's go. We can do nothing for him. Where to?"

Hashi Humma gazed up at the cliff ledge for a moment and said above the shouting Chickasaws, "Come." He turned and ran along the bluff to the left, followed by their men. Behind them, a mob of Chickasaw had grabbed Dupré, still alive but dying, and carried him away. Others picked up their chief, no longer breathing. The rest, thirty or so, trailed after Guy's company.

After bolting beside the rock face, they found a crack in the wall filled with rubble leading upward toward the top of the escarpment. Hashi Humma dashed into the opening and scrambled over the debris. The men followed and reached the summit in minutes, twenty-five feet above the base. The Chickasaw came, too, but wavered in entering the narrow, dark gap, a certain death trap. A few musket shots downward at the enemy discouraged any from following them. The warriors stood below, crying out their threats and anger in high-pitched screams, and then ran further before the bluff, seeking another crevice.

A trooper pleaded, "Captain, what about Sergeant Dupré? They'll torture him!"

Guy turned gravely to his men. "That stab wound will kill Dupré soon enough. Pray it's quick; he'd be gone before we got to him. We must go." He glanced at Hashi Humma, and they led the terrified squad along the crest westward to continue on to the fort. Chickasaw war parties and scouts trailed them the entire way but were always behind by miles.

The attack on the camp had left them without provisions, and they had lived off the land. The Choctaw warriors provided sustenance with rabbits, possums, and squirrels while on the go. Five days later, they straggled into the hastily erected stockade. Fort Assumption, still under construction, sat on a promontory overlooking the Mississippi. Of the thirty men leaving New Orleans, just sixteen trudged into the garrison, starved, weak, and many needing medical care.

Hashi Humma approached Guy when they arrived. He looked downward. "Kersaint, I promised to get you to fort and we are here. I am sorry Frenchmen died."

"What? That wasn't your doing," Guy answered, mouth dropping open.

"Under pines was bad place to camp when they attacked. I chose it and made mistake. Forgive me." His eyes stared hard into Guy's.

Guy shook his head. "Since I'm captain of the company, it's more my responsibility than yours, and I didn't think it was a dangerous location. There's nothing to forgive." Guy slapped his back and walked away.

Lean, dirty, and unshaven, Guy reported to the outpost commander in the small blockhouse in the center of the square-sided stronghold, his voice tired and weak. After introducing himself, he described the trek. "Sir, we scouted an eastern trail to the fort most of the way from New Orleans. We determined it's of no use as a route for the main supply train."

The superior looked at Guy, squinting. "Captain de Kersaint, we assumed they had killed you. Frankly, I'm amazed you made it. The Chickasaw forced blistering attacks on us over the last month. We've lost patrols and settlers all along the Mississippi. After you left New Orleans, Governor de Bienville settled on transporting the supplies, cannons, and regular infantry on rafts up the river. As you discovered, the swampy routes are too difficult. Sit and tell me how many they took?"

The shocking statement and needless sacrifices forced Guy to put his hand over his eyes. He plopped into the chair before the commander's table, dragging off his hat. "Half my men died, sir. I began with seventeen French and thirteen Choctaws and arrived now with my sergeant dead, seven troops, and eight Choctaws gone. The company had two major clashes with the Chickasaw." He shook his head. Tired, sad eyes looked at the dirt floor. "One, a month away from New Orleans, and then a night attack about sixty miles south of here. Had it not been for our Choctaw guide, we'd have perished."

"Captain, see the supply officer for anything you require. Get well. We'll need you and your company healthy for our expedition against the Chickasaw at Ackia."

The men received tents and supplies from the camp provisions officer and pitched them outside the fort near other camps of natives and French regular infantry troops.

Guy slept for a full day before struggling to rise and resume his command. His squad, now without a sergeant, tended their wounds, ate, and got rest. The Choctaw warriors, too, recuperated from the arduous and deadly trudge.

That afternoon, Guy approached Hashi Humma, who sat on the ground by a tent. His eyes were almost closed. "Are you feeling well, my friend?"

The elder gazed upward at the Frenchman as he drew near. "*Ah*." His face, blank at first, shifted to stern. "I am asking Aba to forgive us. Too many warriors will not go to Aba pilla now."

Guy gave him a quick nod. "There would have been more dead without your guidance. Aba may forgive you before he forgives me." He crouched next to the Choctaw.

"Perhaps." Hashi Humma pulled his long hair over his shoulder away from his face. "Many wives and mothers will ask Aba not to forgive."

Guy accepted his part of that condemnation for the deaths. He also recalled their unexpected fortuity, like Dupré seeing Fala's murderer amidst the enemy horde, the enemy's canoes, and Hashi Humma finding a crack in the cliff. Overall, the grueling expedition interwove many fortunate and dreadful outcomes of happenstance or choice.

In the following weeks, more troops and natives arrived. An outdoor baking oven provided Guy's men with bread. Occasional meat put weight back on their bodies. When their strength recovered, they helped finish building the stockade.

Louisiana Governor de Bienville had conceived a plan to draw as many armies as possible from Canada and the forts along the Ohio and Mississippi rivers. Those and more men from New Orleans were to meet at Fort Assumption for a march upon Ackia, the Chickasaw stronghold to the east. The outpost grew from a few hundred to thousands as troops gathered and artillery came on rafts during the summer and fall. By November, de Bienville arrived at the fort to conduct the campaign himself.

The allied natives' camps had divided themselves according to tribes: the Choctaw, Illiniwek, Iroquois, Shawnee, Hurons, Kickapoo, Michigami, Miami, Potawatomi, and other lesser tribes. Over 2,400 warriors, added to the 1,200 infantry, gave the French forces a massive dominance over the Chickasaw. Every soul craved to avenge their losses on the enemy.

─────

Natchez and Chickasaw spies reported to their chiefs the enormous rendezvous of their foes. Unlike attempts years earlier, the vast, new French army with cannons and siege guns to blast down stockades foretold a disaster in the making for the British allies.

Guy and his company sat idle for over a month, awaiting the expedition against the Chickasaw. In late November, engineers, infantry, and native scouts explored trails to Ackia to decide which could support artillery pieces. Three routes existed, with only one suitable for the whole sixty miles to the enemy stronghold. Yet, no plan of attack developed.

Winter rushed upon them, and fodder for the horses and oxen

dwindled. Pathetic bellows from the starving herds sounded day and night. Diseases increased among men and livestock alike. Supplies and foodstuffs shrank, soldiers and natives deserted, and frustrations grew. Each morning detachments carried corpses to a makeshift cemetery. Over five hundred French died of illnesses by the start of the next year. Still, Governor de Bienville delayed an attack.

In February, the governor held a council of war. Although many demanded an immediate campaign against Ackia, he chose to withdraw most forces back to New Orleans.

While that plan took shape, a small party of less than six hundred French volunteers and Choctaw warriors set out for Ackia. Their mission was to test defenses and offer a truce if the Chickasaw were open to negotiations. When a few skirmishes over a village occurred, the seven enemy chiefs gathered. After years of fighting off Choctaw raids, attrition of their men, and thinking the larger part of the French prepared to crush them, they settled for a diplomatic arrangement.

At the end of March, de Bienville and the Chickasaw agreed they burn the fort at Ackia, cease hostilities, and withdraw their fighters. But the French made no promises the Choctaw would do likewise. Regardless of the French agreement, the Choctaw held extreme bitterness toward the Chickasaw and saw their honor still defiled, seeking retribution for past offenses. Disgusted with the treaty, the Choctaw prepared to leave Fort Assumption and journey south to their territories.

With the Choctaw departing, Guy feared his native allies might desert his company. Guy rubbed his brow when he learned many warriors had already left. The very thought of trudging back to New Orleans without their talents raised worries.

He caught sight of Hashi Humma sharpening his knife while leaning on the stockade. The two stood, watching tribes pack up and depart on foot. Most of their horses had died from disease or lack of fodder.

"I'm sure you're happy I promised your payment after the mission and not before. There are so few of the creatures left," he said beside the Choctaw elder. "Are your warriors preparing to go home, too?"

"We wish to return to our families, *ah*." His head bobbed forward a yes. "Those leaving came for war against Chickasaw. Most hoped to get slaves. With no scalps or spoils, they go back to villages. We travel with you for payment and will stay with your company until we are in New Orleans. Do not worry, Kersaint, we keep our promise, as you will keep yours," he taunted, and Guy heard a grunt.

The slightly threatening reminder made him howl, "Ha! The money for your services sits in the bank in New Orleans." Guy's lips spread into a wide grin. "You are a master of subtlety, my friend, like a blowing gale." He shoved the native's shoulder.

Hashi Humma laughed. "Sometimes Choctaw must blow like storms. Frenchmen often forget promises."

"And Choctaw never forget promises?" Guy chided.

The old man grunted again. "Perhaps more than French. But we don't break our agreements with you because you have more weapons."

"Your men deserve rewards for their courage and skills." Guy's voice turned serious. "If not for them, we wouldn't be here. In my reports, I'll commend their actions to the governor and to those in Paris. It will bring the Choctaw fame and honor."

"Choctaw don't need French honor in Paris or New Orleans. We want other Choctaw and enemies to know we keep our promises. French write letters to get fame in Paris." His head shook slightly. "Warriors will tell our bravery at campfires in our villages. There, people will judge if our stories are true or false. Words on paper are tree reflections on pond, not real or proof, only water."

Guy mostly ignored the tribal wisdom and mysticism of the elder. This time, he agreed.

Three weeks passed, and he received orders to return to New Orleans with his company. Guy paid a camp follower so all his men could have a night of drinking.

At dawn, they took a raft to the western side of the Mississippi southward for a trail that passed by Fort St. Francis, following the winding Mississippi. On the much drier and firmer route than the one they used slogging north, the company averaged over twenty miles a day. With no attacks expected, Guy reduced the nighttime sentries. The men ate better, slept longer, and worried less.

On Waves of Glory

In late May, his company crossed over the northern moat bridge and tromped through the palisade wall gateway of New Orleans. The city's rectangular grid, nine blocks wide and six blocks to the water, offered the men a quick march through streets to the military enclosure near the main square. The natives left them to set up camp outside the city.

Guy kept Hashi Humma and his servant Carlos, who also had survived the trek, by his side until he reported to the army headquarters. There he submitted a list of those killed to the young officer, although the man only wrote the French names, ignoring the warriors.

After he finished, Guy, Carlos, and Hashi Humma left to find the tavern nearer the quay, where they'd have their fill of good food and drink. They spotted the large log cabin on the Mississippi River bank.

As they entered, the low ceiling forced tall Hashi Humma to bend his head down to walk, and they found a long table near the single window. Scattered benches and a shorter table also occupied the rustic room.

They ordered a meal and Guy and Carlos asked for rum, which the owner brought in pottery mugs.

Carlos solemnly glanced up from his drink at them. "Sad, Sergeant Dupré not with us. He love rum." He looked down again and spoke into the mug. "Don't understand why he attack chief to save us. He hero and give us time to run."

Hashi Humma slowly turned his head toward Guy, as if he expected him to say something, and paused before he spoke. "Kersaint, you know why, too. I saw it in your face that night. Tell him."

Guy took a sip, and with slumped shoulders, told Carlos why Dupré had thrown himself into single-handed combat with the Chickasaw leader. He ended the story with, "His bravery was for Fala, his wife, more than for us, but an incredible sacrifice, nonetheless."

They sat staring at the tabletop for a few moments, reliving the fateful event until two boisterous men entered to relieve their thirst. As they did, Hashi Humma looked up and his face erupted into a wide smile.

The first man, a trapper by appearance, wore a buckskin shirt and hat, and long trousers with a red fringe sewn on the outsides of the legs. A skinning knife dangled from his red belt. The two men sat on a nearby bench.

When the trapper noticed them, he made a loud clap with his hands and stood again. "Hashi Humma, you old muskrat!" he shouted as he strode toward their table.

Hashi Humma bounded up and hugged the man when they met, ecstatic. In Choctaw, they began an accounting of recent histories.

Guy and Carlos watched, amused, as their friend traded gibes with exuberant gestures. Hashi Humma had never appeared to them so animated and happy.

After a few moments, Guy interrupted their talk. "Hashi Humma, who are these fellows? Introduce them."

The Choctaw, with crinkled eyes, turned to him. "Kersaint, this is my old partner, André! We trapped together in *bayok*, in your tongue, bayou."

"Tell them to join our table." Guy motioned them to the empty seats. "They'll have tales we'll enjoy."

The two trappers sat and the older one, Hashi Humma's friend, spoke first with a grinning face. "Red Moon and I have seen a hogshead of adventures and nearly perished many times." His Creole features showed a stock of European and African traits, with long black Choctaw hair, a true mix of local peoples. "That was long ago. I still trap, but Red Moon spends his days telling tales now." He pointed mockingly.

"Now I know *hashi* in Choctaw means moon," said Carlos. "Never thought to ask—*hashi humma*, Red Moon."

The five of them settled into a conversation about the recent Chickasaw war while waiting for their food. After recounting their clashes with the enemy, they exchanged stories about their exploits and reminisced about wives and children. Carlos's story of his son tugged at all their hearts.

"Red Moon," André said in a quiet tone. "How is Chisha?"

Hashi Humma glanced away with lips pulled downward. "Chisha's spirit walks his path, his body follows if it can."

The enigmatic answer perplexed the others until André added,

"Someday he may walk again if the gods allow it. I am glad he is still with us."

"Ah, he is happy," the Choctaw replied. "I want to take him to village of his grandmother to see her bone house. Kersaint owes me horse." He glanced sideways at Guy.

Suddenly, it became clear why Hashi Humma had pushed to receive a mount, for his crippled son. "How did he lose his legs?" asked Guy.

"Many years ago he fell from tree getting honey. Not in battle and nothing brave. Village shames him for falling like little boy." The elder returned to an impassive face. "My mother's spirit may heat his blood again and make him better."

A broken back hardly seemed likely to heal from visiting a Choctaw bone house, thought Guy. But now that he understood the request for a steed, somehow it made Hashi Humma even more saintly, risking his life to earn a ride for his son.

The next morning he met with his company near the main square, Place d'Armes, after a trip to the town's sole bank in the government building. He paid off the infantrymen in pistareens and hoped they wouldn't spend it all on rum. Then he led his Choctaw natives to the supply warehouse in the military area and distributed their payment in blankets, tomahawks, gunpowder, and musket balls. To that, he added more goods for the families of those warriors who had lost their lives.

His servant stood by Guy's side. "Carlos, the navy will make out your pay tomorrow. Over our time together, we've experienced a great deal, and you're a good confidant and brave man." Then Guy joked. "An old man, but damn brave. I'll be needing a valet once I get back aboard ship in France. If you care to come along, I'd be proud to have you serve me."

Carlos knitted his brow in thought and said nothing. "Yes, change better for me. Nobody for me in New Orleans now. My son gone and no way to find him. I go with you."

"Fine. I'll see you tomorrow morning at the tavern." He turned to the last man of the expedition.

"Come, Hashi Humma, it's time for some horse-trading." Guy put his hand on the Choctaw's shoulder and led him to the stables where mounts were bought and sold.

Hashi Humma inspected them and picked out a former cavalry gelding, a copper-colored bay. As soon as he touched its flank, the animal turned his starred head to him and neighed and stomped, almost as if approving of his new master.

"This is as best a beast you'll find in New Orleans, I imagine. Chisha will not be disappointed." Guy stroked the animal's back, thrilled he had paid off his debt.

"Ah, it is fine horse, Kersaint. Chisha will ride easy." Hashi Humma turned to Guy, his head tilted aside and sighed. "It is time to say goodbye. I have many miles to travel to my village. Along way, I will recall all that happened with you by my side. You walk hard path, Kersaint. I hope you find your peace. Perhaps you might see me once more someday. Then good. If not, still it is good. Everything is as it must be and it is perfect." He let a smile show on his lips and then slowly led his payment out of the stable onto the street.

Guy's eyes filled with tears. "Hashi Humma, I'll always hold you in my heart. Goodbye, old friend." He had more he wanted to say to his companion of the last two years, but found no words.

"Ah," said the Choctaw, again stone-faced, lifting his hand and barely touching Guy's shoulder. "Our spirits are now brothers." He nodded slowly, turned, and sauntered off with the rope bridle in his hand, leading Chisha's gift away.

LISBON AND JEANNE
1740-1744

In late winter of 1740, Guy returned after his Louisiana excursion. Pascal, his old servant in their Brest home, had died, and Carlos agreed to take on the duties until they embarked. With Joseph's church a hundred miles away, only their stepmother stayed in the house while visiting friends in the port, which was seldom.

On the fourth of May, the navy sent word for Guy to report to the naval vice commandant's office. Holding back a smile, the senior officer extended two folded documents.

When Guy opened the first, his face lit. "How I've waited for this, sir." His eyes scanned the certificate, catching the words lieutenant de vaisseau and Louisiana. The expenses and years he spent fighting the Chickasaw had rewarded him. He'd captain his own ship. Then he unfolded the second document.

"In Le Havre," said the officer, winking and spoiling the surprise. "*La Naïade* is a younger man's warship, a 6-gun. She can carry four more cannons if needed when war comes."

When he left, he slapped the papers on his thigh. At last, he thought, he'd garnered recognition for his sacrifices and would captain his own ship.

Guy had three weeks to find a place to live in Le Havre before assuming his duty aboard *la Naïade*. The day was bright, and as Guy walked home, the pounding of shipwrights' hammers reverberated off the many buildings along the road like a line of muskets firing to a rhythmic pattern. As he ambled beside the quay, Guy saw François de Saint-Alouarn in civilian clothing, fifty feet away, his loping gait stepping over puddles and missing cobblestone holes in the paved street.

"François!" Guy shouted.

His old friend spun around and stopped with arms outstretched. "Guy, welcome back! Marie said you were in Louisiana."

With a smile and hurrying, Guy replied, "Well, she wrote correctly. I was there for a while. How have the seas treated you?"

"Come, we need a place to talk. The café?" François beamed and gestured up the hill.

Without another thought, they headed for it. After settling, François told of a great hurricane the previous year off Martinique that almost sank the 64-gun ship he crewed. Then Guy took his turn to tell of the narrow escapes from the wilderness raids, and his friend sat, mouth dropped.

"Oh my, nothing can top that, and you're lucky to survive," François offered, eyes widened. "How I long for action, but haven't seen a shot fired in offense or defense since going to sea."

"It may come soon now that our troops captured Bavaria and draw us into a war with Austria. How are your wife and daughter?"

François's face brightened. "Both remain healthy. God blessed us with a new baby boy the year before last. I have a son now, Louis-François." His back straightened a bit.

"Splendid. A son to continue his father's calling." Guy slapped the tabletop. "Well, you're far ahead of me on that count. But I just came from the naval office and maybe I'm up one on you. They elevated me to lieutenant de vaisseau to command *la Naïade* in Le Havre in three weeks," he clucked.

"Guy, congratulations." François dipped his head. "Then, there will be two new commanders cruising the brine." He winked and put his hand over his mouth.

"Two? They've also promoted you?"

"A month ago." As his brows rose, he took a sip of his coffee and bit into his roll. "They haven't given me a ship yet, but Brest still remains my port. I'm hoping for a frigate or corvette like yours."

Guy, thrilled for him, then remembered François was two years his junior and graduated from the academy later. His enthusiasm dropped into a slump. He'd spent a fortune on Louisiana, not to mention the assaults on his life. Yet François had beaten him in getting a command rank, and in Brest, no less. It seemed, he mused, without fail, his friend succeeded first; with Marie, with having a family, and with becoming a commander. "Have you heard from Marie? A year ago, I wrote, but I've not received a letter lately or seen her in three."

"Marie came to Brest with her husband six months ago for his navy dealings. I hosted them for dinner. She and her two children are fine. Émile is a clever and talkative fellow, perfect for his calling. He's full of ideas, and his admiration of Marie is obvious." François laughed. "Nevertheless, she's the family's captain, of course."

"Two now? How wonderful for her! Marie's husband sounds like a capable provider. Although I still worry about her. Time and distance have little effect on our concern for old friends and lovers."

François looked at him with one eye closed and pointed. "Aha! I know which she was to you, Guy. I always imagined you fancied Marie."

Guy's face flushed. "Oh, perhaps when a youth I entertained amorous thoughts. As we aged, those grew into true caring as trusted confidants. That's all."

The two talked for over an hour and finished their coffee, parting. As Guy walked along the narrow road homeward, his mind wandered back to the conversation about Marie. She seemed happy with her husband and family, and François the same. Meanwhile, he had no one to wait for his return. Guy's lonely, overcast thoughts pushed what had started out as a sunny day of achievement behind clouds of woeful musings as he lumbered home.

Ahead, his stone house sat in shadows on the darkened side of the cramped street. "Thirty-eight and not even a glimmer of a chance for marriage," he said to himself as he reached for the iron door handle.

Carlos greeted the new rank announcement with hand-clapping. Guy knew his valet desired to assume service aboard rather than stay on shore. Although his duties were light, many in Brest looked down upon him, whereas at sea, mates treated one another as equals, regardless of origin or color.

Two days later, the pair rode a coach to Le Havre. As they approached, Guy pointed out his corvette tied to the dock near a tall stone tower by the mouth of the river. She was a small ship, nothing like the big ones he manned before, or even the size of the 28-gun frigate *la Venus* that carried him to Québec and Morocco. Yet he viewed her with pride, with happiness in his eyes. She was his first command.

~

His inaugural cruise on *la Naïade* took Guy on patrol with another corvette to the Channel Islands between England and France in search of smugglers and small pirating ships. Guy assumed the peaceful and routine assignments would continue. But after four weeks, Guy got a surprise message that ordered him to meet with the naval minister Maurepas at Versailles. Requesting Guy to come by July, the orders did not mention the reason.

His first thought was to write to Marie about his planned trip. He hadn't written to her yet about his return to France or of his adventures in Louisiana.

> *My Dearest Friend Marie de Broc Gardinier,*
> *I have the good fortune of coming to Paris in three weeks' time and hope you will find an opportunity for us to meet. There is much to tell you of my recent history in the Americas and of my new command aboard my corvette. Also, I am anxious to see your daughters and Émile. I shall look forward to our moments together and shall contact you again when I arrive.*
> *Your Admiring and Most Obedient Servant, Count*

Guy de Coëtnempren de Kersaint, the 5th of June, 1741, Le Havre.

The entire way, Guy's mind guessed why Maurepas required him, a mere lieutenant, at Versailles. He assumed it was the result of his Louisiana experiences. But drawing closer to the capital, the more Marie occupied his mind. Even if his professional naval career had made headway in the currents of recognition, his personal life still bobbed in backwater eddies of heartache. The few women he encountered never seemed as enchanting as Marie, nor as spunky, or as pretty.

The day after he settled into an inn, he rode to Versailles to confer with Maurepas. In front of the palace, an attendant led him up the enormous Ambassadors' Staircase and along an elaborately embellished hall to Minister Maurepas's salon.

When called after waiting, he got to his feet and entered through half of a tall, gilded, and carved double doorway to the office. Maurepas, seated at a large worktable with a marble top, glanced up and then mumbled to an aide sitting beside him.

"Sir, per your request, I am Lieutenant de Vaisseau Guy de Coëtnempren, Count de Kersaint at your convenience." Guy stood at attention before him without expression.

The minister's eyes darted to him from the stacks of paperwork. "Yes, we expected you. I hope your trip from Le Havre was pleasant." Before Guy could answer, Maurepas continued with a friendly smile. "We chose you from a list of candidates for a special assignment. One that has important political implications, Count de Kersaint. Although you are new at commanding ..." He searched for a slip of paper and then read it. "Hmm, on *la Naïade*, I see. We feel your reputation amongst the admirals supersedes other commanders in the Brest fleet."

Guy grinned. "Thank you, sir. I've dedicated my life to the navy."

Maurepas glanced down at the file again. "Louisiana campaign, it says. That's a courageous undertaking for a naval officer, and you must have seen action there, I presume. The state is indebted for your efforts."

"Yes, sir. The Chickasaw were quite fierce."

"Our alliances with other countries can rest on the most tenuous of events." Maurepas paused once more and pursed his lips. "In our attempts to court the favors of foreign kings, it often necessitates performing otherwise insignificant services. Although a minor charge at the moment, this may have, however, significant lasting effects on our political aims. We are presenting you with a mission that requires an honest, responsible, and apt commander. You fit these qualities."

Guy gave a blink of understanding. "And the mission, sir?"

"To sail to Lisbon and take on board *la Naïade* a small cask for delivery in Paris post haste. Done only by you, with no mention of it to anyone else. The cask will contain four bars of pure gold, each weighing one-quarter pounds, and a pouch of 127 diamonds. This fortune belongs to the Portuguese King Dom John V, to be made into a crown. Naturally, if anything happened to the valuables, our prestige and politics would suffer a blow. Now that things are heating up for war, Portugal may feel less duty-bound to the British if we accommodated their needs. That is why we've picked you for this secret undertaking." He stopped, waiting for Guy's response, with a steady, impassive stare.

"Minister Maurepas, may I inquire why they are entrusting a Frenchman to create their crown instead of an English jeweler?" asked Guy.

"Great Britain doesn't have the world's premier crown maker. France does. You will deliver the materials to him."

Guy lowered his brows and nodded. "Sir, nothing will prevent the undertaking you have requested of me." He bowed low.

"Fine, my clerk has instructions for you to memorize and then destroy. Thank you for your dedication. You may go."

The assistant handed him two folded papers with wax seals, consisting of the mission details and also a letter of introduction to the Portuguese court. When finished, he pointed to the door and Guy exited.

The ordeal left his head buzzing with excitement. To be picked by the marine minister himself, Guy mused, beat anything François accomplished. For a moment, he wondered about Marie's reaction until he remembered Maurepas forbade him to mention it to anyone.

That night at the inn, he studied each step to get the cask in Lisbon, and where to take it afterward in Paris. Memorized, he burned the information in the room's fireplace.

Marie raced down the steps to double-check everything looked proper for her guest. Her children napped and Camille had finished polishing the brass and brushing the upholstered settee. Things appeared in order for Guy to arrive. After the small clock chimed ten, a horse clopped to a stop outside and a uniformed man tied it to the post.

As Marie waited in another room, Camille answered the door and led Guy into the salon to a seat before a large window overlooking the street.

"My darling friend, I'm so happy you came." Marie appeared, swishing her best gown's wide hips through the hall entryway, and her wig's coiffure sported the new pompadour.

He got up and reached out to kiss her perfumed cheeks. "Marie, you look fantastic! Ah, if I might only hold this picture in my mind forever." Their hug lasted long.

"After so lingering an absence, I wore my finest for you." Overdressed for the informal situation, she curtseyed and laughed. "I hope it pleases you."

"Very much, you've succeeded! But where is Émile? You can't hide him from me again."

Marie pulled him to the divan to sit and played with a fan. "No, he's at work already and we'll go visit him. The business is nearby if you care to go later."

"It's a pleasure to walk when I'm not on a rolling ship." A lilt accompanied his reply as he glanced around the room. "It seems your husband provides you with extravagance, Marie." Guy waved his hand across the well-appointed salon, smiling.

She giggled, holding the fan over her mouth. "He'd better, or discover what an angry Breton woman might do." Then her face turned concerned. "On our walk, I have something to ask you, in private." Her eyes glanced at where Camille had left.

"Of course. Where are your daughters? I must see them." A grin spread.

She stood quickly, smiling. "They're upstairs. Come, I'll show you.

Soon they'll have another to play with, God willing."

Guy sneaked a look down at her abdomen, but her full pleated gown hid any sign of pregnancy. "So, you're expecting again?"

Marie patted her tummy lovingly. "Yes, by year's end. Maybe it'll be a boy this time, for Émile's sake. Though I'm sure the girls will enjoy a brother, too."

They climbed the stairs and peeked in the bedroom where her two little ones, the toddler and five-year-old, slept in a trundle bed.

Guy gazed down at them and imagined how he'd feel if they bore his name. Just as warm emotions surfaced, they returned to the salon. Marie sat next to him. "So, now tell me how you survived the swamps and the fierce warriors. Did you get the letters I wrote?"

"Well, I only received one. I suspect the rest are somewhere between New Orleans and Brest." Then Guy told her of his excursion in Louisiana, the hardships, and the murderous attacks of the Chickasaw, seeing her cringes and eye-widened reactions. With each noticeable response, he described the gore and dangers in more detail. Nothing seemed too graphic for her. Finally, he told her about his Choctaw guide.

Focused far away, he said, "Hashi Humma prevented our deaths frequently and never sought praise or more payment than the horse I had promised. It was an education to watch someone with power over people not using it to place himself above others. Hashi Humma said he didn't need to be a chief for the warriors to follow him, just wise. He was, and we followed him, surviving. Had I not been born me, I'd want to be Hashi Humma."

Marie chuckled and said, "Count de Kersaint? A poor native in the forests of America?" She wagged a finger at him. "No, Guy, you weren't ever meant to live in drudgery and impoverishment. I've known you all my life. Your goals are for fame and the glory of serving the king, like your father and grandfather."

The playful rebuff of his idealism reminded him of another thing about Hashi Humma. "I suppose you're right. He also said we choose our path before birth for a reason. The one I'm on must be suitable for me."

Her expression lost its glee. Marie paused, and said with sad eyes,

"Had that direction been different, things between us may have been, too." Then she looked upward. "I wanted to share my heart with a man who shared his with me daily. As a youth, I dreamed of being wedded to you. Did you know that? Although I'm selfish enough to want a husband who puts me above his profession. The love you carry for the mariner's craft blocked any chance we might marry. Otherwise, ..." She put her hand on his, and her gaze drifted to it.

Guy forced a cheerful face. "That's true. Somewhere I became consumed with achieving greatness, or at least notoriety. Perhaps my childhood formed the mold from which I emerged. More than anything, my father's encouragement and expectations caused me to strive for success as a naval officer." He shifted on the seat. "To be honest, it's turning out that way. Few commanders my age warrant an audience with Minister Maurepas."

"Yes, why are you in Paris, anyway?" Marie's eyes perked up and met his.

Guy's mind raced to think up a pretense. "Oh, Maurepas wanted to hear about the Louisiana situation from someone who'd fought there."

The conversation led to his future, de Santec, and even Françoise. Afterward, they rose to leave for Émile's shop. The early spring sky displayed a clear, cyanic curtain behind the buildings on the route and between the tall plane and chestnut trees bordering the walkways. Hoof clops provided a cadence to the background of bird songs in the branches. As they strolled, arm in arm, Guy remembered what she had said.

"Marie, you mentioned you had a topic to discuss when alone," he said.

Lips tightened for a moment before she spoke. "When listening to my husband's explanations about his business affairs, it seems he may border on inappropriate dealings to win contracts with the navy. Whenever I press him for more details, he brushes the questions away with his usual vague answers."

Guy looked at her with kind eyes. "Dishonesty abounds at the yards; carpenters steal wood, armory workers filch iron, and suppliers bribe officials. Unless there is some fraud involved, like selling imaginary goods or faulty merchandise, the navy does little to correct the infractions. Bribery and minor theft are the norm, Marie. It's not openly tolerated, but assumed."

The concern showing on her face relaxed. "Émile is a good salesman, but he separates his work from his home life. I'd like to contribute to it, but he shuns my interest. Of course, he thinks my only responsibility is to run the house. Nevertheless, I wish he'd involve me in a more supportive role to help him. If bribery, which I'm sure he employs as his father did, is common, then I shall let the fears pass." Still, she ended with a slight wrinkle on her brow.

As they neared the shop, Marie pointed to its large grilled windows and a wood and metal sign swaying and creaking over the entrance, Gardinier & Son, Fibers & Fabrics.

When they entered, an old man descended from his tall stool beside a small desk and greeted them. "Madame Gardinier, how pleasant to see you."

"Good afternoon, Alexandre. How is your wife? The last we spoke, she had taken ill." Marie showed genuine concern on her face.

The small fellow raised his hands and grinned at her. "She's recovered and is doing very well, thank you. Here for a visit with Monsieur Gardinier? He's in his office. Go right in." Alexandre resumed penning entries on paper.

Marie and Guy crossed the room, knocked, and opened the door. Émile shut a ledger and rushed to them.

"Finally, we meet, Count de Kersaint!" he said, beaming. "Ah, the dear friend Marie wishes I had, too."

Guy took his hand and pumped it with vigor. "And now you do. I've looked forward to this also, Émile. You've provided well for someone I care about very much."

"In a sense, you provide, too." Émile's lips widened. "With every sail you destroy in a storm, it increases the odds I'll sell more canvas." Then he burst out laughing.

"Then I shall stop reefing them and let them all blow out," Guy replied with a chortle.

After chatting and departing for her home, Guy left impressed with Émile. Marie's husband was gregarious, confident in his appeal, and interesting. He concluded with a wince it justified her devotion.

Back at the house, Guy met their girls, who had awakened from their nap, and then bade Marie farewell, telling her he'd return to Paris soon. The next day, he left for Le Havre.

⁂

It took a few weeks to prepare *la Naïade* for the voyage to Lisbon, loading food, water, and supplies for the two-week trip. The navy also included enough in case of contrary spring winds, or more seriously, an attack by British ships if a war with them broke out. Carlos served him aboard the corvette when they departed, enjoying the sea's freedoms, away from port life. Guy hoped the servant might help him in throwing off any suspicions about the mission. He'd drop a false hint and perhaps Carlos would mention it to other crewmen.

"Carlos," said Guy, with a grave air. "Bad weather in the Bay of Biscay may force us to put in at a Spanish port on our way to Portugal. Do you carry any spitefulness over your enslavement there?"

"Sir, I have no feelings toward Portuguese." He grimaced. "But I never set foot in Spain again unless you command. Then I obey, sir."

"No, no, I'd never force you to go ashore. They ordered me to carry diplomatic documents to Lisbon and pick up ones to take back to Paris." He decided the pretext would dispel questions about why a French ship journeyed to Portugal, a British ally.

The current flowed well as *la Naïade* departed Le Havre in the Channel and made for the western coast of France. Along the way, they encountered fishermen, merchantmen, and an occasional French naval vessel. One day, a British warship, three times larger than his, saluted with a cannon and passed by them. Neither navy, yet, had openly challenged the other at sea.

On the sixth day, the port of Lisbon greeted them in the east. As they drew near in the mid-afternoon, they saw the tall tower of the Ribeira Palace, Guy's destination landmark, rising over five stories high. One side displayed the royal coat of arms and bordered the seawall along the Tagus River outflow. Expansive public squares adjoined the structure on both sides.

As he approached the dock, Guy fired salutes and Portuguese war vessels acknowledged in kind, with loud booms echoing from the harbor. *La Naïade* laid anchor near the magnificent building, and an hour later, his crew rowed him and his first lieutenant ashore.

A small delegation had come when they climbed up onto the stone quay. Four soldiers carrying muskets and two government men waited, ready to receive him. The larger one wore expensive silk clothes.

The smaller gentleman stood in front as Guy crossed the paved square. "Good day, sir. I am Alvaro Falero, a court interpreter. Whom do we have the great fortune of welcoming to Lisbon this wonderful afternoon?" the spokesman said in French and bowed deeply.

"I am Lieutenant de Vaisseau Guy de Coëtnempren, Count de Kersaint, commander of *la Naïade*, on a special assignment for the King of France. This officer is my second in command, Ensign Paul d'Harcourt. Here are my papers." He held out the sealed credentials and made his bow.

The interpreter took the letter and passed it to the taller man behind, introducing him. "This is Dom de Almada, commandant of the garrison, who will escort us into the Casa da Índia." He pointed in the building's direction as the older official broke the seal and read.

They set off across the immense plaza. Gilded trim on the tower gave it a majestic appearance. Its façade exhibited gothic styling but also resembled the Moorish architecture Guy had seen in the North African ports.

Walled in marble and inlaid with ceramic tiles, the foyer looked old, lit by tall, narrow windows. The soldiers departed and left Guy and d'Harcourt and the two Portuguese officials to continue.

The small-framed translator, who looked about twenty, walked next to the officers as Dom de Almada strode ahead. "We'll go to his office for drinks and conversation. Our wine is excellent, though not as fine as your French wines."

They continued to the commandant's office. In front of the door, Guy turned to his ensign and the interpreter. "Please wait here while I talk to Dom de Almada."

Inside, Guy and the commandant stood before a window facing the river. "I understand by the document presented you are to take the gems for making the crown. How do I know you are who you say you are, sir?"

Guy's face dropped at the question. "Sir, who else would hand you an authorization with the king's seal? That should be proof enough." He pinched his mouth shut.

"Ah," Dom de Almada snickered. "Might not you be a pirate in disguise who had stolen it?"

Both tilted their heads and stared at one another with guarded caution.

"Quite true, sir," said Guy, not wanting a diplomatic standoff but with lips pulled tight. "How can I prove to you I am the courier?"

The Portuguese pointed to the harbor. "A naval commander knows warships. See those at anchor beside the docks? Tell me about them."

Guy's burning stare at the other turned out the window. "Fine," he snapped. "The ship farthest is a two-decker. Hmm, looks to be about a 70-gun. She's an old one, though. Maybe built in the '20s. The one to her east is a frigate carrying 30 guns. They look like 9-pounders, and she's seen little use considering her rigging, paint, above-board strakes' wear, and rusting. No older than five years, and oddly, rigged like a British vessel. That three-decker there is ancient. She launched at least four or more decades ago, and from this angle, I'd say she's hogged, too. The one that's ..."

"Who sent you, commander? Quick! A pirate would hesitate." Dom de Almada's brows lifted.

Guy spat out the answer. "The Minister of the Marine Jean-Frédéric Count de Maurepas, of course." His face reddened.

Without pausing, the Portuguese asked, "And who's Brest's naval commandant?"

"General Roquefeuil de Aymar." Guy grumbled, "Have I passed your test?"

Dom de Almada grinned. "If you're a pirate, you are a well-informed one. To please me, an imposter would have responded to my questions with a smile. But distrust would disturb a French officer's pride. It wasn't your answers, but your reaction that proved who you are. Pardon me for validating it."

"Of course it was necessary." Guy stepped away from the window with a smirk. "My ensign doesn't know why we are in Lisbon. It's best if I'm the only one. So please do not mention the reason, sir."

"No. Alvaro is ignorant of it, too. I'll send a message and the treasury should deliver the jewels tomorrow," he said and went to the door to invite the others inside.

After taking places around the desk, Alvaro spoke. "Captain de Kersaint, we have prepared a room for you to spend the night if you prefer to accept our hospitality. The king is holding a concert you may enjoy after dinner."

He had craved an actual bed to stretch out on instead of the narrow portable cot in his cabin. "That would be most welcome, gentlemen. My dress uniform is still on board my ship. My servant can bring it before dinnertime. I shall return to *la Naïade* in the morning to retrieve the documents I am to deliver." He glanced at Dom de Almada.

"*Sim.*" Dom de Almada's *yes* and nod reinforced the pretext. "I'll take the papers to our ministers when you do. They likewise have a batch for you to carry to Paris."

Then the men drank wine and discussed the entangled history between Portugal and France.

"Ensign d'Harcourt, please return to our ship and take command until I come back after dawn. I'm sure Alvaro can accompany you to the launch. Have Carlos gather up my clothing and bring them to me as soon as possible," ordered Guy.

Dom de Almada and Guy then talked about the ongoing conflict between Prussia and Austria and the implications for all the allied countries. Both agreed nothing could keep war at bay. Each would become an enemy of the other.

They socialized into the late afternoon, sipping glasses of wine until Alvaro led Guy to a bedchamber. As one might expect, lavish silk wall coverings and gilded wood furniture abounded. An hour passed, when Carlos, with an escort, brought the uniform, powdered wig, and better shoes.

"Isn't this the grandest place you've ever seen, Carlos?" Guy swept his arm around the room.

"Sir, I never be in a palace. It is what heaven is like." His fingers stroked the bedpost's gold finish.

Dressed to dine, Guy viewed himself in the baroque-framed mirror. "Now that I know the way, Carlos, I'll walk you to the plaza for your launch back to *la Naïade.*"

As they reached the tower entrance, both paused at what they saw.

"Oh, my God! He's you!" said Guy.

Carlos's eyes fixed on a man coming into the building. The well-dressed stranger appeared to be a younger version of Carlos.

"Could it be?" Guy whispered.

The other stared hard when he saw Carlos. *"Papai?"* he exclaimed, his arms rising.

"Oh, my son!" slipped from Carlos's lips as he rushed forward.

In a moment, they were hugging and crying in the tower's foyer. "How did you come to this place?" Carlos asked in Spanish.

In a mix of Spanish and Portuguese, his son explained, and Carlos translated it for Guy. "Diplomat bring him in to Louisiana for house service and return to Lisbon. He no longer is slave and work for nobleman." His tear-filled eyes could not turn away from his boy as he told the story.

"Carlos, if you want to stay, nothing holds you bound to me. But I must sail tomorrow and cannot delay."

His servant and the young man talked for a few minutes with no words spoken without glowing faces.

"Yes, Captain. I stay with my son."

"The search is over, Carlos. It's a miracle." Guy shook his head. "On the ship, pack up your things. Be sure to weigh your decision carefully overnight. In the morning, when I come to fetch the documents, I'll get your pay from the purser. We'll return to the palace together."

Carlos explained to his son he'd see him the next day and sped off, beaming and at a trot to the ship's boat.

Guy dallied on his way back to his room. To lose Carlos created difficulties for him. He depended on Carlos and hoped he would change his mind before morning. Perhaps he'd reconsider staying. After all, Guy weighed, in Lisbon he'd be without a position and more of a burden for his son. Wouldn't it be wiser to stay a manservant, making money, and visit him on occasion? Besides, he had saved Carlos from poverty in Louisiana, and he might remain loyal, Guy trusted.

At supper time, Alvaro took Guy into a large dining hall to join other guests for an impressive dinner. Guy conversed with officers, diplomats, and nobility from many countries. By nine o'clock, the venue changed to the theater for the performance.

"Captain de Kersaint," said Dom de Almada upon seeing Guy searching for a seat in the audience. "If I knew you liked opera, I'd have invited you to join me. I have to attend. The king loves his music, and it befits me to pretend I do, too," the commandant quipped and beckoned Guy. "Come, sit in my loge." He pointed above to the second tier of boxed seats.

Together, they climbed to the little compartments hanging out over the hall. When they entered the box, three women already occupied half, sitting on one side. All wore fine gowns, and one had small pearls sewn onto the bodice. The jewels dangling from their necks and ears could pay for a warship, Guy marveled.

"Here are my seats," said Dom de Almada, pointing to the left of the ladies. Then he leaned toward them. "Donas, you must welcome our French guest, Count de Kersaint, commander of the corvette in the harbor."

Guy stood next to an attractive woman in her late twenties, with curled black tresses trailing down the back of her neck. Her dark eyes caught the candelabra's lights and flashed as she glanced at him.

"Good evening, monsieur." She spoke in a perfect Parisian accent. "Welcome to Lisbon and Ribeira Palace. I'm Dona Carlota da Rocha, Lady-in-Waiting to Princess Maria Francesca Joana." The rouge on her lips seemed redder than the norm in France, and her perfume smelled of orange and lemon.

Guy bowed deeply before sitting. "Oh, a lady-in-waiting for a princess? Can you point her out in the audience?"

"I hope she's not here. Hours ago, we put her to bed. Eight-year-olds seldom enjoy the arias." Dona Carlota laughed and fanned her face. "Princess Maria is the niece of Dom John, the king."

"I'm unfamiliar with the Portuguese court, sorry," he conceded coyly.

"It must be a challenge to be a companion to a royal." Then he realized whom his words maligned. The lady probably was one. "Ah, I mean, not just royalty. Any child can be difficult."

The dona giggled. "My husband often agrees with you when he consoles me after a tiring day. Sometimes the princess exhibits a mind of her own. Although, by far, Maria Francesca behaves well. By coincidence, I teach her art and French. You'd be proud of her progress in your language."

"I'm sure I would if she speaks it as well as you. Your skills exceed my interpreter's." Guy tried to let his shoulders relax, tensed from the unfamiliar and powerful people around him.

The orchestra played a processional tune, and the concertgoers stood. King John V entered the rear of the opera house and walked with his retinue to the front row of red upholstered seats before the stage. A group of seven nuns sat to his left and a line of noblemen to his right.

"Dom de Almada told me King John is a religious man," Guy spoke to Dona Carlota as they sat again. "Although I've never before heard of a king accompanied by nuns to a function. He must be very pious."

She closed her eyes and voiced into her fan. "Captain de Kersaint, these holy sisters provide for more than spiritual needs," the dona whispered with a wink.

Guy's eyes opened wide. "Oh, I see." He turned his head to her again. "Nuns?"

While facing ahead, she wore an almost imperceptible smile. "Only the fairest."

At the king's nod, the orchestra began.

Guy and the Portuguese noblewoman often spoke between breaks, and then he returned to his bedchamber. Exhausted after the stress of the day, he clambered onto the huge four-poster bed and soon fell asleep on the soft feather and cotton-filled mattress.

At breakfast, he again joined others for another gluttonous meal and following that, Alvaro had a boat row him out to *la Naïade*.

Guy hurried to his cabin and found an empty leather pouch that he stuffed with blank papers. Carlos, who had not changed his mind, carried his bag of belongings and sat with Guy and d'Harcourt in the longboat back to the dock.

Once ashore, Carlos spotted his son rushing across the vast plaza.

"Captain de Kersaint, I go with my son. Thank you for bring me from Louisiana. My soul at peace now because of you."

"Carlos, I shall miss you. We've had many adventures, some good, some bad. May your years be long in company with your boy." Guy gave him his military pay and gripped his arm in a last farewell. He turned and continued on with d'Harcourt toward the palace, frowning.

Alvaro met them at the tower door of Casa da Índia and escorted them again to Dom de Almada's office. The interpreter and the ensign waited outside as Guy entered.

Inside on the desk sat a fancifully worked, dark reddish-brown cask, six by twelve inches and about three inches high. Another gentleman stood beside the garrison commander. "So, this is the treasure, I take it." Guy gawked at it.

Dom de Almada patted its ornate eucalyptus lid holding silver inlay, brass hinges, and a keyhole. "Yes. We have some papers of receipt for you to sign and you can be on your way back to France." He picked up a quill, extending it to Guy.

Guy hesitated and made no motion for it. "Before I pen my name, I must know for what I'm signing. Please open it so I may count the diamonds and bullion."

Offended, the commandant frowned. "Do you not trust us, captain?" The other official smirked.

"No more than you first trusted me," Guy laughed.

Dom de Almada roared, "Ha! Let us inspect it together. I admit, I haven't seen what's inside myself." Taking the small silver key off the desk, he unlocked it.

A black velvet bag and letter sat atop four shining gold bars. Guy picked it up, opened it, and let half the contents spill on the desktop. Both men bent down and eyed the king's treasure in glittering diamonds. He poured the rest out and counted them by fives until they tallied the sum. Then he returned them to the box, locked it, and placed the key in his waistcoat pocket.

"It's best if we hide the chest with these," the gentleman from the treasury said. He held out a worn cotton cloth sack and an old cylindrical leather valise with a strap.

Guy agreed and put the precious container in the sack and it into the valise. "Dom de Almada, I greatly enjoyed your hospitality and shall deliver this to the jeweler in Paris upon my honor."

Dom de Almada put out his hand to shake Guy's. "Captain de Kersaint, if ever you return to Lisbon, I'd consider it a privilege if you paid me another visit. If, by chance, we meet in battle, aim poorly."

Guy bowed to the dom and slung the strap over his shoulder. "Whichever it may be, gentlemen. Until then." He turned and left the office.

The voyage back encountered frequent spring storms, and after reaching the Channel, the weather slowed him to a crawl. Gray clouds drenched the decks as he headed against a stiff wind eastward toward Le Havre. Three days from home, white topsails popped up close out of the mist. A squadron of British ships approached, moving fast.

"Damn!" lamented Guy to his first lieutenant, spying them. "With luck, they should leave us alone."

D'Harcourt spoke his mind. "Sir, we may be at war. Can we flee?"

"It's too late for that. We'll pray they just salute." Guy fidgeted with the button on his uniform lapel.

In less than ten minutes, the leading frigate, a 32-gun, came within calling distance. Its captain, a young officer with a speaking horn to his mouth, called out in English. "Heave to, sir, heave to!"

D'Harcourt, who spoke English well, replied. "Why? We cruise in French waters, sir! Are we at war?"

The other captain pointed downward as he rolled out his guns.

Guy scowled at the Englishman but nodded.

D'Harcourt shouted back, "Very well, sir," and tightened his lips as he shook his head.

They gave orders to adjust the sails to slow and stop *la Naïade* as two other British warships boxed in the French warship. Guy paced the deck, fearing they might be prisoners of war and discover the gold and jewels.

Within minutes of stopping, a boat from the British vessel bumped into the side of *la Naïade*, and British marines tromped on the deck. The lieutenant in charge of the squad went straight to Guy in the stern.

"Lieutenant, what right have you to board our corvette? Is this war or a coastal guard inspection?" asked Guy, translated by d'Harcourt.

The brash officer simply answered, "You've entered British waters. You are to come with me to my commander for questions."

A launch carried Guy to the warship. On board, the red-coated marine lieutenant led him to the captain's cabin and out of the drizzling rain.

Seated in the small quarters, Guy asked again, "Sir, why are you holding us? Are we at war?"

The English captain, without any hint of cordiality, replied, "No, not officially yet. We're on border patrol. My orders are to seize French naval vessels in our waters and accompany them to Falmouth, where we will make a disposition on your status. The British officer now on your ship will pilot her. You, sir, must remain a guest upon mine."

"Guest?" Guy, red-faced, spewed one word at the captain. "Unpardonable! We haven't crossed the border."

The four vessels sailed westward along the British coast and, by the end of the day, entered the large harbor under Falmouth's protective forts. Guards shepherded Guy and d'Harcourt ashore to the port's headquarters.

A vice-admiral and two captains behind a long table awaited him. Stacks of portfolios lay to the side, with ink, quills, and papers before the officers.

Guy and d'Harcourt sat before the three, answering their questions. Then an officer asked the reason for the cruise.

"We're on a diplomatic mission for King Louis and Portugal's King Dom John V. Your interference in our task is abhorrent and an affront to political etiquette," Guy said with a glare.

The vice-admiral, in his 60s and with large, bulging eyes, repeated in French. "Diplomatic, huh?" He drummed his fingers on the desk.

Guy had debated whether to divulge his undertaking to them or use the same excuse he had used with his crew. To tell them about the great wealth might tempt them to claim it as a prize. But if he said they carried simply documents, they would open his portfolio to find blank sheets.

"Yes, sir, an official envoy," Guy affirmed. "And if I may speak to you in private, Admiral, I believe you will release us immediately."

Everyone's eyebrows rose. The vice-admiral squinted, and after a few moments, agreed. Guy followed the older officer out of the room to a separate office.

The captor demanded in French, "What is this about, then?"

"Sir, I carry hidden aboard my ship a considerable fortune in materials from Dom John to be made into a crown for him in Paris. Our king has offered this service in a gesture of respect between sovereigns. As Portugal is your ally, I'm sure Dom John would find it very upsetting if you obstructed my mission."

"Then show me these things," he said with displeased eyes.

Guy maintained his stare. "It would be my pleasure if done also in private, sir. Not even my crew knows they are aboard."

Within a short time, Guy, d'Harcourt, and the vice-admiral stood in Guy's cabin as he lifted the deck plank and pulled out the round leather satchel. He carried it to his table, unbuckled it, and took out the small cask. He removed the key from his pocket and opened the box, picking up the letter to King Louis with the king of Portugal's wax seal on it.

A long gush of air came from d'Harcourt as lantern light reflected off the gold. "Oh, my, sir!"

Guy untied the velvet bag of diamonds and let dozens pour into his hand, dazzling, even in the dim cabin. The vice-admiral simply gaped, eyes wide, and motioned for Guy to put it all away.

In minutes, the British marines climbed off the ship and Guy prepared to cast off. The vice-admiral, sitting in his boat, never bothered to look back at *la Naïade*.

~~~

When Guy landed in Le Havre, none except d'Harcourt had discovered what a valuable hoard accompanied them. A day after berthing, he set out in a coach for Paris on a warm summer morning. Earlier, Minister Maurepas had ordered a pair of military guards to escort Guy the moment he stepped off his corvette in port.

Guy presented the bullion and gems for the jeweler in Paris to count and weight, six days later. Given a receipt, he hurried to Versailles to show proof he had completed his assignment.

Again, he sat waiting until the same clerk said, "Minister Maurepas is ready for you." Guy walked into Maurepas's office, smiling. The minister leaned against his desk and thumbed through reports.

The imposing man folded his arms over his chest as Guy neared. "Our admirals were correct in their choice of a commander. You've returned with good news, I suspect?"

"Yes, sir, I've delivered the cask to the jeweler." Guy grinned, his head high. "There was one complication along the way home." After he explained the British disruption, he placed the jeweler's receipt and Dom John's letter on the desk.

"Count de Kersaint, thank God for your quick thinking by putting pressure on the vice-admiral. That incident and the temptation to keep the valuables, no doubt, weighed upon you. With such wealth, one could become a poobah in India," he said with a smile. "It's valued at over 800,000 livres."

"Oh, I didn't know its worth." The surprise showed on Guy's face. "Nevertheless, sir, even that amount falls short in value to my honor and honesty."

"This is why your superiors selected you for the assignment, Count de Kersaint; you've proven your loyalty to the king. That the goods are in Paris and not Falmouth credits your prowess and levelheadedness. With the successful completion of ever greater tasks, we build our confidence in our commanders until we no longer question their capabilities. Someday, you may achieve that level of trust. You show great promise for it."

Guy gushed. "Sir, I am humbled. It was my duty."

Maurepas cut off his fawning. "Yes, the nation appreciates your commitment. You may go now." With a wave of his fingers, Minister Maurepas motioned toward the exit. "Thank you again for your diligence."

After leaving, Guy hurried his rented horse to Marie's home. He expected a warm reception even without requesting the visit as he knocked on her door.

Camille answered and invited Guy inside and sped off to tell her mistress of the unexpected guest.

"Oh, my God, Guy, I'm so happy you've come!" Marie said, smiling.

Guy waited in her fashionable, though small, salon. "I hope I'm not unwelcome. I arrived only today after a mission for the minister of the navy and rushed here when my meeting with Maurepas ended."

"Visits from you needn't ever be requested, dear Guy. Yet more audiences with Minister Maurepas? Meetings at Versailles, and you're still but a lieutenant? Will you be visiting the king when a captain?" She giggled.

They sat on the settee as Guy's face reddened. "No, I don't expect that for some time to come. I'll have to prove myself. Although Maurepas said some very complimentary things to me today."

Marie pouted. "Compliments pay no bills, promotions do. Earlier, you mentioned you need to recover the costs for the Louisiana mission."

"Yes, the expedition drained away a sizable part of my inheritance, and taxes have shot to the clouds for war preparations. At least if it comes, I might have a chance of making prize money from captured ships. Until then, I'll be counting on profits from harvests to cover expenses."

She shook her head and patted his knee. "Well, you're still in a far better financial state than Émile and I. We live in comfort and his business continues to grow, but war disrupts everything. We may face challenges. Of course, it might create more sales for him, too. Brest is preparing for more shipbuilding, he said, and that means they'll need more supplies."

"He should do well. Perhaps you'll have two servants when next I visit."

"What task brought you to Paris this time?" she asked.

He divulged to her the secret trip to Lisbon, the jewels, the sumptuous palace, and the entertaining concert. Marie put questions to him about each scene and event, often followed by her opinion. She burst out laughing when he mentioned the nuns at the concert and sighed when told Carlos's story.

Finally, he told her about the British intercepting him and taking him to Falmouth. She had to know everything about it. An hour later, Guy departed for his inn.

The next day, he boarded the coach with the two guards for the long trip to Le Havre. As they spoke of family, he pretended to nap. With the visit fresh in his mind, Guy allowed his imagination to drift. Marie and the children ran to greet him home, joined him for supper, and he retired with her to bed. The vision soon faded, and Guy opened his eyes to his own reflection in the carriage window. The transparent image looking back seemed forsaken and without substance.

Weeks later, Guy told his new servant to clean his uniform and polish his shoes for the monthly naval ball. In Brest, they abounded with single officers but lacked unmarried women. Le Havre's dances differed with far more choice in prospects.

The event took place in the large military headquarters within the fortress's high walls. Guy dismounted his horse and joined the others in the main hall, where a string ensemble provided background music for attendees talking and a tune for dancing. As expected, a profusion of bachelors circled the available belles like bee swarms drawn to summer flowers.

He meant to make his presence known, drink a glass of brandy, and quickly leave, his usual routine at the obligatory functions. When the time came, he meandered toward the door for his exit.

As he put down his glass to leave, someone called out to him, "De Kersaint!" The distant call slipped to him out of the crowd noise and its familiar sound gave him a tingling rush. When Guy sorted out the speaker's face from others, he beamed.

"De Santec!" he shouted.

His friend made his way and threw open his arms when he stopped before Guy. "I came early, but only now noticed you."

"Ha, I came late and you almost wouldn't have, as I was just leaving," Guy said. "Although seeing you changes that notion."

For the next hour, they exchanged thoughts, including the wonderful news of Captain Daniel's marriage to Sofia, until de Santec leaned in and whispered in Guy's ear. "There's someone who's been peeping at you. Over there." He pointed in her direction with the hand holding his drink.

As Guy caught sight of her, the woman looked again.

"Who is she, I wonder?" Guy asked.

De Santec wrinkled his brow. "No idea. She's young, though, so I imagine not one of the married ladies. Let me find out for you." He spun around on his heels.

"No, that's ...," Guy began to say as de Santec sped off in pursuit of her identity. He took another glance, and she continued eyeing him between comments to her group.

Within a minute, de Santec popped up beside Guy, smiling. "She's Jeanne, daughter of Lord de l'Ecluse, a banker and city alderman."

"Well, she's pretty," Guy said.

"I told her friend your name. It'd be a shame, not to mention impolite, for you not to respond to her interest, Guy."

When they made eye contact again, Guy dipped his head, and she curtsied, fanning her face.

"A banker's child, huh?" Guy squinted with protruding lips. "She's probably spoiled and gets whatever she wants."

De Santec snorted, "Of all seamen, you should not be turning away from opportunities to meet females."

Guy paused and shuffled his feet. "You're right. Your words echo what I've been thinking lately. It's too soon in life to give up on finding a match. If a lady offers her friendship, I must learn to respond in kind. It's just those I've met have never measured up to Marie."

"The solution for that is easy," de Santec laughed. "Change your ruler! Don't compare them to Marie. Every sunrise is unique, and you can marvel at the qualities of each without diminishing the others."

Guy's lips cracked open in reflection. "That is simple, though maybe harder than it sounds. Still, it's an option I must explore before I totally scuttle myself in remorse. Tell Jeanne I'm interested. Would you?"

"Finally, thank God," de Santec mumbled as he worked his way through the assembly to inform Jeanne's friend.

Despite de Santec's encouragement, Guy didn't fully believe he could give up decades of enamoring Marie by simply acknowledging a stranger.

Especially a maiden, who may have nothing in common with the type of female he sought.

As they left the building and their mounts clomped along the avenue, Guy, with a dour face, looked over to de Santec. "Devotion has trapped me in Marie's world since childhood. As you think of your wife when at sea, I do the same, but with Marie. I'm aware she's not my spouse, but it's still satisfying to have that small part of her as a friend. That has always been enough for me."

"To marry could add so much more to your life," de Santec responded. "Promise me you'll be open to a new relationship and allow it a chance to develop. Give her time. It will be worth it."

"I realize I must reform my ways," Guy answered. "But the doing is what's so tough, not the knowing."

Later that week, de Santec cruised the Channel on patrol, telling Guy he'd return within a few weeks. When de Santec anchored, he asked Guy if he had contacted Jeanne.

"Not yet. I thought I'd wait and see." His shoulders gave a slight shrug.

"Guy, don't ignore the possibilities. She may be serious in her intents." He frowned. "When in doldrums, you hang stunsails and more canvas to catch any breeze. Try. Never drift with a current."

Guy let out a deep breath. "Fine. What do you suggest?"

"I'd be happy to coordinate a meeting," he replied with a grin.

Laughing, he said, "Do it. If things go poorly, I'll have you to blame."

De Santec, within two days, planned for Lord de l'Ecluse to invite him and Guy to a luncheon.

"I'm thrilled to introduce you to them," de Santec said on their way to the house. "Please be open to Jeanne and not dismiss her out of hand."

Guy wondered if he was wasting his time as their horses drew up to the de l'Ecluse estate. Similar arrangements over the years had ended unsuccessfully.

The main building, designed in the older Baroque style, featured an entrance embellished with pilasters and topped with a stylized pediment. It dripped wealth.

Once they entered, a servant took them to the grand salon which contained later Régence furniture. In the luxurious room, Lord de l'Ecluse and his wife rested on a wide three-seat sofa. The two commanders discussed with their hosts the important matters of the day; plays, music, and why the king refused to invest more in the navy. Then the time came to meet the rest of the family.

Jeanne entered, followed by a younger sister and brother. Her yellow gown, silk and brocade, played against the highlights in her light brown hair. With the sun beaming into the salon, she glowed in its rays. Flawless, pale skin radiated youth and purity as she curtseyed and sat facing the officers while a governess took the two children away.

Conversations continued for another twenty minutes, with Jeanne sitting and only occasionally dipping her head in agreement.

Then Lord de l'Ecluse addressed her. "Dear, we need a new diversion. Would you play something for us?"

Jeanne went to the harpsichord. "What piece would you like, Father?"

"Mmm, a composition by Dandrieu, perhaps *La Lyre d'Orphée?*" he answered with a smile.

She frowned at the suggestion. "That's so somber and dreary, and doesn't match today's brilliance."

"But it's one of my favorites."

"Yes, Father." Her eyes rolled, and she played the quick tune without a mistake.

Guy spoke after everyone clapped. "Jeanne, your fingers fly across the keys. The notes had me thinking it actually was a lyre."

Jeanne blushed at their first actual conversation. "Thank you, Count de Kersaint. But I'm afraid Dandrieu would have disagreed with you."

"Forgive my daughter, Count, she takes compliments poorly," Lord de l'Ecluse said with his head wagging.

Guy lingered his gaze on her. "What the composer thinks matters not to me. My ears tell me what I like to hear just as my eyes tell me what I like to see." He continued watching her intently.

Jeanne picked a lighter piece and played it equally well, and de Santec poured his praise on her recital. Then he spoke to Lord de l'Ecluse. "Sir, might I impose on you and your gracious wife to show me the rest of the house and grounds? It's such a lovely day." The three exited, leaving Guy and her alone in the salon, as prearranged.

"Jeanne, I was earnest in my admirations of your playing. You're wonderfully skilled at the harpsichord." Guy placed his hand on his chest.

After rising from the bench, she crossed the room to the large windows. "Count, when I saw you at the ball, you stuck out from the rest."

He raised an eyebrow, as well as the ends of his mouth. "How so? With everyone in navy uniforms, I'd think I looked commonplace."

"No, you're more mature than the young officers with whom I'm familiar." Jeanne turned from the window and sat nearer to him on the sofa. "Your naval career impresses my father, and he said you frequent Versailles."

Guy cleared his throat as his fingers stroked the chair's arm. "Well, yes, I've been there a few times in preparation for assignments, but not much more than other officers."

"I was told you delivered a fortune in diamonds and gold to Paris from Portugal for a crown." Jeanne leaned in as she spoke.

"It's not as though I captured it from a treasure ship in battle. I was just a courier between royalty," he confessed. "The king of France offered the Portuguese king a favor, and I performed a cartage service."

She laughed with glistening teeth between her fresh pink lips. "Few deliverymen arrive with diamonds and gold! Where else have you traveled?"

Guy touched on a few of the voyages in a quick version of his missions. As he neared telling about the Portugal trip, the family and de Santec returned. It was time for the guests to leave.

As they rode away, de Santec asked Guy, "Well, how did your new measuring stick hold up?" He grinned widely.

"For the first time in many years, I've found someone who interests me, and nothing what I expected. Actually, opposite. I assumed Jeanne might be demanding, but she's compliant and behaves with more maturity than others her age, and seems to disdain flattery. That speaks well for her vanity." Guy's face showed interest. "I hope she stumbled upon some amenity in me."

"At last! A woman to turn your head." De Santec guffawed. "Soon your frustrations may be at an end."

Two days passed and Guy wrote an expressive note thanking the de l'Ecluses for the pleasant visit. Yet, the one he expected from Jeanne to follow never came.

The next week, after hearing nothing, he set out on patrol and wondered if she considered him unfavorable. At 38 years of age, he presumed himself too old for the budding damsel.

―――

Upon mooring in Le Havre's harbor, Guy sped straight homeward, hoping a response had come from Jeanne. The reason she found him undesirable had perplexed his thoughts the entire week away.

A folded and sealed letter lay on the table in his foyer when he entered. In it, Guy read:

> To the Most Honorable and Respected Lieutenant de Vaisseau, Count Guy de Coëtnempren de Kersaint.
>
> It was a great pleasure to make your acquaintance at our manor. Your flattering words about my talents on the harpsichord inspired me to learn a new piece that I shall enjoy playing on your next visit. Father and Mother expressed delight Monsieur de Santec introduced you and extended hopes you both drop by again.
>
> On Thursday evening, we will attend the drama Zaïre. If the opportunity presents itself, you might find it enjoyable, too.
>
> Until our next meeting, I remain Your New Friend, Mademoiselle Jeanne Armande de l'Ecluse, the 11th of September 1741, Le Havre.

Guy at once imagined Jeanne longing to see him again, and writing the note near a sunny window, the noise of the quill scratching across the sheet. Such fantasizing was unlike him, and he realized it.

The next evening, Guy rode his horse to the largest playhouse in Le Havre. When he looked around, he spotted Jeanne with her parents.

Before long, Jeanne caught sight of him and nodded in his direction. Guy waved his hand with a burning desire to rush over to talk to her, but held himself in check. She seemed not to pay any attention to him, making it obvious to glance quickly away.

He reflected on what de Santec had said about not measuring women to Marie's standards. Guy pictured what Marie would do in a similar situation. She'd run and plop down next to him, not act coy as Jeanne did. Marie never hid feelings under the guise of conventions. The differences between the personalities were stark.

Two and a half hours later, the last scene ended, and Guy delayed no longer. He worked his way around chatting groups of people standing outside, waiting for carriages. To find Jeanne took no time. She stood out, a blossom in a field of weeds, and he wended next to her.

"Good evening, Mademoiselle de l'Ecluse. Did this evening's performance entertain you?" He saw his voice brighten her face.

"Count de Kersaint," she replied, eyes gleamed. "Yes, I found it delightful. The last act, especially."

"Performed with such realism, I imagined myself back on the Barbary Coast," he said.

Her bowed lips opened. "That's right, you sailed to those countries, didn't you? Oh, how exotic! The sultan behaved so lovingly toward her, well, until the end." Jeanne put her fan over her mouth, laughing.

In the background, her mother and father ventured darting glances at them and strained to hear the conversation.

Guy put a finger in the air. "If the sultan's role reflected what the beys are really like, he'd never have let her leave the palace. Someday I must tell you about two slave women I met once. But that is a long story." He studied every nuance when she spoke.

"Slave women? Oh, that sounds mysterious, or should I say romantic?" She tilted her head, waiting.

"Hmm, romantic? Better dramatic. Well, for me at least, although Captain Daniel might agree more to the other."

His comment made Jeanne's eyes wider. "So, this sailor fell in love with a slave? How exciting! At our next meeting, Count, you must tell the story."

"Please," he replied, "you embarrass me with the formality. Acquaintances address me as Guy. I'm assuming we are now friends, no?"

"Yes, we became that when you came to our manor, at least from my perspective, *Guy*." She giggled. "Likewise, call me Jeanne. When can we expect another visit? With the plot of *Zaïre* still fresh in our minds, your adventures in those Arabian lands should mesmerize us."

"Captain de Santec should return shortly from a cruise to Brest," he said. "When he does, I'll send you a message. Your parents enjoy his company, I believe."

"We all do. His stories are equally entertaining. Besides, being away from his family, he needs people to talk to, don't you agree?" she asked.

"At times, the sea seems a lonely place. De Santec, regardless, has never found trouble in making friends or finding others with whom to converse. He's congenial yet persuasive." In Guy's mind, he thanked him for the latter gift.

Minutes later, the l'Ecluse carriage arrived, leaving Guy alone to contemplate the evening's events. He searched for the reason he found Jeanne so attractive. She behaved nothing like Marie; not one aspect of Jeanne's character reminded him of her other than her beauty. Of course, he realized, de Santec's words had changed his perceptions, opening copious possibilities.

Or was it he had grown tired of living alone, and his friend's criticism simply pointed him in the right direction? In either case, he concluded, the blindfold of devotion to an old love had lifted, allowing other women's virtues to debut. His life always constrained him in loyalties. He wondered what other steadfast convictions restricted him with handicaps or self-imposed disservices.

Soon after, de Santec's frigate landed, and they made plans again to spend time with the de l'Ecluses.

When Jeanne and Guy met at the manor, they walked apart from the others, who had gone further into the garden. Jeanne wanted to show Guy her roses. "This is called *Four Seasons*, which I planted two years ago, and is my favorite. See the late bud?" Her hand gently pulled the opening blossom to her nose and sniffed. "Nothing yet," she said. "But soon. This will be the last flower of the year. Perhaps you and de Santec can enjoy the fragrance before it fades."

Looking down at her crouching next to the plant, he reveled in her youth, scent, and freshness, not the rosebud's.

Guy reached down and took her hand, helping her stand. "Jeanne, you've made a deep impression on me, which is peculiar, for I never believed a woman could affect me with such an obsessive hold. Your gentleness and candid regard for the welfare of others sets you in an unmatched niche in my mind."

Her eyes turned downward. "Guy, that's a sweet compliment. Likewise, I've grown fonder of you. I consider the day incomplete without hearing your voice, if just to say *adieu*." Jeanne's gaze floated to him. "My deepest wish is we frequent one another more often."

"Then we share that hope," he said, now holding both her hands and drawing closer. "For too long, I've been with a chilled heart. My compass for happiness steers me toward you."

He held the back of her head and pressed his lips on hers. Jeanne let out a quiet sigh after the kiss, then giggled.

Guy jerked away. "Does this amuse?"

"No, no," her eyes pleaded. "I've looked forward to this moment. It's just … I've never kissed anyone your age before on the lips."

He grinned. "Aha, so you have kissed others?"

"Twice. Although only boys, years ago." She put a hand on his chest. "I had wondered what kissing felt like. Since then, a few have wanted to court me, whom either I found unacceptable or Father did. But you behave far more attentively and are honest in your intentions. Most often men say I'm pretty and my eyes are bluer than the sea." She shook her head. "Whereas you take interest in things I have pride in, not my appearance. Also, you're a bit older and more mature."

"*A bit* underestimates. At 38, I'm at least twice your years." His face warmed saying it, but he continued. "Thank God the silliness, vanity, and self-indulgence of many your age bypassed you. Perhaps my immaturity and your maturity match up as equals."

"You *are* twice my age, as I turned nineteen in July. Although, a person's growth can take leaps through responsibility. To be challenged with adulthood forces one to bloom." Jeanne took his hand, and they walked again.

At day's end, Guy and de Santec stood on the dock, each preparing to check on his warship. Guy's face could not hide the long-sought elation.

De Santec wanted to tease, but let Guy indulge in his cheery disposition. "I noticed you and Jeanne are getting along well."

His smile widened. "Yes, we enjoy each other's company a great deal. Jeanne's so knowledgeable about music, the arts, and science. Every plant we passed and bird singing, she named. When speaking about literature and theater, she knew the titles, authors, and plays. I mentioned navigation, and she's well versed in the planets and stars. Such a quick mind in so many areas, I'd never expected such of a female of her few years."

De Santec put it off no longer and clucked his tongue. "You just threw out a list of qualities you admire in Jeanne that admits to one thing—you're in love."

As his face turned rosy, Guy professed aloud, "Yes, I do believe I am! Even better, I'm certain she is, too. Jeanne invited me to dinner the day after tomorrow."

The night he rode out to the house, tied behind the saddle, bounced a small package containing the finely woven woolen shawl from Tunis. Once planned for Marie's wedding present, Guy decided it unwise after finding out Marie had told Émile about his earlier intentions of marrying her. Not to let such a wonderful garment go unused, he'd offer it to Jeanne.

As they dined, Jeanne's father set his fork down. "Count, do you miss living in Cléder? It must be difficult to run your estate without being there."

"It depends on whom one hires to manage the lands, sir." Guy lifted his head. "I have a capable steward handling the dealings when I'm at sea or stationed elsewhere."

"Ah, of course. With all that farm and woodland, the steward must be very busy, I'd assume." Lord de l'Ecluse's look intensified. "Very busy. It's an extensive holding?"

Guy caught right away her father fished for the value of his wealth. "Not so much. Most of the area was owned by Viscount d'Brézal. The dowager, Lady Marnière, now possesses the land. The dowager is my godmother, and my father was the viscount's registrar."

Lord de l'Ecluse's eyebrows popped upward. "Oh, did the viscount die? I hadn't heard."

"The viscount died the same year as my father, and were close friends," Guy said.

Without a pause, Lord de l'Ecluse continued his questions. "Does your land contain other commodities, Count? Slate, coal, lead mines, and salt come from that region."

"No, the salt marshes are much farther south, and no mines are on our property," Guy explained, shaking a finger. "The de Kersaint's traditional income has been in agriculture and clams. The family, unfortunately, sold off the clamming flats long ago. But I like to think we still sell the best cider in Brittany."

Lord de l'Ecluse's voice lost its charm and said flatly, "Ah, I see, apples."

Guy didn't react to his disappointment and started a new topic. "Jeanne, you understood navigational terms. How were you educated so well?"

With a warm gaze, she said, "Guy, I had the finest of schooling and tutors. One math teacher had been a mariner but lost a leg in battle and switched from fighting to lecturing."

"*Guy?* You should address him as *Count,* my child," said her father, frowning.

Without a sign of reproach, she shot back, "Father, Guy and I are now beyond the formalities of strangers or new acquaintances. Much farther beyond."

Lord de l'Ecluse gaped, as did her mother. "Ah, fine." He glanced at his wife.

After dinner, the group retired to the grand salon where Jeanne again played a piece on the harpsichord, eyeing Guy and only seldom reading the music or keys.

When the piece ended, both parents wished Guy a goodnight and departed, leaving the two.

"Wait. There's something for you," Guy said, exiting the room to retrieve the package he had placed on a foyer console.

With a quick bow, he handed the gift to Jeanne. "I hope you like it. I got it some time ago in Tunis."

When she opened the bundle, the shawl spilled across her lap, and bright saturated colors contrasted with the subtle pastels in her gown. "Oh, this is amazing!" Jeanne replied, fingering the fine fabric. Then she stood and wrapped it around her shoulders. Slowly, she drew it over her head. "Do I remind you of the Arabian beauties you've seen?"

"No, only that they do not compare to the one I've met in Le Havre." Guy jumped up to embrace her.

Jeanne matched his many kisses that carried them to the sofa. Minutes later, they pushed each other away.

"Oh, lord, we must control passions from overcoming our senses," she said with a broad smile.

"I'm sure your parents expected me to leave, and I shall before it becomes impossible to do so." His eyes searched upward, and he laughed.

"When will you come again?" she asked, panting, with hands on his waist, pulling him toward the foyer.

"An hour seems a lifetime. But perhaps the pretense of bringing de Santec with me tomorrow would placate your parents not to think me an overly persistent suitor."

"Yes, bring him. De Santec needs distractions from the navy, too, and Mother and Father enjoy him so."

"Until the afternoon comes again, goodnight, my dear," he said, kissing her one last time.

Jeanne led him toward the door. "Go, before I give in to my desires."

All the way on the ride home, Guy thought the world an Eden and its ills trivialities.

The next day, de Santec joined the two and her mother for an impromptu picnic in the garden. When the light clouds parted, the autumn sun beat down on them. Madam de l'Ecluse, not yet sitting on the ground, placed a hand to shade her face. "Please, let's put up parasols before we burn like field workers."

"Mother, I brought something for myself. Did you not bring anything?" asked Jeanne, reclining on a spread blanket.

"No, I thought the clouds would stay. Will one of you gentlemen accompany me back to the house for a parasol?" Then she smiled at Guy.

"Madam, it is my pleasure."

They strolled arm-in-arm toward the manor as Jeanne snatched her straw bag. She reached in and drew out the new shawl and threw it around her shoulders and arms.

"My, I haven't seen anything that colorful since in Tunis. What a shame such glorious colors are now out of fashion," de Santec said. "Yours reminds me of the ones that Guy and I bought from a stall seller when we helped two Saxon women escape the bey."

"Oh, that's when you smuggled the slaves onto a ship?" Jeanne stroked Guy's gift.

"Yes, he told you about that? The weavers use local wool and designs, and I purchased one for my wife and Guy got one for a woman friend. That shawl looks exactly like them."

First looking down, she fell silent and then peered far away.

De Santec, not noticing the change, continued talking about the differences between Barbary and English sheep until Jeanne's mother came back with Guy. Both carried open parasols.

He bent down and presented the parasol to Jeanne. "Here, may this keep your features from ever aging."

The brimmed hat hid her tear-filled eyes as she reached for it.

Guy plopped down next to her and listened to de Santec amuse her mother with another tale of adventure.

Jeanne turned her face away and wiped streaks off her cheeks. She dragged the shawl off and folded it, putting it in the bag with a lingering look.

Guy caught her forlorn gaze. "You appear sad. Did something happen?"

She stayed silent for a while and stared at the wrap. Then she spoke almost in a whisper, peeping up at him. "Let's stroll so we can talk."

"Certainly, if you wish."

They headed for the trees, now parching their green for brown and yellow. As they walked, Guy didn't speak.

"For whom did you buy the shawl in Tunis?" Jeanne said, emotionless.

Guy paused, his face reddening. "Oh, the shawl? I picked it up as a wedding gift for a friend, but I never sent it."

"Who?" Jeanne's brows furrowed as they continued to stroll.

Guy burst out, saying, "Her name is Marie de Bruc. Our families are old friends. We were practically raised together like siblings." He took a quick peek at Jeanne from the corner of his eye, relaxing when her worried expression faded.

Over the next months, Guy and Jeanne saw one another more often, and by late fall, they became inseparable.

∽

Guy had planned a night at the opera with her. Instead of civilian clothing, he wore his lieutenant's uniform, freshly cleaned and buttons polished. As the carriage drew near the opera house, Guy cleared his throat.

"Jeanne, you have transformed me, setting me on a fresh path in life. Never in all my years have I been so thrilled to see each dawn break, knowing you'll be part of my day, and love you beyond measure. Will you marry me and be my wife?" His eyes craved a consenting response.

Jeanne had assumed he'd ask after her father said Guy had requested her hand. She answered with a bowed head and gazed up, "Of course, my sweet. It's all I want."

The dowry negotiations took days to settle. Once her father agreed, the couple grew even closer and became more intimate, with uncontrollable affection binding them. For the first time, Guy imagined life with a woman other than Marie. More so, his flowering love of Jeanne consumed him.

To stop, Jeanne pulled hard on his hand as they rambled along the Seine one late January evening. The cool mid-winter air blew against their bodies as the sun warmed their faces.

"Now that we're betrothed, we must also make plans for something else." Her face appeared hesitant.

He bent his head to the side, uncertain of anything more needed. "Do you mean where we will live after the wedding? I assumed here in Le Havre and later in Cléder, at the manor."

"No, that's not it." She looked downward. "Just the same, since you mentioned the estate. Does it have a nursery?" She giggled, looking up again.

Guy stammered, "Ah, there's room for that." He stopped, shock showing. "You're carrying a child?"

"I am, at least until July or August. Are you pleased?" Jeanne grabbed his forearm tight.

"My God!" He shouted, beaming. "Yes, of course, I'm happy!"

Jeanne's pregnancy forced the wedding to be held earlier than usual. No one regretted the surprise news, for it tethered their bond even more.

The de Kersaints, known for their ownership of orchards and farmland, stood equal in nobility to the de l'Ecluses. For Jeanne's parents, a union with Guy assured her and her children's future would be secure and add prestige to both families.

Jeanne's father, with little regret, had settled the dowry to marry his daughter at almost eleven thousand livres to be paid in February of the next year. The enormous sum eliminated Guy's fears over his financial shortages.

Over the following months, they spent days touring in carriages, taking in plays in Le Havre, dancing at parties, and playing cards with friends late into the night. Guy had not picked a cultivated summer rose with thorns of caution and distrust. He had embraced a sprouting young jonquil, tender and pliable, to be his bride.

> *My Dearest Friend Marie de Bruc Gardinier,*
>
> *I have a wonderful announcement for you. I am planning on being in Paris beginning the last week of June. The reason for this extended stay in your grand city is to be married to Jeanne Armande de l'Ecluse of Le Havre. Perhaps you may have heard of their name. You meeting my beautiful fiancée is almost as important to me as the ceremony. Please arrange your calendar so you and your family can attend the wedding. Without your presence, my joyous day will be incomplete. I shall contact you when we arrive.*
>
> *Your Loving and Obedient Friend, Guy de Coëtnempren Count de Kersaint, the 12th of April, 1742, Le Havre.*

The nuptials came on June 24th and Marie and Émile arrived late. She took Guy aside after the ceremony outside the church.

"My, she's such a little princess, Guy, so pretty and young. I can see how you fell headlong into those large blue eyes." Marie forced a pleasant face. "I suppose you hadn't a chance to do otherwise."

Guy agreed, looking elated, and nodded. "Nor would I desire any other!"

Marie put her finger against his chest. "Well, you might have waited a week or two after the wedding to have your child. Is she expecting it tonight?" She teased, poking him. Then she added in a sarcastic tone, "All of this is so unlike you."

"Ah, there's the Marie I know, incapable of holding back. You appear not to find our union to your liking," Guy said. "Why is that? I prayed you'd be delighted for us."

"Jeanne's a wonderful girl." Her lips pulled to a side, and her gaze searched upward. "I just always thought you might wed a woman more imaginative and experienced. I'm sure she'll make you happy, though."

"Hmm, do you mean similar to yourself?"

Marie jerked back.

"Yes, my bride is young, although we've much in common. I spent years looking for a person with your qualities, but to no avail." Guy shook his head. "That was time wasted, for you're unique, Marie. Jeanne took me like a sudden gust and nothing like for whom I'd been searching. That's her advantage over me, someone offering a fresh perspective."

"Sorry, I meant no offense, Guy." Marie's brow arched. "Truly, I am thrilled for you. Now enjoy the festivities. I see her watching us and don't want to make her suspicious of you so early in your marriage. Go."

As Guy walked away, she found Émile and coaxed him to take her home. It was true, Marie reflected, she had expected Guy to find a partner like her, not a girl only nineteen years old. Of course, older men often married younger women. Still, it ruffled her that he took such an impressible innocent as a bride. Marie slumped, dejected, shambling along the street.

"What's wrong, dear? You appear unhappy," asked Émile.

"Nothing. It's just that rudeness may have cost me a dear friend."

"Oh, you don't know that. Guy's been like a brother to you for your whole life. One overlooks a friend's sharp or impudent remarks. Besides, matrimony expands friendships, not ends them. Consider Jeanne a new intimate, now. There's an advantage to be gained, not lost, in almost every action. It's all in the outlook people take."

Marie beamed up at him. "Whereas mine is impulsiveness, your hallmark quality is assuming the best. Ever encouraging, that's why I love you."

A week later, Émile left for Brest after kissing his wife, the girls, and his one-year-old son. On the now familiar route, he remembered what she had said about losing Guy the day of the wedding. Marie had powerful feelings for her Breton friends and Brest, and he believed she shouldn't dismiss her childhood relationships.

Nonetheless, the only thing he liked about those unsophisticated rowdy ports and uncultured villages, Émile considered, was the rubes never understood how to barter or haggle well. Even though Marie warned often about using illegal practices, he'd forgive her ignorance of how the Parisian metropolitan business world operated.

The naval stores supervisor Chatroen mentioned a shortage of masts in case the war expanded. Like a dinner bell sounding, Émile hurried to fill the shortfall. He scouted along the coast, and turned up enough in Le Havre and Saint-Malo to satisfy the navy's needs and shipped the wood to Brest.

The rushed purchases cost more and forced him to be trickier to make a profit. In Le Havre, he discovered that timber cutters embossed sawn logs with stamps that graded their quality. He copied the irons and reclassified his inferior merchandise with higher grade embossing marks, looking like originals, worn and old, authentic enough to fool anyone.

After a month from home and Marie, he returned to Paris to spend the end of summer with his family.

"Another successful trip." Émile slapped his hands together. "This sale is the greatest one yet. I've learned so much about spars and what makes a good or bad one. Chatroen said I saved the navy's building schedule by providing what their regular contractors couldn't."

"Did you visit my sister while in Brest?"

He answered with a drooping face. "I did. Charlotte mentioned nothing about it, but it looks as if her husband has lost a great deal of money. I heard it was a poor investment."

Marie wrote to her sister and learned Charlotte's spouse drained most of their wealth on a failed scheme in the colonies. The dowry had disappeared, but he retained enough to manage their expenses.

Upon hearing it, Émile tried to soothe his wife's fretting over Charlotte's finances and almost felt guilty for his own successes. Whatever he did profited him beyond expectations; while others struggled, it seemed all so easy to Émile.

***

After their wedding, Guy and Jeanne prepared for the coming of their child. In Paris, to spare her from the arduous trip back to Le Havre, she gave birth to a son whom they christened Armand-Guy. Jeanne's health rebounded quickly, and the newlyweds departed for Brittany a month later.

They welcomed every friend and naval officer they'd met to show off Armand. Then at the beginning of 1743, Jeanne announced another baby due that summer, catching Guy by surprise. Nevertheless, he rejoiced over the news and had fallen in love with the duties of fatherhood, which the navy's short patrols obliged.

At sea, Guy missed the arrival of his second child, Suzanne, born healthy and spunky, in the warm month of July. His voyages, usually on the Channel and close, afforded him time to enjoy his two new children and Jeanne.

Regardless, he knew the quick missions were temporary, for kings planned their military and political strategies for the coming showdown. The two nations, considered neutral players in the growing conflict, still remained at peace by official agreements. However, in reality, as allies of belligerents, a de facto state of war had enveloped both without a declaration.

During the early spring of 1744, the severity and frequency of bloodshed increased, with most fighting in the colonial frontier forests of America and the farm fields of Europe. King Louis, frustrated over the hostilities, declared war on Great Britain in March.

Guy approached Jeanne with the disappointing news. "I shall likely be at sea for longer periods now with larger patrol areas and perhaps convoy duties abroad."

"And greater peril for you, too, yes?" She sat in bed beside him, her forehead furrowed.

Guy covered his own concerns with a blank face. "Not much while in my small corvette. It's those larger ships going to the colonies in the Americas and India that will see more action. The British will keep their distance from our shores, I believe."

"Then our baby will not be missing your company?" Jeanne's cheeks dimpled.

"No," he replied. "I'll be home almost as often to play with little Suzanne and Armand."

She giggled, her hand covering her mouth. "Oh, you misunderstood. I meant the new one."

Wide-eyed, Guy sprang to his feet. "Another?! When?"

"When we harvest apples for the presses, in the fall." She grabbed him, kissed his cheek, and hugged his waist.

"This is a fitting gift, my dear, to offset the war declaration. None could be finer."

Guy still enjoyed the short convoy duties and quiet patrols chasing away small British privateers. He always returned unscathed to Jeanne and his growing family. In the autumn, the navy assigned him to *la Médusa*, a new, larger, 16-gun frigate. His first corvette *la Naïade* became the ship for his old academy mate, François de Saint-Alouarn.

Sitting in François's cabin, the two comrades met to chat and drink. François bore a tan from trips to the West Indies and grumbled to Guy about his new assignment. "Mind you, I don't find Le Havre any worse a port. Yet, I'd rather be in Brest, nearer to my family. My wife just gave birth to our third child, a girl."

"Of course." Guy leaned over the table, resting his head on his fist.

"It's hard when voyages steal us from the little ones while so young. More than even my babies, though, I miss Jeanne on every cruise."

François stared at his wine glass. "Jeanne is a wonderful young woman, Guy. I'm glad you've found someone. Ah, I never asked. How did Marie take your marriage?"

Guy, remembering her curt comments, frowned. "It was strange. Marie never considered me seriously for courtship, but she seemed upset when Jeanne and I wed, as if covetous. Although she had all those years to have me if she'd wanted to."

"Ha, you don't grasp what happened," François said. "She had you. Despite her marrying Émile, you remained as faithful as a husband to her alone. Marie had two husbands until you mutinied."

"Huh, I suppose you're right." Guy nodded. "I'm still so fond of Marie, yearning for her company always, even now. When with my wife, though, Jeanne's the only woman I love. It's hard to explain."

"Marie has that effect on men." François's stare grew distant. "I often find solace remembering our relationship when we were engaged. She has an appeal that excites men. Émile is a lucky fellow. Though you'll visit her on one of your trips to Versailles."

"I doubt it now that the war is on," he said with a grimace. "The British haven't attacked us at sea yet. But our fleets will soon clash."

"Probably, but you'll survive and have been lucky in your career, Guy. I've never mentioned to you how envious I am of you." François pulled one side of his lips into a smile. "The admiralty holds you in high favor."

Guy blinked and rolled his head back. "To admit the truth, I expected you to get their attention first."

"Me? No, I follow orders to survive while you put yourself in danger's way. Louisiana's Chickasaws? That's not for me. I'll cruise the Channel and ocean to protect our coasts with feet planted on a deck, not seek ruination in Mississippi mud."

"A war thrusts dangers upon all of us," Guy said, eyes sad. "*La Naïade* will sail in the thick of it, as well as my *la Médusa*. Now I'm patrolling from Le Havre down to Portugal. If the British attack, that will change."

Soon *la Médusa*, like British warships, attacked the other's merchantmen. To prevent losing convoys, Versailles increased warship production while Minister Maurepas impressed upon the king the importance of protecting his coasts and colonial holdings. Every sou and livre he squeezed from King Louis's dwindling treasury veered into ship construction.

In early October, somewhere between southern England and the western tip of France, two warships drew near one another. On *la Médusa's* quarterdeck, Guy watched to his lee side as the other approached. She flew the all-white Bourbon flag, like his, but he had not accepted it as proof she was friendly. He shouted up to his lookouts. "Is she British?!"

The sailor far up in the tops checked the decks of the closing warship. "No, one of ours, sir. And I see French officers!"

Guy put his eye to his spyglass once more and waited to identify the frigate. When she stood off a few hundred yards, he still couldn't name her.

After the warship drew a hundred feet away, he placed a speaking horn to this mouth. "What ship are you and who's in command?"

The captain came into view. "*L'Emeraude!* Don't you recognize my face by now?!" When the officer lowered his speaking horn, it was François.

"Heave to, and I'll come aboard!" In fifteen minutes, Guy climbed the ladder to the deck, joining François near the wheel.

"So," Guy said, "you got *l'Emeraude*. A few months back, her hull lay on the slips in Le Havre but didn't have a figurehead. Now I know what she looks like."

François thumped a cannon. "She has twenty-four 8-pounders and four 4-pounders." He pointed to the line of weapons on the main deck.

"That beats my sixteen guns. How many knots does she make?"

"I'm not sure yet. We had her in a weak gale doing over 12 knots before the wind with all her canvas," François said, puffing out his chest.

"Good speed!" Guy smiled, but it left his face in a second. The navy once again offered his friend a faster and more powerful ship.

The unblemished vessel still smelled of fresh paint and tar. Guy caught the zesty odor of fresh-cut oak below decks. In the hold, he noticed the supporting diagonal braces for the sides of the ship, shaped and attached differently than on others. A number of features stood out as unique.

"Quite a fish you hauled in here, François." Guy stared hard at her fine lines. "She'll do you well in a fight. I hope to get one myself someday."

When they finished talking, the two continued on their cruises. As *l'Emeraude* grew smaller in the distance, Guy's envy of his friend grew larger, which bothered him until sunset.

By dark, blasts of rain fell and intensified throughout the night. Flashes of lightning punctuated the constant deep rumbling of thunder and the sky poured a sea of water from high onto the decks. Pushed by immense waves, the craft lunged in one direction and then another, while two helmsmen struggled with the wheel.

By three o'clock in the morning, every crewman had spent his energy on hauling cables and lines, reefing canvas, and fighting the cold elements. Guy did not recognize where he was and feared the mountainous breakers might capsize them, or drive them shoreward onto unseen shoals or rocks hidden in the darkness. Each prayed this would not be his last moment, swallowed by the deep, black ocean depths.

As dawn neared and the sky lightened, the brutal pounding had damaged *la Médusa* almost to the point of being dismasted. The rest of the day held only continuing punishment.

With the next coming night, blasts pushed the warship east-southeast toward the Channel Islands. *La Médusa* shuddered and groaned as each giant foaming crest became a battering ram to smash upon her sides. The men pumped and struggled to empty the ocean from her belly.

Nevertheless, the immense force of the storm propelled them without control until the third day. Ahead, they made out a dark, low shape, the French coast near La Hague. Guy knew to the north lay reefs, and southward, beaches. Only coastline showed before them.

"Ground her on the shore!" Guy shouted to the helmsmen, his hand pointing southeast. The frigate headed straight and fast. They braced themselves. *La Médusa*, driven by the fury, slammed against the seashore, the crew thrown to the deck as a loud cracking shuddered from the hold. The bow rested far up on sand and pebbles, the waves slapping the stern.

After ten minutes, the carpenter and his mate came to Guy. "Sir, the grounding splintered the keel amidships."

"Is she seaworthy?" Guy asked the master, shaking his head.

"Yes, sir. But she'll be hogged bad."

"Do what you can to make her fit to embark for Le Havre." Guy ordered the crew to restart watches and sent the first group to their hammocks for a much-needed rest.

When the final gale abated the next day, they inspected the spars, rigging, and hull timbers for repairs. When high tide came, and using oared boats to drag her off the beach, the battered frigate took sail and crept toward Le Havre to arrive that night.

In Cléder, Jeanne greeted him by presenting his new son, born when he had met François at sea. The couple had a girl and a pair of boys. Armand, two years of age, and Suzanne played at their feet.

Jeanne said, squinting her eyes, "The storm must have been horrific. I worry." It was the first real danger Guy had been in during their marriage.

"Dear, there's no reason for fear. That kind of tempest comes seldom, perhaps once in a lifetime." He rubbed her hand to reassure her. "My ship performed beyond expectations." To shield her concerns, he didn't reveal the British *Victory*, the finest warship afloat, had sunk during it.

Guy said no more about it. His concerns were not over his last storm, but his next command. He had destroyed a new frigate and wondered if they'd ever commission him another.

On the contrary, the Admiralty assigned him to *la Venus*, his former vessel as an ensign, but this time as captain. The old warship lasted long beyond her expected service, but Versailles promised him a new 30-gun under construction in Brest to compensate.

With concerns over the age of the decrepit *la Venus*, she patrolled for British-licensed privateers close by to the coast. For the rest of the year 1744, Guy focused on keeping the shores north of Brest free of the marauders until taking command of the new frigate.

LOUISBOURG AND LA MOTTE
1745-1747

As the carriage horses pulled nearer the ship, Guy noted *la Renommée* displayed the new design trend for frigates. From a distance, she looked different, he thought to himself, sleeker and fast, like a sea hawk. It was the first he had seen of her off the slip.

He strained to pick out other telltale traits when his eyes settled on the gold statuesque figurehead gleaming on the prow. The Goddess of Fame, bare-breasted, held a royal orb and a trumpet of glory.

Her mainmast was high with the foremast placed farther to the bow, making her plow the waves when with the wind, he surmised as he scanned her.

The carriage halted, and the crew rowed the new captain out to his unblemished frigate, still being fitted out on the Penfeld River in Brest. When ready, he planned to hold a small ceremony to put her to sea. On schedule, they had launched her two months prior, in December of 1744. The navy had reassigned him to Brest, and allowed Jeanne and the family finally to move to his mansion in Cléder.

Guy, now forty-one, had matured into a square-jawed, weather-faced, brawny captain who could be mistaken for a seasoned topman. None of his physical characteristics conveyed his noble upbringing. Besides his strapping look, his gallantry and skills continued to impress Minister Maurepas, who had selected him for *la Renommée* and her inaugural mission.

D'Harcourt left to command his own corvette when Guy boarded *la Renommée*. The new first lieutenant, Picquet de La Motte, along with Lieutenant de La Tour and Ensign de Saint Saëns, greeted Guy and showed him to his quarters.

La Renommée's designer claimed she'd be the fastest warship afloat, and Guy looked forward to finding out under full canvas. Still, he assumed she'd handle poorly in rough seas, just like most other frigates. If wind and sea permitted, he'd take her out after the commissioning ceremony and had invited Jeanne to attend.

On a cool February 6th, they readied to leave, and the winds moved in a favorable direction. It was fortunate for Jeanne, he thought, her first visit on his ship, and it'd be without the usual foul odors that might repulse her.

She arrived with little Armand, who wore a miniature officer's uniform. While waiting for the ceremony, Jeanne stood on the side of the quarterdeck. Guy leaned on the rail, eyeing his crewmen below as his first lieutenant walked up beside him.

"Do you want them in ranks, sir?" asked La Motte.

"No. This time, leave them crowded midships." Guy smiled, pointing downward. "What do you see, Lieutenant?"

"A solid band, sir. Every one a veteran and excellent seaman." La Motte gazed over them, chin jutting.

"Make sure, Lieutenant, each gun crew has just two from the same previous ship and only eight per watch."

"Sir?"

"See how they flock?" Guy's hand motioned to them, standing in groups. "Allegiances to their old ships and mates create biases and rivalries against others. We need their loyalty to and faith in every new shipmate. Split them up."

"Ah! Yes, that's a splendid idea, sir."

The priest finished his brief blessing and Guy leaned forward, overlooking those below, with La Motte beside him. The sailors clustered on the main deck and the masters and junior officers lined up on the forecastle. With a chill in the windy air, he kept his speech short.

"Men, I'm honored our navy assigned me to command *la Renommée* and to serve on this exceptional warship for our glorious King Louis XV. The great strides in design made in shipbuilding have culminated in the ship we serve today. Not just another frigate, but one of the best in the wooden sea wall defending our beloved France.

"This new vessel, *la Renommée*, we christened fittingly, for renowned she will be. Under our mastery, this frigate stands as the formidable guardian our nation can rely on for safety from enemies intent on destroying our country. But an innovative weapon must have fearless men to use it. I would have been delighted to handpick every one of you for this crew. Yet, I could not have done better.

"We seamen who sail her will explore beyond the safe shores of our homeland. It is our spirited effort that makes France's naval power invincible, and it will remain the strongest and bravest in the world, keeping France and its possessions protected. That is this remarkable frigate's fundamental aim. Together with our large and powerful navy, we have the essential arms necessary to prevent a sea invasion of our homeland or harm to our sea commerce.

"Three grand traditions merged to create the sound, peerless decks upon which we ride. Brest's shipwrights, the backbone of this famous shipyard, who will prove to develop faster and more superior warships for our navy. You, the loyal stouthearted crew, doing their brave duty. And lastly, our faith, the nation's belief in both our king and our Holy Father to see us through the most difficult of wartimes.

"Even before this war, we have done our utmost to build a fleet of superior vessels that will wipe clear enemies from the seas. Our honorable king maintains we dare not engage in aggression unless trodden on by those countries attempting to end our traditions and beliefs.

"Prussia, Sweden, and Spain pleaded to us for protection in their struggle against the barbarism of Great Britain, Austria, and its allies. In those invading hostile armies, domination is their impetus and cruelty their means. There is no longer any doubt they seek to destroy any country standing in the way of their aggressive desires.

"Our king sent military support to the brave Bavarians and we are paying a heavy price to ensure they live free, unchained from the tyranny of Austria's empress. She can only succeed by defeating us. Nonetheless, defeat is not in our character or in the hearts of true Frenchmen.

"Versailles is moving forward with a mighty treasury for new ships, and never have we designed such frigates to win victory. Never has an enemy confronted such superior warships. And never has there been such brave crewmen determined to bring an end to this abominable war."

His voice grew in volume with each sentence to a near roar and ended with his fist slamming on the rail. "On waves of glory, we will prove the courage lying in each. We shall fight with resolve in our minds, with trust in our hearts for God and King, and with unwavering boldness in our cause. Long may *la Renommée* defend and long live King Louis!"

The crew and officers responded with loud enthusiasm at the end of his oration, cheering and clapping. Guy motioned to the marine guard for a volley of musket shots saluting their voyage. As shouts echoed, Guy joined Jeanne, her face flushed from the speech. They walked back to the large lantern on the stern railing.

"Oh, that was exhilarating!" Jeanne gushed. "I didn't know you had such a talent for speaking." Armand shied away from the muskets' blasts with his palms still covering his ears.

"Thank you, my dear," Guy replied. He'd heard patriotic rhetoric many times over the years, but his emotions were not as exploitable as the young crew and his wife. "Let's hope they'll remember it in the heat of battle."

"Of course, the designer did say she's the fastest ship on the ocean." He laughed.

La Motte told them everything was prepared to weigh anchor. Jeanne kissed Guy, descended, and soon a boat carried his wife and son back to shore.

As crewmen made ready the sails, Lieutenant de La Tour called the pilot to the helm on the quarterdeck to guide the frigate through the narrows to sea. La Motte joined Guy at the stern as *la Renommée* departed.

A cannon saluted them as they passed by the last of the channel's batteries high up on a hill overlooking them. Both turned and raised their hats in salute as a crewman fired a hand cannon in reply.

Guy rubbed his rough hands together in the cool breeze, frowning. "Regardless of what I told the crew, Lieutenant La Motte, even if Versailles had it, I doubt the king would pour livres into the navy's pocket. Maurepas has a hard time convincing him we need more."

Guy paused a moment and frowned. "If the English were to strike at Louisbourg, Saint-Domingue, or maybe even India, we'd find it difficult defending them with our shortage of ships."

"Sir, I don't believe they'll attack Louisbourg. The fortress is invincible, they say."

"*Invincible?* Hah," Guy snickered. "Nothing is invincible. They could starve out even Louisbourg. The citadel is more vulnerable because they count on us to supply them with everything." Guy shook his head.

As they passed beyond the outer bays, around them in every direction, they saw small fishing boats and a few larger topsail ships in the distance. Guy set a course south, and by nightfall, no others cruised the waters.

"Ensign de Saint Saëns, gather the senior officers to my cabin for a meeting," he said.

When they assembled, he disclosed the new orders.

"Minister Maurepas redirected us to Louisbourg in Acadia for a mission of strategic importance. The minister needed a fast ship, and I hope *la Renommée* is such."

Guy's eyes narrowed. "As you know, beginning last year, the British patrolled our harbors in great numbers. This resulted in fewer convoys leaving France and Louisbourg pleading for foodstuffs, ammunition, and men. The Admiralty sent us ahead to find out the port's status and deliver dispatches.

"We'll cruise southward across the Bay of Biscay to Spain, then west to Saint-Domingue for more water and provisions, and afterward to Louisbourg as fast as possible. The navy plans to send a squadron as soon as they're fitted out to meet us for Louisbourg's relief. Men, speed will guarantee success on this mission. That must be our highest priority."

"How large a fleet follows us?" asked Lieutenant de La Tour, whose confident, deep voice drew their attention.

"They're preparing a large new warship, *le Vigilant*, and two frigates to protect Louisbourg and the fisheries in Acadia," Guy answered. "Although to refit the vessels takes time and money, they haven't allocated yet. So, they dispatched us to disrupt the enemy while waiting for the squadron."

His officers asked a few questions, more about Louisbourg than anything else. Gossip was that if Louisbourg fell, in time, all of Canada might follow.

Just before dawn the next day, he woke and climbed topside. Guy stood with the helmsman on the quarterdeck. The waves still flowed low with a gale breeze, perfect for testing the ship's speed.

"Set the topgallants and beat with the wind, Lieutenant La Motte. Today we'll see if she handles well under full canvas," Guy said to the officer amidship. The frigate turned downwind from off her aft and the sails filled, billowed, and strained on the yards.

"Make ready to heave the log-line. Wait for my word." Guy watched the ship's cut through the water.

The vessel picked up speed and swept faster as the gust blew two points off her beam, so the captain kept her there as she gained full momentum. Soon, *la Renommée* split the sea at an incredible clip. The foremast placement let it draw the air that otherwise would have escaped around a closer mast. Guy noticed it pulled the stern up as it forced the bow downward, making her more even-keeled. But it also allowed waves to splash onto the deck, flooding the midships. If needing speed, he mused, a saltwater bath is a small price to pay.

When she achieved her fastest cut through the sea, Guy ordered the log-line thrown. Two sailors ran to the stern with an hourglass and a triangular-shaped piece of wood. One tossed the tied board over the rail. When the hourglass sand emptied, he hauled the rope line in and rushed to the captain after calculating the velocity.

"Sir, she's making fifteen knots!" The sailor beamed.

"My God, fifteen?!" Guy's mouth opened. "Take another reading. No, let Ensign de Saint Saëns do it to check you," the captain said.

After repeating the procedure, the ensign turned with incredible news. "Sir," he shook his head, unbelievingly. "The speed is a fraction over fifteen knots by my reckoning, and that does not consider the slight drift from the wind blowing the line."

"That confirms the designer's brag; she's the fastest ship afloat!" shouted Guy. The crew, hearing the captain's exhilarating declaration, cheered. Such a boon could save their lives or help in the capture of a prize.

The orders to follow the usual trade currents and winds for America would take months longer than their normal short patrols of a week or two.

Speed to Louisbourg remained vital; nonetheless, monstrous storms threw them off course by hundreds of miles. Guy spoke to his lieutenants as they arrived at Cadiz, Spain, to resupply. "We've lost nine days from bad weather," he said to his first lieutenant, worry on his face. "I'd hoped to make port at Saint-Domingue for fresh food after the crossing. That's impossible now. We'll go straight to Louisbourg and resupply there."

"That should shave off a week, sir," La Motte agreed.

"It's not enough," stressed Guy, leaning over his charts in the cabin. "We can run closer to the Sargasso Sea on its southern edge. Head north of Saint-Domingue, then pick up the Gulf Stream off Florida. We'll cut across the current for Acadia. It's a gamble and if we're forced into the doldrums, it'll increase the delay. Still, it's a risk we must take."

"The route should work so early in the year, sir. The hurricane season hasn't begun yet," added La Motte.

"Then that's that. Pray the storms are few." Guy set a course southward.

They crossed the Atlantic, making good speed, bypassed resupplying, and slipped by the British American colonies. But in the northern waters of Acadia, the frigate met fogs and ice drifting from the frozen bays near Labrador and Greenland with a constant danger of icebergs. The ship slowed and their intentions to recover lost time vanished as the harsh winter seas delayed *la Renommée* even more. To make conditions worse, a third of the little remaining food had rotted and forced them to throw it overboard.

By mid-April, the ship closed in on its destination. Unfortunately, Guy soon spied thick ice sheets blocking them from reaching Louisbourg. Through the foggy haze and glare of whiteness on the frozen water, he saw fireplace smoke rising from the houses and buildings huddled within the fortifications, three miles away.

"Lieutenant La Motte," Guy said, his face downcast. "Set a course southwest along the coast toward the village of Canso. We'll resupply there and discover how Louisbourg is doing. Keep an eye out for canvasses. They'll not likely be French or allies."

The sun's glow hid behind the late afternoon clouds as they neared the small fishing settlement. As they verged on it, Guy's lookouts sighted sails. Three British colonial warships approached with a favoring wind. Guy cursed and brought about his vessel northeast to run from them along the coast. Four miles aft of *la Renommée*, a British snow of 24 guns and two 10-gun sloops, closed fast.

"Take us further out from the ice, Lieutenant," said Guy. Although faster under normal circumstances, both the ship hitting sea crust and a weary crew multiplied the danger. Not until nightfall did he see his frigate gain and crawl away from her pursuers, avoiding a nasty engagement where the enemy out-gunned them.

He wondered if the foes searched for French merchants, guarded the British settlements on Acadia, or blockaded Louisbourg. The possibility of more colonial warships along the coast also lurked in his mind.

Snow fell over the next two days, as Guy navigated well away from land and nearer the Banks to avoid patrols and seek the French relief ships.

"Well, La Motte, should we linger longer to confirm Louisbourg is safe from attack, making it even harder on our crew and frigate, or search for our squadron? I presume they took less time than we did in crossing."

La Motte stared seaward, thinking. "Sir, the squadron could help us repel the British colonials and get to Louisbourg if we find them."

"*If* is the key word," Guy grunted and squinted. "Hmm, we'll stay and wait for the ice to clear, enter the port to discover their status, and resupply. Then we can join the fleet."

The next morning, the frigate headed again for Canso to check for signs of a British troop buildup there. Before noon, three sails appeared close by in the fog. They were larger vessels than those that pursued them earlier. Guy, thinking they might be French merchant ships going to Louisbourg or even the missing fleet, signaled to them. Enemy warships answered with cannons. Two frigates, of 20 and 24 guns, and a snow of 14 guns, sent volleys at *la Renommée*.

"Lieutenant de La Tour," Guy called from the forecastle, "tell the helmsman to make southwest along the coast."

Their adversaries followed, firing from the frigate's wake as *la Renommée* made hard headway.

After twenty minutes, more ships appeared in twos and threes until enemy warships of various sizes surrounded their frigate and outnumbered them by many cannons.

"That's nine cruisers, by my count. I guess we'll see just how well our lady will do today. Lieutenant, loose upon them when they are in range after our turn. Prepare to tack to port on my command." He planned to weave a fox's confusing course to slow the enemy's progress. Although it impeded the frigate's speed, finding a route out of danger came first.

For half an hour, Guy zig-zagged in continual course changes, firing when he could as the deadly opponents tried to close in on his frigate.

"There!" shouted Guy as he pointed. On his word, they drove for the opening away as the helmsman pulled hard on the wheel. Wind caught the sails, and they dashed toward the still-unguarded exit.

The colonials attempted to follow but met others in their path or needed to come about. *La Renommée* slipped through the escape route as her cannons sent one last blast at the colonial frigate trying to close the gate. French balls smashed into the targets, and a yardarm crashed to the colonial deck, pulling down rigging and sails to put the ship out of action.

Seven of the ships continued the chase and threw iron, with none falling closer than a hundred feet.

"La Motte, set course southeast along the shore to keep them packed together."

They headed away from the melee and from Canso. Two hours later, dusk came, and the colonials followed in the distance. By dark, the

French frigate had changed direction several times to lose the hungry pack.

Gathered in his cabin after dinner, Guy, La Motte, Lieutenant de La Tour, Ensign de Saint Saëns, and the marine lieutenant reflected on the day.

"Sir," said la Motte, "I believe most captains would have surrendered under such circumstances. We were out-gunned at least tenfold. Gentlemen, let us toast our captain." They got to their feet and took a drink.

Guy waved them to sit again. "Thank you. We need to find our squadron and inform them Louisbourg is now blockaded. While searching, we can harass the enemy and determine their strength. First, however, we need to review the damage to our lady."

The next day, the carpenter reported to Guy. "Sir, I counted thirty-one hits on the hull and masts. Still, we need to repair only ten of them. We'll have to put in somewhere to fix her up properly, though."

Guy calculated the colonials sent at least two hundred balls at the frigate. While he had returned less than half as many, he did more damage. For the repairs needed, he headed to the Bay of Castors located seventy miles southwest of Canso. It held a deep, hidden bay.

During the four days there, *la Renommée* underwent patch-ups and took on fresh water. Then they patrolled the inlets and bays around Acadia and Newfoundland, ever watchful for signs of enemy or troop encampments. Many small French outposts dotted the coast along New Breton and Acadia's shores. At the sight of the frigate, the villagers and troops gathered on the icy shore, waved kerchiefs and hats to her in the distance. *La Renommée* sailed on by, the only connection they had with their distant homeland since the previous year.

Over the next two weeks, Guy sighted many patrols looking for them and, in turn, chased convoys and smaller sloops-of-war. One captured transport held frightened troops, more farmers than soldiers, and Guy released it. His eye was on taking a frigate or snow to add another warship for protection.

Going over his charts, Guy complained to La Motte. "Where's our fleet?! Head toward the Bay of Castors again. Our squadron may be along those coasts. I don't understand why we haven't seen them. They could resupply us."

La Motte spoke of his fears. "We've had no fresh food supplies since we left Cadiz. The men are on rations now. Do you think they ran into the same storms that delayed our arrival, or perhaps the British may have captured the squadron?"

"Who's to say?" Guy thumped his fist upon the table. "In a few weeks, we'll return to Brest if they don't appear. Until then, pestering the enemy remains our objective."

In mid-May 1745, the weather cleared, and they were free from the usual ubiquitous fog. But the scant meals took their toll on seamen and officers alike. Guy's private supplies had run out, and he suffered with his crew. Men became sick, and he feared scurvy might spread among them.

Near the Bay of Castors, the rare sun shone, and the seas hosted low waves. Guy headed westward when they spotted a solitary warship and *la Renommée* set off after her.

"Sir, it's a colonial snow," said Lieutenant La Motte, watching it flee.

"More important, she's all by herself," Guy added with a devilish look. "Let's keep this one from getting away. Hang more sail and close as fast as we can. This time, everything is in our favor."

The French frigate had the wind just off her starboard beam and moved across the water like a skipping stone. Guy discovered that on smooth seas, she didn't need stunsails or even her topgallants to get her best speed. Her low profile and long, sleek hull made her clip astounding.

Guy shouted from the quarterdeck to the crewmen. "Men, this is a chance to increase our defenses. This colonial snow won't escape us like the others. She'll feed both our stomachs and our purse!" The desire for both food and the prospect of a prize pushed them beyond their hunger pangs.

Within an hour, the French frigate came up behind, less than fifty yards away. The colonial snow, *Prince of Orange*, struggled to flee, but Guy fell into the windward side of the ship.

"Take her sails from her if you can," Guy said when they were abreast of her. The loud thunder of the cannons followed and the *Prince of Orange* returned the broadside. Exchanges persisted for most of an hour, the ships' guns hot from throwing cannon iron at one another. The bursts had a shattering effect as rigging fell from above on the snow and damaged the midship hull of the French frigate. Blasts wounded men and volleys of musket balls buried themselves in flesh.

Yet, the superiority lay with *la Renommée*, both in gun caliber and number, and crew size. Guy wasted no time in closing to board the *Prince of Orange* to keep the damage to her light. He ordered grappling hooks thrown, and the crewmen prepared to go over the sides. The snow's deck, lower than the frigate's, gave the French a superior position. Although the colonials had strung a boarding net, bar shot had ripped away half of it.

The boarding parties steeled themselves for the assault and crowded the decks. Marines volleyed on the enemy sailors to force them under cover. As they did, Guy's crew towed the grappling lines, pulling the war machines together. Cannons were muzzle-to-muzzle and continued their dreadful firing. In one exchange, a hit pierced the French frigate's hull and reduced a quarterdeck staircase to kindling.

Lieutenant La Motte readied the first group of twenty to descend on the snow's aft deck near its ruined net. The enemy waited with cutlass and pike for the boarders, hiding behind the bulwarks. Guy and Lieutenant La Tour prepared to lead a group amidship. Guy shouted "Board!" and a wave of men cascaded down onto the snow.

As Lieutenant La Motte jumped to the deck, a young officer attacked him with a pistol and a sword. In the roar of shouts, gunfire, and feet pounding wood planks, he felt the sting of burnt powder and hot air rush by his ear. A pistol ball missed his head by less than an inch.

The colonial then thrust his saber at La Motte, who parried it. Another sailor stepped between them in the scuffling horde of men, and La Motte lost the assailant for a second in the mob.

When he caught sight of him, the glint of a slashing blade flashed and cut through his coat sleeve, just missing his left forearm. The man raised his sword to strike again, but La Motte stood ready and thrust his cutlass deep into his gut. He stepped around the collapsing foe to challenge another.

A jostling crush of fighting men, cursing and screaming, pushed forward across the snow. French crewmen gained foot after bloody foot in the butchery. The colonial captain, seeing they could not stop the overwhelming surge, cut the line holding his flag. Shouts to cease the fight followed in English and French, and the enemy dropped their weapons and backed up to the opposite side of the deck. The Frenchmen advanced, threatening them with cutlasses, pikes, axes, bayonets, and pistols.

The casualties were not as serious as Guy expected. Six of his crew died in the assault and 23 carried wounds, while the colonials lost more than twice as many. He placed a dozen of his 20 marines on board the ship to watch over the enemy and transferred part of *la Renommée's* sailors onto her. After the carpenter reviewed the damage, he returned with a smile and good news.

"Captain, the snow is in splendid shape. Just minor repairs, however, cables and lines need to be laid. There are no holes below the waterline."

At last, Guy had gained the extra protection, and a fine ship at that. She was a newer warship with fourteen 6-pound cannons. To fix the rigging and damages, they headed again for the Bay of Castors.

Guy learned little from their captain, a professional provincial military man, who'd said the province of Massachusetts owned the snow, not leased as many other colonial vessels. Treated as an equal since he wasn't a privateer or a civilian volunteer, Guy handed the crew over to a French outpost as prisoners of war.

After three days of fixing the frigate, they left the bay with two warships flying the all-white French flag, putting Lieutenant La Motte in command of the snow. The prize filled their stomachs and lifted their spirits, confidence, and chances of survival.

Encouraged, Guy took his ships east again toward Cape Breton and Louisbourg, anticipating the fleet arriving. After searching for days, they sighted nothing until just south of the coast. There, on the bright mid-May morning, they spotted a merchantman, a large brigantine, heading for England.

The warships approached the vessel as though a friendly patrol. When flanking it on both sides, they lowered the British flags and raised their French ones, and the merchant struck its colors without a fight. A

Carolina colony ship of two hundred tons. She held a full hold of rice.

Guy placed a crew on the merchantman to run the blockade and get food to the citadel. As *la Renommée* escorted her partway to Louisbourg, Guy detected the sounds of battle. Hopeful that the squadron had arrived, he headed for the clash. Mere miles from the harbor, a large French warship traded cannonballs with three big ships. He recognized her as *le Vigilant* and wondered where the rest of the fleet was. He first thought to aid her, but four enemy warships caught sight of *la Renommée* and the *Prince of Orange*. The colonials outnumbered his guns and forced the two to sail south and away, leaving *le Vigilant* to her fate.

The next day he returned to Louisbourg to find patrols in huge numbers surrounding the harbor. For two more days, Guy continued in vain to search for *le Vigilant* and the rest of the squadron. Discouraged and fearing the enemy had captured them, he departed the cod-fishing waters for France.

La Renommée's swift voyage back along the Gulf Stream was a welcome contrast to her delayed arrival off Louisbourg four months earlier. Storms lessened, and the frigate arrived near the French coast at the end of June with a sizable part of the crew still sick from malnutrition and disease.

The late spring flowers, blooming trees, and warm winds greeted *la Renommée* and her captured escort as they entered Brest's outer bays. Guy docked and hurried to Commandant de Camilly with the news of the blockade and buildup of troops. He feared the squadron never making it to Acadia might be more of a blow than the British and colonial fleet surrounding Louisbourg's harbor.

His good uniform was the only part of him in shape as he entered the naval office. Guy suffered from months at sea in the frigid North and appeared drawn and pale. The meager diet caused a noticeable weight loss, and the officer's coat hung from his shoulders.

"Captain de Kersaint reporting to Commandant de Camilly, please," Guy announced himself to the clerk, who scurried into the inner office to announce the captain's return.

Seconds later, he rushed back to Guy. "The commandant will see you at once! Please follow me, sir."

De Camilly's private office was martial and spartan. Large maps of the world and the Atlantic Ocean draped the walls, and double doors with carved naval crests led to a balcony overlooking the quay. The commandant stood beside a cherry desk with three chairs facing it.

De Camilly rushed to meet the tired-looking captain and offered him a seat.

"Tell me what happened," said de Camilly, his intense blue-gray eyes squinted above his hawk-beak nose.

Slumped in the chair, Guy sighed. "Sir, Louisbourg is safe for the moment, but blockaded by warships and privateers. There's a buildup of troops further southwest of Louisbourg. The men we encountered on transports were only colonial militia and not British infantry regulars. We also discovered the enemy has cannon and cavalry."

Guy let out a deep breath and continued. "Just before I left their waters to return, I encountered *le Vigilant*, doing battle with three big warships near Louisbourg. But we had to flee the oncoming enemy. And I'm not sure of her fate." Guy paused and sighed as he prepared to tell de Camilly the worst news.

"Sir, other than *le Vigilant*, our squadron never arrived." His head bobbed downward. "For weeks, I searched and never came upon a trace of them. My fear is they're lost to either storms or the British." The disheartened captain glanced up at the commandant, saying no more.

De Camilly looked away from Guy, not speaking, and then turned with a knitted brow. "Captain de Kersaint, the rest of our ships never left Brest, only *le Vigilant*. Besides the blockade, Louisbourg has now come under siege; the colonials landed troops and surrounded the fortress just as you departed those waters. A merchantman brought us word of it less than a week ago."

Guy slumped. "The expected squadron, plus the snow I captured, and *le Vigilant* could have prevented a blockade and siege!"

"Yes, it could have." De Camilly shrugged. "But Maurepas couldn't get the funds for them. Nevertheless, we don't think the British will send their regulars to Louisbourg. It can hold out against just colonial infantry if *le Vigilant* reached the harbor with the provisions and gunpowder." The much older man tapped his desk. "We're gathering a new relief expedition. Also, *le Castor*, based on your frigate's plans, is being built in Québec and should be ready to join us."

Guy's head dropped between his defeated shoulders, wagging back and forth. "Sir, we could have averted this."

"I know." De Camilly looked downward. "For now, we must abide until Versailles realizes how serious the Louisbourg dilemma is. Maurepas is doing his best to sway the king." The commandant pulled his mouth sideward. "King Louis believes he must defeat the enemy in the European countries with his army. We may not agree with that strategy; still, we do not make policy, just follow it."

"When will the new squadron be ready?" asked Guy, still glaring at the floor.

The commandant walked to the window overlooking the docks and scanned the warships below. "The plan is to depart next month. *La Renommée* must join it, of course. The fleet will have your frigate and the three frigates anchored near yours." He paced with his hands clenched behind. "De Salvert will command the squadron." De Camilly turned and his saddened eyes looked at him. "I'll explain everything to you later. For now, get things started on your ship, and then take a week's leave. Rest up for the next voyage, which will come too soon for you."

"Yes, sir, I shall." Guy, shaking his head, exited the office to move *la Renommée* nearer the yard for repairs and fitting out for the coming expedition. Two days later, he left for Cléder.

Upon reaching his manor, Guy stepped from the carriage, still looking wan and thin, no longer the handsome, rugged seaman who had gone to sea months earlier. For the first time, he felt beaten.

A servant answered the door, welcomed him, and scampered away to inform Jeanne. Moments afterward, Guy heard quick footfalls coming as he shuffled to the salon.

As he plopped into an upholstered chair, Jeanne entered, her face in shock. Where his battle scars were symbols of courage, his gaunt appearance showed other dangers he faced.

She wagged her head. "Guy, you look exhausted. What happened?"

He sat for a moment, reflecting on the voyage. "Actually, not much occurred at all. Our mission failed. I never did get to Louisbourg and the fleet we waited to meet never embarked. To sum it up, except for a few incidents, we sailed in circles." Guy grunted.

Her eyebrows lowered. "I feared you were injured."

"Only my self-confidence." He moved his head slowly to and fro. But his flippant answer did nothing to rid her creases of concern.

Throughout the next day, Jeanne fed him fruits, foods, and sweets until his disposition improved and a little color returned to his pale face.

When the week passed, he climbed into their carriage appearing fitter. The June day stayed sunny, and by the time he returned to Brest, he had finished making mental checklists of what needed to be done. Guy had two weeks to get *la Renommée* fit for service again.

⁓

Late morning, the hot summer sun melted away the dawn fog. The bright, large gallery windows on the stern of *la Renommée* silhouetted Guy's pacing as the gathered officers watched.

"Captain," inquired La Motte, "will the squadron be docking in the West Indies before heading to Cape Breton this time?"

"First, we won't cross with the rest of the fleet. Again, we'll reconnoiter ahead to see how Louisbourg manages. Then we'll meet the fleet on the Grand Banks, as intended last time."

"Have we any word *le Castor* launched in Québec?" asked de La Tour.

Guy looked down and shook his head. "Nothing yet. The ship remained behind schedule, although she should be at sea by now. Together with *le Vigilant* and *le Castor*, the fleet will have three ships of the line and four frigates, and the transports. That's the largest French squadron ever to campaign in America and formidable enough to break the blockade and siege. We'll find out where *le Castor* is patrolling and join her before rendezvousing with the others." Guy recognized the navy had done the best they could, given the king's inflexibility.

"Shall we be taking prizes along the way?" Ensign de Saint Saëns asked.

"Defense dictates over offense; we'll not be hunting for any. We must be ready to intercept French East Indiamen or other registered merchantmen heading to Louisbourg. They need to be warned the British are blockading Louisbourg." He nodded. "If any enemy ships come our way, though, captures are allowed."

After a week, they split off from the main fleet and set off for Acadia. Fair seas and warm temperatures repaid the crew, who saw the northern waters at their worst during their miserable passage on the first trip to Louisbourg.

The ship pitched as the waves lapped on her sides one afternoon when they saw another vessel headed in their direction. Then the stranger's captain changed course as soon as he realized *la Renommée* was French.

The large colonial mastship carried timber, yet was well-armed. Although to load the wood on her decks, they had reduced the number of cannons from forty-four to twenty-eight.

After an hour, *la Renommée* came close enough to send a warning. The vessel continued and used every sail to flee.

When nearing, they traded infrequent gunfire until *la Renommée* lay to her port aft. Both attempted to disable the other with cannon salvos and musket assaults. The mastship maneuvered many times to throw off her assailant, yet the faster frigate kept pace and sped abreast to loose a series of volleys.

Their engagement lasted hours, with the mastship trying to kill the French crew with small canister balls while the frigate returned chain and bar shot to disable the rigging. Impossible to repair all the damage done to the lines and stays, the mastship plodded with most sails destroyed.

The frigate's attacks subdued the mastship's defenses, and finally, the British captain swore at the victors and pulled down his colors.

"Ensign de Saint Saëns, prepare to board her with marines and search her well," Guy ordered.

"Captain de Kersaint," said de Saint Saëns, after climbing back onto *la Renommée* forty minutes later, "I've brought their captain and a passenger, a government official. Plus, I found a chest of documents and maps, sir. Shall I take the men to your quarters?"

"At once. We need information on Louisbourg. The prisoners must have news of the blockade and siege," replied Guy, and hurried below with the marine lieutenant to his cabin.

"Gentlemen, sit," the captain said to the two captives, pointing to chairs. The marine lieutenant and his sergeant stood behind them while the ship's purser sat to the side, translating everything into English.

"I am Lieutenant de Vaisseau, Guy de Coëtnempren, Count de Kersaint, the captain of *la Renommée*. Tell me from where you came, where you harbored, and to where you traveled," he said without expression.

The mastship's captain told Guy his name, and that they left Boston with 140 men for Portsmouth, England. They hadn't stopped at any other ports since leaving. His frankness assured Guy that it was likely the truth, since it was of no military importance. Then the other introduced himself.

"My title is Lieutenant Governor of the Colony of New York George Clark, on my way via Portsmouth to London for official business. Respect my office and allow me to continue on my journey along with the captain and his vessel. We're of little consequence to you and, I suspect, a burden." The pasty-faced man in his mid-thirties looked more like a skinny bank clerk than a bureaucrat.

"Of course you can continue, but I shall retain your ship. France can always use another shipload of timber," Guy said with a smug air at the official's impotent plea. "Nevertheless, tell me the size of the British garrison and fleet at Louisbourg, and I may reconsider."

The colonial captain leered hard at the lieutenant governor.

Lieutenant Governor Clark sneered and jutted his jaw. "Captain de Kersaint, I won't tell you our strength in Louisbourg. If your aim is to retake it even with an armada of warships, I must warn you they will not surrender without a lengthy fight, unlike the French defenders."

The colonial ships that appeared so clumsy and the farmer soldiers they encountered on their first trip, against the odds, had taken the greatest fortress in North America. Guy showed no outward signs of his dismay.

"Lieutenant, you and the marine guard take the captain to his compartment. There's no need of him any further," said Guy, afraid the officer might caution the lieutenant governor to stop talking. He digested the fortress' surrender before saying anything. If *le Vigilant* had made port, he surmised, then Louisbourg would not have fallen. If the citadel fell, then they either destroyed or captured *le Vigilant* during the engagement he had seen.

Guy replied, smiling, "Yes, that's true. Any plans to assault Louisbourg will be difficult. Especially since *le Vigilant* didn't complete her mission."

"The *Vigilant* could have saved Louisbourg. But now we'll use her against you along with the other ships of the line awaiting you," the proud lieutenant governor replied.

"Tell me, when did you take her?" Guy leaned forward. "I'm curious because I cruised near Louisbourg."

"Yes, the navy warned us of the *Renommée's* presence off Acadia last spring. The capture of the *Vigilant* happened around the middle of May. Her seizure was fortunate because our infantry had run out of powder. We prepared to end the siege and depart for home, but she had over five hundred barrels of it in her hold. Had her captain relieved Louisbourg, *Vigilant* would yet be French, as would Louisbourg." Clark looked up, chin rising high. "It appears her commander failed in his duties."

"Indeed, one never knows the implications of an error," Guy said, thinking more of the official's blabbering than *le Vigilant's* captain. Afterwards, nothing more of importance came out of the talkative man and Guy sent him away as well.

It was the worst of setbacks, Guy thought. The information voided the fleet's principal goal. With the loss of Louisbourg and *le Vigilant*, the squadron's firepower became too mismatched to attack the British fleet or retake the fortress. The quick chat had scuttled, within a few minutes, the months of planning and expenses for their mission.

He had the mastship sent to France. The chest of papers de Saint Saëns found looked official, but the purser didn't read English well enough to translate them. Guy's next worries centered on the fate of the Québec-built frigate, *le Castor*. Had the British also snared her, or might he find her when he arrived in Acadia?

As the frigate continued northwest, *la Renommée* met fair weather and seas. She reached the Great Banks, where Acadians in their schooners pulled in cod at their summer feeding grounds. The fishermen verified Louisbourg had fallen with many British warships protecting it, including several ships of the line and *le Vigilant*. None reported seeing *le Castor*.

Guy cruised along the shoreline for a week and spotted several vessels, but not the missing frigate and only a few topsail ships. Most of the enemy fleet patrolled nearer Louisbourg. It was clear the French squadron could be of scant value to Louisbourg.

With no sign of the Canadian-built *le Castor*, Guy reasoned she had sought a safe harbor in Québec or France, after hearing of the citadel's fall. His observations completed, he set out for the Grand Banks to join the fleet.

After three days of searching in a crisscross pattern, he discovered the warships at a distance, creeping toward Louisbourg.

"Lieutenant, signal them and prepare a boat for me to meet with de Salvert," he told La Motte, his mouth downturned. "This won't be pleasant."

Upon boarding, Guy took a deep breath before telling him the glum news. "Commander de Salvert, I captured a colonial mastship and the lieutenant-governor of New York informed me that Louisbourg has fallen and Acadian fishermen confirmed it. Plus, they took *le Vigilant* when she arrived."

De Salvert twisted his head sideways and closed his eyes. "I feared it from the onset of the mission. Did you hear anything about *le Castor*?"

"No, sir. Perhaps she's safe in Québec or France."

The fleet commander turned to his first lieutenant and sighed. "Send a message to the squadron captains to come for a meeting. Now we must search to warn any French or allied ships heading toward Louisbourg. They'll be easy prey if they assume the port is still ours. Our secondary goal, to attack Annapolis Royal, we'll cancel owing to being unable to resupply at Louisbourg."

For weeks, the warships scoured the waters along the routes to Cape Breton for merchantmen. Their squadron captured a few enemy prizes while encountering fierce gales and heavy fogs.

With the hurricane season underway by August, De Salvert ordered the fleet to Labrador to take on fresh water, food, and firewood before leaving for France. It took three weeks and surviving a hurricane's fury that dismasted the ships before the squadron dropped anchor at Brest. In mid-October, the de Salvert expedition to Louisbourg ended. The second mission to Acadia and Guy's anticipation of success had collapsed again.

He turned over the enemy prisoners and the chest of captured documents. Once translated, the papers proved far more valuable than Guy's mastship prize. The diplomatic letters the lieutenant governor didn't toss overboard revealed a startling plan for a joint British and colonial invasion of Canada. Unfortunately, they were the only strategic benefits of the three-month-long, expensive expedition to save fallen Louisbourg.

―◦―

Not long into the year 1746, Guy burst through the door of his Brest home with exciting news. "Jeanne!" he shouted, dashing for the salon. "They've knighted me!" The proclamation had come to him in the commandant's office.

"Knighted you?" she asked, puzzled.

"I suppose it was for the missions to Louisiana and Louisbourg." His face filled with glee. "De Camilly announced Versailles awarded me a knighthood in the Military Order of Saint Louis. It's an honor that opens many opportunities."

"Then let's celebrate your achievement." Jeanne clapped. "We'll go to the champagne house after dinner."

When they sat at a table in the establishment that evening, Guy reflected on how it would have pleased his father. The knighthood accomplished the last critical step to a glorious career. Those lacking it had a poor chance of advancement into higher naval echelons.

"Jeanne," he smiled and asked, "are you proud of me receiving accolades and promotions?"

"Dear, no amount of praise or awards could change what I've always felt for you. If you enjoy them, then I am happier. They mean nothing to me, though, because I care not what others think about you. You have my whole being already and can stand no higher in my esteem." She sipped from her crystal glass.

His face hung as he put the wine to his lips. Why hadn't his closest love, his wife reaped the joy of his successes, he wondered. Did his triumphs exalt only himself in a selfish need for recognition? The notions doused his pride as he settled back in the chair.

Perhaps Hashi Humma was right, he mulled, and we set our paths before we were born. Marie had told him, too, that he had always sought fame. If so, the struggle for distinction was as much a part of him as his hair color, a predisposition to thoughts, actions, and intent as inherent as his physical being. To reject such might offend God. So, he concluded, it must be his destiny, not vanity.

La Renommée waited again for the first assignment of the year. Guy had recovered from his second unsuccessful voyage to Louisbourg and rested alone in his cabin reading. He recalled conversing with Jeanne about the pitiful, earlier missions, and the king's frustrating neglect of the navy and the colonies.

Regardless, the fall of Louisbourg had devastated the king, he learned. One thing became plain to everyone: they must retake Louisbourg at any cost to save the French lands in North America and even in the Caribbean. Furthermore, the citadel was vital to protect ships returning to France. Their key to the Americas lay in enemy hands.

Then Versailles suggested an expedition to recapture it and forever rid the British threat to their colonial holdings there. Guy sat, tapping his compass divider on a chart with La Motte across from him.

"Sir, two trips to Louisbourg have failed to protect it. A third may end differently if we change our approach," the lieutenant said.

"It could," said Guy. "The new campaign incorporates a massive and complicated undertaking. It requires exorbitant funding and shifts from the strategies we've practiced. The departure must begin in early spring in order to succeed. Versailles hopes to retake Louisbourg by midyear. Afterward, they've created secondary objectives targeting British colonies." The mission made him frown.

Guy inspected the maps, brooding. "They've informed me we'll be leaving ahead, just as in the two previous attempts." He hesitated before delivering an ominous detail. "They chose Duc d'Anville to lead the task force."

"*Duc d'Anville*, sir?" Shock showed on La Motte's face. "He's a Mediterranean commander. Perhaps powerful with the Admiralty, still, does he know anything about the situation in Louisbourg?"

Guy's hand turned into a fist. "No, and his entire career has been on galley ships in the Mediterranean or in Versailles. Duc d'Anville never sailed the Atlantic and is nothing more than an administrative functionary, a commander of pens and oars. I've no respect for his expertise, and he lacks understanding about topsail warships on an ocean. They have experienced admirals available from whom to choose, but this misjudgment could destroy the expedition."

La Motte turned his head aside. "So, sir, we're to scout ahead again, and then?"

Guy took a deep breath. "I don't know all the details. Although Boston and Philadelphia stand out as the gateways to their colonies, just as Louisbourg did ours. Bombard one of their major harbors and it should draw protection away from every other British port in the Americas. We'll see which Versailles considers the most important to attack."

In early cold January, Guy received orders to join the gathering fleet in La Rochelle, on the coast south of Brest. *La Renommée* bobbed in the port's harbor a week later.

Guy scanned those already in its bay. Vessels of all types made berth, filling the sky with masts and the docks with sailors and workers. He'd heard preparations would be immense, and the same occurred in the ports of Brest, Rochefort, and Lorient.

He explained further to La Motte and Lieutenant de La Tour. "There are even more frigates to join, with eleven ships of the line in total, and fifteen additional transports are in the other ports besides here. It'll total over 70 vessels—an enormous endeavor."

The clatter of iron-rimmed wheels on cobblestone sounded day and night. Each port's quays bustled with supply wagons, carpenters making final repairs, and barges carrying supplies to the warships. Regiments of foot soldiers arrived, standing in long lines of hundreds. Smaller boats ferried troops and sailors to and from the vessels. Naval offices burst with officers. For Guy and La Motte to carry out the simplest business required hours of waiting. The fleet in total contained over eight hundred cannon and six thousand crewmen. The drays rolled onto the docks in endless caravans.

Four battalions of French regulars, and one battalion of marines, over three thousand men, assembled to board transports for the attack.

The influx of such huge numbers of people, horses, vendors, and support personnel placed enormous pressure on resources in the ports. Brief delays multiplied to affect other areas, and the Admiralty postponed the departure date many times. Nevertheless, the king's overdue backing motivated the leaders to solve whatever logistical problems arose.

Two months later, the fleet still sat with sails furled. "Well, sir, King Louis has done his part to turn everything around," said La Motte. "This undertaking must cost millions. I hope we depart soon."

"Maurepas estimated it'd reach over five million livres. So now the burden of a victory falls upon us." Guy lifted his eyebrows. "Every day of delay raises the chance of failure."

By April, the remarkable enterprise felt its first blow to invincibility when fever broke out among the troops in their confined encampments. Scores took ill, then hundreds, and finally thousands. Then the disease spread to the civilian population and to the crews onboard. The bedridden occupied every available space on ships and shore. Religious Sisters and surgeons meandered between long rows of the stricken, doling out what little aid they could offer. The death toll rose.

La Renommée received unwelcome orders, and Guy shook his head. "To help the transports, we must board 84 infantrymen and five officers. This means cramped quarters for our crew that will cause the fevers to spread even more. This is insane!" He buried his face in his hands as he sat with La Motte. "Almost three hundred will be aboard instead of two hundred."

La Motte, frowning, said, "Regardless of illnesses, sir, the fleet's departure has to be maintained to achieve the goals before the fall."

"Yes, and we'll cast off with men still stricken." Guy sighed. "It will decimate us."

In May, Duc d'Anville issued a desperate order for the fleet to embark with as many fit as possible, and the impressive force departed over a month late. For days, strong westerly headwinds forced progress to a standstill. Against most captains' opinions, their leader signaled to return to wait for more favorable winds.

<hr>

In mid-June, the mass of naval vessels set off once more. As in both earlier missions, *la Renommée* left the group early and turned for a more northern route to Acadia. The plans instructed the frigate to meet up with Canadian and Mi'kmaq forces at Chebucto for supplies and await the fleet.

The main body continued on but lost time to adverse winds, storms, collisions, and towing disabled ships. Many returned to France, damaged.

Already a month late, near the Azores, two warships advanced from the north, flying the French flag, which Guy assumed were stragglers. When they approached, his spyglass scanned for their true nationality.

La Motte, halfway up the shrouds, called to the captain, "Sir, they're British. One's a 36 and the other a 16. We're out-gunned."

"Prepare to outrun them, Lieutenant La Motte!" Guy shouted back. They spread more from the spars to escape.

The British frigate and sloop engaged them for four days. The violent clashes bashed the ships and killed crew on both sides. Every mast had damages with lines and rigging strewn across the decks, making movement difficult and gun loading slow. The combating frigate captains withdrew often to attend to the wounded and dead and toss fallen wreckage overboard. Guy wondered if the British were also growing short of ammunition and ordered a count after each engagement. The frequent combat delayed Guy almost another week.

On the fifth morning, the enemy warships again came, ready to start the battle anew. He received a grim report from the gun master that they had no roundshot left and only canister and chain links. It meant using his cannon for just short ranges, even the sloop's small cannons had longer reach.

As the foes closed, *la Renommée* cut in front of the larger and peppered the full length of the opponent.

At such a close distance, the smaller, clustered balls and iron links decimated exposed British crew and destroyed the enemy's bowsprit and mainstay. Guy veered to flee, but the closeness opened him to a retaliatory volley. Both British warships returned a last salvo at *la Renommée*. The powerful sledgehammers smashed into the stern and through the gallery windows, killing a gun crew in the cabin, and tearing off part of the port-quarter gallery. Guy, Lieutenant de La Tour, and Ensign de Saint Saëns fell to the deck from the blast.

Guy clambered up on one knee as sailors ran to help him. A flying wood splinter hit him on his left front side near his belly, broke a rib, and took his breath. He also had a wounded leg, gushing blood that Lieutenant de La Tour helped to stop. Guy limped below to the surgeon, who bandaged him to return. Ensign de Saint Saëns, hit in the body with a canister ball, lay dead.

The cannonry over the five days had destroyed his main topmast and carried away part of his rudder, although it still functioned. Guy had twenty-four crewmen lost or wounded. Three officers and the young Garde de la Marine cadet were dead, and the ship, in tatters, needed repair. Nevertheless, *la Renommée* had finally beaten her pursuers and continued onward.

With just a third of the sailors healthy enough to work, the frigate made slow progress in the high seas, stopping often for hasty fixes. When arriving off the fishing banks, they needed medical help, supplies, and ammunition. Held up by over a month and a half, *la Renommée* cruised within sight of Acadia at last.

They put into the Bay of Castors for repairs the next day. While the crew patched the battered ship, Guy rubbed his chin and said to La Motte, "Duc d'Anville should have arrived while we engaged the two warships. We'll fix our damages, but we can't fix our ill crewmen and the infantry on board. We'll go to Chebucto right away to see if they made landfall."

On an early August evening, they cruised toward the village and sighted sails.

"Captain, they're ours!" de La Tour called down from the foremast top. "Most have mizzen braces running fore and not aft, our way of rigging!"

"Thank God!" Guy exclaimed.

Le Northumberland, the flagship carrying Duc d'Anville, eight transports, and a sloop, had moored in the huge bay with another ship of the line farther away. As *la Renommée* approached, Guy made out the distressful conditions of the warships.

Of the seventy venturing from France, just a handful lay before him. Guy boarded his gig and set off for *le Northumberland* to inform the admiral of the terrible passage, battering of his frigate, and sick men. When Guy arrived to report, the distraught leader was pacing in his cabin, surrounded by commanders.

The admiral turned on him when Guy told him about the crossing.

"Captain de Kersaint, please, don't recount your petty troubles," responded Duc d'Anville, his arms flailing. "Can you not see our horrendous condition? I have 1,200 crewmen and infantry dead to the fever. God knows where my warships are. All the king's hopes rode upon this expedition. We're threatened with losing the entirety of our possessions in North America. After crossing, a storm near the Banks scattered everyone. Then, as the fleet reassembled, a hurricane ruined us and two ships sank for certain at Sable Island. How many lay at the bottom? Anyone can guess." His face glowed crimson. "The season is too late to begin an attack; our campaign is useless now.

"I have failed our king and lost our Canadian colony. Nothing can be done," the admiral groaned. The officers in *le Northumberland's* cabin looked at each other with blank expressions.

"Not all is wasted, sir. Within a week, we should account for most ships, and at least part of the mission can go on as planned," an officer offered.

Duc d'Anville, as though he might attack the man, screamed, "Go on as planned?! The entire undertaking is in ruins. The king picked me to rescue Louisbourg. I have failed him!" He strode back and forth, his fists clutched at his sides. "The citadel is gone. There's nothing to be done. We are finished!" He slammed both fists on the desk with tears in his eyes and shook his head. Spittle formed at the edges of his clamped mouth before he opened it again to rant.

The captain of the flagship spoke to Duc d'Anville with pleading eyes. "Sir, give us instructions. We need to recover from this dilemma and salvage what we can."

"Half the troops and sailors lie sick and dying. Exactly what salvation can we plan for? We don't have the ships, guns, or men to retake Louisbourg, nor attack the colonial ports."

"Then perhaps we can take Annapolis Royal on the northern shore of Acadia," the captain urged.

The admiral snorted. "The king expects cake and you offer him a crumb? It is already September and we must soon return." Again and again, his hands went to his head, rubbing his temples. "Too late. There is no hope." His distraught demeanor unnerved every man in the room.

"Had you officers just sped up operations in France, we'd have set off in time." He vented, scowling and pointing at them. "I'm not sure which is worse, nature's wrath or my captains!"

Guy listened to the furious diatribe against the world and men the admiral spewed within the great cabin. During a pause in Duc d'Anville's shouting, Guy excused himself and left to take care of his ship.

Guy learned the mission included many operations, the first to recapture Louisbourg. The next planned on taking Annapolis Royal and other British bases in Acadia. Their last task involved bombarding enemy positions, initially Boston and then other New England cities, including Philadelphia. Afterward, time permitting, they'd leave for the West Indies to capture plantations and destroy Port Royal, the enemy's main naval station in Jamaica.

Overall, it would cripple Great Britain's economic centers and damage or eliminate its military strongholds. Any success, though, would restore confidence in the navy. With the possibility of maiming British power in the Americas, and with the enemy's positions in Europe deteriorating, the French expedition might force a victorious end to the war.

More ships arrived at the harbor the next day. From his anchorage, Guy watched burial details shipping bodies to a common grave on land. His own crewmen would fare better once they got more food and surgeons' attention. Onboard *le Northumberland*, their unhinged leader still fumed.

After returning from another meeting, Guy rolled his eyes. "La Motte, the admiral is beyond reason. Instead of accepting the circumstances and moving on, he continues to rail at fate as if his anger alone will change the past. He listens to no one, wasting the little time left for a mission."

"I suppose he's worried about what the king will say when we return, sir." La Motte lifted his stare upward. "I wouldn't want to be in his place."

Guy smirked. "Nor do I wish he was in his place. Either of the vice-admirals would have been a better fit for the role."

Over the next few days, the admiral did little to ease problems, then soon took ill himself. The surgeon-major announced Duc d'Anville had a history of an undiagnosed malady and usually recovered within a week. Unfortunately, the results he expected from treatment were not forthcoming. Admiral Duc d'Anville, now semi-conscious, appeared to be weakening.

Two days later, a cannon signal sounded on *le Northumberland*. Guy rushed in his launch. In a joint meeting, they announced the admiral had died of an apoplectic fit at three in the early morning.

Guy, stern-faced, reported the passing to his officers on *la Renommée*. "I find it not surprising, considering the admiral's uncontrollable actions and temper. Any new commander will perform better."

La Motte sighed and asked, "Who's next in line for command, sir?"

"Vice-Admiral d'Estourmel should be, but he's still missing."

As if by providence, d'Estourmel and a host of storm-battered ships appeared in the harbor the very afternoon of Duc d'Anville's death. The leadership upheaval forced the fleet to stay put while the new admiral sorted out a late-season plan. Troops debarked to set up camps. Endless days of seasickness, malnutrition, or the fever epidemic weakened most. Guy rejoiced when the infantrymen left *la Renommée* which relaxed conditions for his ill seamen.

At the end of September, d'Estourmel assembled senior army and navy officers to his flagship for a council of war to resolve what actions the beleaguered campaign might take.

D'Estourmel stood with arms crossed. "It is best if we return to France since just seven ships of the line remain at Chebucto. Other vessels of the original fleet have abandoned the mission for home, gone to other ports for repairs, or have sunk. It's useless to attempt anything."

One officer countered with a raised fist, "For honor's sake, sir, we should salvage at least part of the king's plans."

"The invasion force has lost half their infantry to the fever and the Canadian forces haven't arrived," d'Estourmel answered with angry eyes. "To consider invading either Louisbourg or Annapolis Royal remains out of the question until they rendezvous."

De La Jonquière, Governor Designate of Québec, stepped forward. "Perhaps we can try bombarding Annapolis Royal. If the promised help from Canada arrives, the added numbers should provide enough for an assault there. Also, we should send part of the fleet to Québec to ensure we have ample men and supplies to prevent a British victory there."

"No, no. Our orders do not call for such an action." D'Estourmel shook his head and waved his hand before him.

The governor, putting his fists on his hips, said, "Everything has changed. If we had taken Louisbourg, we wouldn't need to reinforce Québec. Now that taking the citadel seems impossible, Québec must have protection."

An army officer spoke up to both senior officers. "Sirs, the Canadians withdrew northward instead of meeting us. A Mi'kmaq runner delivered the message before the meeting."

The expedition commander's mouth opened without speaking, and his eyes widened. He cried out, "All is lost! All is lost!" D'Estourmel shot up from the table, distraught and muttering to himself, and rushed to his private cabin, leaving everyone in silence.

Governor de La Jonquière dismissed the officers and told them they'd issue new orders as soon as d'Estourmel decided.

"Yet another alarmist in command. Heaven save us," Guy said aloud as he left. Others echoed in agreement or shook their heads in disbelief as they boarded their boats for their ships.

That night aboard le *Northumberland*, officers heard moaning coming from the admiral's cabin. When they forced the door open, there upon the deck, d'Estourmel lay curled in a pool of blood, having run himself through with his own sword. Either stress or a fever's delirium provoked him to stab himself. Although the wound was not mortal, its severity left him unable to continue as commander.

The next morning, before the dumbfounded officers, D'Estourmel turned over leadership to his succeeding head, Governor de La Jonquière.

Even the most prescient of Versailles's naval board planners could not have expected such turns. The combination of ill-fated events happening one upon the other, beginning in France and following them to Acadia, seemed inconceivable. It depended on Governor de La Jonquière to save the endeavor.

In a meeting on *la Renommée*, Guy tapped his fingertips together as he talked. "Governor de La Jonquière is a capable leader, even over sixty years of age. He's determined and bold, and fought wars in the field and on the ocean since the age of twelve."

"Have you served with him?" asked La Tour, raising his brows.

Guy smiled. "He was squadron commander on my first visit to Québec years ago. He'll reorganize the expedition into a coherent state. Too bad Duc d'Anville commanded instead of the governor from the beginning. We'd be back in Brest, celebrating by now. Though I doubt even he can save the campaign after what's occurred."

There remained forty-three ships rocking in the waves near Chebucto. Governor de La Jonquière's first orders brought as many of them as could fit into the harbor for protection, giving priority to the least seaworthy. Then he unloaded sick crews and troops.

It took two hours the next morning for the worst ill crewmen of *la Renommée* to take the launch to hospital tents ashore. Over fifty crewmen, a quarter of his crew, had died earlier from the disease or battle, and another fifty were still unfit for duty. Of all those in the fleet, Guy's warship had one of the highest mortality and illness rates of the epidemic.

The governor then arranged camps for the infirmed according to their health, and converted transports into hospital ships, and brought in food harvested by Acadians northwest of Chebucto.

Throughout September and early October, the Acadian villagers and Mi'kmaqs helped the stricken men and received goods in turn. The natives coveted and got wool blankets taken from the general stores. Tragically, the crews had used them, and the disease spread.

First, Mi'kmaq children sickened, and then the parents followed. The pandemic engulfed not only the natives, wiping out one-third of their population, but also the Acadians, and erased entire villages.

Although the governor still hoped to gather enough healthy men to make an attack somewhere, he received ominous information that a British fleet had sailed from England to attack them.

Eyes squinting and brows down, Governor de La Jonquière addressed his officers. "The sum of these troubling events means departing Chebucto without delay before being trapped here. My plan is to meet up with the Canadian forces and together capture Annapolis Royal."

Then he looked at Guy. "Captain de Kersaint, you will escort four troop transports to reinforce Québec. Upon arriving, you are then to return to France. Expect the enemy to be searching for you along the entire way."

At the end of October, Guy set out with the ships, slipping by many British patrols and arriving in Québec six days later.

Meanwhile, just southwest of Acadia, Governor de La Jonquière's fleet ran into another severe storm that scattered them and crushed the weakened spirits of the French. By the time they reassembled, too late for an attack, he abandoned the plans and sailed for France.

Leaving Québec, Guy, with an uncharacteristically dour expression, stood near the helm. "We can head out for Brest now. Set a course east, lieutenant."

"Yes, sir. It's a sad day," replied La Motte, downcast.

"It's pathetic the hopes of Versailles rested upon leaders who possessed so few talents for the task." Guy pulled his mouth into a grimace. "If we had Governor de La Jonquière in command from the first, Boston could be in ruins, and Louisbourg might again be ours. My years of experience lead me to think the king and his ministers won't realize their errors."

Poor conditions lasted throughout November as they plodded east. Just west off the French coast, a half-day from a friendly port, a thick enshrouding fog forced him again to slow. The obstacle demoralized him and his depleted crew, who were at last in home waters yet making rowboat speed. The captain set extra lookouts to avoid a collision or reefs. Soon after, they picked up the sounds of ships signaling one another in the gray mists with drums, and musket and cannon signals.

Guy said, "Lieutenant La Motte, I believe we're amid Governor de La Jonquière's fleet. Silence the men and go to quarters until we discover whom we've joined."

The lieutenant gave the order, and the men rushed on the ship's foggy deck, preparing weapons and going aloft, anxious and waiting to stand down.

Off the starboard side, a stern lantern glimmered. It approached closer in the gray. All eyes watched the darkened silhouette for a sign of the flag she carried. Then the shape on its staff turned blue with a red quarter. It was a British frigate. Everyone held their breath as the ship moved onward until, seconds later, the enemy drummed to quarters. Guy gave the command to fire.

The French iron volley did little to slow the foe's preparations to fight as Guy pulled away from the warship. In addition, the sound of cannons had alerted the rest to *la Renommée's* presence and location.

They converged on him from every direction. Defensive tactics proved tough enough in good seas, but in rough waves with dense fog, it turned hazardous.

As he maneuvered, Guy relied on sound and cannon flash to pinpoint their opponents, shooting at them to force them farther away. During the first two hours of the cat-and-mouse game, *la Renommée* suffered a mangling. Enemy hits reduced his crew, already sparse, beyond the point to man half the guns. He counted thirteen adversaries, from sloops up to third-rate ships of the line. They mauled his frigate, now out-gunned by multiples of ten. His men never once flinched from their duties nor asked to strike the flag.

For the next few hours, the trade of deadly metal continued. The French frigate's guns took a fierce toll on the foe, although for every iron ball that left her cannons, two or more returned from the surrounding ships. Soon, high seas and varied gusts forced the other warships away from *la Renommée*, losing her altogether in the dense shroud. Nevertheless, one frigate persisted in finding and attacking her.

The fight between the two grew fierce, and the French ship had the double handicap of too few sailors and dwindling ammunition. At one close approach, Guy, standing near the binnacle, crumpled as a musket ball tore through his leg, taking part of his thigh. Men rushed him below as *la Renommée* withdrew. The surgeon worked on his wound as Guy lay on his dining table. No laudanum remained to ease his suffering.

Guy looked down at the burning gouge in his leg and shuddered in pain. As the surgeon patched him, he reviewed the voyages to Acadia. Each effort to reach Louisbourg buckled, and this last, regardless of the hopes and support of the entire government, floundered miserably. He gave credit to the British, too, who played their strategies well, outnumbering or outmaneuvering them at each turn. Moreover, luck favored the enemy in every incident.

As the surgeon bandaged his thigh, Guy lay on his side, remembering no other time when all potential factors had turned against him. He wondered if Hashi Humma was right in calling his path cursed, predestined from now until the end to be inescapably disastrous. The beaming confidence that guided Guy throughout his career dimmed.

Since departing, he'd lost almost a third of his crew to battle and disease. *La Renommée*'s condition was pathetic, and supplies had dwindled to nothing. Although he loved commanding the frigate, he realized not one mission aboard her had succeeded. Perhaps old naval superstitions proved right, and he and the warship were just star-crossed. Rather than his crew suffering more for his wretched fate, he'd give in to the worst any commander imagines—to surrender.

The thought of such a defeated action crumbled his pride. Every accomplishment he'd had in life paled under the monumental darkness and weight of giving up the ship. His mind drifted from how other commanders would see him to whether his friends and family might feel ashamed of him.

Someone descending the stairs from the quarterdeck above reached his ears, and he lifted his head. It was La Motte. Both he and the surgeon helped Guy ease off the blood-covered table, and hop one-legged to his cot.

He winced, trying to lie down. Then Guy ordered all the officers to his cabin. When they gathered, he spoke with a weak voice and sad eyes.

"Men, we've fought as gallantly this day as we have throughout this entire cruise. We are out of round and dismantling shot, our mizzenmast is gone and the main topmast and half our yards are in the sea. Most of our topmen are lost, and our crew is decimated, leaving most of the cannon unmanned." Guy looked downward, wan-faced. "I can no longer captain the ship with my wound so severe, nor ask more of you. There is no dishonor if we should strike."

The somber expressions of his officers accompanied his solemn and spent voice. They held back, none wanting to agree, broken and defeated by their plight and his pronouncement. The silence lasted only ten seconds.

"Is that why you've called us here? In that case, I'm returning to my station." La Motte spoke up with steely resolve in his eyes. With that, he saluted Guy and went above to take command of the ship.

Guy gave a nod at his lieutenant's bravery as the other officers, their courage rekindled, joined La Motte at their stations to continue the struggle.

When the room emptied, Guy forced his attention away from his injury, hearing Marie's frequent warnings in his mind and thinking about Jeanne's ever-present fears for his safety. He'd received many a timber splinter puncture and strike to him, and once a pistol ball had grazed his shoulder. They seemed slight in comparison. This time he'd lost a great deal of blood, and the intensity of the pain grew every minute. He had no fear of it, but it reminded him of how closely each walks beside oblivion.

If Jeanne could see him, she'd break down and weep at his side, he imagined. He'd pat her head and try to calm her. She always displayed such sensitivity to the pains of others and their needs. On the contrary, if Marie stood in his cabin, she'd be pointing her finger at him with an

'I told you so.' They behaved differently, body and soul. Yet he held the same emotion for both: one old love from a life of familiarity, and the other, a love for the nurturing innocence of his children's mother.

His thoughts drifted to his children, and his brother Joseph as the noise of the fight above reached him. Then he pictured his father's face, proud of his accomplishments in the navy. Even he would have opted for conceding under such horrible circumstances.

Guy heard a loud crash and knew another yard had fallen to the deck. "One less sail," he mumbled to himself as his eyes closed.

∽

Lieutenant La Motte captained on the quarterdeck with de La Tour, his acting first lieutenant. He repeated the same tactics Guy had used and broke away from the frigate by nightfall.

La Motte continued eastward, so close to the coast of France, yet struggling to escape the trailing squadron. The tenacious British sought to take the smart sailor *la Renommée*. Word of her near the American colonies had spread even to England and made her a coveted target. The enemy persisted with searches in the dark throughout the moonless night and exchanged signals among their warships. The French frigate's crew proceeded in silence and listened in dread.

When the next turbid morning broke, the enemy frigate stood off by only a thousand yards. Again, they renewed exchanges. For hours, the cloudy banks continued to be their sole haven as they headed eastward. When bombarded, La Motte's grit and the crew's handling of what canvas they had left pulled them through the tempest of smashing heavy balls.

That afternoon, the sun started to burn away their refuge. Lieutenant La Motte relied on his nautical skills to avoid the frequent attempts to trap and engage him. When all the fog lifted, he saw only a few of the original thirteen ships still following them. From afar, a large 70-gun warship charged fast over the whitecaps, forcing *la Renommée* into quick course changes to keep from being overrun.

After two hours, the giant man-of-war finally loomed over the frigate. The immense beast cannonballed her and wounded more men than those injured earlier in all the clashes.

As the fighting continued, they were approaching the ninth hour against the enemy frigate and the ship of the line. The melee used up the rest of their ammunition, and nothing remained in the lockers to load into the cannons. La Motte ordered they use ballast in its place. The bits of pig iron, like using canisters, destroyed the foe's jibs and fore topsail in a close-quarters engagement.

Then the fast-approaching two-decker alone stood between them and flight from certain death. The small projectiles would be powerless against the behemoth's sides or spars, twice the size of the French craft. As the British closed again, the giant poured a broadside onto the frigate. The target of the enemy cannoneers was *la Renommée's* stern.

"Lieutenant La Motte?" said de La Tour as he sat on the quarterdeck after the blast. The young officer looked in horror at the rags where his arm had been, dribbling blood into a puddle on the deck. His face turned pale, and he swooned onto his side.

La Motte tied the man's stocking garter around the gushing stump and directed him to be carried to the surgeon. Then, within a minute, as he commanded the helmsman to avoid another such hit, he spun and fell to the deck. His wig and hat flew off ten feet away.

Dazed and confused, he mumbled, "Where's my hat?" It lay across from him, the top missing. Then the penetrating pain of a stabbing, white-hot poker seared the left side of his face. The wound brought him to full consciousness as he kneeled. Reaching up, he could feel soft, open flesh, and his hand dripped wet with red. A cadet rushed up the stairs to the quarterdeck and grabbed him, mouth agape.

"Something hit me," La Motte muttered as he tried to clear his head and rise to his feet.

"Yes, sir. It's taken away part of your cheek and cheekbone, too." The cadet's eyes opened wide. "Come below to the surgeon. I'll help you."

"No! You're in command until I return. Keep us with the wind!" he ordered to the cadet, the gash burning like coals.

La Motte, reeling, stumbled below, pressing his face together to stop the bleeding. The surgeon quickly stitched his flesh and bandaged his face. Patched up, he scrabbled back to the quarterdeck.

The intense throbbing impeded his concentration, yet he forced his mind onto the enemy warship and called command after command as the course changes kept the assailant at bay. Every word he spoke caused torment that resonated in his head.

With the French coast only miles away and the fort in the harbor of Port-Louis in view, La Motte didn't let the injury distract him. As the ship ran on, the 70-gun closed, blocking the path to the frigate's deliverance.

"Closer to shore," Lieutenant La Motte ordered the helmsman. "We'll ground the bastard before she can stop us!"

Before long, the big warship came a hundred yards upon *la Renommée*'s portside. A fearsome burst took away the mainmast, which pulled the damaged fore-topmast into the sea with it. The floating wreckage dragged the ship in an arc, slowing her as the remaining crew chopped at the cables and lines to free her.

The French frigate now carried her lone foresail, and that hung in shreds. To survive, she had to avoid any more broadsides. Ahead of her, the 70-gun prepared to come about to end the fight.

The monster, though, didn't turn. The changing wind hit her head-on and against her sails. La Motte shouted, "She's in irons!" His foresail caught a fresh light breeze as the enemy came to a standstill.

The frigate moved turtle-slow as the ship of the line threw a few shots at her. Then the varying wind billowed *la Renommée*'s foresail enough to run. With it full, she made steady but sluggish progress toward the distant sanctuary.

The harbor lay still a mile away, and the enormous warship again caught a breeze, once more gaining on *la Renommée*. Guns flamed but overshot the fleeing frigate.

Fifteen minutes later, with *la Renommée* within the grasp of the enemy warship's cannons, Port-Louis's fort batteries began roaring. None learned the skills of the fort's gunners. The British two-decker, content with the damage it dealt and fearing the shore-side defenses, withdrew from the dismasted frigate and headed out from the coast.

La Renommée limped into the quiet bay outside Port-Louis and glided up the river toward the docks. Their 36-hour ordeal finally ended. From the towns along the shore, Guy, still below and in agony, counted the church bells ring six o'clock. The tolls replaced the boom of cannons and reminded the crew of the friends they lost in the last struggle for home. They had arrived, now safe from the perils of the expedition to Louisbourg.

When the frigate moored, astonished onlookers gaped at the battered and demolished warship, wondering what horrible scenario had caused so much damage. Within half an hour, military officers who heard of *la Renommée's* return rushed to La Motte on deck.

"Was d'Anville's fleet successful?" they demanded to know. "Is Louisbourg French again?" "Did Annapolis Royal fall?" "Is Boston in flames?"

La Motte couldn't believe the questions. That seemed so long ago, he thought between pangs. Surely they've learned of the mission's disastrous result by now. He explained to them, in an abbreviated fashion, the sad tale of the fleet. They stood dumbfounded.

"How can this be?" officers queried Lieutenant La Motte. Not a man among them believed the fate of such a powerful, strategic undertaking could end in a fiasco.

Later that day at the hospital, Guy dispatched a report to the naval intendant that unfolded the catastrophic events. In the account, he cited, to his best estimates, three thousand men died from the epidemic after the fleet left France. *La Renommée* alone had lost thirty percent of her crew to illness and combat.

Within six days, Guy's description of the disaster shook Paris. It was the first news of the campaign. King Louis and Maurepas grieved over Duc d'Anville and despaired over the tragic outcome. The government spent five million livres on the operation when the fleet sailed. But the final total was closer to sixteen million when adding the loss of so many ships and supplies, not ignoring the massive tally of dead sailors and soldiers. Inflicting further injury to France's prestige and treasury, the effort protected Canada little more than before they departed.

Eleven days after *la Renommée* landed, more arrived. Now fourteen of the fleet were in Port-Louis. The number of ill seamen and troops filled the hospitals. The same occurred in Brest and La Rochelle with the ships that made it past the enemy patrols. Weeks later, the remaining ones, those not sunk, burned, or captured, found refuge in coastal ports.

Their return wasn't the end of the disaster's trials and costs. The navy needed to repair damaged ships, replace lost warships, and heal the sick crews. Civilian women and nuns in the towns formed groups to help the surgeons with their overwhelming tasks. Dockworkers and shipwrights joined in the monumental chore of restoring the vessels, and *la Renommée* anchored in Lorient for repairs.

Weeks later, Guy sat in a chair with his leg propped up on a stool in the hospital. He read an article in a newspaper on the political scene in Paris. The Admiralty at Versailles claimed they had accounted for nearly every vessel except one. Furthermore, they stated the entire cause of the catastrophe was a natural phenomenon and out of their hands. Minister Maurepas dismissed accusations against the navy in the paper. *When the elements command, they can easily diminish the glory, but not the deeds or merits of the chiefs.*

Guy sighed when he finished reading. They ignored the poor coordination of the suppliers and the terrible food quality, and they delayed launching the mission more than once, he reflected. Nor did the Admiralty admit to overcrowding the transports that promoted the disease spreading, or appointing unqualified leaders, and leaving far too late to accomplish their goals. Not one mentioned the entire venture would have been unnecessary if the king provided for a decent squadron on either of the earlier missions.

Guy, still recovering, took leave of *la Renommée*, and with Jeanne rode their coach back home to Cléder. His injured leg stretched out across the seat, the bandages making an enormous bulge on the outer thigh of his breeches. Jeanne stared at the wound for a few moments and peered through the carriage window.

"I know, my dear. It looks much worse, though, than it is," he chortled at her concern. "I lost just a little flesh." Before marrying, combat wounded him many times. Normally, he regarded them as slight nuisances, merely reef scrapes on a hull. This one concerned him. He might have lost a leg, or worse.

Jeanne stared at him, unblinking. "The admiral died and thousands perished of disease, in storms and battle." Her gaze went to the scenery again. "The voyage could have killed you."

"What difference if at sea or tilling a field and dying of an infected toe?" He tried to laugh away her distress.

"The risk, my dear husband," Jeanne answered. "In peace or onshore, there's less chance of injury, and less worry for wives." Her eyes drooped, teary.

"They told me before I left the hospital that they're transferring me to another warship while mine is in overhaul," he said, voice saddened. "If it eases your fears, I'll do whatever I must to be placed on a bigger one. La Renommée, as fine a frigate as she is, has met her share of miserable fortune since I've been on her. I've often wondered if I'm her bane. She needs a new master to change her luck as much as I need a new ship."

The thought of leaving the frigate brought him to near tears as he stared down at his wound. It was a surrender of his ship, not to the enemy, but to fate. In Brest, designers used her as a prototype for newer ones, such was her success as the fastest and most worthy warship. His *la Renommée*, Goddess of Fame, he considered the best he'd commanded, whose reputation spread even among the enemy. To leave her without at least one successful mission, he deemed, tarnished his nautical career. Still, whether it be the timing, circumstances, or luck, captaining her had come to an end, and he'd try to forget the tragedies of her voyages.

―――

By February, Guy was in command of his new warship, *l'Alcide*, satisfying Jeanne. *L'Alcide* was a 64-gun ship of the line. He'd cruise with other big ships and seldom encounter the solo perils faced on the fast *la Renommée*, he told her.

A glow spread across his face when he entered their salon in Brest. "The navy has made me a *capitaine de vaisseau*." His hand raised high the document to Jeanne.

"Oh, that's wonderful." She stood from darning stockings and hugged him. "No doubt you are fast becoming one of their favorite commanders."

"Yes, after two years of horrible missions to Louisbourg, they've rewarded me for my pains." He stroked his healing thigh.

"There was a note from Versailles, too, that praised my performance off Acadia and defying capture while returning to France." Guy smiled. "I first believed they were going to send me back there."

Jeanne interrupted him. "No! You can't go again," she pleaded with a frozen stare.

"No, I'm not." He patted her shoulder. "The king wants to protect Québec and has stopped trying to retake the citadel. In either case, my next assignment is a convoy to Saint-Domingue with two other ships of the line, and at least 150 merchantmen." The very thought of those warm seas and sunny skies pleased him.

A week later, *l'Alcide* shipped off with the large fleet westward and made port in the islands the same month. The voyage was peaceful and fast, with few men dying of disease.

When they put into Petit-Goâve, the ships replenished their water and supplies while new trading vessels gathered for the return to France. But upon hearing of British patrols trying to intercept them off the coast, they postponed leaving.

Guy discovered that de Santec, now captaining the frigate *l'Etoile*, harbored on the southern coast of Saint-Domingue, waited to join Guy's convoy. Regrettably, to avoid encountering enemy patrols, de Santec's squadron commander ordered him to leave at once for France as a separate unit.

Soon afterward, Guy's fleet left and in mid-June, the convoy passed Acadia and the worrisome Grand Banks, and headed east toward France. When drawing near the Bay of Biscay, a broad, dark storm coming from the northeast pushed them much further south, where a large British squadron sped to intercept them. They fled eastward as Guy and the other two French ships of the line positioned themselves in the rear to fight off the enemy. But by nightfall, their pursuers failed to catch up to them.

The morning brought sounds of cannon in the distance, as those merchantmen who had separated or lagged fell to the foe. When Guy's convoy entered Brest's protective outer bays and berthed, they soon learned many of the trading ships, which had separated from the group in the storm, had not made it home.

Later, he sat waiting to meet with the commandant, who had asked him to come for new orders. A tall officer striding out of an adjoining office walked past without recognizing him and then stopped to take a second look.

"People told me you returned from Saint-Domingue," said François, his face older but as genuine as ever.

"Ah, François." Guy stood with a smile. "Yes, the voyage proceeded well, although we lost some of the convoy near Cape Ortegal. Others are still making their way here."

"Glad you're safe. I wanted to tell you I took command of *la Renommée* a few months back. The few cruises we've completed showed her to be, as you said, fast, wet, and often crank. Still, I'd have no other." François grinned widely.

"Regardless if I miss the frigate, I don't miss her missions." Guy held up his hand and shook his head. "Pardon the damage I put on her."

"No need, since I've made holes in her, too." François pointed to himself and chuckled. "We have to careen her. That's why I'm in port. She's been leaking from our patches, too. So, how are Jeanne and the children?"

"My dear wife's healthy and with child," Guy replied as he proudly looped his thumbs in his waistcoat pockets. "Today, she'll join me in town. Is your wife coming to Brest?"

"Not if she can help it. She hates Brest and would rather stay at the manor. We just had our fifth baby, another girl," said François and shrugged.

"Congratulations. Be happy your wife isn't here. To see what our ships look like when we bring them back doesn't allay their worries. God, it horrifies me sometimes. Have you gotten any letters from Marie?"

"I received one months ago, and she complained about Emile being away again. He's been coming to Brest more, she wrote. Perhaps we'll run into him here. Have you spoken to her lately?"

Guy dangled his head. "I haven't seen her for two years or read a post from her in a long time. I must pay her sister a visit."

The captains talked for a few minutes longer before Guy left to go into the commandant's office. De Camilly was waiting for him, writing at his desk. He stood for a moment until de Camilly looked up from his paperwork. Saying nothing, he motioned for the captain to sit in one of the plain wooden chairs that faced him.

When the commandant put his quill in the holder, he looked up at Guy. "How did the trip go? I understand we lost a good number to the patrols." His face appeared tired. "In your report, be sure to include the number and ratings of the British ships you encountered." De Camilly sat with shoulders hunched, looking drained of spirit.

He went on. "Our navy hasn't the strength the British have, I'm afraid. They have us bottled up in our ports. Even our convoys aren't safe, outnumbered in guns three or four to one. It's coming to where we can't send anyone out. If it gets worse, we may lose our colonies." De Camilly stared blankly at a map on the wall. "The latest convoy loss to the British has convinced the king our warships are ineffectual."

"*Latest?*" Guy questioned, his stare intense.

"Yes, didn't you hear? The enemy captured the convoy that left from southern Saint-Domingue just before yours. None of them escaped."

Guy's throat tightened. "And *l'Etoile*, sir? Did the British destroy or take her?"

"Not sunk, burned to prevent capture off Cape Ortegal with most of her crew escaping." His nostrils flared.

"Captain de Santec, also?" Guy's heart raced.

De Camilly, his face downturned, replied, "That's why the king has so little faith in us, so many of our commanders are gone. Captain de Santec died in the action earlier."

Guy's forehead felt cold, and he placed his hands on the commander's desk, eyes unfocused.

"You knew him?" he asked, raising his brow.

Guy barely got the words out. "Y-yes, sir, he was a close friend."

The commandant swayed his head. "You have my sympathy. I'm afraid we will lose many friends before this is over. I think the king feels as hopeless but is bowing out on trying to wage a sea war against the British. We have one more chance to change his mind about our effectiveness in fighting. That's why I've asked you to come today. King

Louis and Maurepas requested you for this next mission."

Later, Guy left the office in a stupor, trudging home along the stone block quay. He tried to recall the last time he saw de Santec, what he said, and how his friend's voice sounded. As he replayed their history together, he remembered how de Santec had guided and changed him for the better since the first day at sea. From training an obnoxious cadet to be a commander to counseling his futile longings for Marie. He encouraged him and steered him into marrying Jeanne. His friend had been more than a naval tutor or comrade-in-arms, he'd been his mentor in life and muse in love.

Over the next four days, he had frequent meetings with de Camilly. After finishing the last of the briefings in Brest, he dashed a note off to Jeanne to come from Cléder.

Later that week, Guy found the family coach parked outside with servants unloading luggage from it. When he entered the bedroom, Jeanne sat arranging her jewelry case.

They soon were discussing news about what had occurred over the past few months, what the children had done, and how his voyage had gone. His tanned skin and cheerful demeanor at once showed her this mission ended well for him.

"So, my dear, the cruise was very successful, and there was no reason to worry. Even when attacked, we held them at bay and I lost few men to it." He said nothing about de Santec.

Jeanne's fingers fiddled with her earrings, and then she forced a small smile.

Guy had brought back for her an expensive gold and emerald necklace from Saint-Domingue and surprised her with it. He made her close her eyes as he hung it around her neck and fixed the clasp.

"It's beautiful, dear!" she said, turning to him. "I'll put it on for the coming ball."

"It won't be the jewelry that makes the other ladies envious. You're still the beauty I married so long ago." He stroked her shoulders.

"Not envy, but jealousy. It is not what I wear, nor looks, but who I wed." Her soft gaze up at him spoke more.

The words warmed him. Guy understood the need for her to make social connections and he no longer objected to the elegant affairs. The balls offered splendid opportunities to learn more about the war from fellow officers.

Before the day turned dark, he braced himself to tell her of de Santec's death, to whom she'd grown close. When he did, she wept for almost an hour, recounting his visits between sobs.

As he waited for them to resupply his ship, Guy spent days searching for captains who had been where De Camilly planned to send him on his next assignment. He sought what to expect about the currents, winds, officials, and people of the region.

In early October, the navy held another social event. Guy put on his uniform and Jeanne, her newest gown. At the ball, they danced and made conversation with other guests. Jeanne overheard the most recent gossip of who romanced whom while he heeded the military and political talk.

"I didn't know La Bourdonnais had arrived back in Paris from Île de France," he mentioned to Jeanne when they finished a dance. "Very interesting."

"Who?" Jeanne looked puzzled, unfamiliar with the man's name.

"One of two governors of our colonies in India. La Bourdonnais was governor of Île de France, an island east of Madagascar. And Dupleix is the governor of Pondichéry, an eastern province in India.

"Tonight, I learned Dupleix conspired with the French East India Company and others to force La Bourdonnais to return to defend himself against unfounded accusations. Dupleix, who's vain and cunning, wants to be the single governor in India. When La Bourdonnais returned to stand up for himself, the king snubbed him, or may even have jailed him. No one knows."

"More political conniving." Jeanne rolled her eyes.

"Much more. La Bourdonnais is an honorable, intelligent man dedicated to the country. It's so unfair he must suffer the results of another's greed. Dupleix is even building a city named for himself."

Someone tapped on Guy's arm. "Captain de Kersaint, have you heard?" It was La Motte, now also a captain.

"Ah, Captain La Motte!" Guy said, bowing his head to his former lieutenant. "What?"

His friend gestured with his hands as he talked. "Captain François de Saint-Alouarn is a British prisoner!"

"When?! How?"

"At the end of September in the Bay of Biscay."

Guy wagged his head. "That happened just after I last saw him."

"François commanded *la Renommée*, carrying Monsieur de Conflans, the new governor of Saint-Domingue, to his post when three warships intercepted him. He fought them for two days, though." La Motte shook a fist.

A discussion ensued about how the British were disrupting and capturing everything they sent to sea. Guy, like De Camilly, feared France's possessions were in great jeopardy. De Santec's death and the capture of François left Guy and Jeanne nettled. As the night wore on, they left before the last dance.

On the way to their house, he lamented over François's imprisonment and losing *la Renommée*. Although she regretted François's new status, she yawned and ignored Guy's long monologue on how the British might copy the lines of the frigate to make faster warships. Jeanne said, "Oh, I see," at the right times and let her mind drift to other interests and her swollen ankles, pregnant once again.

The baby was due in November, and although she was well-prepared and experienced, Guy feared missing the birth while asea.

Before leaving for his next assignment, he received a long-overdue letter from Marie.

> *My Dearest Beloved Guy,*
> *I fear I have troubling news to relate concerning Émile's business ventures. The Intendant of the Navy in Brest has summoned him to a second hearing to investigate for fraud. Apparently, the timber he sold in Brest was not to their standards, and he is suspect. I cannot see how they should accuse him of such malfeasance since he bought the masts from other suppliers and the navy approved the sale after inspecting it. I'm certain it will pass and they will vindicate him of any crime or wrongs. Émile is not concerned over the matter and stated the navy often holds these investigations*

> *to make sure the suppliers and chandlers sell high-quality goods. Also, he reported that the buyer whom we first met at the naval yards, Monsieur Chatroen, has pleaded guilty to accepting bribes and they will sentence him soon. The dear old man was my father's friend and all spoke highly of him. Émile said he was so very near superannuation. It is a great shame he is now to lose everything by not having fulfilled his duties with integrity.*

The letter mentioned other matters, including how her sister Charlotte's family was nearly destitute, relying on Marie and Émile for income. But Marie and Émile's predicament appeared to be more serious. Guy pictured the outcome with Émile slumped over an oar, condemned to a slow death aboard a Mediterranean galley, or shut up in a dark dungeon for life.

A week later, Charlotte received a bank transfer of fifty livres from an unnamed friend. Guy told no one, whereas helping Marie and Émile might prove to be a bigger problem.

The sunny summer days sped by as he prepared for his next undertaking. Guy told Jeanne it would be much longer than even the earlier Louisbourg campaigns.

"No, my dear," he said in bed one night. "You know I can't say where or why. I'll write to you once I'm there. So stop asking," he grumbled, pulling a coverlet up to his neck and pretending to snore.

"I shall worry more, not knowing, and won't tell anyone." Jeanne sat up and crossed her arms.

"Don't put that on me. I feel guilty enough."

"Give me just a little clue?"

Guy rolled over in bed. "Very well." He paused, thought, and then chuckled. "Ship me to any isle of France or port, Louis, the King, wants me to sail to. Now let me sleep." He believed the vague clue should stump her for days, or at least until he left.

"What? That's it? You'll follow orders? That doesn't tell me where," she said, brows knitted.

"Study, analyze, and dissect. You're a clever girl." He closed his eyes and soon snored for real as he lay beside her.

Sometime later, after repeating and rearranging the words, she laughed as she finally understood his riddle.

She spoke her answer aloud. "The king wants me to sail to Port Louis in *Île de France*. Aha! That's why he was so interested in Dupleix and La Bourdonnais. He's going to India." Satisfied and smug, she fell asleep.

The Indian Ocean and Alexandre, 1748-1750

Brest's shipyard intendant, Émile feared, had singled him out. The rules of trade called for permissive discretion, not intense scrutiny, he repeated to himself. If the navy continued such policies, the entire supplier's interchange with the government might crash to a halt. Everyone played the game.

Émile had returned to Brest to argue a defense for the timber shipments he sold. First, though, he found the prison where they held Pierre Chatroen to discover if the jailed stores supervisor told them about the bribes.

Émile, with a worried expression, approached the thin and haggard Chatroen leaning against the iron-gated yard in Recouvrance. "Pierre, you look well."

"Strange, I don't feel so." Chatroen's gaunt face had grown older since Émile last saw him. His hand lifted to the side of his wrinkled brow. "My life is finished, Émile. Decades of work come to this. It seemed so easy, though, and kept growing until out of control." His head bent low, and his hands again gripped the bars.

"Yes, I know. Maybe you can plea for a pardon. When every supplier or officer is taking or giving enticements, it's unjust to punish you. Perhaps someone else would take a bribe to save you from this mess," Émile said.

Chatroen raised his eyes, bank-faced. "Émile, I've known you for many years now. And I've always enjoyed your company, in part because you're so damn optimistic. But now, I must tell you, you're a fool. You revel in the game but ignore the consequences. To subvert honesty, one can lose far more than one wins. Riches pale to the important things in life." He turned and walked away.

Émile called after the man. "But did you mention our arrangement?"

As he continued walking, Chatroen turned with a disgusted smirk. "Of course not."

Émile neither understood what he said to upset him nor grasped what Chatroen meant, since craftiness got things done.

The next day, he appeared before the naval hearing to defend the quality of the timbers. He claimed most were prime growth sawn in Poland and Sweden. After eloquent denials of wrongdoing, he showed certificates of receipt and records to verify the highest standards of his lumber.

The board then questioned him about bribing government agents, but had no proof, nevertheless they suspected it. Émile, in a convincing tone of sincerity, denied any graft.

In a last appeal, he paraded before the officers. "The commissar, clerks, and shipwrights approved the logs after delivery. In addition, I have the supply certificates for them." Émile returned to sit with his head high, certain his half-hour-long oratory had proven his innocence.

Then a captain rose. "That may be true. Yet, the navy based the initial assessments on grade markings embossed on each spar and a cursory inspection of the surfaces. Once carpenters classified them according to our three categories at the shipyard, incompatibilities arose between the grades as marked and their genuine quality. Their actual value emerged far below the brackers' ratings."

Émile popped his eyes and pulled his head back, looking shocked. "The various lumbermen determined the grade markings for each before

I received them. Sirs, you cannot hold me responsible for embossings I did not make!"

"We believe that is exactly the point, Monsieur Gardinier," said the officer. "We cannot hold you responsible for any you did not make, but you *are* responsible for any you embossed fraudulently. The wood came from a number of sources, yet we found all misclassified. That seems unlikely."

Unknown to him, they had summoned another to testify. They called next, an old fellow bent with age, whom Émile recognized in an instant. It was his clerk, Alexandre.

"Please tell us your name and employer," asked the officer.

"Alexandre Moreau. I work for Monsieur Gardinier," he answered without looking at Émile.

"Monsieur Moreau, can you establish if the records in this ledger are the authentic transactions of your employer? Do they look factual?"

Alexandre walked over to the book and paged through it. After a few minutes, he stopped and returned to his seat. "Those are not my entries for the timber contracts."

Dismay showed on Émile's face.

"How do you know this is not the actual merchandise sales tally, Monsieur Moreau?"

"This is not my handwriting. Also, I use a heavier quill nib for entering figures in the debit column. It's an older style of flagging them no one uses anymore."

"Perhaps it's an exact copy of the legitimate ledger?" another asked.

"No, I've kept records for forty-five years the same way. That's fraudulent," he said with a blank face. "Besides, the lumber my employer sold to the navy didn't come from Poland or Sweden nor Russia as these note. I'm sure of it. I entered the original sources. Someone changed the countries and has scribed brackers' marks from the timbers that are false. Both the shipping ports and grade embossing are fabrications."

"How so?" asked an official with slit eyes.

Rising and going back to the table, Alexandre pointed to lines in the entries. "Well, this batch of spars is marked coming from Danzig, which uses a *K* to mean their finest class. We received none that high in the batches, not even a lower *B* quality. The highest we sold would be a *BB* from Danzig. In any event, none arrived from Danzig at all, so these grades and suppliers are fiction. I checked the real invoices myself."

"Alexandre, that's your ledger," said Émile, interrupting as his livelihood collapsed before him. "Why are you saying these things?" His hands and upper lip were moist.

The elderly employee faced him. "Why indeed?" whispered Alexandre to himself, then raised his voice with conviction. "I will not falsify my testimony or compromise my integrity as an honest man to save you, Monsieur Gardinier! For years, I have watched you manipulate people and facts to please yourself and line your pocket. Your disregard for the welfare of employees who might otherwise be loyal to you is loathsome. Your abuse of business ethics is equally so!"

"Are you implying that I didn't treat you kindly?" The treachery and ingratitude enraged Émile. His face turned red.

The officers watched on in smug delight as Alexandre lowered his voice and spoke in a dispassionate cadence. "Kindly? For over eight years, I was a fixture of no greater value than my labor. Your father traded me to you without even asking me. No better than a horse. Do you know my wife's name or anything about my family? Your wife Marie does, bless her. Have you ever asked how they are, living on my paltry salary? To earn respect, it takes more. You will see me no more upon the stool, Monsieur Gardinier."

Émile sat with his mouth agape. The old man had summarized their entire relationship in seconds. He had no rebuttal when confronted with such naked truth.

The board excused Émile while they discussed the matter and after ten minutes, called him back into the room.

"Monsieur Gardinier, you presented falsified records and evidence of changed ratings with false embosses. The commission agrees to a man that the Navy strip you of the military vendor's license. Furthermore, we demand full reimbursement of the monies paid to you for the spars.

"If restitution is not met in three months, by January, the board will recommend taking legal proceedings against you under a charge of defrauding the king's navy. Consider the options with care, Monsieur

Gardinier. This hearing of the General Commissioner is now concluded."

One word echoed in Émile's mind until searing deep into his conscience—*ruin*. He tried to estimate it. To pay the sum back, forced the sale of everything he owned: the warehouse, inventories, and even his house. He'd be homeless with nothing left to restart a business.

The shock blocked all other thoughts. True to his unorthodox nature, a wicked idea crept into his mind. He would sell everything and flee with his family. Since he spoke a little English, they could sneak out of the country to England. French law didn't apply there. He could scrape enough together to start a small chandlery and begin over again. Certainly, it was the best road to take, he decided.

⁓

Marie hadn't expected Émile to spend so much time in Brest. Something was wrong. The night he arrived home, she confronted him at his desk. "Did the board release you from the suspicions?"

"Marie, you needn't worry. I've made plans that will take care of us. There'll be no problems about me going to prison." Émile bobbed his head with confidence.

"What did the naval inquiry say? Answer my question!" she shouted, glaring.

"As I said, you needn't fear," he said with a weak voice, avoiding her stare. "The navy decided to just fine me and the issue is done."

"How much do they want?" Her firm glare demanded answers.

"Well, we may need to move. Everything is unsettled at the moment. You know how complicated things are. I'll check my books, my holdings, and the values. It's complicated, very complicated."

Marie's stare hardened. "What do you mean, *move?*" Standing over him with hands on hips, her look pierced his composed façade. "Dear, I've known you long enough to see when you're hiding something. Out with it!"

Émile shook his head as he looked down, ears crimson.

The words dropped like lead out of his trembling mouth. "The navy has me by the neck. It … it'll come out, eventually. The fine is so large that if I sold all we owned, I can't cover it. The profit of the spar sales paid for the house and increased taxes."

His head still hung as he continued and explained how he had swindled the navy.

Marie said nothing as she listened. Her face reddened with a slit of a mouth drawn across it. Then she turned away and her fingers went to her brow. "In other words, you lied on your holdings to get more for the promissory notes to buy more spars. Much more than what your assets were worth. Then you bribed the navy buyer, sold the below-standard ones to them, and used the money to pay off the bank loans and the house. Now the navy wants their payment back, and we don't own enough to sell to refund them?" Marie placed her hand over her eyes, sick inside.

"Exactly. Similar transactions occur as the norm. The navy rejecting the timbers upsets the routine. I'm one of many chandlers who manipulate account balances the same way to keep commerce flowing between suppliers and the government." His head lifted, and he smirked. "They should give us medals for the creative ways they force merchants to supply them."

"Medals?" Marie's hands knotted into tight fists. "You lied to the note backers, bribed an official, tried to cheat the navy, and lost what we've been building—including my inheritance. And you deserve a medal?!"

Émile looked away, holding up a palm. "Wait. We can still keep almost all we have," he stammered. "By the end of the week, I'll figure out how to sell everything. Then we'll resettle in England and start over there. In Le Havre, I know enough ship owners and traders to find passage for us out of France."

"Oh, Émile." Marie closed her eyes, shaking her head. "Now you want us to run away from your crimes. Should we become criminals like you? How low you've sunk."

"No, not criminals, but a family fleeing injustice," he answered, voice quaking. "Can't you see how unfair it is? The whole interchange works because using bribes and being clever are the underpinnings of trade, the skeleton of the beast. I only used methods every other supplier uses. For them to single me out is hypocrisy!"

"Émile, don't beg us to escape with you. If we lose everything because of your errors and misjudgments, then that's our plight. I cannot forsake France as a criminal, my homeland, whether or not the system is unjust." Tears dropped as she scanned the forfeited furnishings in her house.

"Well, I can't go. No, I will *not* go to prison. It's unlikely we can pay off the debt. We don't own enough. If I'm short of the fee, they'll try me for fraud and imprison me for life. Which is better? If we stay in France, I'll be a criminal and in jail; if we flee to England, I'll be a criminal yet still free."

Marie considered his point. If he couldn't fulfill the demands, they'd imprisoned him. Émile wasn't a man who'd last long among felons. If another prisoner didn't kill him, the terrible conditions of being locked up might. Marie wondered if she acted selfishly in forcing him and her children to abide and suffer for her standards. In addition, how could they survive if he didn't provide for them? She had no actual skills to gain employment.

She wiped her cheeks and replied, "Émile, I need time to think."

"Dear, I've studied the goddamn problem upside down and backward to forward. There is no other way. We must leave France!" Rubbing his glowing face, he slumped in the chair.

"No, wait! Allow me a bit to go over it," Marie said. "I have to give thought to my future and the children's."

"Fine!" Émile slammed the ledger shut.

Marie had always known his principles in commerce were shaded, although she attributed it not to his personal morals but to the work ethic his father forced upon him. The bribery didn't bother her. But never had she envisioned he'd try to defraud the government.

"Can't your father help? If we sold everything and borrowed the rest from him?"

His head made an almost imperceptible nod. "Yes, I've debated that idea, too. I dread approaching him with the problem. Father owns enough and might have extra to loan. Tomorrow I'll call on him and explain what happened."

The next afternoon, he trudged over to see his father and related the sad story. The old man listened silently until Émile finished.

"Why did you over-value the promissory notes? Didn't I tell you years ago never to risk falsifying assets to borrow more in such deals, but to lower costs? If you had bartered as a good businessman should, you could have brought down the suppliers' prices," he scolded Émile.

"The navy contract was a rush. I couldn't be patient or haggle," Émile said, his hands wringing. "The errors are in the past now. Can you lend me funds to stay out of prison?"

His father snorted and looked away. "Do I have the money? Yes, you know I do. The question is: may I give it to you?" His face scowled. "That depends on your older brother. Since I shall be dead by the time you pay this loan back, it's fitting you ask the person who'd inherit it. If Edouard approves, I shall."

"That's fair. I'll talk to him tonight." Émile left in a hurry for his brother's home, arriving just before dinnertime.

Edouard met him in the foyer. "Émile, let's talk in the library." His brother lowered a brow. "You're in trouble with the navy?"

"So, you've heard about the investigation?" asked Émile, again blood coloring his face. "I must pay them back the money. I need your approval for Father to lend it to me."

"That's grim." Edouard rocked his head. "But now what's grim becomes ghastly. This week Father let me look at his records. I saw what you've done, my dear brother. You've taken tens of loans over the years from him. Far more than you'd inherit—my money! Not once mentioning it to me, the one who should get it by rights. Father was so easy to mine for gold, wasn't he? And now you ask for more?" Edouard's eyes narrowed. "Not a sou. No, not a sou."

"It's true. But this is different." Émile's head dropped. "Brother, please, I'm desperate. If not for me, have pity on Marie and the children!"

Edouard sneered and replied in a low tone. "For years, you've flaunted your success in business as of your own making. When, in fact, my inheritance provided for your home and supported your dealings, all without my approval. You be damned. Get out!" In a flash, Edouard grabbed his arm and led him to the front door.

"Edouard, please!"

Edouard closed his eyes. "Go! Your thievery has stricken me to the marrow."

When Émile got home, he sat with Marie. "Neither my brother nor father can help us. They have no spare cash and have unexpected debts themselves."

Marie, again near tears, answered, "That seems odd. Both were doing so well. Did your cheating make them mad?"

Émile threw up his hands. "I don't understand it myself. They showed no signs of being upset with my dealings." He glanced sideways at her. "It must be true they're having hard times, too, or they'd help."

"Then we'll sell what we can and beg the navy to wait for the rest," Marie said, sighing.

By the middle of December, Émile sold his inventory and wrapped up his other finances, including selling the house, shop, and warehouse.

The family moved into a small three-room apartment further south in the city. Besides the navy debt, he kept enough to carry them through until he could find work.

In late December, Émile bought a cheap ride to Brest, and after paying most of the fine money, he pleaded for time to pay the remainder. The officers threatened him with the harsher charge and demanded all the funds. When he replied with a shake of his head, the commissioner stood up and said, "Well, monsieur, you've given us most of the money. We will not place a charge of fraud against you, but expect the remainder. If not, the courts will force it from you."

Two weeks later, Marie spied him from the kitchen window of their apartment as he dragged himself home after the meeting. "My God, Émile, you look exhausted and starved!"

"I'm both, and much more. The navy refused to lower the fine or an extension." His eyes turned downward, dark rings shadowing them.

Marie pointed to the children sitting on the floor, playing. "No matter what happens, we will love you. This setback may only be temporary. We'll figure out some way to keep you free."

Marie had written to Guy about Émile and told him everything, hoping he might feel pity and help. She didn't know where he was, nor learned of the voyage to India.

Ten days passed and a uniformed man, escorted by a very heavy soldier with a musket, came and spoke to Émile as he handed him a summons. "Monsieur Gardinier, I'm here to inform you to attend a hearing on January 3rd at 2 o'clock. The Royal Navy has pressed for the amount you owe and is taking you to court."

Émile nodded without replying. They'd sold off the furniture, pottery and better clothing, and almost all of their belongings, except for necessities, but were hundreds of livres short. They were bankrupt.

When the court date came, Émile and Marie plodded to the session, wondering what verdict lay ahead. The judges ignored his pleas and demanded the full balance.

At the end of the trial, lasting less than fifteen minutes, he received a sentence of *par corps*. He would stay jailed until he, or someone, paid the debt. As a bailiff pulled him away, Émile heard Marie sobbing in the gallery. Guards hauled him to the Conciergerie, an old prison near the Seine, across from the palaces and close to Notre Dame Cathedral.

That evening, Marie walked to Edouard's to plead for money. When she arrived, her brother-in-law acted distant and aloof. After ten minutes, Marie's tears convinced him to support his nieces and nephew, and he gave her enough to buy food for the winter.

"What about your brother?" she asked with moist eyelids. "Don't allow Émile to die in debtor's prison."

"It might be good for him to live with his kind for a while. Émile is just like our father. A month or two in confinement should teach him how to be honest in business affairs," Edouard snapped. "But don't worry, I'll pay his debt in time."

"He's not capable of living with those cutthroats!"

Edouard glared at her, fuming. "Marie, you're not aware of the half of it! Émile spent far more than he earned! For years, he borrowed from Father. Where do you think he got the money to buy and furnish your house? He even wheedled more to dress you in gowns for the plays and for the children's schooling. Father always indulged and coddled him. How much did my brother pilfer that belonged to me as my inheritance? Hundreds? Thousands? Who knows? That's gone, and he's asking for more handouts." He curled his lip and crossed his arms.

Marie listened, stunned, her eyes glazed. The fact he did it was shocking, but that he never confessed it to her hurt deeper. Émile always kept his business dealings secret, and she resented it. The scandalous practices to get the navy contracts had enraged her, but worse, he had deceived her.

Paled, she excused herself and faltered out of her brother-in-law's house. After dissecting it all on her way home, she ground her teeth. Émile had fooled her into believing in his vending skills when most of their money came from his father. Even so, she loved him. She had tried everything to keep him from prison, including asking for help from Guy and her sister Charlotte. It was up to providence to protect him. She could do nothing more.

Marie offered her services over the coming months as a domestic during the day. The children, aged twelve, nine, and seven, had to watch out for themselves until she got home. She scrubbed floors and cleaned stables, unable to find a steady salaried job. The work she found day-to-day, morning until night, allowed her to eke out enough to pay for items needed beyond the food allowance. In the only letter she could afford to mail to Émile after he left for prison, she dared not tell the truth.

⁂

The Conciergerie jailers had put Émile in one of the poorest of cells at the bottom of the levels with six other felons. It held dirt floors, vermin, and small piles of hay on which to sleep. The walls dripped cold and damp from the humidity of bodies, breath, and from the reeking, open sewers. A few distant lanterns in the connecting hallways cast blurry shadows on the darkened stone blocks.

It had rained, and he sat on the earthen floor with his back against the chilling stone wall.

A tough-looking ruffian walked over next to Émile and withdrew a foot from the wooden shoes he wore. He placed it beside Émile's, comparing the size. "Give them to me." It was all he needed to say. Émile removed his shoes and gave them to the man.

They had already taken his hat and a neck scarf. Murderers and thieves became his tutors for survival as a new denizen amidst the dungeon scum. Whatever they demanded, he agreed to, and Émile learned to survive by following the codes by which they lived.

Although he conformed to their ways to avoid beatings, he suffered defenseless against a relentless plague of body lice. The pests crept over his skin, biting every minute, awake or asleep. Horror overcame Émile one night when guards came to remove a dead prisoner from the cell. Their lantern light fell upon the man, whose flesh swarmed with lice, moving in waves over the bare corpse. Disgust washed over Émile as they carried the body out.

Many took sick with gaol disease, an illness that began with flux and vomiting and became a fever-induced delirium that often ended in death. Émile felt certain that in a matter of weeks, he'd suffer a like demise.

Instead, in his fourth week, the jailers took him to a better cell, a *pistole*, luxurious by comparison. Only two other prisoners occupied it, who behaved more civilized than the savages in the lower circle of hell. It contained a wide plank bed, a dry stone floor, and a small table. By far, the most appreciated furnishing was a narrow, foot-tall window a few inches across, piercing the wall ten feet up, allowing sun rays in for an hour each day. The guard told Émile his brother had paid for the move.

He received the letter from Marie. In it, she wrote how they were getting along fine with the money from Edouard and soon they would release him. Émile saw through Marie's lies and sobbed over the bungling of his life.

∽

In late 1747, Great Britain's King George received reports that France's King Louis was open to negotiating a truce. Obvious to all, the continental war had tilted in favor of the French, and the following April, peace talks began at Aix-la-Chapelle in the Germanic states. Soon, Holland, England, and France signed a tentative preliminary agreement, although the countries involved had yet to agree to a final treaty.

Guy had departed on *l'Alcide* for India. As hinted to Jeanne, he headed for Port Louis, capital of the large island of Île de France in the Indian Ocean. His orders sent him in a squadron of four warships to meet up with other ships of the line to attack the British in India.

On the third day out, a strong storm hit that separated his fleet. They found themselves either damaged and forced into port, or captured by the enemy. Guy's *l'Alcide* survived, the only vessel of the Brest squadron to continue on alone.

After he rounded the Cape of Good Hope, Guy headed for Île de France, 350 miles east of Madagascar. The French East India Company used Port Louis as the major port-of-call for trading ships on their way to and from the Orient. Jagged unseen reefs and low wooded hills surrounded the island's bay, creating one of the few protected harbors for French shipping between East Africa and India.

Unknown to Guy, its well-intending governor had placed the colony in a vulnerable position by sending its defenses to help Dupleix on the Coromandel Coast of eastern India. There remained only three hundred inexperienced European inhabitants trained as a militia and seven hundred sailors aboard thirteen merchant ships in the harbor. The island's entire land cannonry consisted of one rusty mortar pulled from storage and a few pieces of field artillery.

At the beginning of July, the strong summer winds of the Indian Ocean carried Guy's *l'Alcide* into Port Louis. Île de France now had at least one ship of the line to defend the capital city. His mind imagined the destruction even a small squadron of British warships might do.

Guy leaned against the mizzenmast, staring at the harbor with only merchant ships in it, and shook his head. What administrator left his capital defenseless during wartime?

He took his gig ashore, spoke to the other ship captains, and hurried to the governor. During their conversation, Guy realized the governor seemed woefully unfit for the task.

The next day, he inventoried the merchant ships and discovered too few cannons to even make one adequately armed warship. Sitting at his desk, he struggled with the dilemma. Then, during a moment of reminiscence, Hashi Humma's trick with the extra campfires came to him. He returned to the governor with a plan.

"Governor David, with your permission, I have an idea. Although the merchant ships have few weapons, they at least can appear like a defensive fleet. I'll place all the merchantmen's cannons on the seaward sides of them. Then I'll reposition the unarmed ones behind with kegs painted black, like cannons."

"Good, good!" complimented the governor, brows high. "So, from the enemy's viewpoint as they approach, we'll look well-defended."

"Yes, but in reality, our fourteen ships wouldn't be a match against even one large British ship of the line. So deception must be our strategy."

He agreed and gave Guy complete control of naval defenses for the harbor.

As if fate overheard, these preparations came not in vain, for only days later, fishermen brought news of a great fleet approaching. Over thirty British warships and transports cruised toward the coast, sending panic throughout Île de France.

Governor David ordered the island's army commander to prepare for the impending attack as best as possible. The much older Count de Restaing found little with which to defend it. He positioned their single old mortar upon a small hilltop facing the harbor and spaced their few field pieces nearby along the shoreline.

Civilians, with ruination on their minds, packed up their valuables and fled to the interior hills. Fishing boats set sail for faraway coastal villages. The colony's most dreaded peril, an enemy's arrival, fell upon them.

The British reconnoitered the coast for five days. Warships then stood offshore of Port Louis, just out of cannon reach.

Guy paced his deck, unsure if his ruse would work. The warm climate and his nerves made his skin hot as he headed for the entrance to the harbor. Once *l'Alcide* reached the opening, he challenged the nearest of the foes, firing at the ship with his largest cannons. When the British fired back, he retreated. Twice more Guy put on a fierce display of preparedness to engage the enemy. Then he hove to the middle of the seaport to face the opposed vessels, as if coaxing them in for destruction by a massed French fleet behind him.

One 70-gun warship bravely set off toward *l'Alcide*. Guy ordered a broadside, hoping his volley would deter it and others from advancing. If she didn't turn away, Guy knew his charade could not stop the port's destruction.

As the smoke cleared from the blasts, Guy stood gripping a line, waiting for the oncomer to change course. "Oh, please, turn back," he said to himself.

Seeing the potential failure of their plan, Comte de Restaing, from on land, ordered his aged mortar to shoot at the warship from the overlooking hill. After its enormous boom filled the air, its shell landed close, sending up a shower of seawater. This unexpected bombardment, along with *l'Alcide's* pluck, forced the British captain to reconsider and retreat.

Guy let out his breath. "Thank God!"

Within minutes, the flagship raised signal flags, and Admiral Boscawen began to withdraw his mighty fleet to the Bay of Tortoises, five miles northeast of Port Louis.

As night drew near, the enemy had all but departed for the protective bay. Count de Restaing's artillerymen prepared to lob one more shell at the last warship leaving. When they ignited the touch hole, the ancient mortar blew itself up.

When morning came, a powerful enemy 60-gun ship of the line revived hostilities when she ventured to destroy an apparent large French redoubt along the coast. Not a single cannon struck back from land as the ship began a dreadful onslaught. The attack laid low the mounds of dirt and battered the timbers into splinters as fusillades of iron smashed into them. Over two hundred cannonballs flew to crush the position.

A French scout observed the devastation and spurred his horse back to Port Louis to report the assault. Count de Restaing, who had heard the cannons booming afar, ran to him. "Well, what are they attacking? What have they taken? What?!"

"Sir, after forty minutes of an intense, annihilating barrage from the British warship, they laid asunder our entire month's supply of kiln wood."

The count's head skewed. "What?"

"They thought the piles of kindling logs were a coastal battery and split them up for us, sir." The scout's tight lips curled and held in his amusement.

Then the commander and scout burst with laughter at the ludicrous mistake. When word of the great bombing of the sticks spread around the seaport, it lightened the fearful spirits of the population.

Guy realized his trickery had caused the enemy to fear a frontal assault on the harbor. They would flank the port's nonexistent defenses and invade with ground troops. Guy, the governor, and the count strategized several plans, depending on where the attack might occur.

"Governor David, although they could pick anywhere along the coast, it'll be near the city where there's a good beach and deep water. Then they can use their ships for gun support. Therefore, they'd land at la Petite Riviere. The anchorage lies close to shore with the river mouth only eight miles southwest of us." Guy tapped the map and nodded with confidence. "That's where the amphibious assault will disembark."

"If they do, we have nothing to stop them," said Count de Restaing, putting his head down and closing his eyes. "We have so few weapons, troops, or ships, they'll overrun us."

"No," Guy chortled. "We have the same defense we used to deter them from entering our harbor."

The governor lowered his eyebrows and pouted. "But we have no real defenses there at all."

"Exactly," Guy said.

Count de Restaing had stationed lookouts along the shore to spy on the enemy and report their movements, and held ready to defend his port.

Early the next day, two British warships approached la Petite Riviere. The wide beach with rocks and sand sloped up to low and thick wooded knolls, perfect for an effortless infantry march into the unguarded southwestern corner of Port Louis.

French lookouts relayed the sighting to their commanders, who started their cunning maneuver.

Guy and Count de Restaing rode to la Petite Riviere and followed the river almost to its mouth. Guy dismounted and could hear the clanking and noises of infantry being ferried to the beach beyond the ebony tree woods that lay between him and the sea. "We'll have time to set up. They won't start pushing inland until all the troops are ashore."

The count nodded, agreeing. "This had better work, or we may as well surrender the entire island before they even reach Port Louis. I ordered a cannon placement about a hundred yards from the shore, near that curve in the river," said Count de Restaing, pointing to the spot.

"I hope they don't send out scouts. They'd discover immediately what we're doing. Do we have any men in place on the enemy's side of the woods?" Guy asked. His palms had begun sweating, although the heat of the day was still hours away.

"I sent five infantrymen to try to scare back anyone from leaving the beach." The count wiped his head with a kerchief. "That should keep them there until we're ready."

As he spoke, they saw French cannoneers pulling the single artillery piece up to the river's edge, almost within sight of the shore that lay just over the trees. As they prepared the cannon, a small company of twenty men scattered among the near treeline. Five French lieutenants went with them and hid themselves with their troops behind trunks and thickets.

Guy pulled out his spyglass and scanned the area, his sweaty head dripping. "You know, the enemy outnumbers ours thirty or more to one. Maybe the gods will favor us again."

"If so, their admiral is the dumbest fool alive." The count clucked to himself. "It'll take less than an hour, I assume, for them to start marching inland."

"Yes," answered Guy, "By noon we'll either be victors, dead, or prisoners of war."

Guy had checked his pocket watch at ten-thirty and twenty minutes later, they heard orders being shouted and drumbeats from the shoreline. "Here they come, Count!"

The old count stood out from behind the bushes and raised a red flag.

As the British regulars advanced on the shore toward the dense wood growths, the French cannon roared and a shot fell and planted itself on the beach, missing everyone.

On Guy's side of the trees, their two drummers stepped out, beating the signal to advance, while a lone trumpeter blew the attack call for phantom companies of soldiers. Infantrymen fifteen feet apart in the dark shadows thrashed around in the bushes and fallen branches. It sounded like entire battalions moved to counter the invasion. Shouting to no one, the five French officers yelled out orders as if thousands of fighters were eager to charge the hapless enemy backed up to the sea.

"Is it working?" Guy asked, running a thumb across his sweaty upper lip. "Is it working?"

"Watch for a yellow flag waving in the woods, Captain de Kersaint. That'll be the signal of our salvation." The count put a spyglass up to his eye, his aged hand trembling.

The two leaders waited and paced while troops continued to thwack the bushes with sticks and stomp on underbrush. But before a quarter hour had passed, a lone French infantryman came sprinting from the dark trees with his musket.

"You didn't tell me." Guy turned to the count, his eyes riveted on the streaking man. "If the British advance, what color is the flag?"

"There is no signal for that, Captain, just our men fleeing," he grunted as he continued to watch the trooper run.

As soon as the soldier cleared the treeline, he stopped and raised a stick with a yellow flag and waved it frantically.

"Oh, my God!" Guy shouted. "It worked!"

Both rejoicing men clapped one another on the back repeatedly as the sounds of boats ferrying the enemy back onto their ships reached them.

The warships departed two hours later to rejoin the others in the Bay of Tortoises.

When Guy and the Count de Restaing returned to Port-Louis, they enthusiastically informed Governor David of their incredible success.

"Might not they try again?" the governor asked, his eyes darting to each.

Guy admitted it. "They could, of course. But anywhere else along our rocky coast is less accommodating for an amphibious attack and much farther away. If they've run from us when so close to the port, it's unlikely they'd attempt a longer campaign. Although, they still might consider a naval assault on the harbor again."

Early the next morning, riders woke Guy and the count, who had slept in the governor's mansion, with good news. The enemy ships had hauled up their anchors and headed outward bound to sea.

At breakfast in the governor's dining room, the three relaxed around the table. The view out of the open, floor-to-ceiling windows showed fishermen docking in the harbor again and the port sounds returning to normal.

"I presume their admiral found attacking the well-defended Île de France meant massive losses," mocked Count de Restaing.

Guy laughed. "No doubt against so many intrepid French regiments and our warship-filled harbor, their only course should be to withdraw with honor and sail away." The three men roared and toasted the frightened enemy admiral with a glass of wine.

By late morning, the largest British fleet in the Orient was nowhere to be found on the horizon. The devastating and imminent invasion of defenseless Île de France had failed without a single man dying in combat.

In Paris, the scant amount Marie earned seldom paid for anything besides rent. With no postage money, she sent no letters to Émile nor got any. Marie sold off the last of her pewter spoons and bought wooden ones for a small price. They ate cheap, coarse, black bread and green bean soup for most meals. The children hated the taste, but after a few weeks, stopped complaining. Months passed with no news of Émile's fate.

In March, she received a message from Edouard telling her he paid for Émile's transfer to the *pistole* with better conditions. This relieved her somewhat, and she told the children their father was doing well. Marie wondered if Guy had gotten her letter and when Edouard would pay the debt to release Émile. The days moved in a slow grinding procession of hard work when she got it, to hours of worry.

Spring arrived but offered no renewal for them. The money Marie had received from Edouard ran out. Just as quickly, their landlord forced them onto the streets without a mote of concern.

Marie towed the children that morning to Edouard's house, only a half mile away, where she hoped he'd feed them the first proper meal they'd have for the day.

When the maidservant opened the front door, she glared at Marie. "Yes?"

"Good morning, I'm Marie Gardinier, your master's sister-in-law. Is he at home?"

"Oh, no, madam. They've gone to Reims to visit the mistress's family."

Marie's legs weakened at the response.

"Please, may we enter? We've been walking all morning and my children haven't eaten a thing today."

The old lady inspected them and gave pause, seeing their dirty, worn clothing.

The servant's nose thrust upward. "I'm afraid you'll have to come back when the master and mistress return."

Marie asked, "When will they return home?"

"Not long, perhaps a month," she said, and slammed the door shut.

Marie needed to find food for the children somewhere out of the frigid spring breeze. Then she remembered her former cook's home on the other side of the Seine in the poorer section of Paris. It meant another hour of trekking in the cold.

Along the way, Marie went further than needed to cross the river. A closer bridge lay near the Conciergerie, but seeing the prison would force her to break down.

As they crossed over the Seine, a variety of performers and vendors dotted the span, with her small ones laughing at the spectacles. Then the scene changed from well-kept buildings and houses to dilapidated apartments and squalor. The narrower roads were full of rubbish and open sewers. Poverty stuck out everywhere, and likewise, unemployed men, beggars, and women of loose morals crowded the walkways of every street. The children didn't notice. Their eyes stayed on the laundry hanging above that looked like so many holiday flags in the chilly wind.

After asking people, Marie found the small building where three families lived, one on each level of a narrow house. The entrance had no handle. She pushed it open, climbed the uneven steps to the second floor, and knocked at the apartment door.

It spread a crack with a slow creak, and Marie caught sight of a young teenage girl peeking out of it. "Hello, are you Camille's daughter?"

The girl nodded, her foot wedged at the door's bottom. "Who are you?" She squinted.

Behind her, Marie spotted two children playing on the floor. "My name is Marie Gardinier. I used to employ your mother as my cook. Do you remember?"

"Ah, yes. What do you want?" She remained guarding the entry.

Marie smiled widely. "Well, I need your mother's help. Is she home?"

"She's at work." She eyed them again. "I can't let anyone into the house."

"Yes, I'm sure she told you to always protect them," Marie said, pointing at the tots. "I wonder if we could stay here and just wait until your mother returns. My children walked here from the left bank and are exhausted. May we come in to rest?"

"Well, I guess it's all right since you know Mother." The girl appeared to be fourteen or fifteen and dressed in clean but tattered and patched clothes.

She let them in and Marie sat and talked to her in the cramped room. The apartment held two, a kitchen, and a smaller one serving as the bedroom. The tiny place could have fit into the front salon of her old house.

Marie explained the problems she had and how her brother-in-law left for Reims, and there was nowhere to stay. The teenager responded older than her years, although still leery of Marie. Yet, she soon warmed up as the conversation continued.

The girl told Marie what had happened after Camille lost her job. "Mamma took another position right away, but the man died. Now she's a baker in the morning at a government office near the river. She cooks pastry for breakfasts and lunches for noblemen. She'll come home after one o'clock."

Soon after the church bells called out the hour, Camille arrived, and her eyes snapped wide when she saw them. Marie explained as Camille slouched exhausted in one of the two chairs.

"Then you'll stay here with me until either your brother-in-law returns or they free Émile," Camille said.

"Oh, Camille, thank you! I don't know what I'd do without your help. After Émile lost his business and the word of his cheating the navy got around, we became lepers."

A week later, a letter with a money draft arrived in Paris from Jeanne. Because Marie no longer lived in her old home, it sat in the post house to be claimed when or if she returned.

∞

Émile weathered the pistole for two horrific months, punished by the boredom and terrible jail food, and missing his family. All three cellmates, thieves of varying trades, told their life histories and love affairs many times, or anything that provided entertainment.

In mid-March, the oldest convict became ill and for five days lay on the wood plank bed, chilled, moaning, and feverish before dying. The next month, the second man became ill and followed the first. Émile's solitary confinement without cellmates both blessed and plagued him with memories. He smiled when he recalled his wife and children at home and then cursed the naval inquiry board that condemned him to his present state. Still, the possibility of Edouard paying off the debt gave him hope, waiting until time sated his brother's revenge.

Edouard returned and visited Émile in May, and spoke to him through the cell's barred window, appearing self-pleased. "Well, I see they moved you to the nicer place. It cost me more, but I didn't want you to suffer."

"I am very grateful you helped me get out of the dungeons," replied Émile, his face blank. "Have you seen Marie? How are my children?"

"No, I haven't seen or heard from her in many months. I wrote to Marie at your apartment before leaving for Reims. Now that I'm back, I'll try to contact her once more. I've good news, though. I'll pay off your debt so you can leave prison."

The next week, after they released him, Edouard took him home to recuperate. Émile had lost weight and a deep cough and sore throat afflicted him. Regardless, he was in ecstasy, knowing he'd soon embrace Marie and his children.

Marie had found an all-day job working as a sweeper in a weaver's shop that paid a paltry sum but helped contribute a little for her keep at Camille's. Toward the end of May, hopeful that Émile's brother had returned to Paris, she again walked to his house in the evening, a weekly practice.

Marie stepped up, rapped, and the maid opened the door. Seconds later, she stood with Edouard in the foyer.

"Marie, where have you been? I sent word to the apartment," he said, his hand pointing upward. "Come, Émile's here, resting in the bedroom."

Marie rushed past Edouard, nudging him aside. "We don't live there anymore!"

Her brother-in-law ran after her with a warning as she raced to the bedroom. "Marie, there's something, ah, Émile returned from prison over a week ago and took ill. It started out as a nasty cough but turned quite serious. The brief stay in jail, I'm afraid, was just too much for his constitution."

When they got to the room, Marie wondered if it was the wrong one. The person looked old, with sunken eyes, pale cheeks, and a bloated neck.

"Marie," Émile croaked out, seeing her standing at the foot of the bed.

"Oh, my God," slipped from Marie's quivering lips. "What's happened to Émile? Is it gaol disease?" she asked in a hushed tone, looking shocked first at his brother, then again at Émile.

"No, but the surgeon said it's croup," Edouard said with a sad face. "You can't go nearer."

In a raspy and weak voice, Émile whispered, "Marie, you mustn't. I would give anything to hold you again in my arms. But ... ."

"Are you in pain? Where does it hurt?" she asked.

Émile pointed to his throat and chest as he coughed, and then placed an open hand on this heart.

Marie started for him, but Edouard grabbed her wrist.

"No, don't," Émile mumbled. "The children. We might spread it." Then his outstretched arm fell limp to the bed as the exertion of speaking tired him.

"Dear, we'll make you better. Finally, you're home and out of that place."

"Enough, Marie. Émile needs to sleep and is in a great deal of pain," Edouard said. Together they walked out, and he disclosed more about Émile's condition and how life had been for him in prison. "Perhaps I should have had him released before the trip to Reims." He bowed his head.

Marie turned on her brother-in-law. "Perhaps?!" The venom flowed out. "You let your own brother lie in that stinking, dark hole to teach a lesson, remember? Now you wonder if you might be blamed? Think on this, if he gets worse it will be by your doing! May you be damned for your vengefulness!" Marie, crying, ran to the entrance and opened it. "I'll be back tomorrow."

At home, she told the children their father was resting at their uncle's house, but hid the news of the illness. Marie and Camille knelt and prayed for Émile's recovery after the children fell asleep.

In the morning, Marie returned and rushed straight to the bedroom. Émile looked paler, although relaxed. Edouard, who said nothing, left and went to his library.

"Marie, my lovely girl. Waited for you." Émile muttered with half-closed eyes. Perspiration covered his body, sopping the clothing and bed linen. He let out a small groan.

Everything seemed unfair that she couldn't see him as before, she thought. After all he'd been through, he didn't deserve to suffer.

Tears blurred her vision and dropped as Marie held back her voice from cracking. "Émile, we've missed you so much. The little ones ask for you and want to visit. But I haven't mentioned your illness, and shall bring them when you get better."

His breath came in uneven gasps that ended with another groan as he attempted to speak. "The children ... you kept me alive. Never could have made it." His eyes closed shut. "Times I heard them playing outside my cell in my mind. Brought hope ... gave strength." Émile's words were faint whispers, and he grimaced with each drawn out phrase. His pallid lips were dry and cracked.

Marie tried to smile for him, but more tears fell when she noticed his shallow breath. She knew the signs. Her head felt faint.

"Darling, you must get better and come home. We need you!" The words ended with her grabbing the bedpost to keep from collapsing.

"Yes. Nice, ... wasn't it, Marie?" Émile mouthed it with little sound but continued smiling.

His hands turned into fists and his chest stopped rising.

"Émile?" Marie whispered. "Émile?" she repeated louder.

But there was no answer. Émile lay there with the faint smile still upon his lips and eyes closed, poised in a serene portrait beyond the boundary of existence.

In that heartrending instant, she understood her old life had ended, too. Nothing would be the same again. "Émile," Marie sobbed, waiting for something that could never come. "I love you," she sighed, taking one last, long look at her beloved, and left.

Few attended the small funeral. Most of Émile's former friends shrank from the convicted criminal who died of a prison illness, although the surgeon said his heart had stopped.

Marie and the children said little to Edouard, leaving for Camille's apartment to grieve.

"Here is something for helping me. When I had no one to turn to, you sheltered us," she said when Camille returned from work, holding out a handkerchief tied at the top.

Camille took the gift, and her brows peaked. "What is it?" She untied the knot, and the cloth opened to glittering gold coins. "Oh, my God. No, don't pay me for your stay."

"Dear friend, it's a present for your kindness. You must take it or I'll never speak to you again." With a smile, Marie reached and tightened Camille's hands on the money.

"Marie, I've never had so much at one time in my entire life! What should I do with it?" Camille's face lit.

Marie looked around with a raised brow. "Move to a nicer home, I suppose. It cost me nothing. Edouard gave me a hundred livres and you deserve half." Then she frowned and shook her head. "It's blood money that I don't want at all, but I must think of schooling and food costs."

"Please thank Edouard for me when you see him." Camille grabbed Marie's arm.

"That won't happen. I shall never speak to him again." Marie narrowed her eyes. "He doesn't know where I'm living and I wish to keep it that way. The children no longer have an uncle or grandfather."

⁂

Marie rented an apartment a week later and searched for cottage work, finding a position as a needlewoman. She had embroidered and sewn since childhood. The work required embroidering rococo-style flowers onto ribbons, the fashion in Paris on women's dresses and men's waistcoats. The task was small, meticulous, and strained the eyes.

Marie enjoyed sewing the pre-drawn patterns and later sketched new ones of her own. Her natural talent for color matching created a harmonious blend of compatible hues. Designs of her own came to her with ease as she drew upon memories of nature with curling leaves and blossoms, vines, and swirling Jack Frost on windows. She experimented with her favorites in various shades of thread. Soon the seamstress shops making gowns and clothing for the rich bought her versions over others.

Marie stitched long hours into the late night while still taking care of the children. If she lived off only her sales, they couldn't afford the two-room apartment she rented. But the small amount of money remaining from Émile's brother covered the rent and school costs. The rest of the expenses depended on her talents.

Soon after Émile's funeral, Marie wrote to Guy to inform him of the tragic event and prayed for a reply, but none came. Perhaps, she thought, he cruised on a long voyage or even moved to the Caribbean like many other sea captains.

To keep Camille's teenage daughter from debauchery in the mills and factories, she tutored her in embroidering and hemming handkerchiefs. One morning each week, Marie visited the men's clothiers to sell them for her.

In early fall, she received a letter from Jeanne.

> *My Dearest and Beloved Friend Marie,*
>
> *I lamented over your message about the tragic conditions of Émile's passing. One's sympathies cannot console what you and the children are suffering, but know in your heart I join your grief. Émile was a loving spouse and an amiable acquaintance to many.*
>
> *Émile's quick demise will shock Guy when he learns of it. Your old friend and my cherished husband, is in India after departing last year. I am confident news of the war's end should hasten his return, so he may offer solace to you.*
>
> *I am anguished over the dire circumstances you find yourself in financially. In response to your earlier letter explaining Emile's troubles, I sent a bill of exchange to your old home's address. I noted that you have yet to draw upon it, and gather you are not aware of its posting. If the amount is insufficient for your needs, please reply with any value you wish. I pray this message arrives in your hands and gives you succor.*
>
> *Your Loving and Obedient Friend, Jeanne Countess de Kersaint, the 28th of September, 1748, Cléder.*

After Marie read it, she left for the mail office the next day, nearly running. Along the way, she reflected on the tragedy of Émile's death and her situation. The quaint neighborhood she passed through, one she once loved for its simpler life, reminded her that everything diverges. Beneath each seemingly calm and controlled interlude writhed disorder and sources of calamity but a twist of chance away. She cringed over her believing Émile's lies, and for inferring the role of a wealthy and dutiful wife was absolute. She chided herself over her ignorance of how quickly things can change.

⁂

Months later, in Port Louis, Guy learned of the British plans to recapture Madras, take Pondichéry, or seize Île de France had collapsed, and they departed the waters in October.

In the East for over a year, he completed arming seven ships at Île de France and sailed to Pondichéry on the Coromandel Coast. Dupleix, at last, had a naval force, a goal and dream he had held since first trying to expand the French colonies in India into an empire.

Many months after signing the treaty at Aix-la-Chapelle, the military officers stood in the elegant meeting room in the gubernatorial palace in Pondichéry. Dupleix scanned the terms of the new peace proclamation sent from Paris.

"Oh my God, such foolishness!" Dupleix cried out after reading it. "The king returned Madras. After we won it all, he gave it back." He crumpled into his large upholstered chair, his head hanging and the document dangling from his fingers.

The men looked at one another in wonder. "Sir, what's the news from Paris?" urged an infantry officer.

"I can scarcely repeat what I've read here," he said, cheeks aflame. Dupleix had performed well, removing any other French competitor and playing local rulers against each other to take over more territory for France. He had dared brilliant strategic military moves against the Indian and British forces. By every right, he was the de facto nawab of southern India.

Dupleix pounded the arm of the chair and continued. "The war is over. What they agreed to in April of last year has become a reality. The king conceded to the return of Madras to the British." He paused, shaking his head.

"Here are the terms. First, France has given back the regions in India taken during the conflict and also the cities we conquered in the Netherlands. The British returned the territories in Cape Breton and

Louisbourg to France." Then he skipped across the legal phrases, trying to pick out more affecting the French.

When he finished reading, he hesitated and then spoke to no one in particular. "In brief, he's given back everything we've accomplished. The British have done likewise. The carnage was for nothing!" His hand smacked his knee.

To Guy, who stood off to the side of the large polished mahogany table, the exception was obvious. Dupleix achieved a considerable deal he'd keep. Even in yielding Madras, he had proven himself qualified to face both British and Indian leaders and armies. He ruled as the Governor General of French India. Plus, he wrangled himself into significant importance and had to be dealt with cautiously, a ranking he didn't have before the war, nor did his finances suffer. He had become fabulously rich. Perhaps for France and Great Britain, the conflict resulted in a stalemate, for Dupleix, his holdings grew both politically and financially. The bloodletting had ended well for him.

"Gentlemen, I also have dispatches regarding reassignments," Dupleix added, a hand over his eyes. "New orders will come later. You may go." He sat again on his grandiose throne as he mumbled oaths against Versailles.

Guy left and analyzed the provisions of the pronouncement. The *status quo antebellum* agreement seemed more of a temporary truce since it resolved none of the issues that began the war.

There would still be strife over territories in North America and the West Indies, and continuing conflicts in India. The lack of a definite victor or consensus did not bode well for a peaceful future, he surmised.

A few days later, in Dupleix's office again, Guy learned the admiralty ordered him to stay in Pondichéry and promoted him to lead a new fleet to protect France's interests there.

Although his upgrade to squadron commander pleased him and completed the next step in distinction, he regretted his absence from Jeanne and the children. Just one letter from her had come since arriving in India. In it, received six months after written, he learned of Guy-Pierre, his new son, born soon after he left Brest. The boy was over a year old and he had not yet seen him. It read:

> *Dearest Beloved,*
> *May this letter reach you in good health and safety. Our precious new baby Guy-Pierre is doing well, as is the rest of our household. Armand asks for you each day, and Suzanne misses her father dearly. As for my longing, I pace the rooms, awaiting word from you or your footsteps in the hall.*
> *Your close friend Marie hasn't sent any news. Additionally, rumors spread in Brest that the navy has tried her husband and he is now in prison. I wrote to her at her home, but she has posted nothing in response. I assume she is financially still well-provided. Nevertheless, I shall write to people in Paris, inquiring about her situation …*

Three long years in the cyclone seas and heat of Coromandel passed before Guy set off for France.

⁂

By the fall of 1750, Guy returned with accolades for his efforts with Dupleix and on Île de France against the British fleet. The homecoming more than achieved his expectations. Almost every waking hour, relatives and friends visited once word spread that he had come back from India. On the second day home, he wrote Marie about plans to go to Paris as soon as the navy permitted.

Marie's sad situation fouled his triumphant return. Instead of satisfaction in the tributes he received, Guy mulled over the despicable behavior of Émile which had cast Marie into despondency.

"I find it so unbelievable that he'd jeopardize their marriage and security by taking such risks." Guy grumbled to Jeanne again, "Had Émile no thought of consequences or concerns for his family? Poor Marie! Poor dear Marie!"

Jeanne sat on the settee, not replying, and stared unfocused. "Some men only see their goals, not their family's needs, never noticing. Many are like Émile, unfortunately." She glanced up at him. "I'm sure he didn't intend the outcome, but his fixed ambition doomed them." Her eyes stayed on him.

"The fool." Guy rolled his eyes.

Fate again intervened in Guy's intentions as Minister Maurepas requested his presence within a month, and both Guy and Jeanne rode their carriage to the capital. They entered the city in the late morning and told the driver to head straight to Marie's home.

The neighborhood where she now lived seemed better than Camille's. When it stopped, they hurried to the apartment. Their pounding brought a call.

"Who's there? What do you want?" It was Marie's voice, defiant and challenging whoever knocked.

"Marie, it's Guy and Jeanne. Let us in!" he shouted through the old, unpainted wood.

Within a second, the door flung open and Marie threw herself into his arms. "Oh, how I've needed and missed you!"

She pulled them inside. The apartment held a tiny bedroom and another larger room with a fireplace, kitchen table, and chairs, and near the single window, an old, worn divan. Across from it sat a bookcase that contained most of Marie's sewing materials, two books, and a few toys.

Guy clasped her shoulders and lowered his gaze. "Marie, I want to tell you how grieved we felt over Émile's passing when we read your letter. Things changed for the worse for him so fast."

Her eyes also dropped, joining his. "Guy, I needed you during that nightmare. But distance worked against us. I'll never get over the loss, nor will the children," she lamented, tears springing up on her eyelids.

"Are they in school? I'd love to meet them," Jeanne asked. It was her first time to visit and talk to Marie since the wedding.

"Yes, they're in class now. The children missed two years of schooling." She managed a contented front, but wiped her nose with a handkerchief. "They hadn't attended again until this spring. They'll be home in an hour and will be excited to see you. I often talk to them about you. How are yours?"

Jeanne's eyes brightened. "Armand is eight now and the younger ones are all well."

Guy raised a finger to interrupt. "Marie, I hate to bring this up. Did you use the money Jeanne sent to you? When I left Cléder, someone had cashed the bank draft."

"Yes, dear friend, I got the note of exchange." She patted his cheek. "You know, I could've spent it, but I didn't have the need for it. I received a sort of inheritance from Émile's brother that's provided for us. True, this apartment isn't the best and humbler than the house we used to have." Marie glanced around at her shabby abode. "The children don't seem to mind the inconveniences and I've adapted."

"Well, never think about repaying it. I insist. If you want better quarters, move to them and use it to cover the cost and rent," Guy said, and Jeanne agreed with a nod. "So, please, spend it on whatever you need. If you require more, write to me. After all, I am your daughter's godfather."

"Thank you, I'll keep the money for later."

"What are those? Silk ribbons?" Jeanne noticed a stacked pile of Marie's handiwork looped and tied with strings on a shelf.

"Oh, yes. That's my job, a needlewoman. I put designs on the ribbons. I've quite a few clients now that provide for our basics. Although it's hard on the eyes and fingertips." Marie wiggled her fingers and her mien shifted from morose to a happier countenance.

"In Brittany, every girl learns needlework and lacework. Your patterns are clever and pretty." Jeanne narrowed her focus on the intricate, small flowers as she inspected each ribbon.

"Thank you. I'm starting something new. The shops keep asking for more of my designs, but I don't have the time to do them, especially with the children and housework. So, I made a batch of sketches and gave them to other needlewomen to copy onto ribbons. Then I pay them and sell the ribbons to the shops. I have four working for me."

"My God, he left his legacy to you! Émile taught you how to become a merchant," said Guy.

With a sad voice, Marie said, "His enthusiasm for business inspired me when starting out. I remembered how he did things. Émile had such a talent for buying and reselling. Oh, there's much we have to recount." She paused and swallowed. "First, I want to hear about your adventures, Guy. The battles must have terrified you."

"Put away your threads, Marie. When the children come, we'll go out for supper and we can tell our stories." He wore a cheerful face, but the dark circles under Marie's eyes and her tattered and much-patched gown made Guy look to Jeanne and raise his brows.

Soon the children arrived, and they all left to eat, returning after impressing the children with their first four-course meal in a fine café.

Well into the night, Guy and Marie exchanged their stories, her life as a ribbon-maker, and the dreadful conflicts and foreign sights Guy experienced in the navy. Marie and the children sat enthralled by his adventures until bedtime, while Jeanne squirmed in her seat.

Guy and Jeanne left for an inn, promising to return the next day, declaring it a holiday. The children stayed home from school and they rambled off for an autumn stroll through town. In the morning, a marionette show in a park and a traveling fair featuring trained monkeys entertained the small ones. After that, they visited Notre-Dame Cathedral to light candles for Émile.

When daylight faded, the group bought an abundance of food to cook for an impromptu feast. On the way home, they stopped and invited Camille and her children to join them for supper.

Camille, excited to see Guy after so many years, arrived with her children. Everyone ate more in the crowded apartment than they had in days. Guy enthralled them with more tales of Hashi Humma, the fall of Louisbourg, the clever trickery of the Barbary beys, and his exotic life in India's Pondichéry.

Guy and Jeanne returned on the last day. "Well, my dear friend, the week has come and gone and time urges us to depart. Visits pass too swiftly and we attend too much to things of small consequence." He hugged her. "Being with you, though, has balanced everything. I feel better now than I have since coming back from India."

Jeanne glanced at them.

Marie spread her lips wide. "Oh, Guy, you're also what I needed. My struggles of late have tested my abilities to a profound extent, but your encouragement, whether with me here or in a letter from afar, gives me courage. Thank you."

Before they left for Cléder, Guy slipped Marie fifty livres, dropping the wrapped gold coins into her apron pocket as he hugged her farewell.

Armand and Quiberon Bay
1751-1759

The next few peaceful years saw Guy taking quiet voyages to the West Indies and French ports along the Atlantic and Mediterranean. The navy gave him the command of the new *l'Illustre*, a 64-gun ship of the line. Meanwhile, Jeanne gave him three more children, a girl and then twin boys.

For his services, he received eight hundred livres from the king's personal treasury in a laudatory meeting at Versailles with King Louis. While in Paris, Guy stopped to visit Marie, learning with great delight she had found a better home.

Seated on the newly reupholstered divan in her salon, Guy turned to Marie. "Where does Camille live now? You mentioned she also moved."

"Yes, she's here in the Sainte-Antoine District, too, a few blocks closer to the Bastille. Now she helps with my customers and her daughter still works for me, making the handkerchiefs and doing well. Your goddaughter is being courted by an accomplished musician. Is Armand in the Garde de la Marine, yet?"

"No, he's ten now and won't enter the academy until thirteen. Their lives will be so different from ours. When children, we never imagined you'd be running a successful ribbon business, did we? Do you ever pick up a needle anymore?"

"You're right. The last time I did any embroidery was a year ago, I believe." She grinned. "Now I have twenty-eight women working for me and twelve customers buying the ribbons. Up above, I bet Émile takes pride in his gift to me." Her chin lifted. "I supply trim materials for hatmakers and dressmakers all over Paris."

Marie left her chair and sat down next to him. "It seems you're in Paris at least a couple of times a year. And King Louis can't do without you." She laughed and slapped his arm.

"The thing I've learned about the king and his ministers is they love you until you make a mistake. They'll turn on you the moment you give a sign of being human. But who knows how long my luck will hold?" said Guy, raising palms in the air.

"Is another war coming with the British? News from the American colonies isn't good."

Guy answered, frowning, "There's no doubt it will. The last ended as an appetizer for the main meal. Each side uncovered enemy weaknesses and strengths, and they'll try to take advantage of the knowledge. The next war should be much broader and worse than the previous one, I'm afraid."

The prospects of a new, dreadful conflict approached on the horizon. Whispers he'd heard at the Admiralty involved preparations for invasions everywhere. The only thing holding back the plans rested on the funds available.

In 1756, at the war's beginning, King Louis found himself a naval champion against Great Britain. The brilliant naval commander Captain Guy de Kersaint now wrote letters of his opinions on matters to the monarch. The Admiralty rewarded his valor, promoting him to squadron chief on board *l'Intrepede* of 74 guns.

With British aggression gaining strength, Versailles devised a clever scheme to strike at their commercial centers. At the same time, the plan protected France's own colonies while keeping their precious few warships safe from enemy encounters.

In the cool Brest fall, Guy spent his last day with Jeanne before departing. They stood above his fleet in the harbor near the citadel. "I'll have two squadrons. The first squadron holds two ships of the line, a frigate, and a corvette." He pointed down to the vessels. "The second contains one ship of the line and a frigate to attack commerce at a different portion of the African coast. Then the divisions will unite afterward and proceed together to Martinique in the West Indies."

Both had agreed Armand, now fourteen, could go with Guy on his next mission.

"Armand will be so excited to be with you on the voyage, Guy. Since finishing Garde de la Marine, it's all he's talked about. Watch over him. He's so enthused and may act rashly." Jeanne looked up at him, her brow peaked. "Don't let him take chances."

"Of course, I shall do my best, my dear. Although risks are part of training, too. Still, I won't send him into any danger he can't handle."

The next day, the fleet set out and in a week headed south toward Africa's western coasts.

"Sir, what's Guinea like?" Armand had asked questions about the mission ever since coming aboard. "What do the British outposts get from there?"

"The coast is hot and green, with forests right up to the sandy beaches and many rivers emptying into the sea from its shores. The settlements are few, though," Guy answered. He found difficulty being both a commander and a father to Armand. On deck, he tried to be Armand's captain, using emotionless responses.

"Like us, they get spices, wood, gold, and slaves there. Slave trading is the main reason, so, we'll probably encounter slavers on the trip. The Dutch, Portuguese, and Danes engage in it, too, to a lesser extent. And France buys more of theirs near Angola."

Within five days, they were off the coast of Guinea in search of ships, settlements, and all things British.

"We'll be raiding the trading posts and forts at Dixcove and

Komenda," Guy told the squadron officers in his cabin. "They're unprepared for us and will put up little defense. I want marines to go ashore to spike cannons and burn buildings. If they find any valuables or food, bring them back."

The raid at Dixcove met slight resistance even though merchant ships, caught surprised at anchor, tried to defend themselves. The marines boarded and captured the vessels without loss.

Guy remembered the thrill of his first combat in Louisiana, and the imprudent risks he attempted that Hashi Humma's wisdom dampened, and sought to temper Armand's youthful impatience. To learn valuable lessons impossible to teach at the academy, he had let his son go ashore during the raid.

The next onslaught at Komenda met stiffer opposition. When Armand returned, he rushed to tell his father about the engagement.

"They put up a tenacious fight, sir!" Armand, who led a squad of men, spoke quickly with gestures. "I took my marines around the village and attacked from the rear. Enemy infantry fired upon us, but we soon overran their defenses. They fled like mice." His chest puffed out.

Guy held in his amusement. "That's the thinking we need to take the posts without suffering casualties, my boy. Good work!"

While cruising eastward, the first lieutenant informed Guy, "Sir, we've made out a British topsail, three leagues windward."

Guy climbed up onto the deck and watched her through his spyglass. "Very well, make for her, and tell me her size," he answered, returning to his cabin.

This was the only merchantmen they had seen at sea and in an hour the slow ship fled less than half a league ahead. *L'Intrepede* opened up on the smaller vessel.

"She looks like a slaver, making her way from Cape Coast Castle," said Guy on deck to Armand. "It's the main British slave-trading center."

Abreast of *l'Intrepede* came *l'Opiniâtre*, firing bow chase guns at the escaping vessel. The two ships of the line on each of the slaver's stern quarters forced her to surrender.

"Armand, take a squad of marines and let me know what's on our prize."

Excited to inspect his first captured ship, Armand took a launch over to her.

He came back after half an hour, his face concerned. "Sir, her hold has hundreds of slaves bound for Port Royal, Jamaica. What should we do?"

Guy paused, looking aside. "She's a prize now. I cannot return those on board to land. They now belong to the French government. Send a crew to man her and we'll continue on toward Cape Coast Castle, less than five leagues up the coastline."

"Are the defenses at that fort strong, sir?" Armand asked, smiling.

Guy said, "The garrison itself is small, with low, armed battlements, I'm told. We won't be there to capture it, though. By now, they've learned of our presence and are prepared. We don't have enough men or time for a ground attack. So, we'll inflict as much damage as possible."

The next morning, they sighted the fort with stone and cement walls just fifteen feet high built on rocks beside the sea. Guy raised signal flags for them to pass offshore for a bombardment. As he did, the ill-equipped castle loosed its guns, most balls missing the ships.

Armand stood on the poop deck with his father. "They're few and the defenders show no skill, sir. Couldn't we subdue it with an amphibious landing?"

Guy waved his finger before him. "No, we needn't take the fort. Besides, the enemy has armed a large company of natives in case we land. Look left, there, under the trees." The deep shadows of palms hid hundreds of men with muskets.

After half an hour, Guy called to his lieutenant, "We've spent enough iron on the ramparts. Concentrate a barrage on the town and government buildings for the rest of the afternoon." The bombardment caused extensive damage to the structures, while the return volleys put only a few holes in their canvas.

Guy said, "Well, lieutenant, I believe we've forced the British to protect their forts. That was our mission. Signal the others to continue eastward for Accra."

The fleet set out and hammered the slave-trading post in Accra, and captured merchantmen there. Guy patrolled the coast for the enemy for weeks. By the next month's end, the time came to meet up with the second squadron.

The first lieutenant found Guy at the stern. "Sir, we've gathered a convoy. We now have nineteen prizes with their valuable cargoes of merchandise and slaves. This should demoralize London."

"Yes, and encourage Versailles to place confidence in our navy again. We'll set out tomorrow for the Canaries to meet the other division. I hope they were as successful as we were."

"If I may, sir. There is one other thing I must mention." The young officer's face reflected something serious. "I've talked with the other lieutenants. They all agree Armand has impressed them with his grasp of tactics and his dogged determination to attain an objective. Although only fourteen, he revealed exceptional leadership skills when leading his men during the raids."

Guy grinned. "Thank you, lieutenant. That means much to me."

The assaults at Guinea soon rattled the London stock market and Parliament. Not one senior officer of the British Admiralty had the foresight to predict French strikes on their remote posts. Pressure from shipping businesses, insurance companies, slavers, and the public fell upon their navy to do something about the costly surprise attacks. Many warships that had attacked or patrolled French ports, now left to protect Great Britain's investments in Africa and elsewhere.

Guy searched for the other half of the French raiders to begin the rest of their mission. After waiting days without catching sight of their sails, Guy continued west, as planned, to pick up the currents for Saint-Domingue.

A week later, in the sea near Martinique, Guy and his officers located their comrades in a group heading in the same direction. They merged with the others and in Saint-Domingue unloaded the cargoes and the eight hundred slaves captured from the enemy. With the original mission completed, he gathered a new convoy of merchantmen and other warships to return to France.

"Sir, we have five ships of the line, two frigates, plus the convoy's merchant vessels. Now that it's late autumn, the storms are weakening, too," Armand mentioned to his father, hoping he'd order the departure.

He wanted to go home.

"Yes, Armand, we're going to leave Saint-Domingue in just days. First, however, we must wait. Merchant ships have reported four enemy warships patrolling off the coast to intercept us. When we get a strong gale that pushes them away, we'll cast off."

Word had reached the West Indies of Guy's successful raids in Guinea, and revenge festered in their foe's mind.

On an October morning after a stormy night, he assembled his convoy outside Cape Town's port and set out to chance a crossing homeward.

Within miles of leaving the harbor, they encountered three ships of the line leeward.

"Damn." Guy pounded his fist on the mast at the warning. "Armand, signal our cruisers to follow in a line of battle. At least the wind blows in our favor."

L'Intrepede led the French formation. By mid-afternoon, the two enemies approached.

"They're close hauled. When in range, give them doubleshot," Guy commanded.

As soon as a few of his cannons sounded, it met a sharp reply from the British's lead 60-gun warship. After a confused hours-long battle, both sides retired.

The British squadron limped back to Port Royal, where they lay held up for months for repairs while both squadrons claimed the fight as a victory in their reports. Guy, however, incurred a serious wound that healed slowly.

Three weeks later, he led his fleet homeward and arrived in Brest the next January. As he reviewed his successes at home, he felt compelled to write to Marie in Paris. After so many years, things still needed to be told.

> *My Dearest Friend and Beloved Marie, As you may have read in the newspapers, my recent missions to Africa and the West Indies delivered me back safely. Many of those who voyaged with me, alas, fared not as well. We made port in Brest in January with scurvy and consumption ravaging*

my crews and forcing us to anchor in quarantine until the threats passed. The diseases that harm sailors by far outweigh the dangers of enemy cannons. With each cruise, I am thankful for my return.

Whenever the talons of fear grip my heart at sea, I find sanctuary in memories to calm my nerves. One I hold precious is of you and me when young, around twelve years, as I recall. You had climbed upon the roof of our stables to see the sun setting. I forced myself to join you, although afraid of falling off the slates. With your face full in the sun's last rays, you stood facing the golden spectacle. At that moment to me, you were dauntless. Nothing cowed you nor could dominate your resolve—a divine heroine, a warrior goddess. It stands as a vision I cling to for courage during my darkest trepidations. That might seem simplistic. To me, it's always been an inspiration from my childhood that strengthens me. So, my dear, in many of my triumphs you share in the victory ...

When Marie entered the darkened apartment, it was already late after a day of seeking new buyers. She lit a candle stub by the window and watched its dim flicker for a few seconds, struggling to burn before it grew into a flame. Mostly used up, she thought, like me.

Now that her girls had married and her son lived at a print shop as an apprentice, she spent her evenings designing and reading in solitude. She sighed as memories of life in their former home drifted through her mind. The thing she missed more than her children's dependence upon her was her dependence upon Émile. The ten years since his death left her lonely for his company and wanting for things missing.

She often passed back in time to when she met Émile at the tailor's shop, recounting their hopes and intimacies. Sometimes, she remembered Guy's and François's flirtatious conversations. Their words of adoration gave her comfort. Marie had loved them, too, though differently, and when melancholy overtook her, fantasized a marriage with one or the other.

The next day Marie went with Camille, who assisted her, to stop by her customers and many other shops to sell her ribbons and fine Dutch and Bretton lace. She saved the last shop as a treat to herself. The proprietor always seemed pleased to see her and engaged her in amiable conversation.

When they entered the millinery store, their eyes caught one another, and he held a lingering gaze.

"Madame Gardinier," said the millinery owner, "I haven't seen you in months."

"Monsieur Bertin, so good to visit you again. How are you and your children?" asked Marie, her face glowing.

"The children are fine, two married and two soon to be. My wife would have been so proud of them," he answered, smiling.

"Mine are all on their own, too," said Marie, making a faux frown. "In the evening, I fill my time with memories and reading."

"Then we're a pair. If it weren't for this business, I'd probably join my wife." He laughed aloud. "I assume you have some new lace designs for me to see?"

Marie pulled a large flat book from her straw basket and handed it to him. "Here's what I have right now. There will be others later and we can change patterns if you have new ideas."

The tall man, distinguished looking and near Marie's age, opened the folio and leafed through the pages with pasted ribbon and lace samples. He identified which he liked and could use as Camille wrote the page numbers and quantities he wanted.

"And ribbons?" asked Marie.

A slight wrinkle on his nose formed. "No. No ribbons right now," he answered, rejecting her samples.

Marie made a wry face. "Monsieur, be frank. Should we update ours?"

"Well, the work is beautiful, though I'm afraid passé for the current style." He tilted his head with a sheepish expression. "Metallic threads are becoming more in fashion again."

"Are there any ribbons in your shop you find more fashionable? I'd like to discover which you prefer." Marie widened her eyes.

He took them to his shelves in the workroom. Together they inspected ribbons he purchased from other sellers. Soon Marie and Camille recognized the slight but important differences for the new vogue.

She looked up at him as a warm glow grew in her chest. "Monsieur Bertin, would you mind if I drew up some new patterns and showed them to you? I honestly respect your opinion and knowledge of the latest styles."

"I'd love to help you," he said with a smile. "Return tomorrow, and we'll take a trip to tour other millineries and clothiers with popular design trends. To introduce you to them will be my pleasure."

During the week, Marie and Monsieur Bertin were inseparable as they marched from shop to shop and discussed materials and concepts.

―※―

At Cléder, Guy relaxed and healed from his wound, with Jeanne caring for him. Armand was unaffected by the terrible epidemic ravaging the fleet upon their return from the West Indies and transferred to a different ship. Guy had stayed with his crew until the dangers passed.

At 55 years of age, he moved more slowly and more than once had considered leaving the sea for life ashore. Guy wondered when his legs failed to sway with the rolling waves, if he could leave the navy to stay landbound. Still, a pitching deck and the sea's beauty would hold him captive as long as his body permitted.

In March, the king presented him with a thousand livres for his outstanding accomplishments. Guy, at last, regarded himself near the summit of his career with the prestige and fame that he had sought throughout his life. Versailles welcomed him. He held the position of a fleet commander, and they had knighted and granted him awards. Guy believed it was a wonderful legacy for his children.

One night, as he fell into the visual aberrations of deep sleep, Guy's dream didn't seem the same as others. Every detail seemed real. The deck boards beneath his boots felt solid, and the railing pulled at his fingertips like actual weathered wood. The sky dazzled his eyes with a brilliant sun surrounding the horizon in all directions and gradually darkening at the zenith. His head back, he gazed up at stars in the dark navy blue over him. Every luminous speck emitted a warmth he had never experienced, not heat, but pulsations of unquestioning love. He tried to stare at as many as he could to fill himself with the uplifting sensation.

The ship he stood on extended outward in all directions as an enormous round vessel with no bow, nor stern, and no levels. Sailors scoured the deck with gold holystones that made its planks radiate a faint yellow glow. Only one mast ascended upward from the middle, with seven shrouds attached to its unseen top. As the crew sang a shanty, some climbed as their breaths filled the great silver sail that stretched up beyond the clouds.

"*Ah*, you see truth of it." Hashi Humma stood at his side.

"It's wonderful," he said to the old native, much more aged than when he last saw him. "To where do we journey?"

The Choctaw pointed to the surrounding sea. "Look, there."

Guy stared at the iridescent waters of pearly hues around them. As he watched, the ship and waves swirled into sparkling colored flashes. Then, in an instant, he and Hashi Humma sat on the shore of the Mississippi, gazing into the last embers of an evening campfire. Along the bank from the right approached a beautiful native woman who emitted a blue aura. Guy recognized both Jeanne and Marie in her. The maiden said nothing but pointed to faded purple mountains far away. "Where is she taking us?" Guy asked.

Hashi Humma, his eyes happy, rose. "I go to Aba pilla to see Chisha, now."

"*Ah*," Guy answered in Choctaw. "But I must stay longer."

As he spoke the words out loud, Guy awoke. It was still night, and he lay in bed.

A week later, he received a letter from Marie.

> *My Beloved Guy,*
> *I am overjoyed to tell you Claude Bertin, a former millinery customer, and I united in matrimony three days ago. My wonderful new husband, whom I've known for*

years, asked for my hand only last month. Camille attended me in the private ceremony with our children accompanying us, yet your presence would have made the occasion more joyous. We married at my old church, Saint-Sulpice. I am so happy with Claude. He is considerate of my wants, and I reflect often on how twice I was given the blessings to wed amazing men, my Émile and my Claude. I pray for you every night and cannot wait until I introduce you to my remarkable spouse.

Your Loving and Obedient Servant, Marie de Bruc Gardinier Bertin, the 9th of September, 1758, Paris.

Guy sent her an overly expensive wedding present.

～

In May of 1759, Guy became captain of *le Thésée* in Admiral de Conflans's squadron at Brest. The news of the constant defeats over the last year frustrated him. They had lost Louisbourg again, and Canada soon after Québec fell. The British had attacked the coasts of France and their colonies in India and the West Indies. Even his fellow commanders were losing faith in their ability to halt the enemy.

Guy joined François, who commanded the large warship *le Juste*.

"Yesterday, I reflected on our dismal efforts to recapture Louisbourg again, just like in '45," Guy said with a frown. "The complexity of such missions tends to work against their success. Perhaps this one will prove fruitful."

François tilted back his captain's chair and nodded. "If this expedition fails, we will lose the war, Guy. We're the last real naval force protecting the coast and our colonies."

"Oh, if only we had realized how things would turn out when we attended Garde de la Marine so many years ago. Of course, we still might succeed and be in our wives' arms in two weeks." He grinned at the hope.

"My wife is used to my absences and running the estate on her own." François laughed. "She'd barely note my return!"

"Hmm, not so Jeanne, I'm afraid." Guy shook his head. "She's by far the more concerned of the two. We found some fine women to marry, didn't we?"

"That's something I often ponder," François said, his stare vacant. "Had I married Marie de Bruc, things might be so different. She'd have forced me into an officer-of-the-pen position on shore, no doubt."

"Ah, our Marie," Guy's thoughts flooded with pleasant memories. "She always set us straight, didn't she? Never a restraint, never coy or quiet. She's been the cannon in our lives, saying what needed to be said and doing her job—a blast and fury." His hand thumped the top of the cannon next to his chair in François's cabin. "God, I've missed seeing her lately!"

François shook his head. "No concern. You'll be in Versailles after this voyage to reap the laurels of victory again. Give her my best when you see her." He paused and sighed. "You know, we've done well in our careers. Both of us received Saint-Louis knighthoods and became captains, profited from our prizes at sea, married well, and reared fine children to carry on our names. What more could we ask, my friend?" He looked at Guy with raised brows.

Guy held up two open hands. "A lasting peace after this expedition succeeds, I pray! Where is your son stationed, by the way?"

"He's in Martinique right now. And where is Armand?"

"The same. He left a week ago. Perhaps they will meet." Guy locked his fingers behind his head and leaned back in the chair. "I have two of my boys onboard my *le Thésée* for this trip. The older one, Jacques-Guy, is a cadet now. Oh, he's going to make a fine officer someday. And Guy-François is six. One can never start them too young. There's so much to learn. But more than that, I wanted them both with me to witness the invasions and what I hope will be a victorious conclusion. Imagine the stories they'll tell of this expedition when captains themselves!" He clucked his tongue.

Versailles had decided to end the war by attacking with several precarious campaigns. The king's treasury emptied to provide a vast number of supplies, warships, and transports. Foremost, the plan called for multiple invasions of England and Scotland. But enemy patrols, unfortunately, had cruised offshore for weeks and kept France's forces blockaded in ports.

In mid-November 1759, the large fleet prepared to embark from Brest's harbor after a fierce storm pushed the British away. Little Guy-François had waited beside his father on deck for hours in his small cadet's uniform until he tired. His tutor took him below to his father's cabin to nap as the ship hauled anchor. When a new gale blew down from the northwest, they turned south along their coast to join another squadron near La Rochelle.

The British in England learned from spies of the French fleet's departure, got underway, and set out after them. With the wind full at their backs, the enemy sped southward. Two days later, the vanguard of their ships caught up with the French formation outside Quiberon Bay, just eighty miles southeast of Brest.

"Sir, British flags three leagues on our stern," the first lieutenant said to Guy in his cabin.

"Where, port or starboard?" Guy lept up from his desk and strapped on his sword.

With a look of worry, the young officer answered, "Both, sir. It's an enemy fleet."

"Have they signaled us to form up to take them on?"

The first lieutenant shook his head. "They're attacking in mass, sir, like hounds on a scent."

The enemy's admiral, Guy saw, had disregarded the usual and begun a melee attack rather than form a battle line.

The French admiral, Marquis de Conflans, grasped the jeopardy he faced and tried to head into the bay. It lay amid rock pinnacles, shoals, and sandbars, too dangerous for the enemy to follow without knowledgeable pilots. Guy and François's warships veered east toward Quiberon's large bay.

Guy's *le Thésée* shielded the French fleet's trailing end with three other big ships as the rearguard. In time, a British warship passed windward of his ship and engaged him. After a heated exchange of volleys for an hour, their opponent ran afoul of another and slowed, allowing *le Thésée* to continue on ahead toward the bay. Guy, free from the first, came within range of a second ship of the line. He fired at the closing foe of equal size, the enemy 70-gun, *Torbay*.

High seas and darkness in the driving downpour limited the warships' fighting power. Rough swells climbed two to three feet above the closed bottom-tier portholes as waves crashed against the hulls and forced Guy to keep their lower guns unused.

Other French ships fought off the British as the battle disintegrated into one-on-one action. Huge 70- and 80-cannon ships of the line pounded away at one another. *Le Thésée* and the *Torbay* continued to trade broadside for broadside in a horrendous hours-long bashing.

Cannonballs whizzed overhead and Jacques glanced up at each. "Don't panic over those, Jacques," said his father. "The ones you don't hear are the danger. As an officer, you must stand your ground and show no fear of what may come. Remember, son, you're a de Kersaint—born to lead!" Guy winked down at his budding cadet.

The effect showed with the next volley, as Jacques stood, chin up and fists on his hips. Guy chuckled to himself.

As the intensity of the shelling increased, it took its toll on the hull. Guy saw his youngest boy, Guy-François, leading his tutor onto the poop deck.

Guy screamed at the man, "For heaven's sake! Why have you brought him up from the cabin?!"

The tutor reached down and grabbed the running child's arm. "I didn't, sir. He sped up the stairway before I could stop him!"

Guy-François's eyes, big as coins, begged for his father's security. "Papa, I'm scared!"

"Oh, my dear boy, it's just a bit of noise and the enemy knocking on the wooden sides of our ship. But we'll be brave and won't let them in, right?" He smiled down and picked up his son, hugging him.

"No, Papa, we won't." His son said, burying his face in Guy's shoulder.

"Now we must not let those rascals see us cry. You go with your tutor and stay in my cabin. It's far better there than up here, where they can spot you." He kissed his head and handed him to the man. Then he motioned with a nod for Jacques to join them to help calm Guy-François.

Guy waved and watched them go below, thankful that Jeanne,

oblivious and safe at home, had missed the episode. He scanned the dark horizon and sea and tried to expect what the *Torbay* planned to do. Both ships used only their top decks of guns, a serious handicap.

Soon Jacques stood beside his father again.

"Is he settled?" Guy asked.

His cadet son smiled. "Not entirely, but the tutor is reading him a story. It'll hold him until we get out of this mess."

"My two brave boys," Guy said out loud. "God, I'm proud of you both. Your mother has done a fine job of raising you."

"And Father, you've done a fine job of keeping this from her." His mouth pulled to one side as he pointed at the *Torbay's* cannons.

Within the hour, the winds weakened and blew less sea foam to show the scene farther away. Ships in clusters fought throughout the seascape. *Le Thésée* plied on, still clashing with the *Torbay*.

"Captain," said Jacques to his father, standing with his musket near the first lieutenant. "Look, the admiral!"

"Sir, the enemy flagship is making for the admiral's *Soleil Royal!*" shouted the first lieutenant over the noise of cannons and storm, pointing starboard to the flagships.

Wiping mist off the spyglass lens, Guy saw the admiral's flagship had collided with another French warship in trying to flee from the British.

"We must help him!" Guy yelled to the lieutenant. "The winds and waves have let up. Open the lower gun deck ports. We need more firepower to disable the *Torbay*. We're close enough for chain shot." He strode over the poop deck, sword in hand, shouting orders to put an end to the *Torbay's* threat.

Across the short span of water, he caught the *Torbay* taking the same risk and rolling out the lowest guns. As both ships began a deadly duel, blow for blow. Every barrel hurtled balls from all tiers as Guy tried to shake off the opponent and pull away.

Never known for timidity, Guy pondered intercepting the much larger 110-gun rascal on his own. Without another of his size joining him, it was a suicidal task. Yet the crisis demanded intervention. "We'll make for their flagship!" He shouted to his second-in-command. "Close the lower deck hatches!"

The first lieutenant raced for the stairs. When he scrabbled down to the lowest gun deck, a cannonball from the *Torbay* tore through the side of the ship. Shards of wood launched outward in all directions. As he opened his mouth to shout the order to shut the ports, nothing came out. He had taken a long, sharp splinter through his neck. He fell, and a sliced jugular emptied his life.

Guy waited for the call from below to confirm the ports shut. Through the dimming light, he spied the enemy closing in on his admiral. No confirmation reached him that the crew had finished the crucial task. He held back any actions. The minutes passed. He looked over the side, knowing the lower hatches were not visible, but their blasts were. Smoke and flame still belched from the bottom guns and his fist pounded the railing. When the first lieutenant did not return, he suspected a holdup to the simple procedure.

The foe's enormous ship continued to bear down upon the admiral's *Soleil Royal*. Guy struggled to keep from ordering the helmsmen to head for the impending clash as he waited for word they had secured the openings. Each second passed in agonizing frustration as he envisioned his admiral under attack.

After holding off far longer than the time to make fast the hatches, he spied his son Jacques with his musket firing at enemy marines on the *Torbay*. "Jacques!" Guy shouted. "Speed below and order the lower gun deck ports closed. We must tack to help the admiral. Now!"

The young cadet raced off, leaping down the stairs two steps at once until he reached the bottom level. There he stopped, aghast. The first lieutenant lay dead. Crimson covered his neck and chest. Jacques ran toward the first officer he saw and jumped to clear a gun's breach rope.

Above, Guy again paced and stood by as he awaited and watched the flagship draw closer to the admiral. But as before, he heard nothing. After holding up for almost five minutes, far more than needed, he could delay no longer. "Hard to starboard! To the *Soleil Royal!*" he shouted to the men pulling on the wheel. His sword pointed toward the great ship of the line.

As *le Thésée* turned to come between the two flagships, an intense gust of storm wind caught the sails full. The ship hove leeward under the rogue draft and continued to tilt rather than righting. In just over a second, Guy realized what happened below and what must follow. The sudden blow had pushed le Thésée's starboard lower hatches into the waves. They had not been closed. The sea spilled through the bottom tier openings, and the water's tremendous weight rushing onto the lowest gun deck, pulled that side further downward. The ocean flooded inside the hull.

For a few moments, a last panicked search raced through his thoughts to correct what had happened. But decades of experience stopped the review. His mind only envisioned the inevitable catastrophe unfolding.

The whole of the deck, masts, and sails began leaning into the sea. No command would alter that they were doomed.

His glorious warship slowly rolled deeper leeward. The deck angled more each second. Guy climbed up on the railing and wove his trembling arms between the mizzen shroud lines and held onto the ratlines. The tight grip of his hands pushed the rope deep into his skin. He placed his shoe heels over the railing as everything steepened seaward. Guy felt the timbers shudder below and heard masts strain and crack. His mind sought any refuge from the unfolding chaos. Still, his focus only could dive further into the terror of their impending annihilation. Just moments passed when came the screams, curses, shouts, and prayers of over six hundred and fifty crewmen. The cries rendered him guilty of the horror's indictment.

His thoughts yielded to Jacques and little Guy-François, their innocent lives lost to his irrevocable command. Tears and rain mixed upon his face as he remembered disregarding the dangers. And how, over the years, he lied to Jeanne about the likelihood of harm. He had even placed fame above them! He wondered if her forgiveness would ever come.

The depth of love he felt for them forced his eyes closed. Then he recalled Carlos and Hashi Humma. Guy had questioned their sacrifices for their sons. Dupré, out of love, had avenged his wife, and Émile might have fled but died for his family. Guy, at last, understood why.

His attention leaped to all he'd condemned. "My sons," Guy whispered to every soul on board, "my sons, forgive me." His head hung. He might try to escape the disgrace and cast himself into the sea to swim away. But if he survived, despair from guilt would forever brand him.

Le Thésée continued to sink starboard and deeper. The water advanced upward from the hold, level by level, almost to the gun deck amidships. A strange quiet overtook the scene, with only nature's lashing waves playing its rhapsody. No more crew screamed, no cannons thundered, and the ship timbers settled into a silent wait. The *Torbay*, too, had ceased its attack.

Flashes of shame, regret, and anger passed through him until the load of emotions, consuming his focus, surrendered to unburden his mind.

The fear and panic waned to be replaced by a calm acceptance of the end of the race he had dashed toward his entire life. In that instant of his gravest decision, all the brave and dangerous actions he had ever taken summed up to this ultimate moment. This time, the ever-rewarding odds played against him, and he could do nothing.

Guy realized the risk he had taken in opening the lower deck ports. The brilliant achievements in service to the king dissolved before his eyes in the warship's ruination. All would point to him for leaving the hatches open, a mistake even cadets learned to avoid. It cast his entire glorious career into a shadow of incompetence. He clung to the shrouds and asked himself what purpose his life had been.

His eyes opened. Rather than wondering, Guy accepted everything is as it should be. His calmed thoughts professed all occurred exactly as they should. Every action he had ever taken, regardless if mundane or profound, fit precisely into the great mosaic of his being. It concluded in a defining realization, that the world's physical structure only existed to support his invisible feelings. The true riches, his love of Jeanne, his children, and Marie remained intact forever, a simple sensation expanding into infinity.

No longer afraid, his frenetic emotions had converged on a single consoling thought, Hashi Humma's message, sounding in his ears above the sea's roar, ... *it is perfect.*

The glory, victories, and greatness he chased throughout life now ended with the last scene of the role he played. To an unseen Choctaw, Guy uttered his last words, "I do see the truth of it." As the cold waters crept up the deck toward him, a slight smile appeared on his lips. There was no hell for him. It would not be a violent death—no screams or thrashing about. He accepted his cursed path. His blood unspilled, he would go to Aba pilla with his boys.

Amidst *le Thésée*'s destruction, *Torbay*'s captain turned windward to take on fewer waves after closing his own gun ports. The British crew watched silently, transfixed as *le Thésée* continued to turn over on her side until a quarter of the ship was underwater.

The bow began to sink in that position but rolled back upright with just her forecastle and poop deck visible. There, among crewmen grasping for hopeless salvation in waves flooding the decks, stood Guy upon the railing, his arms woven into the ratlines, prepared to accept his end. His head turned skyward; no emotion showed on his face as the chilled waters washed over him. In less than a minute, with just twenty-two swimming to safety, the last of *le Thésée*'s topmasts and crew disappeared under the water; and Captain Guy de Kersaint's warship glided to the sea's bottom.

∽

Within days of the battle, word spread. Joseph, his parish nearer the scene, received news of it before those in Brest. He sped north on horseback to Cléder to be with Jeanne in case anything had happened to his brother or nephews. Five days after the devastating anguish and shock over the disaster hit Brest, the Admiralty informed Jeanne of Guy's death and that of their two young sons. Often she had worried but had never seriously conceived her husband or children might die at sea. His faithful return after countless dangerous missions gave her false confidence in his abilities and God's safekeeping. Jeanne's unrelenting mourning lasted many months, shared by her remaining four sons and three daughters.

In Brest, Armand's captain informed him and sent him home

to Cléder. His father's death gave him much to contemplate, no less than whether he should continue his career in the navy. Regardless, he remained and was to follow his own path to greatness, surpassing even his father's former glory.

King Louis XV granted Jeanne, the wife of one of his favorite commanders, a pension of two thousand livres. A month after Guy's passing, Jeanne sent a letter with a package to Marie.

> *My Dearest Marie,*
> *I am sure that you, as all in France, have learned of the tragic demise of our beloved Guy and my two sons. I grieve for them without pause and my tears do not cease to fall, although my deepest sorrows have no display or voice. My hope lies in the passing of time to heal the wounds of my heart. If only those long days and nights might become minutes to lessen the suffering. No doubt you relent his passing with equal heartache.*
> *The package contains a gift Guy had meant to give you long ago. Perhaps regard it as a keepsake of his affection.*
> *For many years, I have realized the love he held for you was greater than that which he held for me. I do not write this in contempt or jealousy but in honest reflection. Guy loved you like no other woman. This is the man we knew, one who adored others deeply. It is what made Guy the captain I shall forever cherish. May life fill you with happy memories of Guy and bliss with your new husband.*
> *Your Loving Friend, Jeanne, Countess de Kersaint, the 6th of December, 1759, Cléder.*

When Marie recovered from the shock of the letter, she opened the parcel to discover a finely woven shawl of Moorish design. She reminisced about how Guy had loved, encouraged, and even financially supported her throughout her life. Though his advances didn't sway her into marrying him, had she not torn her cloak one winter's day, she might have wed Guy instead of Émile. Marie imagined how things would have turned out, the home, the family, and the endless waiting. Although after she contemplated her lifetime choices, she concluded she'd have changed little except trying harder to save Émile.

Marie also learned François de Saint-Alouarn had died aboard his ship in the same battle the next day, struck down by a musket ball. His warship, along with others, wrecked on the shore with all but a few crewmen surviving the violent surf.

None of the strong connections she had with men from Brittany had survived the years. Marie's sole consolation lay in Claude, who comforted her through the difficulty.

Time and fading memories separated her from her history, and she poured herself into the business and her future. With Claude as a guide, she discovered a new artistic outlet in hat design. Marie's fresh ideas took hold and soon their hats topped the coiffure of the wealthiest in Paris. Although other designers copied her styles, she felt her greatest pride when she hired a young woman from Brest, whom she mentored to surpass even her own creations.

When, after a long, adventurous but contorted journey through the world, she passed, she was buried with the colorful woolen shawl draped around her shoulders.

Guy affected many during his life. His contributions to the French navy escalated with each mission. He sailed from cadet to squadron chief and set an example for others to follow. To lose such outstanding captains as him and François left France with a loss of her best commanders. The destruction of the Atlantic fleet at Quiberon Bay enabled the British navy to dominate the seas for decades and establish their empire.

His lifelong quest for fame ended the way warriors favor, in battle in the pursuit of glory. Yet, before Guy's end, he came to understand life's greatest treasures ... *and it was perfect.*

Other Books by D. E. Stockman

TWEEN SEA AND SHORE SERIES
The Ship's Carpenter
Captains of the Renown

About the Author

D. E. Stockman wrote articles for a printing trade magazine and also for an e-zine before creating historical nautical series set in the mid-1700s. For most of his career, he worked as a graphic artist for the imprints of Simon & Schuster, Harcourt Brace & Co., and Pearson Education. He lives with his wife Valerie in the winters-here-aren't-too-bad Chicago suburbs.

The award-winning novels in his *Tween Sea and Shore Series: The Ship's Carpenter, Captains of the Renown, and On Waves of Glory*, offer more than the usual tall-ship tales. Portraying lovers as well as adventures, the author illuminates the fuller and intertwined lives of the British and French characters. Based on over ten years research into naval archives, the story follows those linked by fate and the fastest ship of its day, *la Renommée*—the frigate Renown.

Be sure to go to https://stockmanbooks.com/downloads for the free pdf booklet, Addendum, a handy aid to the book series with maps, a pronunciation guide, and other material. Also download *La Renommée, Story of a French Frigate*, containing factual information on the warship.

If you enjoyed **On Waves of Glory**, *please leave a review where you purchased the book.*

Other Titles You Might Enjoy

PRISONER OF WALLABOUT BAY
Jane Hulse

A young woman's daring quest to free the . . . Prisoner of Wallabout Bay.

Sarah's relentless digging uncovers a story that nobody wants to even talk about, no less print. The British have set up decaying prison ships in the waters off New York. Risking everything, Sarah fights to expose rampant cruelty and wretched conditions, and in the process just happens to find love.

"The novel plunges the reader into a series of perilous adventures, at the same time opening our eyes to a little-known war crime that still haunts our history."
—**Ellen Pall**, author of *Must Read Well* and *Among the Ginzburgs*

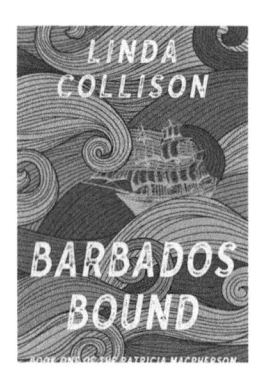

BARBADOS BOUND
Book 1 of the Patricia MacPherson Nautical Series
Linda Collison

Portsmouth, England,1760. Patricia Kelley, the illegitimate daughter of a wealthy Barbadian sugarcane planter, falls from her imagined place in the world when her absent father unexpectedly dies. Raised in a Wiltshire boarding school sixteen-year-old Patricia embarks on a desperate crossing on a merchantman bound for Barbados, where she was born, in a brash attempt to claim an unlikely inheritance. Aboard a merchantman under contract with the British Navy to deliver gunpowder to the West Indian forts, young Patricia finds herself pulled between two worlds—and two identities— as she charts her own course for survival in the war-torn 18th century.

"*Barbados Bound* is a rousing and engaging tale of the almost impossible challenges facing a young woman cast adrift in 18th Century British Empire."
—**Rick Spilman**, The Old Salt Blog

For the Finest in Nautical and Historical Fiction and Non-Fiction
www.FireshipPress.com

Interesting • Informative • Authoritative

All Fireship Press books are available through leading bookstores and wholesalers worldwide.